The LOST BRANCH

DONNA COOK

To Anna,
For the magic hidden
in all of us.

Cook

Also by Donna Cook:

Gift of the Phoenix
Nashua's Choice

Published by Penrose House Press, LLC
United States of America
www.penrosehousepress.com

www.donnacookauthor.com

ISBN 978-0-9882089-6-4

Printed in the United States of America

Acknowledgements

My deepest gratitude to my editor, Elyse Ross, for always pushing me to do my best, and for her sincere friendship. I can't imagine writing a book without you.

To Kim Foster, the only proofreader on the planet I would trust with my baby.

Many thanks go to my fabulous beta readers, Alexandra Amor, Carina Anderson, Michael Arbon, Melissa Burnham, James Chapp, Kim Foster, Ruth Hallows, Kira McCain, and Jim Ross. Your input made the book even better.

My fellow writing peeps, Louise Berlin, Debra Anne Bishop, and Devri Walls, for your cameraderie, advice, and encouragment. Thanks for inspiring me to reach ever higher.

To my loyal readers for all the enthusiasm you've shown for this world and for these characters. This story is for you.

To my mother, Barbara, for her unfailing support.

To my beautiful boys, John, Ben, and Chris, for the deep joy you give me.

To my stepdaughters, Kira, Sheahan, and Annika, for always bringing a smile to my face.

To my loving husband and partner in crime, Kevin McCain. Thank you for your encouragement, wisdom, humor, and patience. I cherish you.

To John, Ben, and Chris.

My Three.

The Lost Branch

PART I

The Orsini Colony

One

Thrayce Island rose out of the gray sea like a hunched giant, quiet and waiting. The little boat bucked over the waves, riding close to shore. Corren gripped the edge with a hand numb from the cold, the other hand loose on his staff.

Marcellus stood next to him, somehow holding his stance in spite of the rocking boat. His hand rested on the handle of the sword at his hip. "I don't see a vessel," Marcellus said.

Corren nodded. He'd noticed too.

Nicolai leaned forward, sitting on the bench behind them. "Maybe on the other side."

"Maybe she didn't use a boat," Marcellus said.

Yes, Corren thought. "But what about the others?"

There were no signs of habitation. No buildings, no boats, not even a lean-to. If Aradia had been on this island—and they all agreed that she had—she may have come to one of the island's many other coves. However, she left the island from here, so for now, this cove mattered most. Even two days later, the magic Aradia had used to travel from here to the Gateway lingered in the water. Corren followed the sensation of it all the way here, like following a trail.

The two knights rowing in the stern brought them close to shore, the boat jumping in the tumultuous water. Marcellus and Nicolai leapt out and pulled until the bow wedged in the sand. Corren, in his long wizard's cloak, clambered out and onto dry land.

Marcellus and Nicolai wore leather boots, but their trousers were wet to the knees. Corren thought the incantation to dry and warm them and immediately saw the effect this had on his brothers. They startled, looking down at their legs.

Marcellus gave Corren a wry look. "You could warn me."

1

The two knights hopped out, one making a concerted effort to avoid getting himself wet. He gave Corren plenty of distance.

A billow of wind cut past them and rushed inland. The sandy cove stretched away to a rocky inlet, which ended in a thick line of towering trees. The sound of rustling branches rose up as all along the tree line they swayed and undulated in the wind. That was when Corren saw them. "Footprints."

His brothers drew to his side and together they looked at the trail before them. The footprints were faint, the wind dusting away bits of sand from the shallow indentations even now, but they were there. The footprints came from the direction of the treeline and ended nearly at Corren's feet. He took a step away.

Behind him, half a dozen little boats, filled with knights, dotted the water as they bobbed toward shore. They'd been launched from the king's grand sailing vessel, anchored in deeper water half a league out.

Far beyond, the rearing Cliffs of the Realm of the Phoenix cut through the horizon, dominating the sky. Up the coast of the mainland, the Cliffs came to an abrupt halt and the nation of Caedmonia began. Her sprawling capital city, Stonebridge, claimed the bay and climbed up the hill where the castle perched on the crest. Between this city and the Cliffs of the Realm, on the coast, the ancient Rock of Light stood sentinel. At its tip, the Eternal Flame burned like a beacon.

Two days ago, when Aradia had been standing here—right here—the Eternal Flame would have been a mere pinprick in those hours leading up to the Phoenix's death. He imagined how the distant coastline would have looked to her: dark, quiet, unsuspecting. So far away. *How did she get there so quickly?*

Whatever magic Aradia had used to propel herself through the water and to the Gateway, it had begun in the water. Corren wouldn't have known where to look next had it not been for the footprints. He wanted to follow them now, but waited, gripping his staff in his right hand.

Even when not in use, the staff held a kind of radiance. An energy seemed to reside at the very core, the origin of which was the hardened ash at the tip, wrapped in the clawlike fingers

2

of the wood. The ash was the only remnant of the three stones the brothers had used to help protect the Phoenix from Aradia.

Together the Three waited as the boats came to shore. The knights hopped out with military precision, far more graceful than Corren's awkward deboarding. Corren hoped they wouldn't need the knights. Marcellus hoped they wouldn't either, but they had reason to believe Aradia may have been holed up here with troops of her own, and Marcellus wanted to bring along a battalion as a precaution. Marcellus kept an alert eye on their surroundings, but there didn't seem to be anyone around.

In fact, the entire island had an eerie sense of desolation.

The knights settled into a predetermined pattern. Marcellus assigned two small groups as lookouts and another as scouts. The rest he commanded to follow him. He looked at Corren. "Ready?"

Corren nodded and led the way, Nicolai on one side and Marcellus on the other. They crossed the sandy beach, their strides awkward in the deep sand but settling into their normal gaits as the sand relented and the ground under them grew firm. The footprints were gone by now, but if they kept on in the same direction, they'd end up at a break in the trees. It seemed to lead to an opening of some sort. They continued toward it without discussion.

The wind shifted and the Three came to a halt. An unearthly stench, darkly familiar, assailed them. It smelled of maggots and rotting flesh. Corren heard the knights reacting to and complaining against the rancid odor.

The Three exchanged glances and Nicolai's light green eyes darkened as he said, "I know that smell."

Images flashed through Corren's mind. Some unknown soul extracted in the forest. Theo's remains in slimy piles in Aradia's hidden stronghold. Flesh and entrails and bone. He wished he knew a spell to suppress the cold chill crawling under his skin.

He and his brothers continued to look at one another. They already knew she'd been extracting souls to use as a protective shield once in the Realm of the Phoenix. What they did not know was how many.

Corren was not keen on stumbling across more evidence of Aradia's killing. Mercifully the wind shifted, the trees roared in front of them, and they had a reprieve from the stink. Thus released, they got in motion again.

They entered the break in the trees. Branches and bushes stopped abruptly on either side of them, as if they had been magically carved away. Charred bits of wood and leaves littered the edges of a path through the forest ahead. Corren hesitated briefly then pushed on. Though there was no immediate threat, he gripped his staff tighter.

The path was barely wide enough for two, so Marcellus stayed by Corren's side and Nicolai fell slightly behind. The knights fell in line behind them. For a time, all they heard was the trudging of their march and the occasional roar of wind through the trees. Were it not for the path, the forest would nearly be too thick and damp to traverse.

The path curved to the right and circled past the base of a rocky knoll. The stone face was dark and covered in lichens and, as they came round it, presented a narrow opening. Like the path itself, this seemed an unnatural occurrence.

The Three stopped and the troops immediately behind came to a halt. The action worked down the line until the knights stood waiting along with the rest. Corren sensed the magic humming around the edges of the opening.

Marcellus made to go through it but Corren grabbed his arm, stopping him. He felt the protective spell, which dropped over the opening like a shroud. Sharp and waiting to bite. He waved his staff, thought the appropriate incantation, and felt the protective spell dissipate.

It had only been two days since the Phoenix had resurrected itself in the Realm. Two days since they'd nearly lost their lives defending it. Two days since the Phoenix, in a moment of glowing transcendence, had taught Corren the before-unheard-of skill of nonverbal magic. Every time he used it, a deep warmth reminiscent of his moment with the Phoenix hummed though his bones.

Corren released his brother's arm and nodded. "Alright."

Marcellus only gave the opening an appraising look, however, so Corren led the way. He stepped through the opening, his brothers close behind. For a few steps it was nothing but a narrow passageway, progressing darkness, and the smell of damp earth, but this soon opened into a larger space. Among the objects in shadow, Corren discerned a familiar shape and sent a spell toward it. Light bloomed in the lantern, revealing an inner room carved out of the rock.

A lounge with deep mahogany fabric sat to one side. A knotty pine table dominated the rear, its worn surface covered with various implements: a spindly iron *ambitus*, brass scales, a silver inkwell, Aradia's enviable mortar and pestle collection, and boxes and vials that Corren knew contained an array of potion ingredients. Clustered on one corner of the table, half a dozen hourglasses of various sizes sat abandoned, the sand lying mutely at the bottoms. Two massive cauldrons sat on the ground near the rear wall.

Corren had hoped to find Aradia's belongings on the island—it was part of the reason they were here—but he was unprepared for the emotions they caused in him. Aradia's presence wrapped round him, taking hold as he stood in this strange place with all her familiar things. That's how she was in his mind: familiar and foreign all at once. Perplexing. A known thing he did not know at all.

Unbidden and unwelcome, memories assaulted him. Tossing her head back in a rare laugh after he'd done something to amuse her as a boy. Her calm presence in front of a class as she demonstrated a fiery spell that went out in a haze of purple smoke. Her eyes on him, cold and unflinching, as she shut the carriage door and sent him to his death. Aradia leaning over the book he was studying, giving some instruction, her long silvery hair falling in a sheet over her shoulder and wrapping them in safety.

That's how he'd felt at the time. Safe.

Now these memories of her that he wished would stay away... memories that had been trailing after him like cobwebs... they gained fresh substance being in this place. They pulsed through him, tangible and without mercy. The staff in his hand felt a mere stick. Corren stood among Aradia's things not as the powerful Head of the Order he had become, but as the boy he'd once been. Her boy.

The flame in the lantern sputtered as it caught hold of bits of grime on the wick. The lounge, the table, the vials, the hourglasses, they shuddered in the flickering light, seeming to press toward him, nearer and nearer.

"Corren?" It was Nicolai, at his shoulder.

Corren flinched almost imperceptibly. He'd forgotten they were here. His awareness extended to include his brothers, but he would not look at them. He forced himself to glance around the room, as if he were looking for the things they sought. As if he didn't already know every object in sight.

Everything was clearly visible. There were no trunks to look through and not a book to be seen. He should have been disappointed but was too grateful for the freedom to take his leave.

"They're not here," Corren said. He escaped into the narrow passageway, the smell of dank earth expanding in his lungs. The tendrils of Aradia's presence reached after him. He came through the entrance and into weak sunlight. He took several steps until he finally stopped.

Marcellus appeared beside him. "I'm sorry."

Nicolai came to him next.

Corren looked at his brothers at last. Nicolai gave him that concerned, piercing gaze of his. Corren did not try to hide from this—there was no hiding things from Nicolai anyway—but neither did he wish to discuss it. He did not wish to do anything but forget it.

Aware of the gaggle of knights surrounding him, watching him, he forced himself to breathe normally. Indeed, away from Aradia's things, out here in trees with the brooding sky above, he was able to get some hold on himself. He was being foolish. It was over. It was all over.

His heartbeat slowed down in great gulps. He hadn't realized it had been racing.

He held the smooth wood of his staff, a reassuring presence once again. As the emotions he felt in the cave sank back into that place deep inside himself, he remembered why they were here. They still faced the same problem that brought them to the island to start with.

"Where are her books," he said, his voice hinting at his earlier emotions, "if not here?" Of course, they had already checked her office at Tower Hall South, and this was her only known hiding place; he didn't know where to look next.

"Further along perhaps," Marcellus said. For indeed, the path Aradia had carved through the trees kept going past the cave.

Corren nodded but did not move. This time it was Marcellus who led the way, with Nicolai by Corren's side. The knights followed in silent obedience.

They had not gone far when Nicolai said, "Here it comes."

Marcellus, who had been walking with his hand on his sword, drew it in response, followed by the ringing of dozens of swords behind them doing the same thing. "What?" Marcellus asked, looking around.

Corren looked around too. He saw and heard nothing.

"No," Nicolai said. "The earth. It's up here."

Corren understood. It was Nicolai who had led them to the first extracted body they'd found in the woods of Caedmonia. He had felt the evil of the act leeching into the earth. He must have been feeling it now. Marcellus must have understood too, because he gave a signal and all the swords went back into their scabbards.

Corren didn't want to investigate. He didn't want to see. As before, they stood there a moment. Corren wondered if Marcellus was remembering Theo. He'd witnessed the whole horrible scene. Corren could not be more grateful he didn't have that memory to add to the others.

Mercifully, the wind was at their backs, but as they continued on and, apparently, drew nearer to what Nicolai sensed, the stench overpowered the wind. Their steps slowed, but they pressed forward.

The forest, and therefore the path, gave way to a meadow stretching over a rise. They crested the hill and that's when they saw it. A virtual field of extracted bodies. At the sight of it, Corren felt as if he'd been knocked from head to toe with a stone wall. Darkness squeezed the edges of his vision as he looked on pile after pile of remains, flesh, stench, slime, bone, rot, black, black, black. "Oh, god."

He turned away, swaying, his knees soft and thighs trembling. He pressed his eyes closed and leaned on his staff. Gripped it with both hands. Willed himself to stay upright as he felt the world swaying around him. But he knew what lay right behind him, and felt compelled to move away. He took a step, not sure he could hold himself up. Someone took him by one elbow then the other—his brothers?—and he managed to put one leg in front of the other as they escorted him away, back through the mass of knights who stepped aside and murmured and it all buzzed in his ears and in his bones.

They were back on the path. No knights. The air smelled only of impending rain. Here Corren raised a hand and they stopped. Nicolai slowly let go of Corren's arm. Corren held steady. Marcellus did not let go until Corren took a deep breath and looked up at the sky. Gray clouds, starting to lift, and a patch of blue, as if the sky didn't know any better.

"Sorry," Corren said.

"Now we know what happened to her followers," Nicolai said, visibly sickened.

Marcellus nodded, looking a little green himself. "The troops will finish scouting. Let's go, Corren."

No more was said as they retreated down the path, past the cave, and back to the cove with the hulking shape of the ship off in the distance. They waited for the knights to finish scouting the island, but Corren doubted they'd find anyone. He thought he knew what fate Aradia's followers had met.

What Corren didn't know was how. How could she have done something so horrific? Aradia had raised him. Had taught him everything he knew about magic. Had made him want to be the man he'd become. How could he have been so wrong about her? So blind?

The Eternal Flame shone bright on the distant shore. Even by day, its light was clear and steadfast. He wished he could be there now, away from this place. He wished he could somehow forget it all.

But even if he could hide in the uppermost room of the Rock of Light, basking in the healing glow of the Eternal Flame, another mystery awaited him there. A mystery everyone was looking to him to solve.

Two days earlier, after they'd defeated Aradia in the Realm, the Phoenix resurrected itself and brought its gift—the egg of ash—to the Rock of Light. After Corren had removed the egg from the pillar of receiving, he had conducted the ceremony that evenly divided the ash between the seven branches of the Order. After so many centuries of too little ash for their needs, at last the branches of the Order would have ash in abundance. They could rebuild the magical communities that had been stripped to the bare necessities and sometimes far less. They could restore the Order to what it had been before: a glorious magical organization created and sustained by their beloved Phoenix.

But they soon discovered a new problem.

When Corren lifted his glass orb of ash off the altar, it glinted in the light of the huge Eternal Flame. All around the altar, the other Heads of the branches lifted their orbs in one fluid motion and raised them high above their heads.

All but one. Sage Kennard's orb remained on the stone slab, his hands cupping the glittering glass, his face a palette of confusion and panic. The orb would not be lifted.

It sat there even now.

As newly appointed Head of the Order, everyone looked to Corren for an explanation. He was as puzzled as they were and could not lift the orb any more than Kennard could. Corren had gone to the Vaults of the Order seeking answers. But the Inner Vault, that which only the Head of the Order could access, had been stripped bare.

So in addition to stealing the secret books of each branch of the Order, Aradia had squirreled away the books from the Inner Vault as well. Since Thrayce Island was her last known location, and since all of her other belongings and magical implements were indeed here, it only made sense that the books would be here.

If he didn't know Aradia better, he'd wonder if she'd destroyed them. But she would never do such a thing. She was a meticulous record keeper. In addition to the missing books, Corren knew she had dozens of folios of her own notes over the years. They had to be somewhere.

A realization took hold of him. Her office in the cave did not have a single book. Not even the innocent ones, her herbologies or encyclopedias. Nothing. Aradia never traveled without books. A folio at minimum.

Corren watched the waves rolling toward him, roaring as they hit land, lost their steam, and retreated.

Aradia never traveled without her books. Never.

He turned away from shore and headed back for the path.

"Where are you going?" Marcellus asked.

"The cave. Let's look again."

"There's nothing there," Nicolai said.

"So it would seem," Corren replied, but did not slow.

They followed him in silence. The stone face of the knoll came into view. They again came round to the entrance. This time Corren felt his heartbeat accelerating. His temperature rising. Down the dark passageway he took a deep breath. And another.

They entered the inner room, the light still pulsing in the lantern. Looking around, the lounge, the table, the vials, the hourglasses... they all stayed put. He felt as hard as the stone walls surrounding him and turned his attention to them now. He knew what went wrong the last time he was here: he'd been too overcome by emotion and memories to sense what now seemed obvious.

He approached the wall on the right and put his hand on the rough surface. It was cool. Solid. He felt the rock beneath his hand, but he felt something else. He grunted and waved his staff. The illusion of rock disappeared, revealing an alcove with shelves carved into its walls. The shelves were loaded with books.

Nicolai made a noise of surprise. Corren could only concur. It was an impressive illusion, one that not only tricked the eye but tricked the sense of touch as well.

That old feeling of awe at Aradia's abilities, even the sense of pride that always came with it, entered his heart. But it was tainted with the truth of her. Such clever wickedness in that woman. And he never saw it, all those years. How could he have loved someone so evil?

He felt a new emotion then: shame. So thick and hot he felt it leeching through his skin.

"Very good," Marcellus said.

"Is that it?" Nicolai asked.

Blood pulsing, Corren glanced at the two empty trunks sitting at the bottom of the hidden alcove and flung open the lid of the one on the right. He grabbed the nearest book and slammed it onto the bottom of the trunk.

"I gather that's a yes," Marcellus said.

Corren leaned his staff against the wall, took two books in both hands, and dropped them on the other.

"Want help?" Nicolai asked.

Two more books. *Thunk*. Three. *Thunk, thunk*.

Nicolai stayed where he was.

Corren cleared two shelves, filling one trunk, and began working on the other. He set one massive volume on top of another then finished with stacks and stacks of her folios.

He wanted to fling them across the room.

Aradia would've flayed him alive.

He set each stack in the trunk, doing no damage, but feeling his blood pulse and his face burn.

A few knights appeared in the cave's entrance. "The island is clear, my Lord."

Corren loaded the last few folios and closed the lids.

"Take the trunks to the boat," Marcellus said, eyeing Corren.

Corren grabbed his staff and watched the knights retrieve the trunks and haul them away.

"We got what we came for," Nicolai said.

Corren nodded.

"Want anything else?" Marcellus asked.

Corren looked around. He had spent the last many years coveting her extensive mortar and pestle collection. Her fine brass scales could discern the slightest pinch of powder. Her heavy cauldrons were worth a tidy sum. The knights could load it all up in the boat and he could take it back to Tower Hall South where it could be put to use.

Corren shook his head.

They did not press him. His brothers turned to leave and Corren followed them. At the entrance to the inner room, Corren stopped and considered the lantern. The fire in its belly illuminated the remnants of Aradia. Corren remembered the first time he saw her. He was lying on a cot in an empty room in Tower Hall South, orphaned for the second time in his life, and here was Aradia, leaning over him, her long silver hair falling over her shoulder like a shimmering veil. Aradia, come to save him.

Corren raised his staff and slashed it through the air like a sword. Her lantern, her couch, her table, her hourglasses, everything in sight exploded and disintegrated in a haze of ash and splinters and smoke.

When he turned he saw his brothers' astonished faces, but did not linger. "Let's go," he said and pushed past them.

Two

Two days after the regeneration of the Phoenix, the cobbled square that had—for over a thousand years—led to the Bridge of a Thousand Ages was now merely a square. The Bridge was gone and the square teemed with people who, regardless of recent events, had work to do. Carts loaded with goods lumbered over the uneven stone. Men stacked empty wooden crates outside open warehouse doors. Fishermen hollered to one another, mended nets, and launched boats into the gray water, hoping for a good haul before the sky decided whether or not to make good on its threat of a storm.

Out in the water, one being scrutinized them all.

Had anyone noticed—and no one did—they would've merely thought him a dolphin.

But though he appeared in that form, Faatin was no dolphin. He swam through the bay, the cool water gliding over his smooth body as he came to the surface and slipped below. He had been there early that morning, when the square first came to life. He was there when the boats set out and there when, late in the afternoon, they came in again. He lingered all day, searching, just as he had the day before.

And just as the day before, he didn't find who he was looking for.

A few times he had swum all along the shore, thinking maybe they would be elsewhere, but he kept returning to this place where he'd seen them before. After the Eternal Flame had renewed to its full glory and the Bridge of a Thousand Ages went up in flames, four figures had appeared in the square. Delivered, it seemed, by the power of the Phoenix itself. These four. Not Aradia. Them.

Faatin had felt despair in that moment. He had to admit it.

13

And what had he felt next? The presence of four who were not like the other people swarming the square that day. Three males and one female.

He felt them clear out in the water.

He'd been back looking for them ever since. As the day's light waned and the crowd of people on the square thinned, Faatin came to a reluctant decision. He descended deep below water and transformed at last.

The water faerie shot through the water, his arms at his sides, his legs stretched out behind him, using his magic to manipulate the water and propel himself forward. He did this without thinking much. His mind was on other things.

Faatin headed north in the bay, away from the city of Stonebridge and the Rock of Light. Away from Crescent Island and his fellow faeries, whom he had not seen since he and several fellow conspirators had fought alongside the witch Aradia.

She was supposed to be the solution to their problem, promising she would harness the magic of the Phoenix to heal them at last and return them to their former selves. She would help them regain their former home, the once-beautiful realm of the water faeries. Naida, its underground caverns hidden under Thrayce Island, had fallen into murk and decay since the water faeries' failed attempt, hundreds of years ago, to steal magic forbidden to them.

It was the reason for their disfigurement. The reason they could no longer maintain their beautiful home. The reason they'd been living for hundreds of years like castaways on the barren rocks of their own creation: Pearl and Crescent Islands.

But Aradia failed.

Even before that, she was treacherous.

Faatin hugged the algae-covered drop-off under the bay. Brown seaweed reached out from the rock, swaying slowly in the water. Sometimes long tendrils escaped and spiraled far below.

He came to a series of openings, black holes gaping open like silent screams. Swimming into one, the water turned chill as

14

darkness fell around him. He sensed his way through the tunnel and soon saw the water lightening above him.

He ascended until he broke through the surface, water running off his scarred face. The pool let out into a cave, much like the under-surface caverns at Crescent Island. There was just one opening, high above and behind him, that led to the outside. This was minimally sufficient to provide air and light for his human companion.

Bricker sat on the ground, leaning against a rock. His rough pants and leather vest were streaked with dried mud and dust. His brown hair fell in matted clumps to his shoulders. An intricate gold symbol glinted on his dirty forehead.

At his feet, a small campfire sputtered. The fire's smoke lingered in pockets on the low ceiling before finding its way out of the opening. It filled the cave with the sharp smell of fire. All five fish Faatin had left that morning were reduced to scaly carcasses, tossed aside into a pile.

Bricker had glanced at Faatin when he surfaced then went back to his task. He was using his knife to carve a piece of wood into a spear. His head was cocked and his eyes sharp on the tip as he ran the knife over the rough wood.

"Anything?" Bricker asked without looking up.

"No." Faatin pulled himself out of the pool, water running off his body and puddling on the rock. Keeping an eye on the human and his spear, he grabbed his cloak of seaweed from a nearby rock and wrapped it around himself, relishing the firm, waxy feel.

"I told you," Bricker said, holding knife and stick in one hand and running his thumb along the tip with the other. "They're inland."

Bricker had accused Faatin of being obsessive and wasting time. He was probably right.

Bricker glanced up at Faatin. "Sit down," he said. "It's unnerving the way you stand around all the time."

Faatin had noticed the human's tendency to sit. He didn't see much point in it and attributed it to his inferior, mortal body.

15

He ignored the command. "Do you still want to go to Hathmirr?"

Bricker stopped his carving, looked up, and rested his spear on the ground. His leather vest creaked as he moved.

"You know I do."

"And can you," Faatin went on, "guarantee my safety?"

Bricker sheathed his knife into the casing on his leg. "No. Not without talking to them first. But I won't bring you to them unless I know it's safe."

"Maybe I don't want to go all the way to Hathmirr without a guarantee," he said, just as he had said two days ago when Bricker first laid out his plan. He did not feel the same conviction now though. After two days of wandering the harbor, two days of failing to come up with a plan of his own, and two days of realizing he had nowhere else to go, a trip to Hathmirr felt less of a gamble.

"What else do you suggest? We can't stay here."

"*You* can't."

Bricker scowled at him. The dirt caked in the creases on his face gave him a hard look. Harder than normal.

Faatin did not respond to the man's scowling. This human may have found the idea of living here impossible, but it was not much different from the living conditions Faatin had already endured at Crescent Island. When it came down to it, he could go on living here indefinitely. Far past the time the human would age and die, or starve to death, miserable in this dank little cave.

But Faatin didn't want to stay here either. Just as he hadn't wanted to stay on Crescent Island in his mutilated form for the rest of time.

He'd wanted out. He'd wanted his old life, his old home, his old form back.

He'd thought Aradia would be the answer. Before she'd turned on them all.

Faatin and Bricker had sensed it coming. Others too. But only Faatin and Bricker managed to escape the carnage undetected.

Bricker, bathed in that anger that is so typical of humans, raged about Aradia's treachery and his plan for revenge and justice. Though he would not say how, Bricker seemed to believe that if Faatin would help him get home, there was still a chance the water faerie could be healed.

Aradia had said the same thing. The only difference was Bricker made no promises. He only said, "I think. I think it will work." With a dark glint in his eye.

Faatin had no reason to trust him. But Bricker was all he had, and the small chance of finding salvation in Hathmirr was his only hope.

After coming so close to redemption, Faatin could not stay in this cave any more than the human could.

He looked at Bricker. Bricker looked back, his arm resting on one raised knee and the half-finished spear lying by his side in the dirt.

Neither one quite trusted the other.

Nevertheless, Faatin said, "I will go."

When Janus entered the Grand Cavern in the underground realm of Amon Tunde, Salerno was there to greet her. The king of the earth faeries stood next to the sparkling pool at the center of the cavern. The clear, blue water that sprang up from the earth broke off into first one underground stream, then another, winding its way through the many tunnels and caverns of Amon Tunde.

The ceiling soared high above him. Moss and flowering vines hung in great curtains over the glittering walls. Hollitas, buzzing buttons, yewlies, and trumpet bells—flowers unique to this underground realm of the earth faeries—bloomed from arched ceiling to grassy floor. They were joined by flowers found above ground: roses and lilies and tulips. Nearly every flower known to man, and a great many more besides, bloomed somewhere in

Amon Tunde. Many of them flourished right here in the Grand Cavern.

Salerno's wild hair fell past slender shoulders, and his eyes mimicked the intense green of the soft moss so often found here.

"Janus," he said, uttering her name in that old familiar way. Like he knew everything about her.

She hoped he didn't.

Though Janus had left her boots, heavy commander's overcoat, and bows and arrows above ground at the invisible border of Amon Tunde, she stood barefoot on the dewy grass aware of how human she looked. In her trousers and tunic, she did not look much like her fellow faeries, draped in cloaks of moss or soft *undanna* cloth. Though all faeries had a distinctly human look about them, most bore the distinguishing marks of their race. From all corners of the Grand Cavern, they watched Janus with their bright faerie eyes—brilliant greens, blues, purples, and oranges. Like so many of the flowers that bloomed here. Only a few had more muted, earthy-brown eyes like Janus. Some had smooth, humanlike hair, as Janus did (bound in a thick braid hanging down her back); others were more leafy or laced with twigs. Still others, like Salerno, were somewhere in-between.

Though she looked and dressed like a human, and sometimes even felt like one, the first thousands of years of her life had been spent underground, here, in the realm of the earth faeries. Differences or no, Janus felt the familiarity of her home seeping into her bones.

Since leaving twenty years ago—after her fellow earth faerie and friend had died giving birth to three sons—Janus did not return often. She had found new homes among the humans including, recently, the sons whom her friend bore by the human King Clement: Prince Marcellus, the wizard Corren, and the farmer Nicolai. Well, no longer a farmer. The son of a king. The son of a faerie.

Of course, until recently, he and Corren had not known their royal identities (much less their faerie ones); they were

18

secreted away at birth to protect them until the time came for them to fulfill the prophecy and save the Phoenix. Only Marcellus had been raised by their father as the prince he was.

And what about Marcellus? He was the latest detour in Janus' life that she didn't intend to happen. Like nearly everything else in the human world.

"Salerno," Janus said, giving her king a slight bow. This subtle gesture was more rare in the faerie world than it was in the human one, but she saw her king so little and loved him so sincerely she often greeted him this way.

With the steady calmness that was so common to many of her people, Salerno studied her as if he were looking for something. His pale brow drew down. Thinking of last night, she grew nervous, wondering what he could see.

"What is it?" she asked.

"Hmm," he said. "You are come to tell me of our three victors?"

He was not going to answer her question or tell her his thoughts. Being a faerie with private thoughts of her own, she did not press him. She had grown used to the human tendency to pry. That inclination had even rubbed off on her a bit during the years she'd spent living among them. But here in the sanctuary of the faeries, she fell to her old ways.

She nodded—she did indeed come to tell him about their three victors—and he gestured that she should follow him to the Royal Cavern and his throne. As they passed through the quiet throng of faeries, she thought of the secret she was keeping.

The night before, Marcellus had called to her in that glowing way of the faeries. She followed the call, meeting him on the castle grounds at the gate to a private spring—filled with seawater she declined to touch.

They talked nearly until dawn. For the last several hours, as fatigue pulled on them more and more, one of them would declare they should get some sleep. Then they'd talk more anyway. It had been a conversation with a mind of its own. They talked about the extraordinary events of the last few weeks, of course, but they also talked about the most random things. Horse breeding, the merits of broadswords over sabers, the rocky shores of Southern Caedmonia, Janus' favorite hollow deep in Amon Tunde, and the proper way to prepare tuna fillets (seared not baked, according to Marcellus).

As they talked and teased one another, Janus frequently wondered at the undercurrent of feelings that were entirely foreign to her. A surprisingly tantalizing combination of exhilaration and terror.

As Janus and Salerno walked silently along the central tunnel toward the Royal Cavern, her cheeks blushed hot at the thought of Marcellus kissing her. The first one had been a week ago, at night, on the training grounds after he'd beaten her in a duel. That was one. Her one and only kiss—a truly human thing—until he went and kissed her again. On the shore after the Phoenix had brought him and the others back from the Realm. That was two.

She'd since lost count. Who knew humans kissed so much? Yet even though she'd lived thousands of years without a single kiss and had gained more of them in the last week than she thought anyone could need in a lifetime, she wouldn't mind a few more. She wouldn't mind one bit.

Of course, the dilemma for Marcellus was that he'd kissed her right in front of everybody, and now she was no secret to anybody. The night before, he'd explained.

As members of the royal family went through the process of selecting a companion, they were supposed to follow strict rules for courtship. There had to be chaperones and a certain number of public appearances so the whole thing could happen under the eyes of the kingdom. Of course, many a king had had his share of secret and not-so-secret mistresses, whether there was a queen sitting on the throne or not.

"But such women are never anything more," Marcellus had said. He lay on the ground, propped on one elbow, a glint of moonlight on his face. "Of course, courtship would not be proper so long as the kingdom is in mourning."

"Which lasts until the funeral?" Janus asked. She sat barefoot and cross-legged on the ground, twirling a stray piece of grass in her fingers.

He nodded.

"There are a lot of rules about how you're allowed to see a woman. I notice you're breaking all of them."

He smiled ruefully. "Well."

Then she wondered. For one hot, piercing moment, she wondered if he were telling her he wanted her as merely a mistress. Until that moment, Janus had not given much thought to what it meant to be with a king. She had only been drawn to the man, Marcellus. But a king would need a queen. Of course he would. She had given no thought to this until she realized she was not being courted, but rather meeting him secretly at night, away from prying eyes.

A sick knot of distaste formed in her stomach. She did not care about being queen, but did not want to be this way—this human way—with Marcellus, only to have him be that way with someone else.

She remembered a young fisherman's daughter she'd once witnessed crying in despair over a boy who broke her heart. Janus had thought she'd understood then and had compassion on the girl. After all, Janus had suffered loss too. But in this moment with Marcellus, she understood this sort of loss was something entirely different.

Marcellus took her hand then. "So... I thought... after the funeral, if you want, I can arrange for a more... formal courtship."

"With me?" she said stupidly, her hand limp in his.

"Only if you want to. You don't have to." Even though he held her eyes with characteristic strength, she felt the trembling in his hands. The same hopeful trembling she felt within herself.

"Do *you* want to?" she asked.

He nodded, his voice low and thick as he said, "Very much."

And like that, all those sick feelings turned into something light and playful, dancing in her chest. She clasped his hand

and he responded in kind. "Well," she said, giving him a mischievous look, "you can't get rid of me as a commander that easily, you know."

He broke out into that broad smile of his that made her want to kiss him. Yet again. "I wouldn't dream of it."

Now, thinking of these secret, human things in the depths of the faerie world, Janus felt as though anyone who looked at her would see it on her face and in her walk. She hoped not.

She stole a glance at Salerno, relieved he was looking ahead and not scrutinizing her again. She knew she would, eventually, have to tell him what was happening between her and Marcellus. But not now. Not today.

And she would keep certain details to herself.

They came at last to the Royal Cavern. Unlike the throne rooms of human kings, where sometimes large crowds of humans gathered both to hear and be heard, this room was for Salerno to meet with only a few at a time. When speaking to the faeries as a whole, Salerno joined them in the Grand Cavern. Thus, the Royal Cavern was not large. In that modest space, however, it did capture the kind of glory fit for a king. Salerno was fond of golden kitonas. They bloomed out of the walls, their large petals giving the room a rather glittery feel.

Salerno crossed to his moss-covered throne adorned with tiny, white flowers. He settled in, his robes puddling comfortably around the base.

She sat on a raised bench near his side, her fingers resting on the soft moss covering the surface. "You sensed what happened at the Rock of Light?" she asked him.

"I did, but I would like you to tell me more. How was it done, in the end?"

She told him about the battle in the Realm and the defeat of Aradia, and how the Three had discovered the role of their different stones. Marcellus, whose blue stone had bound him to the element of water, used the stone to get through the magical Gateway at the end of the Bridge of a Thousand Ages; it transported him to the Realm of the Phoenix. Praea, whose secret identity as a Tulaga bound her to the air, somehow

22

managed to carry both Nicolai and Corren up, up, up the Cliffs and to the dizzying heights of the Realm.

"A Tulaga?" Salerno asked, his brows furrowed.

"They are of the Order," Janus explained. "They use Phoenix ash to transform into golden birds. It's really quite magnificent."

Salerno stared at her. His intense green eyes grew distant. Janus felt an uneasiness creep over her skin.

"Salerno?"

There was a shift in his countenance, as if he had gone somewhere and was back, staring at her.

"Is something wrong?"

He waved his slender hand. "Go on."

She resisted the human-like urge to interrogate him and did as she was told. She was eager to continue her tale anyway. With increasing energy, she told the story of the battle in the Realm, just as the Three had told her. Sometimes gesturing with her arms, she laid out every detail she knew, including Corren's act of sacrifice. He used his red stone to give up his life in order to bring the Phoenix back from the brink of death.

"Corren thought he would die by doing so?" Salerno asked.

Janus nodded. "He did in fact die, from all accounts. It was Nicolai's yellow stone that restored him." Nicolai was the only one of his brothers the Phoenix bound to the element of earth, even though they were all half earth faerie.

"And where are the stones now?"

"Gone. Disintegrated into ash. Except Corren's stone." It had been encased in the tip of his staff, which he had forged in the lava lake of the fire faeries. Instead of disintegrating like the others, his stone turned to petrified ash, giving his staff a unique power indeed.

Janus concluded with a dramatic account of the Phoenix destroying the Bridge of a Thousand Ages as it brought the four of them—"the four elements of the prophecy!"— back to shore.

Finished at last, she rested her hands on her lap, beaming. The Three were triumphant. They did it.

Salerno nodded his head slowly. "That is good," he said.

His response was muted, even for him. Her enthusiasm waned a bit in the face of it and she furrowed her brows at him. "Are you not pleased?"

"The Tulaga," he said. "I thought they were extinct."

Janus opened her mouth to answer, but then looked at the faerie before her more closely. "The Tulaga were believed to be a human myth," she said slowly. "What do you know of them?"

But Salerno would say no more.

Three

There is a man whose name has been blotted from every record to ever mention him. He is known to history only as the Mapmaker. Only a few know him even as that.

It began long ago, when the world was still new.

The Mapmaker had already charted the mountains of the northern realms and the shoreline along the west. He had discovered soaring waterfalls in the king's mountains and deep canyons in the vast desert plains.

Carrying his burlap pack stuffed with thin leatherskin maps, writing implements, and his folios of notes—along with bothersome necessaries such as hunting weapons, food, and a waterskin—the Mapmaker headed into the previously unexplored territory of the East and an unnamed forest.

A grand forest it was. The grandest he had ever seen. Not merely because he had the sense, upon entering them, that it was vast and would carry on for some time. Not merely because the trees were larger and more magnificent than any he had seen in all his years of traveling. No, this forest held some intangible glory that seemed to vibrate within all he saw.

He stepped under the sweeping canopy of a massive oak, placed his hands on the rough bark, looked up, and saw the leaves winking at him as he heard the wind whisper through.

When he looked down, he saw a rather unusual man he would later learn was named Salerno.

It was the first time human and earth faerie ever met eyes.

The human and the earth faerie found one another equally fascinating, but the human was not so prudent as Salerno was. Before discovering Salerno's forest, the Mapmaker had already sent a report to his distant king, detailing the shoreline he had mapped. Within a short time, the king sent a handful of leaders and citizens to populate the area. The new settlement was still a mere speck on the very edge of human development. In many thousands of years it would become Stonebridge, the helm of a kingdom that had not yet been born. It would also, very soon, become the center of an Order the Phoenix had not yet created.

But the Mapmaker knew none of that. He merely considered the new settlement, which was only a few hours walk from the realm of the earth faeries, to be a convenient home base. Naturally he told a few humans what he had discovered. When next he returned to Salerno, he had three humans in tow.

Salerno, who had told no one, was not disconcerted by the increase in their numbers until the next time the Mapmaker returned. This time with nearly twenty more humans.

"How many more of you are there?" Salerno asked, looking from face to human face.

"Hundreds," the Mapmaker replied. "Thousands."

"Tell no more about us for now. I cannot teach thousands at once."

How many he could teach at once soon became irrelevant. Though the humans longed to learn faerie magic, it did not take long to discover certain limitations to any training Salerno might offer. One woman among the humans, Madera, explained that some had magic and some did not. It is something humans were born with, or were not, and the abilities of magical humans seemed to vary widely. She had wondered if the non-magical humans could perhaps perform faerie magic.

Not only could they not, but it turned out even the humans with magic could not duplicate faerie magic, which seemed a variety all its own. Many of the humans left and did not return, disappointed that the oddity of the forest yielded so little.

The few who stayed were rewarded for their persistence. Over time, these magical human friends of Salerno formed into three groups.

Madera, a woman with red hair so wild and thick she almost seemed a faerie herself, became the unspoken leader of the

26

small group of witches and wizards who seemed to have a particular skill for, and interest in, the faeries' ability to magically conceal.

The second group was led by Eala, a woman so aged she created more fascination in Salerno than he did in her. She was shadowed by three young ladies who asked question after question about the faeries' transformative skills.

And the Mapmaker? He wasn't sure if he had no magic or had so little it did him no good. After hearing Salerno and the others talk, he learned he could sense things in a magical way, but struggled to do even the simplest human spell.

This created a strange ache within him, different from the unquenchable yearning he had to explore new lands. This was an ache he could not quite sort out. Did he wish he could perform magic as he had seen the others do? Or did he just not want to let go of this world he'd discovered? Did he not like the others laying claim on Salerno in a way the Mapmaker could not?

Salerno scheduled certain days for their training, often with weeks in between, for faeries had a lower tolerance for interaction than humans did.

While Madera and Eala and their followers were away, they practiced their magic and developed new skills, inspired by what they'd seen Salerno do.

While the Mapmaker was away, he did what he did best. For while the humans were not allowed in the belowground realm of Amon Tunde, it was not long before he knew their lands above ground as well as Salerno did.

Sage Kai'Enna stood in the Upper Room of the Rock of Light near one of the rough openings that faced toward the Realm. The slight breeze coming through the opening felt chilled compared to the warmth of the Eternal Flame behind her.

Her aged arms wrapped around herself, the glass ball at the end of her necklace resting in the soft hollow of her neck. This magical object, within which lay the potent Phoenix ash, made her transformations into a Tulaga possible. She had worn the necklace for close to forty years. For over thirty of those years, she was the only Tulaga on earth.

It was a necessary risk that had been so terrifying she felt the echoes of that fear even now. Once she had found and trained Praea, the risk had lessened slightly. Now that her branch finally had more ash, enough not just to survive but to thrive for many hundreds of years, she should feel peace at last.

But she didn't.

Kai'Enna frowned, looking at the Realm of the Phoenix far in the distance. The sheer Cliffs of the Realm rose high into the sky, impressive even at this distance. Elsewhere, Kai'Enna knew, snow had reached the caps of the highest mountains, but not so for the Cliffs. Perhaps they produced their own heat, for snow never dusted the top, even in the deepest days of winter.

Behind her, the newly regenerated Eternal Flame filled the room with a dull roar. It dominated the huge altar, where it would burn night and day, day in and day out, until the Phoenix came again in hundreds and hundreds of years.

Their beloved Phoenix.

After all the fear they'd had for it, after all the worry that someone would steal both its life and its power—and still she could not believe Aradia had been their enemy all along!—they already faced a new threat.

Kai'Enna turned and glanced over her shoulder. The Eternal Flame caressed her face with gentle warmth as she considered the orb of ash sitting on the altar. The smooth surface of the glass glinted with the reflections of the dancing reds and yellows and oranges from the Eternal Flame.

The reflection morphed into the rising figure of the Phoenix, wings outstretched and aglow. Then it was gone. The reflection was merely a reflection again, without any distinguishing shape.

This vision happened so quickly, she would've questioned whether it had happened at all if it hadn't occurred many times over the last few days. She wasn't the only one who'd witnessed it. It seemed the Phoenix was reminding them this was a problem they could not ignore. As if they needed reminding.

She turned back to the Realm. What did it mean that the ash could not be lifted from the altar? She wondered, not for the first time, if the secrets jointly guarded by her branch and the Madera branch might simply be lost to humans now. She hadn't yet told Praea about it—she was still in training as a future Head of their branch—but Kai'Enna couldn't help but wonder... what if she never told Praea everything?

What if she destroyed her branch's records of their most important secret? The knowledge Kai'Enna guarded would go with her when she died.

Wouldn't it?

After all, with the Madera branch extinct these last four hundred years, surely she was the only one left who knew the secret. Even the Heads of the Order did not know anything of it. Maybe all Kai'Enna had to do was take it to her grave and the secret would at last and truly be safe.

But, Kai'Enna wondered, absently rubbing the glass ball at her neck with one finger, while she could destroy her own records, what of the records of the Madera branch? What if they were still out there somewhere? What if they fell into the wrong hands?

Kai'Enna lifted both hands, the transformation complete by the time she brought them down again. The aged and massive Tulaga flew from the upper room of the Rock of Light resolved.

She would wait. She would wait and see what Corren learned.

29

The funeral procession advanced down the broad avenue from the castle, turning onto a network of narrower streets that angled through the city and on toward the cemetery. Citizens lined the route along the cobbled lanes, many clasping small bunches of wildflowers tied together by flaxen cords and the traditional seashell garlands. They held these aloft when the marble casket came into view. The seashells fluttered and tinkled as a brisk wind came in from the sea. The bedecked mahogany cart bore the white marble casket—within which lay King Clement's remains—that was topped with a glistening relief of the beloved king lying in state. A dozen royal carvers had been working on it ever since he had passed away fourteen days ago.

Lord Marcellus, atop a grand black stallion, rode alone behind the casket. Horse and rider were adorned in Caedmonia's colors: red crushed velvet and smooth silk, gold braided trim and soft tassels. Behind him, two abreast, came Corren and Nicolai, some dozen royal advisors, and a host of knights dressed in their finest. As the procession advanced, the mourning citizens along the route closed in behind, joining in the solemn march, but not before paying close heed to the royal assembly as they passed by.

Lord Marcellus, their soon-to-be king, did not fail to notice their scrutiny.

He knew that Corren, in his fine wizard's cloak and holding his distinctive staff, would draw notice regardless of the situation. What Marcellus made note of, however, was that most eyes lingered on Nicolai the longest. Dressed in finery fit for a prince, but without the adornment Lord Marcellus bore, Nicolai valiantly withstood the skeptical gazes of the people.

By this time, the citizens knew who Corren and Nicolai were. To a degree. The Phoenix brought the Three and Praea back from the Realm and deposited them in the crowded square. Witness to this extraordinary event were citizens, knights, and members of the Order alike. At that point, Marcellus felt it best Caedmonia understood what it all meant. The royal storyteller wrote the official tale, now recorded in the *History of the Kings*, and Marcellus sent criers to the squares of every village and town in the kingdom. The story would take months to reach the far corners of the land. It included Corren, the eldest son, renouncing any claim to the throne, though he would still make a public pronouncement before the Coronation.

Nicolai, however, was an official prince of the kingdom, though younger. He would need significant training to fill that role. Should something happen to Marcellus, the kingdom would need to accept Nicolai as their leader. As a newcomer to the stage, the kingdom would not be likely to do so now. Still, he had come to the kingdom's attention as one of the Three, quickly becoming stuff of legend. Since most of the events surrounding the Phoenix and the Three happened underground and involved a world most people knew nothing about, it was all very shocking. Marcellus had a lot of work to do to get the kingdom to accept Nicolai as a potential ruler. Nicolai had a lot of work to do too, for he was not prepared to rule. Hopefully it would never come to that, but as future king, Marcellus was responsible for making sure his country was prepared for any eventuality, including his own death.

Not included in the official tale spreading across the land was the fact that Queen Elana had been a faerie, thus making her sons— Corren, Marcellus, and Nicolai—half-faeries. The earth faeries wanted to stay hidden, preferring the humans to think of faeries as only a myth. The Three would honor that wish, for now. No one knew how the kingdom would react to the knowledge their king was a half-faerie. Marcellus didn't quite know how to handle that himself and decided to leave it be until he gained more clarity.

But first they had to bury his father. Something he never wanted to have to do.

He'd known, as much as any child can know, that this would happen in due time. That one day his father would die and be gone forever. But in that part of his heart that made him who he was, he hadn't believed it. Not really.

Part of him still didn't believe it.

The procession curved and climbed the hill to the walled burial grounds of the kings. Knights stood guard at the open gate, a throng of citizens waiting anxiously nearby. The lane into the cemetery itself was empty save for the single row of knights on either side. When the cart bearing the king crossed through the gate, the knights drew their swords and pointed them heavenward.

Individual graves with massive headstones dotted the grounds. These were for lesser royals or people of honor. Soon they would move Nashua's remains here, erecting a statue and headstone that immortalized her great service and sacrifice to the Phoenix, and indeed to them all. The royal mausoleum dominated the center of the cemetery. A magnificent structure built by the second king of Caedmonia to honor his father, King Revelle, it lent the appropriate air of reverence and finality. Every king and queen of Caedmonia was buried here. In time, Marcellus would join them. And who would take over then?

He better understood why his father had pushed him to marry. The kingdom did need heirs. With his father gone, the kingdom suddenly felt vulnerable.

Concerns over Nicolai aside, his kingdom gave him plenty to worry about. For one, he had the neighboring countries to consider. Rather than coming himself or sending one of his children, as would be proper, the Sakkaran king merely sent a delegate to the funeral. Marcellus could not fault him. After losing two sons to murder and nearly his daughter Praea, along with the shock of learning she was a Tulaga, King Jareth wanted to keep his children close to home.

Then there was Norrland, the kingdom to the north that was still rocking from the recent coup by the younger prince. Marcellus at least didn't have to worry about the Norrland troops and wizards who'd followed Aradia—they'd met their fate on Thrayce Island—but given the Norrland prince's willingness to murder his own brother in order to gain the throne, it was safe to say Marcellus could not count on their prior alliance with them. It was a small country and not much of a threat on its own, especially given their recent troop losses, but he would have to make sure they didn't form an alliance with Hathmirr, the country to the west.

Caedmonia and Hathmirr had never been on friendly terms. They *always* had to worry about Hathmirr.

Then there was the matter of the unclaimed ash. Quite apart from Corren's concern about it, the whole thing gave Marcellus a sense of unease. He often wondered what the Phoenix meant by it.

Still, there was nothing to do but leave such matters in the capable hands of the wizard in charge. Marcellus had the whole of Caedmonia to worry about. His country had suffered a large loss of knights during the wizards' attack, was still recovering from the devastation caused by the destruction of the Eridanos Dam, and now had a new, young king at its helm with two previously unknown princes.

All in all, Caedmonia was reeling.

Not to mention the fact that the citizens who witnessed the extraordinary events at the Rock of Light also witnessed Marcellus kissing the only female in his army. He'd already fielded questions from a few people, wanting to know just who this Janus person was. They would find out soon enough.

The cart stopped in front of the grand mausoleum made of smooth, dark granite and anchored at each corner by massive, gold-plated pillars. From the top of each of these, sculpted dragons spread their wings wide, eternal sentinels of Caedmonia's past rulers.

Marcellus dismounted, the horse's bridle jangling, and landed firmly on both feet. A page slipped discreetly to the horse's side, taking hold of the reins. His brothers came next to him, the royal advisors behind them.

Before them, the cart and casket waited.

Ten knights worked with surprising grace as they slid the heavy casket off the cart. They carried it inside the mausoleum and walked the short distance to the stone pedestal destined for the king, the marble casket of Queen Elana waiting next to it.

The casket in place, Marcellus entered the cool bowels of the tomb and approached alone.

Bowing one last time to his king, his bow turned into mute longing. He placed his forehead on the stone relief of his father's chest and his hand on his father's clasped hands. The marble was smooth and cold and he breathed in the clean smell of stone as he inhaled deeply. A moment of scent and silence and stillness, then he rose and the moment was over. He left the shadows of the tomb and joined his brothers in the sun.

The rest proceeded with the mournful elegance so typical of such events. The resonating echo as the mausoleum doors swung closed, the precise movements of the knights, the shouts of "Hail, King Clement!"

Someone handed Marcellus his own bouquet of flowers. The seashell garland gently brushed against his hand, and the aroma of roses and lilies and daisies rose to meet him. He laid the little bundle at the base of the doors.

Corren and Nicolai placed their flowers next and returned to Marcellus' side; it was tradition for the children of the passing king to watch over this final rite. The rest of the nobles and knights followed suit, then led their own procession back to the castle. The citizens of Stonebridge likewise left their final alms before their king and wandered away in silence. They would break off from the funeral route at various places, returning to their homes or the inns at which they were staying, though many of them would linger on the street for the final recession.

By the time the last mourner left, the Three, along with the ten knights who bore the casket, faced a mound of flowers so large it nearly overtook them. Part of the mound lay in the shadow of the hulking building, but the rest spilled out into the late afternoon sun. The many little petals fluttered in the wind.

At last, Marcellus led the group away: his brothers behind him and the ten knights. It was the smallest formal procession the kingdom ever saw, this final march back to the castle. It was intended to signify how even great men are made small in the face of death, and to remind the city that while the king is

34

mourned by his citizens, he is also a father mourned by his children.

The next time the city would see these children, it would be to see their new king crowned.

Four

The first light of dawn crept over the horizon and slipped into Corren's tiny office. The room was illuminated by a simple, wooden chandelier hanging above the desk, where Corren sat leaning on one elbow. He had used this office for a number of years and, though cramped, was unable to bring himself to take over Aradia's old one.

The wall to Corren's right was lined with mismatched bookcases, packed tightly with bound books of various sizes and wooden boxes cradling smaller folios. More stacks teetered on the floor next to the cases, creeping outward as if contemplating a coup.

The wall opposite this presented a small, stuffed chair and a massive cupboard with carved doors. The cupboard's interior overflowed with Corren's modest stash of magical instruments, potion ingredients, scales, hourglasses, spare quills, ink, and parchment.

Across from his desk, above the narrow door, an ancient-looking slab of mahogany bore an inscription. It read, *Magic is to the soul as breath is to the body.* It had been there when Corren inherited this office several years ago and was the only item of decor he'd kept from the previous owner.

To the left of the door, Corren had placed a small painting he'd found in a shop near the old bakery on Cobblers Street in Stonebridge. It was of a young boy kneeling at his mother's feet and laying his head in her lap. Her hand rested on the soft curls on his head, while he reached his hand to a white and tan spotted dog that sniffed tentatively toward them.

His desk, made of fine maple, was a substantial piece of furniture at least a hundred years old and entirely too large for the space it occupied. He'd often wondered if a bit of magic had been used to get it through the door, or if perhaps Tower Hall South had been built up around it.

In spite of Aradia's insistence that a tidy desk fostered a clear mind, Corren never could seem to avoid some degree of clutter. As of late, however, he'd reached new heights. Every spare surface of his desk held either his own folios and notes, or else piles of the books and folios he'd rescued from Thrayce Island. More were stacked against the wall under the window behind him.

Corren dipped his quill in the inkwell, yawning widely as he scratched his latest note on the parchment in front of him. He'd been trying to catch up on his sleep but kept waking in the middle of the night. Once awake, his mind would start whirring and he would inevitably find himself shuffling down the quiet stone halls of Tower Hall South to his office until he was entombed by books and questions alike.

Added to his recent swell of books were several volumes of the *History of the Order of Ceinoth*, which he'd retrieved from among the hundreds kept in the Vault at the Rock of Light. He was interested in the histories that recorded the years when the Madera branch had gone extinct four hundred years ago.

Due to the scarcity of ash during the last age of the Phoenix, the Madera branch had run out and thus could not maintain their magical traditions. The other branches of the Order could not share their own ash, thanks to a binding spell that sealed each branch's ash to itself. After the extinction of the Madera branch, the Order split the Wysard branch—Corren's branch—into two to preserve the magical number of seven branches, and thus the Guard was born.

But of course, Kennard, Head of the Guardian branch, could not lift the ash off the altar.

Nor could anyone else.

And no one was quite sure why or what they were to do about it.

Corren set the quill down and rested his head in both hands, rubbing his temples with his fingertips. He had skimmed through the massive histories that included the last days and years of the Madera branch but found no answers. The books sat in a pile on the corner of his desk, awaiting a more thorough inspection.

Of course the first thing he'd done, after bringing Aradia's stash of books to his office, was look for any records kept by the Madera branch themselves. Aradia had stolen the secret books of all the other branches of the Order, which he'd found on Thrayce Island and returned unread, but there was nothing like that for the Madera branch. Either she hadn't been able to find them or the records of the Madera branch didn't exist anymore, extinct like their members.

He was now in the middle of sorting the many personal notes Aradia had taken over the years. Some he recognized; others he'd never seen before. So far, their contents were harmless enough. Nothing more about what she had been doing in the months leading up to her attack on the Phoenix. Certainly nothing about the Madera branch that might help him figure out what to do about the ash left on the altar.

He skimmed a folio of notes taken years ago, set in her familiar, slanted hand. This one seemed to be dedicated to certain potions and their variants. He set it aside in a pile of folios he intended to leave alone for the foreseeable future. There were still dozens left to examine. Tired of the task, he stood, grabbed one of the histories, and sank into the chair to read.

Some time later, a knock on the door roused him from the nap he'd descended into. Judging by the light in the room, he guessed it was midmorning. He rubbed the pain at the base of his neck and called to the knocker to enter. In came Delossa, cradling a stack of folios.

Corren sighed inwardly. Only somewhat gifted in the arena of magic, Delossa was nevertheless adept at managing things and thrived at Tower Hall South as Counselor of Procedures. She managed the day-to-day operations at the Tower so the Head (now Corren) could focus on nurturing and sustaining their magical traditions.

She had been trying to corner him for the last few days and now here he was, literally in a chair in the corner, with his only way out blocked by Delossa herself.

"Sage Corren," she said. "I was hoping I could review things with you. Now that... well, now that..." she fumbled about for her words.

"Now that Aradia's gone. Yes."

"Well, yes. I need to go over things with you. There's the new recruits and the training to think about." Perhaps she sensed his hesitation, for she added with hopeful emphasis, "The schedules in particular?"

Under normal circumstances, the schedule at Tower Hall South could be set without him, but two things complicated matters and she needed his direction.

The first was the replenishment of the ash. They were now back up to normal levels, although "normal" referred to a period over twelve hundred years ago and therefore not a state of operations anyone could recall. He needed to decide how to go about reinstating some of their former activities. He didn't even know what all of them were.

It was a problem faced by every branch.

The second complication was the introduction of nonverbal magic. It was an incredibly effective way to perform magic and everyone was eager to learn it. Trouble was, he wasn't sure himself exactly how he was doing it, so he wasn't sure how to teach it to others. But as recipient of this new form of magic, he had a responsibility to pass it on to the rest of the Order.

Along with everything else he had to do.

Just thinking about it exhausted him. He remembered Marcellus' recent counsel to get sufficient rest and wished he could go back to bed. He gestured for Delossa to sit and wondered if Marcellus was having better success following his own advice. Somehow he doubted it.

Corren stood and cleared a stingy area of his desk, into which she plopped her stack of folios. The sight did nothing to ease his sense of burden.

She opened the top folio.

"Let's begin with the schedules," he said.

She stopped and looked at him over the open folio. Apparently she'd had it in mind to begin elsewhere and had to decide whether or not to argue with him about it.

Delossa was only a few years older than Corren, and he'd known her since he came to Tower Hall South as a scrawny, eight-year-old orphan. He had advanced quickly, so for a period of time, they'd had several classes together until he advanced again and joined the next group up.

While many of his peers had pelted him with their jealous comments, Delossa was never one of them. Even after Aradia had discovered Delossa's skill in operations and moved her into supervisory positions, they had always had a casual, friendly relationship.

He sensed she wanted to take his suggestion and tell him what he could do with it, but then said, "Of course, Sage Corren." Replacing the folio, she removed another further down the stack.

She quickly and efficiently went over the existing schedules, outlining key decisions that needed to be made before making any adjustments.

"Put the Apprentices and head teachers into the first rotation for learning nonverbal magic," Corren said. "Work the administrative heads into the next session. We'll see how that goes before deciding when to teach the lower-level students."

Delossa nodded, taking notes in her folio. If she were bothered by being excluded from the first round of training, she didn't show it.

Pausing in her note taking, she held her quill aloft and looked around on his desk.

He retrieved the inkwell from behind a stack of books and moved it closer to her.

"Thank you," she said, dipping her quill. "The new session begins next week. Do you want—"

"I'm not beginning next week. There's too much to do. Work it into the second half of the session."

She allowed herself a moment of surprise before shaking her head and then nodding. "Of course, of course. You've been through a lot recently." She was no longer looking at her notes, but now at him.

She let things hang there and seemed to be waiting for some sort of confession.

He had no desire to divulge confidences or go over recent events. "The second half of the session," he said again. "Put them on my schedule once a week. Mornings. It doesn't matter which day. Work around their class schedules and let me know."

She nodded, now back to her note taking.

A knock caused Corren to look up and Delossa to turn round. His door still hung open from Delossa's entrance. There stood Sage Bellamy, Head of the Layrin branch. His long, dark hair, streaked with gray, was pulled back from his round face. Olive hands gripped a staff of smooth, dark ebony. One of the symbols of the Layrin branch graced the back of one hand, pale against his skin like a tender scar. The top of his staff bore the same symbol.

"Ah!" Corren said, standing. "I didn't know you were coming."

"Neither did I," Bellamy said, smiling calmly. "Do you have a moment?"

"Of course." Corren looked at Delossa. "You have enough to go on for the schedules, don't you? Can we finish the rest later?"

Delossa again looked like she wanted to argue, but she knew the Head of another branch took precedence. She took another tack. "When could we meet again? This evening?"

Corren glanced about the stacks of books on his desk.

"Or in the morning?" she pressed.

"Yes. Alright."

She smiled, stood, and gathered up her folios. Bellamy stepped aside to let her through but lingered in the doorway.

"Please come in," Corren offered.

"Might we go outside?"

41

"Yes, of course." Corren retrieved his staff from its place in the corner, and they took to the grounds. Bellamy explained he wanted to examine the old site of the Silent Circle, so they went to the far west side of the grounds where a mound of hedges grew wild and unchecked.

Long ago, before the ash became scarce, the Silent Circle was one of the magical hedges the Layrin branch tended on behalf of the members of Tower Hall South. The Layrin branch was one of the branches that intertwined with the others the most. In addition to their own magical hedges (including the Labyrinth, which Corren and Aradia had both used to see visions of their futures), the Layrin branch maintained the enchanted auditoriums and gazebos of the Chanters, created protective symbols for the Murano branch, and more.

Some of these things were critical and maintained at minimum levels during the shortage of ash. The Silent Circle was not considered critical, thus the current state of decay.

"Quite overgrown," Bellamy said, looking at it.

"Sorry about that."

Bellamy waved his olive hand in dismissal and began to circle the hedges. "Not at all."

Corren had never given much thought to the Silent Circle. He knew it was a complex device, having many uses, though it was most often used to remove magical blocks. Aradia had once said she wished they could use the Silent Circle to help Corren get over his block with healing spells.

As Bellamy progressed around the circle, he bent here and there to hover his staff over one section or push an overgrown branch aside to investigate what lay underneath. As Corren watched him work, he remembered, not for the first time, that he wasn't the only one coping with the recent, painful revelations about Aradia. Unlike the other Heads of the Order, Bellamy considered Aradia more than just a colleague. He'd considered her a friend. They would never know if she'd ever considered him the same.

Bellamy had attempted to discuss Aradia with him, to find out how he was coping as Aradia's former charge. Corren had only shrugged and said something noncommittal before changing the subject. He didn't want to discuss it. Then or now.

When Bellamy circled back to him, Corren said, "I imagine you have a long list of hedges to repair."

"Yes," he said as they headed back, their staffs leaning forward and back as they used them for walking sticks. "We are forced to prioritize." Across the tree-studded grounds, the sprawling stone complex of Tower Hall South rose ahead of them. "Most important things first. We will get to it all eventually, but some members may have a difficult time waiting." Bellamy smiled good-naturedly.

"I understand," Corren said. "We're in no hurry."

"Oh, but no. Yours will be one of the first."

Corren looked at him. "The Silent Circle? But why?"

"It may come in handy," Bellamy said calmly. "Who knows what will happen if you reabsorb the Guardian branch back into yours."

"Do you think it will come to that?"

"It's where they belong anyway. The Phoenix seems to think so."

They passed beneath the shadow of a sprawling elm. A black-and-white warbler had been pecking at the ground nearby, but issued a feeble cry of protest at their approach and flitted off.

"But then," Corren said, "who will take the ash?"

"I wish I knew."

"I don't understand why Kennard cannot take it. It seems it should be him. The old branch is gone. He's already one of the Heads. Already part of the Order. Maybe... maybe he just needs to learn the magic of that branch before he can take the ash?"

"Perhaps. I don't envy you the task of sorting it out."

They came to the central fountain and Bellamy stopped. Corren paused with him. Up ahead, several students advanced along the walkway at the base of the main building, but here, they were still alone. The water gurgled and splashed tirelessly.

Bellamy gave him a thoughtful look.

Corren sensed a change in subject coming. He did not want to find out what it was. Though it was clear Bellamy was about to say something, Corren spoke first.

"Will you be staying with us for a while? You're more than welcome, of course." And this was true. "I have much to do though, I'm afraid, and I'm due at the castle for evening meal. I'll see that you're well fed here, though."

Bellamy smiled faintly and gave Corren a knowing look, seeming to understand that Corren was steering the conversation away from potentially painful topics. There was no offense in what would be Corren's gross lack of hospitality under ordinary circumstances. The two knew each other too well for that. To his relief, Bellamy did not press him.

"I'll be staying with Solesmay tonight, but thank you. It will be another week or two before I'm home, then I'll send word about the repairs on the Silent Circle. We'll tend to it soon."

Corren nodded.

Bellamy gave him a meaningful look. "Please. Let me know if there's something I can do for you."

Corren shook his hand and lied to his old friend. "I will."

He saw Bellamy away and returned to his office. He closed the door behind him and stood in the center of the room, facing the calamity that was his desk. Above him, the lights in the wooden chandelier still burned, though it was nearly midday and no longer needed.

He waved his staff and the lights within puffed out. Drifting to the window, Corren rested his head against the glass. Off to the left, the stone fountain glistened in the courtyard. Ahead, some distance away, lay the unkempt remnants of the Silent Circle.

One of Bellamy's first priorities.

Corren stood staring in the direction of the neglected hedges for some time, pondering.

Five

Marcellus rode down to the sea on a bay roan from the king's stock. Over the past few days he'd been switching from one horse to another and hadn't yet settled on a favorite. Today's mount was a decent horse with a strong gait, but he had no particular fondness for it. Certainly not the connection he'd had to Kedron.

He'd had a strange dream about Kedron the night before. It started out as more of a memory.

They were back in the Realm. Marcellus lay helpless on the scorching earth, held immobile by Aradia's spell. He again saw Aradia slash Kedron's throat with Marcellus' own sword. Again saw his beloved horse fall to the earth, bleeding.

In the dream, he experienced this in a kind of haze, without any of the horror he'd felt when it happened in real life. Then the dream shifted to something new. He was sinking into the earth, folded into it until he was wrapped in the dark. It wasn't frightening, but rather oddly calming. He lifted back up through the earth until he was embraced by the sky. Though he couldn't see Kedron, Marcellus sensed his horse had been going down into the earth and back up again right along with him.

Marcellus woke feeling comforted for some reason. He went to the stables and approached Kedron's stall. He half expected to see Kedron there, nibbling his hay.

But the stall was empty. The dirt floor swept clean.

Now, down by the shore, on a horse that was not his horse, Marcellus dismounted and tied the animal to a tree close to the cliffs. The wind lifted and fell, playful and buoyant, drawing him to the sea. Not that he needed any encouragement.

He removed his boots and socks, the firm sand still cool in these early morning hours. He rolled the cuffs of his trousers and headed for the water, knowing it would be brisk. It was, in fact, biting cold. He trudged in up to his calves anyway.

Closing his eyes, he inhaled the crisp air. He wondered if the Phoenix had bound him to the element of water from birth, for Marcellus had always found it rejuvenating, cold or not.

He glanced far down the shoreline to the Rock of Light. The Eternal Flame burned at the top where, Marcellus knew, a portion of ash waited. Waited for what, he couldn't help but wonder. A sense of unease settled into his chest, but Marcellus turned away. He had enough to think about without claiming the worries of others.

He took another deep breath of clear sea air and let his gaze stretch into the distance. The ocean worked its magic. The rest of the world dropped away. He knew only this unending mass of rolling water. The seagulls crying overhead. The wind caressing the sea, coaxing waves both big and small. He fell into the rhythm of it. As if he, like the ocean, were a great, powerful calm.

As each wave roared onto shore and slid back out again, the water pulled sand from beneath his increasingly numb feet. He allowed himself to sink in, a smile tugging at one corner of his mouth.

That was when he felt it. A subtle change in the water. Somewhere in the distance.

And off in the distance, the green underbelly of a wave rose above the others. The biggest one he'd seen yet today. Maybe ever. Whatever strange thing he was feeling in the water was coming from that wave. He was sure of it.

It gained in strength as it came closer to shore, and he realized it was big enough to knock him off his feet if he didn't move.

And move he did. He took one step back and then another, unable to take his eyes off the wave as it roared toward him. Back and back he went, steps quicker now as the wave reared and crashed in front of him. The wave flattened and reached toward him as he retreated onto dry sand. As the wave gave its last and stretched as far onto the shoreline as it would go, it kissed the tip of his bare toe.

It was like being kissed by light itself.

Standing still now, Marcellus watched as the wave retreated. But part of it did not retreat. Part of it stayed. Made of swirling water, a formation of sorts rose up as if it were an entity unto itself. Like part of the sea taking on a life of its own.

The shape moved. Rearranged. And took the form of a great horse.

A great horse made of nothing but sea.

One slender, watery leg stepped forward, and the animal shape came toward shore.

Marcellus could not move. Held in place by this apparition or vision, he could not breathe. Could not even blink.

Nearer the strange specter came. Starting at the head, the water fell away, down the neck and back and tail until there was nothing left but a magnificent horse. Its white coat gleamed in the sunlight. Its cream-colored tail flicked once, then relaxed. Leaving the water, it came to him on dry land, the ocean roaring benignly behind it.

Its great, glassy eye, black as coal, blinked at Marcellus, who at last blinked back.

The animal looked as real a thing as Marcellus ever saw. Though its coat was pure white, a faint mark the color of honey stretched across its neck in the same place Aradia had slashed Kedron's throat.

Marcellus' skin tingled and he felt his blood pulsing through his veins.

The horse did not look like Kedron. He stood a full hand taller and his coat was lighter. But his eyes... though they looked different, they felt the same.

The horse took a step toward him and Marcellus moved closer as well. It was a massive animal. It radiated something that reminded him of the sea. He had the feeling of floating on calm waters, arms stretched out and warm in the sun.

Marcellus cautiously placed his hand against the soft mark on the horse's neck. The beast let him. Its velvety coat felt as any

47

horse's might, but something about touching the honey-colored mark brought an ache to Marcellus' chest.

"Alright, boy?"

The horse nuzzled his massive head against Marcellus' shoulder. So firm and real. He smelled of horse and seawater.

Marcellus ran his hand along the horse's neck. Solid. He continued along his back and hind haunches, feeling the taut muscles underneath. Even his father's old horse could not compare to this one.

He came back and looked the horse in the eye, considering. The horse blinked calmly, waiting patiently. A name came to him. "Ryafan," he said.

The horse neighed softly in his throat.

Marcellus nodded slowly. "I like it too." He smiled, patting the horse on the neck. "Yes, I like it very much."

He turned and headed back for his boots, sand sticking to his wet feet and the air chilling his legs. He looked over his shoulder.

Ryafan watched him.

"Come on, then."

And the horse followed.

Corren went to the training grounds near the stables, where he was told he could find Lord Marcellus. Some forty knights gathered in a semicircle, facing away from him. They were talking and pointing at something, but he couldn't see what. A general uproar excited the group, followed by laughing.

"I told you," he heard Marcellus say. "He'll have none of it."

Corren worked his way through the crowd, spotting both Marcellus and Nicolai near the front. On the far side of the broad training field, a rather large, white horse trotted away from a knight who was picking himself up off the ground.

48

Corren drew up between Nicolai and Marcellus, the latter of whom glanced at him. "There you are."

"What's going on?"

"Behold," Marcellus said, gesturing, "my new steed."

The horse trotted across the grass with a regal gait, then reared up slightly, shaking his head and mane as his front hooves came down with commanding thuds. He sped into a trot then slowed into a saunter. Stopping, he stood lengthwise in front of the assembly and turned his majestic head in their direction, as if granting all the privilege of admiring him. He had no harness, no saddle, and seemed to be wandering the grounds at will.

"He's not broken yet?" Strange for a full-grown horse not to be broken.

"Not exactly." Marcellus proceeded to tell Corren about the horse's origin, and how even though he was taller than Kedron and his coloring was different, the mark on his neck was where Aradia had killed the other horse.

"He just feels like Kedron," Marcellus said.

"Resurrected?"

"I don't know. Something. I call him Ryafan."

"Not Kedron?" Corren asked.

"No. He's Ryafan."

The horse was on the move again, taking a wide arc in Marcellus' direction, coming so near the semicircle, the knights had to take several steps back as he approached. Several of the men laughed, seeming to enjoy the animal's spirit. Corren furrowed his brows. Resurrected from the Realm? Was that possible?

"It's strange," Marcellus said, "but not the strangest thing from the last few weeks. However it happened, he's my horse. He won't let anyone else ride him, and I didn't need to rope him to get him here. He just followed me."

The horse advanced until everyone had retreated except the Three. Massive hooves clopping, Ryafan came up and sniffed first Nicolai, then Corren. His soft muzzle pressed gently against Corren's stomach, where he exhaled with a burst of warm air. With the horse this near, Corren felt the faint magic humming within it.

"The strangest thing is he seems to understand me," Marcellus continued. Ryafan turned his attention to Corren's staff, sniffing the tip before proceeding to Marcellus.

Ryafan nuzzled his shoulder. "He's hungry," Marcellus said, patting his alabaster neck.

"Looks like you can understand him as well," Nicolai said.

"I suppose so. Let's take him to the stables. See if he'll eat."

Marcellus dismissed his knights, who wandered off reluctantly. The massive, white horse and the Three entered the stables and proceeded down the long corridor. A few curious horses poked their heads out of their stalls to watch as they walked by.

Marcellus stopped in front of a spacious stall and opened the gate.

As the horse wandered in, Nicolai patted his haunches appreciatively. "Another gift from the Phoenix."

Corren hadn't thought of it that way but realized Nicolai was right. "If the Phoenix gave me my staff," he said, looking at Nicolai, "and gave Marcellus his horse, what did he give you?"

Nicolai looked at Corren like the answer was obvious. "Praea."

Corren considered his staff. *Praea?*

"The staff doesn't seem so great now, does it?" Marcellus said slyly.

Nicolai laughed, but Corren shrugged. "I suppose we each got what suits us." It was all well and good.

Nicolai gave him a perplexed look. "Don't wizards..." He trailed off.

"What?"

"Marry?"

"Not usually."

Marcellus followed the horse into the large stall, but Nicolai and Corren hung back just outside the door.

"Is it forbidden?" Nicolai asked.

Corren shrugged again. "No, it's not forbidden. There's an old married couple at the Tower. But their magic's rather weak. The more magic resides in a person, the less likely they are to marry."

"Why?" Marcellus asked, watching Ryafan sniffing around the perimeter of the stall, twitching his long, white tail.

"No room for it, I suppose." Aradia had once explained that magical minds tend to be highly consumed with their craft and therefore less interested in romantic dealings. "Magic takes over everything. Although, it seems to depend on the kind of magic. Some branches have more married couples. The Chanters tend to marry quite often. I don't think the Layrin ever do, though."

Nicolai and Marcellus exchanged glances. Why did they both look so mystified?

"You've never been in love?" Nicolai asked.

Corren considered the question. He hadn't been in love or lust or anything close to it. There was no debating that. But that wasn't really what Nicolai was asking. "There's the idea of a thing, and then there's the thing itself. I see love makes you both happy, and I'm happy for you. But it's nothing I've ever sought for myself."

The horse, having fully investigated his new quarters, turned toward Marcellus and snorted.

"No hay, I know. We'll get you some." Marcellus stepped out of the stall and gestured to a stable boy at the end of the row. The young lad responded with a quick step. "Hay for Ryafan," Marcellus said. "Keep it stocked. The water as well. Keep the gate open though."

"Open, my Lord?"

"Better yet, have it removed. It will only get in the way."

The boy looked at the horse questioningly.

"He is not to be contained," Marcellus said. "He goes wherever he chooses, understood?"

"Yes, my Lord."

"Make sure my orders are broadly known."

"Yes, my Lord."

Marcellus dismissed him with a wave and he hustled off.

51

"I think we're a different breed," Nicolai said to Corren, picking up the thread of their conversation. He crossed his arms and leaned against the doorpost, smiling. "I've always been aware of the opposite gender."

Marcellus laughed. "Speaking of the opposite gender, here comes Janus."

They left Ryafan in the stall and headed back down the stable halls, but the only thing in sight was the long corridor that smelled of horse and the stable boy hauling a bundle of hay. Corren knew about the connection between Marcellus and Janus that allowed them to sense one another at a distance, but hadn't quite gotten used to it. They were halfway to the entrance before she came into view.

She was still wearing her knight's uniform even though Marcellus had moved her from the barracks to the east wing of the castle. Apparently she had initially resisted this move, wanting to stay close to her troops, but Marcellus thought it might be easier to establish proper courtship rituals if she were residing in rooms reserved for honored guests and visiting heads of nations.

Though still courtly and composed, Marcellus' face softened at the sight of her. Marcellus and Janus were not prone to displaying affection in front of others, though Corren had once spied them in a private moment and so knew things were different when they were alone. Even around others, though, there was an undercurrent of fondness that was not difficult to detect.

Though Corren had never considered having a relationship, watching his brothers interact with the women they loved created a strange feeling in his chest. Almost an ache.

Was it longing?

He didn't think so. He decided it must simply be the isolating feeling that comes from being so different from others.

Janus approached and passed her greetings to each one. "Donnelly said I could find yo—" Janus stopped mid-sentence, her eyes widening. Ryafan had wandered out of his stall.

Marcellus smiled at her reaction and turned to the horse, watching him approach.

"This is... strange," Janus said. "A horse, but... more than a horse. Where did you get him?"

"The sea."

"Ah. That explains it."

"Does it?"

"He feels like the sea."

Marcellus again told the story of Ryafan's beginning and the inability of anyone else to ride him. Marcellus looked at Janus. "I wonder if you could mount him."

Janus shook her head. "I wouldn't dare."

Six

The human named Bricker and the water faerie named Faatin sped through the bay, far beneath the dappled surface. Below, the seafloor rose in mountainous formations and fell into deep rifts that tore through the bottom and sank into blackness. The water faerie traveled faster than any man or dolphin could swim and the water whipped around them like an assault.

When they had been fleeing Aradia's carnage, Bricker had been grateful for the speed, but it was a long way to Hathmirr, and now he wearied of the journey. He was famished and wondered if the water faerie had need of food. Or sleep.

He was a strange creature, just as unsettling in his current dolphin form as in his faerie form. Bricker longed for the dusty trail he'd taken from Hathmirr to Caedmonia three weeks ago. It'd been a long, miserable trip, but at least they'd had food and shelter.

He thought of the half-dozen companions who'd come with him. All dead because of Aradia.

More than once he wondered if Faatin were tricking him, if they weren't going to Hathmirr at all. But he could think of no reason why Faatin would want to do so at this point. And besides, the faerie had nowhere to go. Bricker knew perfectly well Faatin was considered a traitor among his own people.

At last they neared the surface and broke through. He squinted against the sharp, white sunlight but took a cleansing breath that smelled of sea air and fish.

Faatin transformed back into a faerie. Bricker made a point not to look at him. He had seen enough of his disfigurement: silvery skin stretching down one side of his face, as if he'd been burned.

"Hathmirr," the faerie said.

Bricker was willing to take his word for it, but they were nowhere he recognized. All he saw was uninhabited shoreline. No city or marker of any kind. They continued down the coast until he got his bearings and they were soon upon it.

"There it is," he said nodding.

Mingren, capital city of Hathmirr, stretched away from the shoreline. Its squat, adobe buildings crouched together as if for protection. The city spread over the flat landscape until it petered out and scrubby plains of desert took over.

Not far from the city, they found a deserted cove where Faatin agreed to wait. Bricker had been worried Faatin would insist on coming into town with him, which would've been difficult to manage. Faatin, however, bluntly said he would never go so far from the water's edge and they both left it at that.

Bricker followed the rocky path into town. Though not the most direct route, he cut through the busy market, drawn by the sweet smell of baking *askinos* and the growling of his own stomach.

At one stall, canvas flapping overhead, he pilfered a couple of hard rolls, a stick of dried sausage, and a ball of cheese that he soon discovered was too sharp for his taste. He took a handful of dates from a barrel in another stall and, after he'd finished those, a sweet *askinos* from a booth at the edge of the market. The woman who made them along with other baked goods caught him doing it but spied the gold symbol on his forehead and looked carefully away.

She wasn't the only one. As he walked through the fabric district—bright folds of cloth stacked in pile after teetering pile—most passersby gave him plenty of space.

He polished off his treat, sucked the remnants of sticky glaze off his fingers, and rubbed his hand on his pant leg.

The street narrowed and the two-story buildings on either side cast him into shadow. At last he came to it. The imposing stone complex of the Orsini Colony headquarters. It consumed several city blocks and was surrounded by walls taller than any of the neighboring structures. The front wall of the compound presented only a single set of carved double doors. Bricker approached and pulled on an iron chain, which rang the bells inside. Their tinny summons sounded considerably more muted on this side of the door than the other.

Peridot answered. A gaunt man, he seemed consumed by the many folds of the bright orange tunic wrapped around his shoulders. He immediately drew his brow down as Bricker stepped inside and closed the door. "Back so soon? Where's everyone else?"

"I need to talk to Lord Tivoli."

Bricker and his fellow brother crossed the spacious, tiled foyer and ascended the iron staircase to the floor above. This led to a covered walkway. A series of painted doors lined one side, and the other opened to a broad courtyard below. Several Orsinians, intricate gold marks glinting on their foreheads, joined them as they made their way along the walkway and deeper into the interior of the building.

Someone must have run ahead to get Lord Tivoli, for he was coming to meet them in the middle of a wide, stone corridor.

Lord Tivoli was wrapped in a maroon, multilayered tunic that hung to his knees, underneath which were loose, tan breeches and soft shoes. His gold mark shone above hard, dark eyes and thick, brown brows. It was all the hair he had on his head, for Tivoli's servant shaved both crown and jaw every morning.

He carried a staff—the only such thing in the entire colony—but it looked more like a stout walking stick. His hand grasped the gnarled top, which came to his waist. The pointed base rhythmically knocked the tiled floor as he walked.

Both men and the assembled Orsinians came to a stop and Bricker offered a deep bow.

"My Lord," he said to the floor before rising and meeting his lord's eyes.

Lord Tivoli took in the sight: Bricker alone, unkempt, somber. "Where are the others?"

"Murdered."

A cry of outrage rose from the group, questions pelting him from all directions.

Lord Tivoli hollered out once: "Quiet!"

The gathering stilled.

"Aradia betrayed us," Bricker said. "When we got there, she had another group of followers with her. Wizards. They weren't with the Order, but they were helping her. She took us all to an island to wait for the final Song of the Phoenix, but turned on us before then. Another... follower... and I felt it coming and barely escaped. When we went back, everyone had been slaughtered."

He briefly shut his eyes against the memory, which was still so vivid the stench stung his nose even now.

"Niall? Siliom?"

Bricker nodded. "Everyone."

"I told you," Lord Tivoli said, his face hardening. He swept one pointed finger around the group. "I told you all. The Order cannot be trusted!"

Various members chimed in their agreement, nodding and shuffling slightly nearer.

Bricker proceeded to tell them about the water faerie and how it was he who watched the Bridge of a Thousand Ages disintegrate into nothing but fire and smoke, and how four people appeared in the midst of the fire at the end of it. He told them how Aradia was absent from it all and presumed dead.

"Then the Order went into the Rock of Light and retrieved the ash. I would have gone to them and demanded our portion myself, but after what Aradia did, I dared not do it alone." He bowed his head. "Forgive me, Lord Tivoli."

Tivoli grunted. "No. You were right. This time we go en masse." He turned and started retreating back down the corridor, the tapping of his short staff echoing off the tiled floor. "They can give us the ash," he said, "or we can take it from them."

Nicolai stepped into his office and locked the door behind him. The room was dark, except for the faint glow from the coals in the fireplace. He allowed his eyes to adjust to the lack of light before crossing the room. He reached out, feeling for the furniture to guide his way: side table, back of the couch, chair, corner of the desk.

He held a message in his hand. It said simply, "On the night of the new moon. Your loving Praea." Setting the note on his desk, he groped his way to the double glass doors leading to the expansive stone balcony.

He swung open the doors and stepped into the crisp, night air. The sky was nothing but black and a few dim stars. Leaving the doors open, he crossed the balcony, placed his hands on the cool stone of the railing, and listened to the crickets chirping on the grounds below.

The grounds of the castle were cloaked in darkness. He could not see the wall or the guards on the wall and knew they could not see him either. Beyond, the city was only a few flickering lights, but otherwise, a black mass of indistinguishable shapes.

She could not ask for more perfect conditions.

Heart beating in almost painful anticipation, Nicolai perked his ears, waiting for the sound of great, golden Tulaga wings. He didn't have long to wait. He heard her before he saw her. With a swooping feeling in his chest, he retreated to the doors in order to give her space.

She flew in front of him, brought her wings down, and finished her transformation just as her feet touched the ground.

Groaning, he pulled her inside and into his arms. He whispered her name and tightened his embrace. She squeezed him in return, nestling against his neck. She smelled of lavender and night air. She smelled of Praea.

They loosened their embrace enough to tilt their heads toward one another. Wrapped in each other, they kissed deeply. Through every separation from her, he seemed to carry an ache in his chest wherever he went. Holding her now, being in her arms, kissing her so deeply, the ache melted out of him until he felt warm and whole once more.

At last, he pulled away and looked into her eyes. He cradled her face in both hands and planted a kiss on her nose.

"I've missed you," she whispered.

He sighed. If only he could marry her now.

"How is your father?" he asked, taking her by the hand and leading her further into the room. They settled on the couch by the fireplace, whose belly glowed with the burning embers. Her features slowly came into focus in the near dark as she told him what was going on at home.

Her poor father, the king of Sakkara, was badly grieving after the deaths of two of his three sons. Aradia had mistakenly thought the three princes of Sakkara were the Three prophesized to stop her and had them brutally murdered before realizing her mistake.

Praea, who was secretly being trained by Kai'Enna as a Tulaga, came under Aradia's notice as well. The existence of the Tulaga was such a carefully guarded secret that they were long regarded as a mere myth among humans, and even her father did not know what his daughter was up to. Aradia had been privy to the secret, however, and sent her henchmen after the princess.

Now that Praea's secret was out and her father—indeed everyone—knew she was a Tulaga who'd helped the Three defeat Aradia, Praea made the mistake of telling her father everything, including her own brush with death. It had only added to his emotional strain.

He struggled to manage the affairs of the kingdom and some days did not even leave his bed chambers. Prince Akren was quietly attending to things in his father's absence and insisted their father only needed time to heal. Praea had to hope he was right.

Meanwhile, she was often away, doing the work necessary for the survival of her branch. Kai'Enna had just finished teaching her how to find new recruits, and they were about to begin that process. If it weren't for her branch's dire need, Praea would wait until her father was stronger, but there were still only two Tulaga in the world, and that needed to change as quickly as possible. Her brother supported her in this, at least, but her father was another matter.

"He wants me home all the time," she said now, clearly pained that she could not grant him his wish. "But even when I'm home, he usually wants to be alone. I try to get him into the gardens or out to see his people, but he won't go. He doesn't seem to be getting any better."

"He will," Nicolai said quietly, though he was not so sure himself. "It's hard to lose a child and it hasn't been that long."

"I do hope you're right."

Her father's fragile state was a frequent topic and the reason they met in secret instead of courting in the open. No one wanted to add any more shocks to her father's system, and no one wanted to risk the possibility of him refusing to allow their courtship. The citizens of Caedmonia weren't quite sure what to make of Nicolai; what would her father think?

No. Everyone agreed to wait for a more opportune time, but that did not make waiting any easier.

No one knew about their secret meetings. Marcellus thought Nicolai and Praea were maintaining their relationship via letters, and Nicolai was not keen to correct him of the impression.

He pulled Praea closer and she rested her head on his shoulder. He could only be grateful for her gift of swift flight or who knew how little they'd see of one another.

They moved to discussing the ever-approaching coronation and the days they'd spent since they saw one another last. After a time, he noticed her arms felt chilled. He kissed her forehead, then got up and stoked the fire, which gave them some light at last. After arranging the logs to his satisfaction and replacing the poker on the rack, he turned to see her gazing into the flames as if her thoughts were far away.

Realizing he was watching her, she glanced up at him, thinking.

"What?" he said softly, returning to her side and sinking into the couch. He expected her to curl against him as she had been doing, but instead she observed him, brows furrowed.

"Nicolai, may I ask you a question?"

This preamble seemed strange. They shared almost everything two people could share. "Yes, of course."

"Remember that day we went to the Wilds? After you found me in the gorge and were taking me home?"

Nicolai was not likely to ever forget finding Praea at the bottom of the gorge, injured and stuck in her transformation between human and bird. Well, a little girl had found her and he had found the little girl. It was how he'd discovered Praea was a Tulaga. He'd intended to take her home through the Wilds, but of course they'd never made it. A series of delays and events led them to Aradia's cave instead.

"Yes," Nicolai said, "I remember."

"Remember the man we met in the forest? Who was that?"

The one thing.

The one thing he still couldn't tell her, at least not for now. The faeries were still a secret, so he had to hide his identity as a half-faerie, even from Praea. Until Marcellus decided how he was going to handle letting the kingdom know that their king was a half-faerie and their future queen immortal, Nicolai could not say a thing. As king of the earth faeries, Salerno had rather firm opinions on the matter.

It was a tricky situation. Marcellus had bemoaned at least a dozen times that he wished he knew what their father had planned on doing about that same situation, before their mother died in childbirth. Elana and Clement had been married for thirty years before choosing to have children, and in all that time, the kingdom had no idea who Queen Elana really was.

They couldn't have kept it a secret much longer. What were they planning to do?

Marcellus and Nicolai didn't know of course, but as Marcellus said, "If my father could be a good king and still make a faerie his queen, so can I." That seemed to alleviate any hesitation Marcellus may have felt about courting Janus. If he'd ever had any. But the intricacies of the situation weighed on everybody.

In the end, nothing weighed on Nicolai more heavily than the oath he'd sworn to Salerno as a young boy. He'd promised he would never reveal the faeries to anyone and he meant it. He knew Salerno trusted him to keep that promise.

Were it not for that, Praea would know who Nicolai was already.

And here she was, asking him about it directly. He was not prepared for the subject to come up like this.

"The man?" he asked.

"The man in the forest. The man you spoke with. Who was he?"

It was bad enough keeping things from Praea when he'd first met her. It was even worse now. He forced the lie to his lips. "A friend."

"But why was he there? Does he live in the forest?"

She looked at him earnestly and he saw the determination in her eyes. She wasn't going to let this go.

"Praea—" He would have to settle for what truth he could give her. "I'm sorry. I can't say."

She did not seem surprised by this. Rather, it seemed to confirm something for her. She sat back and looked at the fire. He sat back as well, holding her hand and watching her expression. The firelight flickered on her face. The little glass ball resting at the base of her neck glinted and winked.

"It's not my secret to tell," he said.

She glanced at him sharply. "Not your secret? It's not?"

Well, maybe technically it was. The land of the earth faeries, the land of Amon Tunde, it was partly his home. Had, in fact, always felt like home.

"I made a promise to someone, Praea. I would tell you, but I can't. You can understand that, can't you?"

"So..." she said thoughtfully, "it's not to do with you? You just know things you can't tell? Is that it?"

He furrowed his brows and stroked her hand. "What is this about?"

She sighed and shook her head. "Nothing. It's nothing. I only got to thinking about it. I was merely wondering. It's nothing." She smiled and curled into him, as he'd expected her to do earlier.

But now he was the one left feeling it was Praea who was hiding something.

Seven

A few years after the Mapmaker discovered the earth faerie king, the red-headed witch Madera concocted a plan to thank Salerno for his training. She decided they should throw him a grand feast in the tradition of humans. She also, she said, had a surprise for him. Something to show him. Eala, the aged woman with her young followers, had a surprise as well.

The Mapmaker had already wearied of their constant discussions of a new magical Order recently created, they said, by the Phoenix, who supposedly had selected humans to start seven unique branches of magic. The Mapmaker, meanwhile, had made only moderate progress on his own magical abilities. He could crush twigs into fine powder and extract the essence of lemon balm with a word but nothing more complex than that.

He had, however, explored every knoll and glen of the sprawling forest, about a third of which belonged to the earth faeries. Their realm, Amon Tunde, was mostly below ground, an area he longed to see. But he did, at least, learn the aboveground boundaries of Amon Tunde, thanks to Salerno's help.

When Madera and Eala came to the Mapmaker for help with the feast, when they talked excitedly about the surprises they had in store, then refused to tell him what they were, he decided he would not be the only one without a gift for Salerno.

He settled into his room at the boardinghouse by the bay, spread out a large, semitranslucent piece of leather fit for a king, and set to work.

* * *

When Madera invited Salerno to the feast, promising a day of surprises, she had to explain both the concept of a feast and that of surprises.

"We will have it on the three-year anniversary of our first meeting," Madera said.

Given humans' rather tentative hold on time, Salerno thought they would do better to forget about the time they'd lost, rather than highlight it. But he was intrigued by the promise of human food and human surprises. He had yet to tell his fellow faeries about the humans—it had only been a few years since meeting them after all—and wondered if a surprise might be the way to do it when the time came.

On the day of the feast, Salerno and the humans met as arranged in a grassy glen surrounded by sweeping oaks. Madera had decided to forgo tables, an object foreign to faeries and something that would have been cumbersome to arrange in any case, and instead spread the dishes for the feast on a length of emerald-green silk she'd obtained just for the occasion.

Madera and her followers, five men and women of various ages, sat along one side of the silk, fluttering with anticipation. The aged Eala and her group of three young women sat along the other side. They placed Salerno at the short end of the silk, explaining it was the place of honor according to their customs. The Mapmaker, as the one to make the discovery, sat at the opposite end. It also made for convenient sitting arrangements, as the Mapmaker had no followers, but rather came to Amon Tunde alone.

The Mapmaker had his satchel and a long wooden box sitting on the grass nearby. In spite of the tantalizing feast spread before them—stuffed figs and glazed lamb, the scent of cinnamon promising a satisfying meal—he kept glancing at the wooden box. It was made of rich mahogany, intricately carved by an artisan in town. Upon her arrival, Madera had exclaimed at the beauty of it, but the Mapmaker silenced her.

"The box is not the surprise," he said.

Her reaction had been gratifying. He did not know what their surprises were, but he knew no one here could give Salerno what he had designed.

Salerno was delighted by all the unique food, some of which he politely refused to touch (the stuffed pheasant), and some of which he subtly kept nearby for frequent tastes (the candied walnuts).

"This reminds me of our own Gatherings," Salerno said. "There is not as much food and nothing of this sort, but we sing much and tell the stories of our histories."

"What stories?" Madera asked.

"Hmmm. It is not always the same. However, we always begin with the Story of Origin."

It took little persuasion to convince him to grace their feast with the story, but he prefaced it with the familiar warning: "This is not information to take back to your villages."

"We agree," they said in unison, as they had regarding many other things many times before.

"Deep in the earth," Salerno began, "is the origin of all things faerie and the origin of many other things beside. Deep below ground is a vast network of tunnels we call the Shoals. On and on it goes, far beyond the boundaries of Amon Tunde. There in the Shoals, the earth is not like itself. It is smooth and hard and does not allow us to manipulate it the way we do the earth everywhere else. It feels unlike anything either above or below ground. It is like magic, but more than that. Much more than that.

"At the heart of it all, the Vortex claims its place."

Salerno furrowed his brows, looking around at each of them. "I have not before had to describe what it looks like, for all faeries have seen it." He narrowed his eyes, thinking.

"It is... it is like wind swirling around itself." His graceful hand moved in a circle. "And the wind is all colors. Purple. Blue. Yellow. Swirling, like this." Again, his hand circled, but it did so slowly. He looked at each one of them, holding their gaze with him.

The gentle breeze that had been playing with them all day stilled. The scurrying of little animals and fluttering of leaves grew silent. As if all things had turned to listen to the tale.

"The Vortex," he continued, "isn't wind. It is the perfect harmony of the three elements: earth, water, and fire. It is the place where the elements first reside before they go out to all the world." He gestured his arms outward, his mossy cloak spreading wide.

The gathered group and the forest alike witnessed him do this.

"It is this power, this force, that we draw upon and sense in our magic. Yours too. But everything is fed by these elements. The trees above ground and the mountains and the fires within the mountain and the water in the ocean."

In his deep and soothing voice, Salerno explained that the Vortex spun and spun, deep in the earth, sending each of the three elements off in their own directions through the maze of tunnels that comprised the Shoals. "The element of water goes west, deep into the bay," Salerno said, gesturing a slender hand, "and somewhere there the water faeries were born. The element of fire goes south to the Mountains of Vitra where it gave birth to the fire faeries.

"We, of the earth, know more about our own creation than we do of the others. From the Vortex, the element of earth formed our Tree of Origin, and in this way the earth faeries were brought to life.

"So you see," Salerno said, "the Vortex is a power far beyond what we faeries can do. We do not tread there often. It is a sacred place. A powerful place. The place where all faeries and the elements of the world find their beginning."

The little group sat in silence around the emerald silk.

Eala was not looking at Salerno. She had turned her eyes downward, gazing at her aged hands softly folded in her lap. Brown sunspots and wrinkles covered the youthful hands she once knew. Sometimes her own body was a stranger to her. She had long feared death, that ending she hoped, as others did, would mark only another beginning. Her recent magical work had given her new purpose and hope, but nothing had touched her quite like this telling of Salerno. She thought of the vast Shoals, hidden underground beneath them, and felt wonder. She thought of this origin of beginnings and felt curiously at peace.

Madera had not taken her eyes from Salerno once during his telling. She felt as if the swirling of the Vortex was swirling also within her. She was dumbstruck by it. She was hardly aware of her crossed legs on the grass or her wrists resting on her knees. This magic she had within her, the magic within the faeries, even the very power of the sea to roil and the wind to roar—it came from someplace. Someplace Salerno had seen with his own eyes.

He had used the word sacred. Only one other time had that word come to her mind, and it was the one and only time she laid eyes on that glorious creature known as the Phoenix.

Madera did not yet know how this reverence for the Shoals and the Vortex would affect not only her life but generations after her. But the time for that was not far off.

Meanwhile, the Mapmaker, who had seen more of the world than any of them, could think of only one thing.

He wanted to see the Shoals and the Vortex. He wanted to see them for himself.

When the pheasant had been picked clean, the bread taken down to the crusty ends, the remnants of plum pudding dried into a gel at the bottom of the bowl, and the last of the candied walnuts consumed, it was time for Salerno's band of humans to deliver their surprises.

Madera went first.

She stood and walked barefooted on the grass to the edge of the glen. Here she stood by the trunk of a grand oak, her full red hair bobbing as she looked up at its sweeping canopy.

She took a pinch of something out of a small pouch that hung at her waist. The Mapmaker thought it might be a kind of powder.

Turning her attention back to the oak, she raised her arms high and chanted, "*Asphalos asphalos allay mah las.*" Opening her hands, the powder—or whatever it was—floated in the air and spread out in tiny specks, visible only because they blazed like cinders. Like tiny fires.

"*Alla poa lene,*" and here the glowing specks settled on the tree. The trunk and limbs took on a glittering quality. Then the tree itself gave way to a fluttering kind of translucence.

Murmurs escaped the group, transfixed by the image before them.

The Mapmaker narrowed his eyes and cocked his head. In that moment, the oak disappeared.

They gasped as one. Salerno stood as Madera spun and looked at him, triumphant.

"What is this, child?" he asked.

"Come," she said, gesturing with her arms. "Come see."

No one moved as Madera held one hand toward Salerno and the other toward where the oak had once stood. The Mapmaker watched as Salerno approached, placed his hand next to hers, and did something Salerno had never done before. He laughed.

Beaming, Madera explained how she took the principles of faerie concealment and combined them with what she had learned from the Phoenix. "I couldn't do it with my magic alone," she explained. "It took Phoenix ash to make it work. Come, everyone. Come feel. It's still here."

And so they did, exclaiming and wondering as they gathered around the oak that was invisible but plainly still there. The Mapmaker approached last, quiet and pondering, as he placed his hand on the rough bark of the hidden oak.

He could not imagine the use of such magic. By the time Madera said the spell to make the oak visible once again, the Mapmaker bristled with an emotion he did not enjoy having. He did not want to be jealous of her.

By the time they settled around the silk, he found it within himself to send Madera a smile of congratulations. The smile felt bitter and he hoped she did not know it.

Eala was next, but she did not stand alone. She and her young women stood in a line, several steps back from the silk and several steps apart from one another. Eala was also part of the Phoenix's Order, but Head of her own branch and therefore privy to different instruction from the Phoenix.

"I also found a way to blend faerie concepts with Phoenix ash," Eala began simply, lightly touching the delicate glass ball she wore around her neck. "We begin now," she said, nodding to her companions.

Eala and the others raised their arms. When they brought them back down, the Mapmaker flinched as they transformed into great glittering birds. Golden feathers. Massive wings. Clear, dark eyes. His heart pounded as they took to the air and circled the glen. The others clapped and cheered as the birds landed and transformed back into women. As if that's all they had ever been.

"Extraordinary!" Salerno exclaimed.

The Mapmaker rubbed his sweating palms on his pants. He did not belong here. Salerno, Eala, Madera. They all had skills—incredible power—he did not have. He watched as Salerno came to Eala and her young women, asking them questions and praising their ingenuity.

"You are something new now," Salerno said. "What do you call yourself?"

Eala smiled her ancient smile. "We have not thought of a name."

"May I suggest one?" Salerno asked. Eala and the others nodded. "Tulaga. Guardians of the Air."

Eala frowned. "Is the air another element? Does it come from the Vortex?"

"The air is indeed another element, but it is unique. It is born in the wind on the earth and in the waves of the sea and in the breath of the fire. Tulaga," he said again, nodding.

She nodded too and smiled.

The Mapmaker looked at his mahogany box and thought about what was inside. He had no place here. Truly.

Then the Mapmaker heard his name.

It was spoken by Salerno. He loved the way Salerno said his name, as if all he knew and cherished about the Mapmaker was conveyed in that one utterance.

"You have a surprise for me too?" Salerno asked. "I am enjoying this idea of surprises."

The others laughed, but the Mapmaker only shrugged, avoiding looking at his box. "It isn't much," he said.

Salerno didn't respond, only waited patiently.

The Mapmaker looked at the others, with visions of disappearing trees and flying women in his head.

His eyes landed on Madera.

She smiled at him, her mop of red hair seeming to smile right along with her. "Go on," she said. "Show us what's in the box."

Resigned to it, the Mapmaker rose.

He picked up the mahogany box and carried it to Salerno. As planned, he placed the box in front of Salerno, knelt down next to him, lifted the heavy lid, and withdrew the leather roll inside. As he laid it on the ground, he sensed the others shuffling to get a better view. Just as he'd imagined it. But he did not feel the pride he thought he would feel.

He felt shame. He felt small.

Wearing a mask of calm, he unrolled the massive piece of fine leather to reveal his hand-drawn map of the aboveground realm of Amon Tunde.

He had drawn the boundaries and landforms in rich, smooth ink the same color as the mahogany box, but the illustrations were brought to life with pigments imported from the king's capital: emerald, lime green, orange the color of poppies, lavender, crimson. Highlights in gold matched the intricate border and embellishments in the corners.

He had spent weeks on it and it seemed silly now. A mere thing.

For a long, long moment, no one spoke.

At last an exhalation of wonder. The Mapmaker looked at Salerno, whose eyes were fixed to the map. "What is this?"

"A map. A map of Amon Tunde."

"It's magnificent." This from Madera.

The Mapmaker glanced at her to see if she were teasing him, but no. She came and gathered near them, the others following suit. "I've never seen a map like this," she said. "It's so beautiful."

The others nodded in agreement and the Mapmaker began to take heart. He explained the map to Salerno, showing him how to read it. Faeries know their own lands; they need no map. But Salerno's delight was apparent.

"There," Salerno said, pointing, "that is where we are."

"Yes."

"And that," Salerno said again, "that is the Hidden Door. And the Great Oak here."

"Yes."

Again and again Salerno pointed at different places he knew, and some of the others did as well. At long last, when it had been studied from one corner to the next, Salerno surprised the Mapmaker for the second time that day.

"Thank you for showing me this," he said, placing his hand on the Mapmaker's wrist.

That one gesture did away with any thought the Mapmaker had about leaving and not returning. They had never once seen Salerno touch anyone.

"It is for you," the Mapmaker said.

"For me!" Salerno looked back at the map. He spread his arms wide and lifted it before him. One corner of the thin leather curled softly, and Salerno smiled. "For me," he said.

Thus it was that Salerno became captivated by a human object. For the first and last time.

Eight

In the form of a great, glittering bird, Praea flew across the flood-ravaged plain of Rheita Valley. The expanse of the Wilds blanketed the land to the right. Even though she'd once spent several days in the Wilds with Nicolai and had become acquainted with its beauties and dangers, she had not known the true mystery of the Wilds until recently.

During her latest training session, Kai'Enna told her the earth faeries lay hidden in the Wilds, and their branch's founder formed a friendship with the king of the earth faeries. Inspired by faerie magic, Eala used the power of Phoenix ash to achieve the first Tulaga transformation.

It had been a magnificent revelation. Like the Tulaga, the faeries had hidden under the cloak of myth but were, in fact, real. It explained some things about Nicolai too. Somehow, he must have discovered the existence of the faeries. Became friends with one.

And she'd seen one without realizing it. A faerie. How she longed to see one again.

But the wonder Praea felt was soon darkened by Kai'Enna's stern admonitions. She was not to discuss the faeries with anyone, and she was never, ever to go into the Wilds again. Even now, Kai'Enna's warning rang in her ears: "Stay away from Amon Tunde."

It was almost as unsettling and puzzling as Kai'Enna's concern about the ash stuck on the altar. She refused to say why this bothered her so much, or even admit to the depth of her concern, but Praea saw the weight of it etched into the lines on her Sage's face.

Something about that ash waiting on the altar felt ominous.

She banked left, away from the Wilds, over the rise toward the city of Stonebridge with its castle on the hill, and past the castle toward the wood directly north of it. The last time she was in these woods, she had been hunted by two of Aradia's henchmen and gone careening over the cliff's edge to the river far below.

Praea glided above the treetops, their branches rushing just beneath her. The trees came to an end and the ground fell away. The gorge, with the sparkling river in its belly, looked different to Praea now than it did the last time she was here. The memory of falling still echoed through her, but she was not falling today.

She owned the currents in the air. Owned the sky. She felt as if she owned everything she saw.

The majestic cliffs cut a picture of beauty as they led out to the sea. She pulled in her wings and dove down. Picking up speed, heart thrilling, she swerved in time to avoid colliding with the water and circled over its rustling surface.

The trees on this side of the bank thickened as the gorge opened up on its journey to the bay. Praea flew above the aspen and oak, coasting now, in search of the dwelling she'd seen once before.

It was closer than expected. It had seemed she'd been tossed about in the water for a league before coming to shore and being saved by the miller's daughter. But there it was already: the small clearing with the longhouse and the miller's shed at one end.

She found a place to land, out of sight, transformed back into her natural form, and went in search of the miller's daughter.

As she walked across the clearing, it all looked familiar to her, but altered. Bright and cheerful. The tree under which Nicolai had found her looked just like any other. It was a crabapple tree, gnarled and still in the warm afternoon air and betraying no signs of Praea's former injuries.

As Praea crossed the meadow, she heard the bleating of a goat. Then the miller's daughter came around the corner of the longhouse, holding the baby goat in her arms.

The girl spotted Praea and stopped. She wore a faded yellow dress that hung to her knees and heavy, brown work boots that gaped around her calves. Her expression went from surprise to recognition to delight.

From somewhere behind the house, a woman's voice called out, "Jesaray, stop playing with that goat and tend the tomatoes!"

Jesaray, Praea thought.

The girl did put down the goat, but she didn't go to the tomatoes. She came running toward Praea, boots clomping on the ground, brown hair flying out behind her.

Praea's heart ran toward the girl as well. She still needed to talk to the girl's parents, explain the apprenticeship of the Tulaga, seek their consent, and settle any concerns. But looking at Jesaray running toward her, stopping just short of her and beaming up into Praea's face, she knew: this girl was one of them.

Hers.

Nicolai stood in the antechamber, looking toward the door leading to the Throne Room. The swell of noise coming from the crowd of citizens waiting on the other side reverberated off the walls and in Nicolai's own chest. The antechamber held several couches and chairs but was otherwise empty save for Nicolai and two pages, dressed in red, who stood on either side of the door. It would be cozy if it weren't so terrifying.

Nicolai could not stop fussing with his cummerbund and the red, silk sash tied from shoulder to waist. The thick linen of his pants and coat hung heavily on his body. He felt as bedecked as a peacock. Gold buttons, rubies, sapphires, and emeralds studded his belt. They matched the jewels in the small, gold crown that would be placed on his head during the official coronation, in which Marcellus would be crowned king and Nicolai, prince.

He glanced at one of the pages, who was regarding Nicolai uncertainly. The page's eyes snapped forward and Nicolai looked away.

He tugged at the sleeves of his coat. Though tailored to his body, he longed to shed the restrictive jacket, throw on a loose, cotton smock, and run for the fields. Of course, his former home was almost as changed as he was. His father—at least, the father who raised him—was dead and buried seven weeks now. His adoptive mother had been moved to the east wing of the castle and was, presumably, dressed in finery and in her place of honor in the Throne Room, waiting with the rest of the kingdom for the ceremony to begin. The old house stood empty, surrounded by barren fields.

Nicolai took a deep breath.

He thought Corren would be here by now, not to mention Marcellus. He had a fleeting thought that maybe the whole thing had been canceled. Could he be so lucky? But Corren, Marcellus, and Janus came into the room, bringing with them the air of finality.

Corren was in the striking white wizard's cloak the Head of the Order wore for ceremonies and, apparently, more formal occasions. The fine material did lend a majestic feel, but it was relatively simple garb compared to the others. Since Corren was publicly renouncing his claim to the throne, there was no need to dress him up as they'd done with Nicolai.

Janus was in a blue satin gown that gathered softly at the floor. It was the first time Nicolai saw her in anything other than a knight's uniform. He could not help but react to the difference; he saw a glimpse of the queen she was destined to become.

Marcellus had always borne the mark of a prince, but today he truly looked the king. His broad shoulders displayed his uniform with all the power and grace of royalty. His double sash of red and white offset the magnificent sword hanging at his waist. The water sword, given to him by the king of the water faeries, hung in a jeweled scabbard on his other hip. Though Nicolai may have resembled King Clement in looks, Marcellus reflected their father in grace.

Nicolai had small opportunity to soothe his nerves in the presence of the others, for mere seconds after their arrival, Commander Perry swept in after them.

"Lord Marcellus," he said, bowing, "the citizens have filled the Throne Room and almost all the guests of honor are in place." He glanced toward Janus. Perry would no doubt prefer Janus be in her place as well, but Nicolai noticed Perry was a quick study. Perry knew Janus would take her place when she was good and ready. Marcellus was no help as he would have it no other way. Nicolai suspected Marcellus would have Janus accompany him through the door and stand by his side as he was crowned king, if he thought he could get away with it. Nicolai would certainly have Praea by his side if he could.

"Commanders Donnelly and Lance are ready in the west anteroom," Perry continued. "The trumpeters and musicians are in position. The knights await their signal in Jade Hall. All is ready, as soon as Commander Janus joins the other guests of honor in the Throne Room."

"Very good," Marcellus said.

Perry began going through the order of the ceremony for Corren's benefit. Nicolai had been told the order of events many times earlier in the day, as if Perry thought he couldn't manage to remember it all.

Nicolai stood apart from the group and looked toward the door leading to the Throne Room. In a few minutes he'd be walking through it. This was going to happen whether he wanted it or not.

"Nervous?" Janus had come to his side, speaking softly as Perry droned on.

Nicolai nodded.

"I don't blame you," she said. "All I have to do is sit and I'm glad for that."

"I think they should have put you right in front of everyone. That would solve any questions about your courtship. You look like a queen." He nodded toward Marcellus. "And Marcellus looks like a king." He shrugged, considering Corren and his wizard's staff. "Corren looks like he always has, but he's not pretending to be a prince."

Janus raised her brows. "Are you pretending?"

Nicolai looked at her. In the few days he'd been getting to know Janus, he was already fond of her honesty and directness. She now looked at him with so much openness and so little judgment, all the anxiety he'd had about the situation came bubbling to the surface, as if she were conjuring it out of him.

From the moment he'd learned his true identity to now, he'd felt swept along in the tide, driven toward a future that looked nothing like the one he'd always envisioned. Over the last several days, he'd often been reminded how ill-prepared he was for such a future.

Marcellus frequently had Nicolai shadow him as he went about the business of the kingdom, following up with private teaching sessions at the end of the day. Some half-dozen times, Nicolai had sat in Marcellus' office like the local castle oddity he was, and watched as advisors swept in one after another, decisions made, and various letters drafted. Marcellus handled it all with such calmness. Such authority and efficiency.

Meanwhile, Nicolai's head would be spinning to understand one thing while they were already halfway into the next. Often he found that he'd moved back and back and back until he was hovering against a wall, watching the great machinations of the kingdom at work, and wondering what on earth he was doing here.

"I don't know how to be a prince," he said to Janus now. "I'm a farmer and every person in that room," he said pointing toward the door, "is going to know it. Everyone is going to wonder what kind of prince I could possibly be. It's what I would think myself."

He did, in fact, think something very similar when he thought Corren might try to claim his right to the throne. As much as he liked Corren, loved him really, he did not want him to be king. As a citizen of Caedmonia, he knew and trusted Prince Marcellus the Protector. That's who they needed at the helm of the kingdom.

"What do I know of ruling a country?" he asked Janus. "It's ridiculous. Who would ever take orders and direction from me?"

Her expression sharpened so much he felt as if she'd reached out and shook him by both shoulders. "Nicolai of Knobby Tree," she said sternly, "you are Yellow Brother, defender of the Phoenix, son of Elana Priestess of the earth and the great King Clement, and a *prince* of Caedmonia. You don't know what to do? Learn. Your brother and his advisors will teach you everything you need to know. If the people out there don't think you'll make a good prince, well then you just have to prove them wrong."

He blinked at her.

"What? Do you think anyone saw a knight when they looked at me? No. I spent years proving I could do it. I'm better than most of the others too, if you want to know the truth of it. I had to be. I had to prove it until they could no longer deny it. You can do the same thing."

"But..." Nicolai said. Her words and earnestness seeped into him. He forgot about the peacock suit and the skeptical page by the door. Forgot about the crowds he would soon have to face. Still, though the truth of what she said was sinking in, there was one flaw. "But you wanted to be a knight. I don't want this."

"Oh, yes you do," she said casually, her sternness fleeing as quickly as it came.

"I... What?"

"You want it quite plainly. You're scared. That's not the same thing as not wanting it."

He looked at her. "But..."

She raised her eyebrows, waiting. A smile teased at the corner of her mouth. She looked perfectly amused.

"But..." he said again. She was right. How did she know it before he did?

"But what?"

"But... I want to be in my old tunic," he said, feeling rather stupid now.

She laughed. "So, tomorrow, throw on your old tunic if you want. Do you think I'm wearing this dress tomorrow?"

The others approached. "Commander Janus," Commander Perry said, holding out his arm, "may I escort you to your seat? The ceremony will begin shortly."

Ignoring Perry, Janus put her hand on Nicolai's arm and leaned close to his ear. "Live up to your own expectations and you will not disappoint anyone."

She gave him a squeeze, a strange thing for a faerie to do since faeries rarely touched others. But Janus was no ordinary faerie.

She took Perry's arm and allowed him to escort her away, looking back over her shoulder and giving Nicolai a wink as they left the room.

Nicolai smiled. Yes. He was quite fond of his future queen.

Soon the trumpets blared and the pages swung the doors open and he had a clear view of the two thrones that sat waiting.

By the time they placed the crown on Nicolai's head, he'd made a vow to become the kind of prince he himself would be willing to follow.

Nine

Two months after the coronation, Corren navigated the dusty street of a busy market. Open stalls lined either side and vendors called out their wares: fish, vegetables, fruit, often in unfamiliar varieties. Though disguised in the garb of the Hathmirrians, with the tip of his staff hidden beneath a woolen wrap, he worried he may not blend in as easily as he might wish. He hoped his deep skin tone, dark hair, and brown eyes would be enough to keep people from wondering too much about his place of origin. His accent was another matter.

A man with olive skin and brown eyes hollered to him from a stall, holding out a strand of colorful beads. "Look how beautiful. Come, buy one for your lady."

Corren pulled the top layer of his crimson robe back onto his shoulder and kept walking. He hadn't quite mastered the art of wrapping the multilayered robes common among the Hathmirrians, so some of the fabric kept sliding out of place. He'd prefer the black cloak hidden in the bottom of his traveling bag. The bag contained little else besides a few folios, writing supplies, a map, and the bulk of his traveling money. The small bag was well hidden beneath the many folds of his disguise.

The Hathmirrian market consumed many city blocks. Corren had become disoriented in the maze of side streets and canvas-topped stalls. He passed row after row. Each corner he came to presented him with more vendor-filled streets. It all started to look the same: baskets of strange green vegetables, tables of peculiar varieties of fish, and hunks of some sort of meat hanging from hooks.

The bread, at least, felt familiar. As morning drew on, he bought a hard roll and a ball of tangy cheese from a particularly enthusiastic woman in a bright yellow shawl.

He soon came to the market's edge, which butted against the city wall. Here he could get his bearings at last, but he was too turned around to rely upon the directions he'd received earlier in the day. He'd have to ask again.

He shored himself up for the task.

He glanced at the various vendors, most busy haggling with customers or trying to draw them in. Citizens of Hathmirr, in their colorful skirts, tunics, and head shawls, bustled past, too concerned with their own affairs to pay him much heed.

A woman selling dates, nuts, and a host of unidentifiable items caught his eye. She was a meek-looking thing, though she bustled about with quiet determination. Unlike her neighbors, she was not hollering to the passersby. Her stall did not seem to suffer for customers, however. As he drew near, Corren understood why. An enticing aroma wafted through the air, originating, he now saw, from a small kettle in the rear set up over a tiny open flame.

No need for her to shout. The sweet smell drew everyone in.

He wandered about her stall, waiting for a break in the traffic so he could speak to her privately. When the moment came, he pointed to her simmering concoction and asked the price.

She held up a small copper and three fingers. He reached into the pouch hanging from a cord around his waist and produced the desired currency.

She scooped out a measure of the caramel-colored, glossy substance and poured it onto a flat block of marble. She began scraping it with a wooden slab, folding it again and again as it cooled rapidly.

"I wonder," he said, trying to affect the lilt of the Hathmirrian tongue, "if you might tell me how to get to the Orsini Colony?"

She flinched and looked at him, her hand hovering over the board. Catching herself she went back to work, shaking her head vigorously. The substance was a pale tan by now and had

82

begun to solidify. She patted it into a square and handed it over.

It was no longer pliable but still warm and carried a sweet aroma. It must be a type of candy.

"I've lost my way. It's that way, isn't it?" He pointed at random, for he had no idea which way it was.

Her eyes grew wide and fearful. She shook her head again, this time bringing three fingers to her mouth. She patted her lips again and again.

He realized he had not once heard the woman speak and that she was pantomiming. He exhaled in frustration. He'd asked directions from a mute.

She began gesturing wildly, shaking her head no, and pointing at her forehead. This, he gathered, signified the mark of the members of the Orsini Colony.

"Don't worry," he said, but she was shooing him now, urging him out of her stall. The top layer of his robe shifted again and he tugged it back into place.

She was right on top of him, practically pushing him, and he was backing up in haste to keep his distance. "Sorry, sorry. I'm sorry to have bothered—"

A hard shove from his right sent him toppling to the street, candy flying. He landed hard on his back, staff in his right hand, and someone else landed on top of him.

"What—?"

"Oh—!"

A young woman in a bright red shawl trimmed in gold lace was scrambling to get her weight off him, and he was trying to get out from underneath her.

Two things happened at once: she noticed the tip of his staff and froze and he noticed the curling gold mark on her forehead. The mark of the Orsini Colony. Their eyes met. Her eyes were so dark he could hardly see the pupil.

She looked again at the tip of his staff, concealed under coarse, woolen cloth, as if she knew—sensed—that it was something more than a walking stick. Their eyes met once more. She scowled at him, resumed her scrambling, and got to her feet.

He did not dare speak, for his accent was not something he wanted to add to the situation. As she glanced back over her shoulder and hustled away, he realized he did not back into her as much as she had run into him.

Moments later, he saw the cause of her haste: two men in the traditional garb of Hathmirrian soldiers ran past, shouting and pointing after her.

With a moment's decision, Corren gave chase as well.

That very day, deep in the heart of the earth in the glittering caverns of Amon Tunde, a faerie lay on a bed of moss, sweating and shivering.

Salerno, king of the earth faeries, leaned over her. He placed a hand on her cheek, and the faeries gathered around shuffled with discomfort; faeries sensed one another in a way far more intimate than touch, so touch was a boundary they didn't often breach. But here this faerie, Lily, with her delicate face and luminous orange eyes and leaf-like hair that looked like autumn rustling in the wind—Lily lay sick.

And faeries didn't get sick.

Her cheek felt hot under his touch. Her slender fingers rested on the moss, slack and pale. He cupped one hand over hers. Unlike her cheek, her fingers lacked any warmth at all.

She looked at him. He saw the pleading in her eyes but felt it even more in her spirit, which tugged at him. "Salerno," she said, "what's happening to me?"

He thought of the Mourning Chamber, where five faeries lay buried. They had been instantly killed after the witch Aradia's attack on the Tree of Origin destroyed the branches that gave life to those faeries.

The Vein of the Earth, which led from the Royal Cavern to the Tree of Origin, had been closed off to Salerno ever since, but Salerno knew the Tree well. He knew exactly where Lily's branch lay on the Tree.

It was adjacent to the others.

He looked at Keck, one of the guards. "We need to take her up."

The other faeries shuffled and murmured. Keck nodded. He was one of the few unafraid of the world above ground, a characteristic that made him well suited to keep intruders away from the forests of Amon Tunde.

They crafted what they needed from the earth: two long shafts and a mat of moss, magically bound together to create a carrier. It took four faeries to carry her. Salerno led the way, sending her silent feelings of reassurance.

They brought her through the tunnels, past the sparkling pool in the Grand Cavern, and to the Hidden Door that led to the forest. The band of faeries who had been accompanying them diminished once they emerged above ground, but several continued to follow even though they had not so ventured in thousands of years.

Salerno led them to the Old Oak. Several hundred years old, its base was as far across as he was tall. The canopy lifted high above them.

Surely this will help, he thought.

"Bring her close. Closer." They lowered her carefully to the ground at the base of the tree.

Without having to be instructed, she laid her hand on the trunk. A golden glow emanated between her palms and the bark.

A soft moan escaped her lips.

The assembled faeries drew closer.

The color on her skin deepened. The leaves in her hair, which had begun to wilt and curl, grew full and healthy again. A breeze came through and rustled the autumn-colored leaves of her hair and the oak alike.

Though Salerno could both see and feel her healing, something deep inside of her was still wrong. She had been pulling health from the tree into herself, but now her healing stopped.

She drew herself up on her knees and opened her arms wide, embracing the broad trunk, pressing her cheek against it.

The others exchanged glances.

"Is it working?" Keck asked.

Salerno knelt next to her. "Let me help you," he whispered.

She moved her hands near to him, still on the bark, and he placed his hands over hers. He could pull greater healing powers from the tree than Lily could, and he felt the strain on the Old Oak. What would be enough to kill a smaller tree, however, was not too much for this majestic beacon of the forest. This oak was like an old friend and Salerno pleaded with it now. *Heal her.*

More of the sickness within Lily surrendered to his healing, but then even Salerno could go no further. A knot of blackness persisted deep within her and Salerno could not remove it.

They dropped their hands. Lily furrowed her leaf-like brows. "I don't understand," she said. "Can you not heal me?"

She sat on her makeshift cot, her orange eyes brighter, but looking at him with confusion.

"I cannot."

But thinking of the Tree of Origin and the faeries they'd lost already, Salerno thought he knew who could.

He sent the call without delay, sent it until he felt it reach the person he sought, far away in Stonebridge.

Nicolai, Salerno thought. *Nicolai, Nicolai, Nicolai. Come quickly.*

In the few months following his coronation as prince of Caedmonia, Nicolai's days had been full of battle training with

Knight Whittaker, history lessons with Lang, reading and writing lessons with Himmel, and diplomatic exams with Marcellus. Any remaining time was consumed by meetings, formal dinners, tours of the city, and sitting in the Throne Room while the king heard his citizens. That was Nicolai's favorite part, even more than battle training with Whittaker (which he enjoyed in spite of the knight's fondness for yelling). The more Nicolai saw the citizens of Caedmonia, the more he came to love them and wanted to learn how to serve them well.

He admired Marcellus' ability to handle such a myriad of situations, from land disputes to family conflicts. As citizens laid out their troubles or made requests, Nicolai mentally determined how he would've handled the matter and compared his responses to those of the king. More and more frequently, he'd known what was called for. Marcellus seemed particularly pleased with Nicolai's progress in this area.

That almost made up for the difficulties he was having with his studies. His head swam with a bevy of historical facts. Names, dates, battles, treaties, laws, rebellions, famines, proclamations... it all merged together until it was a muddied mess in his mind. To his tutor's frequent frustration, he often mixed up which king did what and when. Lang, no doubt, considered Nicolai a sorry, dim-witted excuse for a prince.

In times like that, Nicolai sustained himself with encouragement from Marcellus, Janus, and Praea. Most of all from Praea.

Their covert meetings often kept him up until the wee hours of the morning some two or three times a week. It was a wonder either of them was able to function the next day. Sheer determination and an apparent inability to stay away from each other kept them at it.

Today, however, Nicolai was enjoying the benefits of a full night's sleep. He was on the training grounds with Whittaker, the sun having long since burned off the morning's mist. While they frequently trained with real swords as they practiced specific moves, today was different.

"Anything goes," Whittaker had said, tossing him a wooden sword, "just like on the battlefield. But I'd rather not run you through."

Nevertheless, Whittaker fought as though he were determined to prove that if a knight *could* run someone through with a wooden sword, he'd manage it.

Though Nicolai was gentle by nature, he'd long since learned it was another matter during battle training. Whittaker may have wanted to beat Nicolai but not nearly as much as Nicolai wanted to beat him.

The two men circled one another, lunging, blocking, thrusting. Several knights had gathered nearby, watching the contest. Whittaker brought his sword down but Nicolai blocked him, the loud crack of wood echoing across the field.

Sweat dripping, hearts pumping, muscles taut, the two men were a constant dance of movement. Nicolai lunged and nearly struck Whittaker square on the chest—what would have been a fatal blow in real battle—but Whittaker blocked him just in time, ducking backwards. It threw him just slightly off balance.

It was the moment Nicolai needed. Capitalizing on his opponent's temporary disadvantage, Nicolai swung his sword through the air.

That was when he heard the call: *Nicolai, Nicolai.*

The urgency in Salerno's call broke his concentration and he slackened his swing. His sword cut through open air, missing Whittaker completely.

Turning in the direction of the Wilds, he heard Salerno again. *Nicolai, come quickly.*

Searing pain tore through his shoulder as Whittaker's sword came crashing down.

Nicolai turned, raising his sword to defend himself, but it was too late. In seconds he was flat on his back with the tip of Whittaker's sword on his chest. The hulking, sweating man loomed over him, scowling. "What in the name of the gods was that?" he hollered.

"I—"

Nicolai, Nicolai.

"Never turn away from your opponent! NEVER! Now you're dead and Caedmonia's down a prince."

"We had a spare anyway," someone hollered from the back of the group.

A few chuckled at this, but Whittaker barked at them to shut up and get back to work.

Come to us, Nicolai. Concerning as his present situation was, it wasn't nearly as concerning as the feeling of Salerno's call. Something was desperately wrong.

Whittaker humphed in disgust, gave Nicolai one final push with the tip of his sword, and walked away.

Nicolai heaved himself off the ground, his shoulder hot and throbbing. He knew Whittaker well enough to know he was supposed to follow him. Likely he would allow Nicolai to rest a bit; Whittaker would not allow a practice session to end with such failure.

But Nicolai did not follow.

Instead he retrieved his horse from the stables and headed straight for Amon Tunde.

Ten

Panting and overheated in the Hathmirrian sun, Corren stood at a busy intersection trying to decide which way to go. He'd lost the soldiers two blocks ago but gathered they had lost their quarry as well, because they'd come back in his direction, looking this way and that, pointing and arguing. He shadowed them until it became clear they were giving up.

He gave up as well. He didn't even know if the woman in the red shawl was heading for the Orsini Colony headquarters or not, though the mark on her forehead clearly branded her a member.

Not knowing if the soldiers would head back to the market or some other direction, Corren let them go. He'd need to ask for directions yet again, but he knew enough not to ask them.

The noise on the crowded street was not much better than it had been in the market. As he weaved through the throng, the stark foreignness of his location began to press on him. He sought temporary refuge in the shadows and relative silence of a narrow alleyway.

He sank down, held his staff close to him, and rested against the stone wall. His legs ached and his feet complained sharply. The top layer of his robe slid off his shoulder and he let it. Nonsensically, he wished he had his piece of the mute's candy.

Corren could not allow himself to rest long. As he had been for most of the long journey through Hathmirr to the capital city of Mingren, he felt driven by the problem of the ash, still waiting on the altar at the Rock of Light. Exhausted or not, the Orsini Colony headquarters was somewhere in this city and he had to find it.

He stood, readjusted the confounded robe, and stepped into the bright sunlight of the street just in time to see a bright red shawl disappear around the corner opposite him. A shawl he recognized.

Corren hurried after her.

He followed the young woman for several blocks but lost her around a turn.

He realized he must have gone the wrong way. He doubled back and checked an alternate path but was soon back in the maze, wandering, certain he'd lost her for good.

He was now in a more residential section of the city. Two-story buildings lined both sides of the street. The ground floors were no more than narrow wooden doors set in the stone walls. Shut against the heat and the dust, no doubt. The doors were colorful though, some painted green, others red, blue, or orange. The upper stories revealed terraces filled with hanging baskets of flowers and laundry hung out to dry. Rather than the browns, tans, and muted colors so often seen in Caedmonia, the bright colors worn by even the common people here swayed on the lines. Were it not for the fact that he was deep in enemy territory, Corren likely would have enjoyed these colorful surroundings.

Occasionally he passed a ground-floor shop, the owner's living quarters in the floors above. He selected a friendly looking shop that sold clay jars and pots and entered the cool and darkened interior. The shopkeeper, a thin man with shocks of gray in his short, brown hair, hesitated to tell him where to find the Orsini Colony.

"Why do you want to go there?" he asked.

"I have a meeting."

The man eyed him. "You should know where to go."

"I've lost my way." Corren retrieved the fold of fabric escaping off his shoulder as nonchalantly as possible.

The man watched him do it, puzzling his brows at him. "Where are you from? Everyone around here knows where they are."

"North," Corren said vaguely. Then, remembering his studying, "Sunderland."

"Ah."

For whatever reason, that satisfied the man. He gave Corren directions and called out to him as Corren was leaving his shop: "Be careful."

Corren repeated the directions to himself over and over, determined not to lose his way again. After the prescribed number of turns, Corren came to the massive building so suddenly he had the illogical feeling he'd arrived there by accident.

The dusty street running alongside the building was nearly deserted, as if the city's citizens were avoiding it on purpose. The stone walls climbed two stories high and lacked a single window. He suspected a courtyard or open area lay on the other side, for he heard mumbling voices, both male and female, and it sounded like a lot of people. Thirty maybe?

Farther down the wall were two massive, forbidding doors and an iron chain, which, he assumed, rang a bell on the interior. He approached, still listening to the voices within the complex. He considered the chain, thinking again about his strategy, wondering (not for the first time) why he felt it so important to do this alone.

The voices fell silent. He held his breath, waiting. A lone cart rumbled farther down the street before turning a corner and disappearing from view.

With one accord, the voices returned, this time as a song. No. It was more of a chant, and resonated through the air like so many drums.

Corren creeped back along the wall, the voices growing louder as he drew nearer to whatever was happening on the other side. He came to the end of the building and an alleyway. He followed it, plunging himself into shadow, keeping his staff close. The voices grew louder. He realized they had been farther away from the street side of the wall than he'd thought and indicated a larger gathering than he'd first realized.

Now he felt the magical residue of whatever was happening. A pause interrupted the chanting. One lone voice boomed across the air and the group answered in unison.

He came to the end of the wall: another corner, another street. This one more deserted and ramshackle looking than the last had been. The alleyway opposite was full of trash, discarded crates, rotting food.

The voices grew louder. Corren wanted to see what was happening for himself. He crossed to the alley and grabbed a crate.

Corren climbed to the top of a rather unstable tower of crates, magically supporting an otherwise impossible contraption. He'd built it high enough that he could stand and see over the wall, though he crouched at first, raising himself incrementally. Slowly, the layout of the complex revealed itself. Stout buildings—one with a covered walkway and the rest with a smattering of narrow windows—opened to a massive courtyard, but the courtyard was off center. The buildings ran along two sides of the perimeter walls, leaving the courtyard in the corner closest to him.

The chanting of the group rose to a crescendo as he straightened enough to see them at last. Wrapped in layered robes of orange and red, a circle of at least sixty people surrounded a cluster of six, set slightly apart and standing by a stone pillar. The gold mark of the Orsini Colony glinted on each forehead, though he noticed the marks differed from one person to the next.

He scanned the faces of the men and women in the circle, wondering if he would recognize the woman on the street if he saw her. He did. Though she no longer wore the gold-trimmed, red shawl, he recognized her high cheekbones and dark eyes. She chanted with the others.

A bald man held a short staff aloft, circling the tip over a large copper bowl sitting on top of the stone pillar. Corren sensed the chanting of the rest of the members likewise directed magic toward the bowl.

The magic had an unholy feel to it.

Corren came to Hathmirr to investigate this notorious magical group because of some notes he'd found in one of Aradia's folios. He came because those notes suggested this group may help him unravel the mystery of the ash waiting on the altar at the Rock of Light. But Corren knew what kind of people these were. Watching them now, he wondered yet again: *What could the Orsini Colony have to do with the Madera branch?*

The chanting of the group came to an abrupt halt. An eerie silence fell over the courtyard. The six figures nearest the pillar drew closer to the bowl and together lifted it high.

The surrounding members answered with a raucous noise, like cheering the slaughtering of some sacrificial animal. Noting the blood-like appearance of the liquid inside the bowl, Corren wondered if there had indeed been some sort of sacrifice. He saw no evidence of such but held his judgment in check. He could not, after all, see what was on the ground immediately on the other side of the wall.

The cheering ceased. The bowl was replaced on the pillar and a chalice produced (Corren could not tell from where), which the apparent leader dipped into the bowl.

The group then commenced a low chant. It was so soft he wondered if he would have been able to hear it from the street. The chant itself did not feel magical, but as the leader took the chalice to first one member, then another, he heard the leader say an incantation and each member repeat it after him. Following the incantation, each individual took a sip from the chalice.

It felt a dark rite and Corren would have liked to turn away except that he could not. As Head of the Order, suspecting this group was somehow tied to the mystery of the ash lying forsaken in the Rock of Light, he had to watch. Though, being the man he was, always thirsting for knowledge even when he should not, he wanted to know just for himself. What exactly was going on here?

The man with the chalice made his way around the circle. When he was but two people away from the young woman, Corren's attention turned to her. Unlike the others, she did not watch the leader circling the group. She was chanting but kept her eyes on the ground in front of her. Corren could not look away from her face.

The leader stepped in front of her and she stopped chanting, as the others had done. She looked not at the leader but at the chalice in front of her.

He said his incantation and she said hers back. Corren felt the magic in these incantations as he'd felt all the others.

Then he felt something else. It felt like an incantation, but no one said anything. Not a mouth moved. She took a sip from the chalice, and the lingering sense of magic lasted until the chalice left her lips.

The leader moved on.

If something unusual had happened, he seemed not to know it. As before, Corren could not take his eyes off the young woman, but now it was for an entirely new reason.

His mind raced to work out what he thought he just saw.

Eleven

By the time Nicolai returned to the castle, the evening meal was nearly finished. Only a few knights and citizens lingered at the many long tables in the Great Hall, and the king's table at the head of the room sat empty. A knight noticed Nicolai, leaned toward his dining companion, and pointed in Nicolai's direction. He said something and the two erupted in laughter.

Nicolai ignored this, leaving the hall. He realized too late his disappearance earlier probably looked like he was fleeing the scene of his defeat at the hands of Knight Whittaker. That was damage he'd have to undo later.

There were more pressing matters at hand.

He found Marcellus in his office, alone, save for the dutiful young page standing by the door. Nicolai dismissed the lad, who gave his king a questioning look as Nicolai scooted him out the door.

"One day you'll manage to get them to obey your orders without physical provocation," Marcellus said lightly but then saw the look on Nicolai's face as he marched across the room. "What's wrong?"

Nicolai began without preamble. He told him about answering Salerno's summons and discovering the strangest thing he'd ever seen in Amon Tunde: a faerie lying sick on her bed.

It had been such a shocking sight. Almost as shocking as what Salerno had said next: "Heal her, Nicolai."

Nicolai had merely stood there. He was never one to refuse help when asked for it, yet he could not begin to imagine why Salerno thought he could heal Lily. He knew better than anyone what Nicolai could do... and what he couldn't. This was far, far beyond his capabilities.

He'd wished for his yellow stone, which had turned to ash in the Realm of the Phoenix. Though, he likely couldn't use it to heal Lily anyway. The stone had always had a mind of its own.

Salerno told Nicolai to place his hands above Lily's stomach and sense the elements inside her the way he'd been taught to do with plants. Still feeling the entire situation somewhat preposterous, he tried anyway. After a few false starts and with instruction from Salerno, Nicolai managed it.

But sensing Lily was an experience far beyond that of sensing a flower. Lily was just as pure and bright, but much more complex. There were countless layers to her and they unfolded to him, one after another. It brought a tenderness of feeling for Lily he never had before. He hadn't really known her, but in one instant he came to know, really know, who she was. Her gentleness, her trust, her purity. The rawness of their connection brought an ache to his chest. He wanted to cradle her in his arms and soothe her like a child.

The next thing he discovered came as a painful blow. There was something dark and menacing deep within her. It branched out in thin tendrils like so many sharp claws.

Chilled by the memory, Nicolai now asked Marcellus, "You remember that Aradia stole a leaf from the Tree of Origin?"

Aradia had been above ground with the Tree far below. No one knew how she'd removed a gold leaf through the earth, but however she did it, she'd killed five branches—and the faeries connected to them—in the process.

"I remember," Marcellus said.

"Aradia did more damage to the Tree than Salerno first realized," Nicolai said, "and it's spreading."

"What do you mean, spreading?"

Nicolai explained. Whatever blackness was in the Tree had spread to Lily's branch, infecting her with a sickness no one seemed able to heal. "Though..." Nicolai said, "Salerno asked me to try."

"You! Why you! Why can't Salerno do it?"

"I'm not sure, but I couldn't heal her either. Not that it was surprising. I can't do half what Salerno can do."

"Then why would he ask you to heal her if he can't?"

"Because the earth is still blocking Salerno from getting to the Tree of Origin."

For as long as the earth faeries could remember, only Salerno could go through the tunnel that led to the Tree of Origin. After Aradia's attack, however, the earth no longer allowed him. In their quest to defeat Aradia, Nicolai and his brothers had needed a single leaf from the Tree. Salerno wasn't sure if the earth would allow Nicolai to approach the Tree and warned it might be dangerous to try. It had indeed been a harrowing experience.

The earth had tested him—with pits that fell out from below and rock that collapsed from above. That's how it felt at the time anyway: a test. As if the earth wanted to see if he were worthy enough. Or determined enough. Whatever it was the earth wanted from him, Nicolai apparently delivered. He'd obtained the leaf they needed to defeat Aradia and journeyed back out of the tunnel with nary an obstacle in his way.

"Can you still get to the Tree?" Marcellus now asked.

Nicolai nodded. He had gone to the Tree that very day, in fact.

It was Salerno's idea: "You must try to heal the Tree, Nicolai," he'd said. "You are still the only one the earth is allowing. It must be there's something you can do."

Though Nicolai didn't know what that might be, he did not refuse. In fact, he went to the Tree of Origin full of hope. After all, it wasn't the first time he'd gone to the Tree with a mission he didn't know how to fulfill. During his first visit, the earth had provided exactly what he needed: a spear borne of the rocky wall. It was the only thing strong enough to remove a leaf from his branch. He bore the scar on his back to mark the occasion and wore the spear strapped to his calf even now.

But the earth had provided no such solution today. Nicolai followed Salerno's healing instructions without success. He tried one thing, then another. He looked for clues and hoped for inspiration. He practically begged the earth to give him insight. Nothing he did helped.

He stood in the golden light of the Tree and looked at the blackened branches high at the top. They'd been there last time, of course, destroyed in Aradia's attack, instantly killing the faeries connected to those branches. From his position on the ground, Nicolai could not see if the blackness was truly spreading.

At that point he removed his weapons and began to climb. Barefooted, he placed foot then hand on one golden branch after another, rising slowly and silently. He climbed so gently it was like taking a woman tenderly into his arms. He was encircled by golden limbs, and as he climbed, the leaves shook and tinkled softly like so many little bells. The golden energy of the Tree seeped into his skin and deep into his bones and made him feel as if he were made of nothing but light itself.

He climbed until he was nearly to the top, the ground far below.

Here, he saw.

Black streaks marred the base of two golden limbs that were adjacent to the dead branches. A few other limbs were also close to the blackened branches but did not yet show signs of damage.

He placed his hand on a section of smooth bark streaked with black and nearly recoiled as he sensed the evil within. He gathered all the magical knowledge and strength he had and tried to push the sickness away. But the bark was impenetrable. His magic couldn't reach through.

He continued to try anyway.

For a long time, he refused to leave until the Tree was healed, but eventually he had no choice. He descended to the ground and left the Tree just as he found it.

But he himself left changed. Instead of hope, his heart was full of fear. What if the Tree were damaged beyond repair?

"If Lily is sick," Marcellus asked now, "who else could get sick? What about Janus?"

"I don't know."

"How fast is it spreading?"

Nicolai shrugged helplessly. "Let us hope we can stop it. Salerno believes he can teach me what I need to know to heal the Tree." It seemed an almost impossible task, but Nicolai had faith in Salerno and would do as he was asked. Still, there may be another way to heal the Tree: if a witch had caused the damage to start with, surely a wizard could stop it.

"I was hoping you'd heard from Corren," Nicolai said. "I checked at Tower Hall South, but they still have no word on when he'll be back."

No one there even seemed to know where he'd gone, let alone when he'd return. They knew he planned on being away for a while and that his absence had something to do with the ash still stuck on the altar in the Rock of Light, but that was the extent of it.

Nicolai had asked them to send messages to the other branches and to the members working at the Rock of Light in case Corren showed up in any of those locations. Marcellus was his last hope. "Have you heard from him?" Nicolai asked now.

"Unfortunately not," Marcellus said as he looked toward the door and stood. He made it halfway across the room before Janus entered. "There you are," Marcellus said. "I've been calling and calling for you."

Nicolai was aware that Marcellus could use the faeries' ability to sense and call out to one another, but only with Janus. He suspected Marcellus could learn to do it with other faeries, but he didn't seem interested.

Janus arched her brows at Marcellus, amused. "You've been calling me for two whole minutes."

"Are you sick?" Marcellus asked.

She furrowed her brows at him, still smiling, as if trying to determine the jest. "I'm a faerie, Marcellus. We don't get sick."

"Nicolai said Lily is sick."

Janus looked at Nicolai. "What? Our Lily? She can't be."

Nicolai launched into his explanation, and by the time he was finished, Janus was sitting on the couch, her face drawn down in shock.

"So, are you?" Marcellus asked her.

"Am I what?" she asked distractedly.

"Sick."

She shook her head, looking like she was trying to get a handle on the situation. "No. And you said they tried the Old Oak?" she asked Nicolai.

He nodded.

Marcellus was still eyeing Janus. "You're certain?" he asked.

"Certain about what?" she asked, this time with some irritation.

"Are you certain you're not sick?"

"Marcellus," she said firmly, "I am not ill."

He settled a bit but continued to regard her with concern. She softened and put her hand on his knee.

They all looked at one another in silence.

No one said anything about what would happen if the sickness spread unchecked, but Nicolai did not doubt they were all thinking it. An entire race would be eradicated, including each individual present. It would affect not just one kingdom, but two.

"I'm going back in the morning," Nicolai said at last. If Praea didn't show up tonight, he'd have to send a message to the Rock of Light and hope it got to her. He didn't want her to show up at the castle not knowing he was gone, but he couldn't delay either.

"I don't know if I can do anything, but... I have to try. Who knows when Corren will get back and Lily can't wait."

Janus nodded grimly. "I'm going with you."

As the ceremony continued around the circle, Corren gripped the top of the stone wall, still puzzling out what he saw the woman do. If she did what he thought she did, what were the implications?

A sharp voice commanded his attention. A man was pointing at him. Several faces turned in his direction as he ducked behind the wall, lost control of the crates, and came tumbling down. He thought the incantation just in time to stop himself from landing on his head on the stone alleyway.

Commotion and shouting swelled on the other side of the wall.

Clambering to his feet and letting the crates fall where they may, Corren hustled down the alleyway. He ran away from the front entrance to the complex. There must have been a rear entrance as well, because as he exited the alleyway, several robed men and women came swarming in his direction.

The bald man was near the front, pointing his staff at Corren.

Corren raised his in response.

Covered or not, he surmised the leader knew Corren held a staff as well, for the man stopped. The group halted and the two men sized each other up.

More robed members came running down the alleyway, but Corren kept his eye on the leader. The man gave a signal and several members of the group rushed toward him. Corren sent up an invisible barrier, holding them at bay.

Amidst their shouts of displeasure, the leader of the group raised his staff and said an incantation.

Corren blocked the spell then sent another to obstruct the entrance of the alleyway, where the members of the group bottlenecked, complaining and groaning.

If he'd wanted to escape, he'd just run. But that wasn't what he wanted.

"I wish to speak with the Lord of Orsini."

The man snorted. "I am Lord Tivoli. You dare spy on us then say you wish to talk?"

"I—"

Red-faced, the Lord of Orsini spat out, "We should hang you for what you did! We should—" Lord Tivoli stopped mid-sentence and narrowed his eyes at Corren.

Corren realized he forgot to disguise his accent.

"Where are you from?" Tivoli asked.

Corren debated his answer. He wasn't ready to fully reveal himself yet. "Stonebridge."

The group exchanged glances and murmurs. Corren spied the young woman from the market toward the back. She spoke with no one, but watched intently.

"Enough," Tivoli said as they continued to murmur. "Enough!" and they fell silent. "A spy from Stonebridge. I may or may not decide I want to talk to you. You can await my decision in the dungeon."

Corren pulled his staff close. He sensed he would be able to speak with Lord Tivoli eventually, but he would have to act like it was on the leader's terms. Even more than talking to the Lord of Orsini, however, Corren wanted in that building. If he had to start out in the dungeon, so be it, but he would not go defenseless. "I will go, but my staff comes with me."

The members waited in silence, looking between Corren and their leader. Lord Tivoli regarded Corren with a calculating expression. Corren did not forget the man held a staff in his hand as well, and knew he may or may not have seen the full power of it. He had no idea what kind of strength this man and his staff had.

"Take your staff if you wish," Lord Tivoli said. "I warn you now not to use it against us."

"As long as you give me no reason to," Corren replied.

They all stood a moment longer on the dusty street, the mass of Orsinians gathered around the lone Caedmonian, unmasked in spite of his colorful and disheveled Hathmirrian disguise.

Tivoli finally gestured to his men. "What are you waiting for? Take him away."

Twelve

After banishing the stranger to the dungeons, Lord Tivoli sent the Brotherhood to his office. Since the Brotherhood included both male and female leaders in the Orsini Colony, Lini would go too, but she had to clean up first. As Steward of the Archives, part of her job included setting up and taking down the ceremonies. She had to mend the drapes and ceremonial robes, make sure they had ample supplies for the potions, and wipe down that infernal bowl before putting it away. She was also responsible for maintaining their catalogue of books and folios, keeping track of borrowings, and doing any necessary repairs on bindings.

It was an underling job with a minimal amount of respect. She never looked forward to Brotherhood meetings—they didn't ask her opinion on things anyway—but she didn't want to go within reach of this one.

An outsider. Witnessing the Ceremony of the Way of Orsini.

That was disturbing enough, but it was Lord Tivoli she really wanted to avoid. It was best to steer clear of him when he was in a mood in any case, but after a crime such as this? Who knew what he'd do.

Lini recognized the wizard, of course. She'd quite literally run into him in the market. But who was he and why was he spying on them?

She slowly wheeled the cart of ceremonial items to the Archives, a vast room full of books and folios and a separate cabinet for ceremonial supplies. She took her time with the drapes, straightening them with a firm snap before folding them in half, then in half again.

She unlocked the cabinet door and stacked the drapes on their shelves. She placed the ingredients back into their drawers and the bowl in its place of honor on a rounded stand built specifically for this purpose. All was neatly tucked away.

Lini stood there staring at it all.

She did not want to go to the meeting.

On a shelf below the bowl sat a simple wooden box. It was without ornamentation and lacked the distinguished feel of the other items in the cabinet. It wasn't the box that was important but what was inside.

When she was first assigned to this position, she was shown the box and its contents with only a minimal amount of instruction. Everyone knew about it anyway, especially these days. She had just never seen it before. Still, she was ordered to leave it be and of course she did.

Only recently had she violated that command.

Only recently had she taken the box down from the shelf (as she was doing again right now), lifted the lid (her hands felt the rough edges of the wood), and removed what was inside.

It was a book. A very old book. *The* book.

She felt a familiar surge of warning when she lifted the cover. She'd grown used to disobeying such feelings. Those feelings that she shouldn't be doing something but was doing it anyway.

Her hand rested on the old parchment and she inhaled deeply, loving the smell of the ancient pages.

The first time she'd done this, she'd only dared to read the cover page. Last week she'd carefully turned a few more pages before coming to her senses and putting it away.

As she should be doing right now.

Her fingers ran along the uneven edges of the parchment.

She lifted a page then—

"What are you doing?" A voice boomed across the room, shaking her.

She jumped as Lord Tivoli marched toward her. Half a dozen leaders lingered in the door behind him.

She snapped the book closed and he yelled, "Don't—!"

They both froze.

Lord Tivoli rushed forward and seized the book from her hands. She offered a hasty bow as he gripped it, arms shaking.

Lini knew this kind of rage. She didn't like being so easily within his grasp but dared not shrink back. If all were as it was supposed to be, she would stand there and wait.

She forced herself to lower her hands and take on a guileless expression. She felt moisture on her palms.

Dark brows drew down over dark eyes as Lord Tivoli scowled at her. She had seen this look prior to him doling out brutal punishments. She knew she shouldn't have looked in the book, but the severity of his reaction was surprising even to her. Of all days to get caught. Why did she do this when he was already upset about the snooping wizard?

Her only out was to feign ignorance.

"This book is not for you," he said, the rage in his voice rolling over her like thunder.

"I'm sorry. I didn't know," she said meekly, not even needing to fake her subservience. She knew too well he could do anything he wanted and she would be helpless. Even if she dared fight back—and she wasn't sure she wouldn't—it would only make matters worse.

"Want to see what's inside, do you?" he growled. The others crept toward them, drawn to the promise of carnage.

She shook her head. "No, I'm sorry my Lord, I—"

He reached out and grabbed her arm, squeezing his fingertips into her flesh. He yanked her forward and leaned over her, his breath hot on her face.

"I'm sorry, my Lord."

He raised his eyebrows and jerked her arm. "Are you?" Sharp pain radiated outward from where his fingertips dug deeper and deeper.

He squeezed harder and she couldn't help releasing a gasp of pain.

Satisfied, he released her and stood up straight. "Go ahead," he said, without taking his eyes off her. "Open it again."

Lini shook her head. "No, my Lord. I'm sorry, my Lord. I did not understand."

She thought he was making it clear she should not touch the book again, but he thrust it at her. The heavy book gouged into her breasts. She allowed no expression of pain or shock to escape her lips.

She fumbled for the book as he released it. Her arm was still throbbing from his grasp.

"Open it," he said again.

Lini knew she could not hesitate. She knew that alone would call her into question. But she found it more and more difficult to maintain her mask of obedience, especially in the face of such danger. She feared he had already doomed her and was making her disobey one more time before pummeling her until she bled all over the cold, concrete floor.

"Open it," he said lowly.

Lini could not take her eyes off his as she slowly lifted the cover.

Lord Tivoli snatched the book away and she flinched and gasped.

He looked down at its pages, staring at the evidence of her treachery. No one moved. He slowly turned a page. Then another. He looked at her, as if taunting her.

"I did not know, my Lord," she whispered. "I swear. Please."

Her only defense. Outright disobedience was rare, but misunderstandings. Misunderstandings could sometimes be forgiven.

Lord Tivoli turned away from her, the book still in his hands. "Take her to the chambers."

By the time they escorted her down to the chambers, Lini's fear had left her. Now she was just angry. Angry with herself for being so foolish. Angry with Lord Tivoli. Angry with everyone around her. Routt and Jatvia had her by the arms, leading her along.

They took her down the stairs and underground to the rock passageway. Little cavelets flanked each side of the dank and dimly lit corridor. The cavelets were fronted by iron bars and doors. Most were empty. They didn't have many prisoners now, aside from the foreign wizard. They marched her past him and his guard to a cell clearly meant for her.

She pulled her arms free. "I'll go myself."

She stepped into what felt like a hole in the earth, and the iron door clanged shut behind her. There were no windows. No light except for the torches in the hall. A few air shafts in the ceiling kept prisoners from suffocating. Barely.

She turned around and faced her fellows, crossing her arms. Giffen, who was guarding the wizard asked, "What now?"

"Lord Tivoli had one of his rages," Routt said. He looked at Lini. "She asked for it though."

He and Jatvia left while Giffen, a friend of hers, pointedly looked away from her. She couldn't blame him. She was in bad with Lord Tivoli. Ignoring her was his safest course of action.

The wizard was diagonally across the way. He lingered not far from his own bars, wearing a long, black cloak and holding that tall staff. He was watching her.

Lini turned her back to him and sank down in a dark corner, out of his line of sight.

Thirteen

Lini spent that night and part of the next day in the chambers. She and the wizard had caught each other's eye more than once, but neither mentioned their meeting in the market. They were under guard, of course, and so it would be impossible to speak of anything anyway. She sensed they would be tiptoeing around one another even if they were alone.

She stood in a weak circle of light cast by the torch in the wall, examining the little bruises on her upper arm where Lord Tivoli had grabbed her. Light and shadows flickered on her skin, making it difficult to see clearly, but they were there. She felt them plainly enough too. She was lucky this was the worst that had happened... so far anyway.

She readjusted her shawl and wrapped it tightly around her shoulders. The musty air in the chambers gave her a chill and made it hard to breathe.

"Giffen," the wizard called, his voice jarring the deep quiet. She glanced up. There he stood, in his long, black cloak, near the bars of his cell. "I'd like something to eat," the wizard said.

It was not for prisoners to request anything, not even food, but that morning she'd noticed he had a mattress and blanket in his chamber. She had no idea when he'd managed to obtain such things. She herself had slept on the dirt floor.

Giffen was a hulking man, well suited to guard duty. He nodded toward someone at the far end of the chambers, whose job it was to watch the door. "Bring food for the wizard," he called.

"Giffen?" Lini asked.

He turned to her. The light from the torches flashed on his face. He looked at her without expression, but she held his gaze hopefully.

109

He huffed and called again, "Bring something for Lini too."

Giffen approached her, clearly thinking he'd ignored her long enough and could safely talk to her now. She noticed the wizard watching them but refused to meet his eyes. She wished he would go back to his mattress.

Giffen came close to the bars and looked down at her; she took half a step back. He seemed even taller than usual in the low light of the chambers. "What'd you do?" he asked.

"I..." She glanced up at him, saw his dark eyes on her, and looked away. "I looked in a book."

"Looked in a book?"

She wasn't about to give the details. If he knew which book, he wouldn't be so confused.

"Why would Lord Tivoli care if you looked in a book?"

She wished he would go away. "He just did."

Giffen made a dismissive sound. "Ever notice your curiosity gets you into trouble?"

Across the way, the wizard perked up at this. He held her eyes longer than she meant to allow. Unsettled, she forced herself to look away.

Giffen was still hovering near her. "Mind your own business," she told him.

He laughed and went back to his post.

With nothing left to see, the wizard went to his mattress and lay down, seemingly unconcerned about his fate.

Anger flared up in her chest. She walked along the front of her cell, drawing closer to his. "You should've been hung for spying," she said, her face getting hot, "instead of just being our prisoner."

"Prisoner?" he said without looking at her. "No, I'm not a prisoner."

Foolish talk for a man behind bars. "Why don't you leave then?"

"I will if it comes to that. I think he wants to talk to me though. I'll wait."

"I think you're waiting for the noose."

He didn't respond, just lay there on his mattress.

She turned away and went back to her corner where it was dark and free from prying eyes. Instead of sitting, she leaned against the wall and crossed her arms, her blood charging through her veins. She was angry at the wizard, at Giffen, at Lord Tivoli. Most of all at herself.

A few moments later, Routt came to release her. Her punishment was, apparently, over. She marched out of the dank chambers, having never eaten.

In a sun-drenched glen in the forest of Amon Tunde, Nicolai watched Salerno carefully. He hoped Salerno's demonstration would show him what he needed to know to heal the Tree of Origin.

The king of the earth faeries stood under the massive canopy of the Old Oak. His thick, mossy robe hung from his outstretched arms. Turning his palms upward, Salerno began.

Faint strands of light, barely visible, started trailing downward from the many branches of the tree. They flowed together and gathered at a single point near the base of the broad trunk. Here, the patch of light grew brighter, glittering at the edges.

Salerno gently curled his fingers inward and the light obeyed his command. It arched off the bark and through the air to his open palms. The healing light absorbed into him and disappeared.

He lowered his arms. Nicolai had never seen Salerno do anything so beautiful.

Salerno began walking toward the tree and gestured Nicolai to him. Beautiful though it was, Nicolai struggled to understand something. He hesitated for a moment, the sun warm on his skin, then followed.

"This is what you will learn to do first," Salerno said as Nicolai drew close.

"But, you took healing *out* of a tree. How will that help the Tree of Origin?"

Salerno smiled mildly. "You learned to walk before you learned to run, did you not?"

Nicolai nodded.

"It is the same with this. You must learn to draw healing out of a tree before you can learn to put healing back into it."

Salerno patted the bark, indicating Nicolai should put his hands on it.

"But..." Lily was sick *now*. How long could she wait while Nicolai trained? "Do we have time for that?"

"We do not have a choice," Salerno said, his expression darkening, "but you are right. We have no time to spare." He patted the trunk again.

Nicolai put his hands on the rough bark, and Salerno placed his slender hands on top. He began again. This time, Nicolai closed his eyes and concentrated on feeling the elements within the tree.

As Salerno repeated his demonstration, the elements moved so rapidly and what they were doing was so complex Nicolai could hardly keep up with it. Head spinning, he opened his eyes in time to see a glowing light emerge from the space between Nicolai's hands and the bark.

As Salerno directed the tree's healing energy into Nicolai, warmth flooded through him.

They dropped their hands and Nicolai took a step back, feeling energized.

His heart was beating rapidly. He'd healed using flowers and herbs, but this... this was something else entirely.

"You see?" Salerno said.

No. Nicolai did not see at all.

"Do not worry. We will begin with identifying the elements. I do not believe you've yet learned them all."

Nicolai shook his head.

"Do not worry," Salerno said again in his soothing voice. "I will teach you as I've taught you before. The faerie in you will learn quickly enough."

"Then I'll be able to do it as you did?"

"Well," Salerno shook his head. "Not quite like that. Perhaps I should not have shown you in that way. I do not need to touch the tree to draw out healing as the others do. But you saw what must be done, did you not?"

Nicolai already knew that as king of the earth faeries, Salerno had capabilities far beyond those of the others, but this served as a stark reminder. He wondered yet again, *If Salerno can't heal the Tree, why would I be able to do it?*

Salerno seemed to sense his thoughts. He raised one finger and gave Nicolai a stern look. "Remember, you have unique abilities of your own. We need this from you, Nicolai."

Nicolai took a deep breath.

He placed his hands on the bark. "Alright."

He had no idea what his unique abilities might be, but they had no time for his hesitation. "I'm ready."

Barefoot and in only her trousers and knight's tunic, Janus walked through the Great Cavern and headed down the tunnel that led to the faeries' private dwellings. She'd come with Nicolai to Amon Tunde that morning but left him in the glen to train with Salerno. She had her own reasons for coming here.

Even though they said Lily was sick, she half expected to find her just as vibrant as she always was. Janus couldn't help it: there was a side of her that disbelieved.

But... Aradia's spell had killed five faeries instantly. Was it so hard to believe that same spell was now spreading?

It was hard to believe.

And Janus had to see for herself.

She passed the little hollows dug out of the earth, the doorways draped with curtains of moss. A few of these were pulled back to reveal lush interiors and faeries reclining within.

As she neared Lily's chambers, she sent the silent faerie call asking permission to enter. The frailty in Lily's response gave her pause. Hand hovering for a moment over the mossy curtain, Janus finally drew it back and stepped inside.

Flowering vines covered the walls. Their gentle scent filled the air. A trickle of water fell from a spout into a rocky hollow, serving as both washbasin and drinking fountain. Several cloaks made of moss and green leaves hung from a series of hook-like branches. On the opposite side, a raised platform of moss-covered earth served as her bed, and there lay Lily.

Her body looked frail and slight. Even her fingers, resting on her stomach, seemed diminished. Her sallow skin lacked the usual vibrancy. Instead of full and bright leaves of hair, they lay flat against her head, wilting slightly.

"Lily," Janus breathed softly. She had only ever seen a human look so ill. Never one of her own.

Lily turned her head toward Janus. It seemed an effort for her to do so.

Crossing the room, Janus sank to her knees by Lily's bed. Her orange eyes watched pitifully. Normally such a lovely orange, even her eyes were dimmed.

The two reached for the other in the faerie way. More intimate than an embrace, this ancient way of conversing surpassed words and allowed for a depth of understanding Janus had yet to experience in the human world. Janus had no words for the situation anyway.

Janus sensed Lily's fear. Her sorrow. Her regret. She wanted nothing more than to comfort her friend and make her well.

"You've managed to get yourself in quite a bind, my darling," Janus said at last, trying to tease her gently.

This did not bring a smile to Lily's face as Janus had hoped. Lily nodded in agreement. "I fear I've made a mistake." Her voice was weak and slightly raspy.

Janus tried to appear as if she hadn't noticed. She smiled stubbornly, determined to cheer her. "What mistake would that be?"

"I think I waited too long to tell Salerno." The smile faded from Janus' face. She shook her head slightly, wanting to dismiss Lily's fears, but she went on. "I didn't understand what it was."

"Of course not," she said. "How could you have?" Furrowing her brows, Janus turned her attention to Lily's cloak. Some of the cloth had bunched up and looked rather uncomfortable.

"This illness is... so strange," Lily said as Janus took to straightening the soft folds of her cloak. "It feels... it feels as if..."

Janus stopped, looking at Lily's face.

"I don't know what it feels like. I've never felt anything such as this."

Janus sat back on her heels, her hands in her lap.

"Maybe if I'd told Salerno right away, he could've healed me then."

Janus felt the pang of Lily's fears and couldn't help but wonder herself. What if Lily had told Salerno right away? Then again...

"It's the Tree that must be healed," Janus said, "not you." And this was true. "You've done nothing wrong. Please don't blame yourself." She fussed with one last fold in Lily's cloak, as if that would make everything better. "It will be alright."

Lily nodded and closed her eyes.

Janus felt the weariness within her friend. She looked again at Lily's strangely thin fingers and the curling leaves in her hair. She longed to take Lily's hand in hers but did not think Lily would find such a thing comforting. The room was silent, save for the trickling of clear water falling into the basin.

A ledge nearby held Lily's collection of pine cones, stones, egg shells, and leaves, all arranged in an orderly pattern. She had obtained them one at a time over the course of hundreds of years. Many of the items were brought to her by the few faeries who guarded Amon Tunde's aboveground realm, for though Lily enjoyed her treasures, she did not care to venture into the world above.

Janus remembered when she and Elana had found the little blue robin's egg, long ago. It was so neatly hatched into two halves they decided to bring it to their friend. Janus could still see the way Lily had cradled it so gently in her open palms before carrying it away. This was long before their adventures above ground started getting them into trouble and they'd earned Lily's stern disapproval for their wanderings.

But the little blue shells lay there still.

When Lily opened her eyes again, she looked at Janus and furrowed her leafy brows. "It is always strange to me," she said sadly, "to see you in your human clothes."

Janus always felt self-conscious here in her knight's tunic and pants, but she felt doubly so now. This was not just about looking out of place. Janus sensed the mournful longing within her fellow faerie.

"What ever happened to your lovely *undanna* cloak?"

"It is here," Janus said. "In my chamber."

Lily looked at Janus a moment, her orange eyes searching her. How grief-stricken she was. Janus sensed such a deep sorrow within her it brought tears her to eyes. "I wish things were as they were before," Lily said. "When we were all still here together."

Then Janus understood. Recent years had unexpectedly taken away so many of their friends. First their dear Elana, who'd taken a human weakness into her when she chose to conceive and ultimately died giving birth to the Three, then fully five faeries who'd been killed instantly during Aradia's attack. Now here lay Lily. Would she be next?

And who after that?

But as Lily looked at Janus—who appeared for all the world like a true human—she seemed to think she'd already lost Janus as well: lost her to the human world.

And in a way, she had.

◆　◆　◆

116

On Janus' way out of Amon Tunde, she went to Nicolai and Salerno to say goodbye. Nicolai intended to stay here at Amon Tunde until he healed the Tree or...

Or not.

Nicolai practiced on the Old Oak while Salerno saw her to the borders. As they walked along in bare feet on the softened ground of Amon Tunde's realm, she wondered why Salerno had called Nicolai but not her. "Why did you not tell me about Lily yourself?"

"I was going to," he said simply.

It was all the answer she needed to understand him. Her people were never in much of a rush. Thus, he saw no need to tell her immediately. He'd called Nicolai when he did, simply because he'd needed him.

They took a few more steps in silence. A warbler called in the distance, soon answered by his fellow.

"Why do you think the earth is blocking everyone from the Tree except Nicolai?"

"These boys are unusual," Salerno said. "Being both human and faerie seems to give them unique strength. However, there is something different in Nicolai that is not in his brothers. They are each half earth faerie, but the other elements are strong in Marcellus and Corren. I can only assume this is the work of the Phoenix. Nicolai, however... Nicolai resonates the earth in his very bones. This must be why the earth allows him. There must be something only he can do."

Janus hoped Salerno was right. He wasn't often wrong, though if he were, it wouldn't be the first time. What would they do then?

They came to the border of Amon Tunde and stopped. Her boots, knight's overcoat, and bow and arrows were in a neat pile only a few steps beyond the border. Her horse was tied to a tree not much farther, watching them benignly.

"How is Keck?" Janus asked.

Even though most of the faeries had never seen the Tree of Origin for themselves, they all knew exactly where their branches were thanks to Salerno's stories. She knew Keck's was dangerously close to Lily's.

His wasn't the only one.

"He is starting to show signs," Salerno said.

A cold shock of fear gripped at her chest. It was spreading. Truly.

"How are you, Janus?" Salerno asked. She felt him sensing her in that deep way only Salerno could, searching for anything amiss. "Feeling alright? No signs?"

She shook her head. She didn't want him looking for illness within her and gently resisted him.

He relented, respecting her desire for privacy. "That is good."

She nodded, looking away to her horse. She did not want to discuss it.

"Your branch is so near the others," he said.

She turned back to Salerno, alarmed. "You haven't told Nicolai, have you?" But it was not Nicolai she was thinking about. She didn't want this information to make its way back to Marcellus.

"No," Salerno said.

"Good," Janus said, stepping beyond the border at last. "Don't."

Fourteen

Kai'Enna lingered in the doorway of her little stone cottage with her aged hand resting on the wooden frame. A breeze swept through, thick with the scent of pine. Her cottage was high in the mountains on a cliff plateau and had offered both shelter and security for many decades. In the sun-drenched meadow in front of her house, half a dozen young women were gathered in a circle.

Standing among them was Praea. She transformed, took to the air, and circled above the group. A swell of wind trailed after her, gaining in strength as she gathered more and more elements into it.

She caused the wind to whirl around the girls, who laughed as they grabbed long hair with one fist and held down skirts with the other.

Kai'Enna watched them soberly. The air around her was still, untouched by Praea's windstorm.

Praea tamed the whirlwind with her magic, landed in the center of the circle, and changed into her natural form. Looking thoroughly windblown, the girls broke into enthusiastic applause. Little Jesaray, youngest of the group, bounced on her feet and clapped in glee. She was never far from Praea's side and seemed to take special delight in her.

While Praea's demonstration was meant to give their little flock a glimpse of what was to come, they would not master such skills for some time. She settled them on the grass and set to the less exciting task of delivering the day's lecture.

While Praea was not yet fully trained to take over as Head of the branch, she was well on her way and Kai'Enna was grateful for it. She felt all seventy-three of her years deep in her bones. She'd spent most of those years waiting for the Phoenix, longing for it, wishing for the time when their branch's magic would no longer be in danger of extinction.

Now here they were. All eight of them. But oh, how young those girls were, and already she would have to ask so much from them.

Much as she had tried, Kai'Enna had not been able to quiet her fears surrounding the Golden Canyon.

The Golden Canyon had once been the headquarters of the Tulaga. It was, from all accounts, grand and beautiful. After the shortage of ash, the Tulaga withdrew their presence from the many cities and villages across the country—which they had protected for thousands of years—and only maintained the villages near the Golden Canyon. They kept the dragons at bay, restricting the wild beasts to territories elsewhere in the mountains.

But as the life of the Phoenix lingered on and on, it became clear just how in danger of running out of ash they were. They were forced to reduce the number of Tulaga further and further and watch helplessly as the dragons slowly took over the mountain villages.

Finally, the Golden Canyon itself became too dangerous. Unable to defend themselves from the dragons, the Tulaga had to flee their beloved home.

The dragons had claimed the Golden Canyon ever since.

Kai'Enna knew that must change, and soon. In addition to needing a place with room to grow, there were other reasons to return to the Golden Canyon. Small and inexperienced or not, their branch had certain obligations. It had been dangerous enough to neglect them as long as they had. Now that they had the ash they needed and their numbers had increased slightly, she could ignore them no longer.

Praea stood and gave their young charges permission to transform. The beautiful, glittering birds scattered in the air, trying to control the elements around them. They had accomplished their first transformation only a few days ago and had not yet learned how to fly together in formation. But after much training, these young girls were finally Tulaga at last.

120

Kai'Enna could not quite delight in their progress, too weighed down as she was by the knowledge that she must intensify their training. After all, it took time to learn how to defend oneself from dragons, let alone fight them.

But these young girls would have to learn.

The Golden Canyon waited for them.

Five years would pass before the Mapmaker would see either Madera or Eala again. Salerno said they did not visit often, busy as they were with their duties within the Order. The Mapmaker cared little, for he and Salerno had been working on their own project.

It all began with Salerno's surprise for the faeries. He had gathered a few of them above ground—Keck, Cyri, Ivy, and Spri—and presented them with the Mapmaker and his map of Amon Tunde.

If the surprise went well, Salerno would show his human friend to more faeries, and perhaps ask Madera and Eala to demonstrate their faerie-like skills as well. He sensed, however, that he should proceed slowly.

He was wise to have thought so. The faeries did not much care for the surprise, and Keck was quite vocal about his feelings regarding the human and his strange device. He would have liked the human to go home and not return, for his kind belonged elsewhere, he felt. "This is the realm of the faeries," Keck said.

Still, Salerno was their king and he would have his way. He did not tell them about the others, but he did insist the Mapmaker would have a place among them for a time.

Salerno wanted another map, this time of the underground realm of Amon Tunde.

He created a chamber for the Mapmaker away from the others, who found the presence of a human among them too strange for their comfort. In spite of this discomfort, Salerno escorted the Mapmaker through their tunnels and into their caverns, while the other faeries, with only a few exceptions, kept their distance.

The Mapmaker worked on the map in his little room, and Salerno stopped by regularly to see his progress, exclaiming at his representation of the sparkling pool in the Grand Cavern or the arched ceiling in the Throne Room.

Of course, the Mapmaker could not enter the Vein of the Earth, the tunnel that led to the Tree of Origin. Only Salerno himself could pass through. Instead, Salerno described the room and the Tree, later marveling at the Mapmaker's final rendition. He had even used gold leafing to capture the glittering brilliance of the Tree that Salerno had described.

When at last the map was finished and Salerno stood over it smiling, the Mapmaker pointed at the entrance to the tunnel that led to the Shoals.

He remembered the day Salerno had shown him this entrance. It was smaller than most tunnels found in Amon Tunde, just wide enough for two, and lined with luminous moss. The Mapmaker could not see very far into it, for the tunnel spiraled downward like a staircase. A soft, steady breeze came out of the opening and smelled of freshly turned earth.

"This is the Way Beneath," Salerno had said, then led him away.

"I wonder," the Mapmaker now said carefully, "if the earth would allow me here."

His heart beat so soundly in his chest he wondered if Salerno could hear it.

"Hmmm," Salerno said, "the earth faeries have all entered the Way Beneath. It is not like the Vein of the Earth in that way."

"I was thinking," the Mapmaker said quietly, listening to his heartbeat reverberating in his ears, "your collection doesn't seem complete without a map of the Shoals." He hadn't wanted to ask before. He'd wanted to present Salerno with a map even grander than the first in the hopes that Salerno would want more. And now the moment had come.

Salerno did not reply for a long time. He only stared at the place marked on the map. It was illustrated in such a way that the opening seemed to recede into the paper, as if inviting the viewer in.

He knew Salerno was admiring it. The Mapmaker was admiring it himself.

"I would like to see such a map," Salerno said at last.

So it was that the Mapmaker descended the spiraling tunnel called the Way Beneath and began charting the Shoals. He spent the next few years mapping both the area of the Shoals that lay beneath the faeries' realm, and the area that extended far beyond the invisible boundary of Amon Tunde that the faeries would not cross.

He would take his pack into the rocky tunnels and disappear for weeks, living in the constant presence of the faint light unique to the Shoals.

He showed Salerno his progress on the map as he went, informing him of the network of tunnels that headed toward the bay only to turn into water and the tunnels that spread outward under the Mountains of Vitra and turned into magma.

Salerno suspected these led to the realms of the water and fire faeries. "Perhaps they have their own gateways to the Shoals," Salerno said.

"Can fire faeries travel through magma?" the Mapmaker asked.

"I could not say for certain," Salerno said, "but I do not think the element of fire harms the fire faeries any more than the element of earth harms me."

It mattered little to the Mapmaker, for regardless of what the fire faeries could or could not do, he certainly could not pass through magma himself.

What interested him far more was the fact that he found two other ways into the Shoals that Salerno did not know about. The Mapmaker kept the existence of these entrances to himself.

They were far past the boundaries of Amon Tunde, located in fissures in the earth.

One was at the westernmost edge of the Shoals, where the aboveground climate was hot and unforgiving. He named this the Desert Entrance.

On the opposite end of the Shoals, in the East, another fracture in the earth likewise provided access to the Shoals. The scenery in this location could not be more different from that surrounding the Desert Entrance, however. In fact, it was nothing short of stunning, with a nearby mountain lake, broad canyon, and soaring cliffs that glowed in the light of dawn.

He dubbed the glowing cliffs the Golden Canyon and the entry point into the Shoals nearby, the Golden Canyon Entrance.

He said nothing to Salerno of any of this. He also said nothing about how often he visited the Vortex. It truly was a thing more grand and breathtaking than anything he'd ever seen.

His greatest find yet.

The Vortex was in an immense cavern, more vast than anything within Amon Tunde and the only cavern in all the Shoals, so far as he'd been able to tell. In the center was a large pit so black and so deep that when he dropped a large stone over the edge, he never heard it touch bottom.

Hovering directly above this pit was the Vortex itself. The swirling mass could indeed be described as wind, as Salerno had once done, but it was more than wind. It streaked round and round in purples and blues and oranges and yellows in a pulsating form fully five times his height.

The entire cavern resonated with its energy. He could not see the elements of earth, water, and fire flowing out of the Vortex, but even his scant magical abilities were enough to sense the presence of the elements in such raw form.

Though the Vortex was one of the first things the Mapmaker saw down in the Shoals, he had not yet drawn it on his map.

"I want to save it for last," he'd told Salerno.

In truth it was the one thing he'd discovered in all his years that he did not know how to claim on a map, but it was more than that.

Again and again, he'd end up back in front of the Vortex, sitting on the stone floor, silent and awestruck and nearly blind with the colors sweeping in front of him. He soon stopped wondering how he could ever draw such a thing and began thinking about something else entirely.

He wanted to own it.

The Mapmaker was not a powerful magic holder. Any magic he held was so slight it was nearly nonexistent. But near the Vortex, he felt different. He felt as if he could reach out and capture a tiny piece of that power with his own two hands.

And he wanted to. He sensed that if he did, he would no longer be Salerno's only apprentice with too little magic to be worth mentioning. No. With power from the Shoals he could join the others at last. Perhaps surpass them.

He already felt he would be known throughout history for his explorations and that his name would be known for generations. But what would people say about him if he had magic too?

Salerno's most powerful student.

These were his thoughts as he sat gazing at the Vortex. This is where his heart lay when he heard Salerno say his name.

Salerno stood observing him, brows furrowed, and the Mapmaker scrambled to his feet. He hadn't heard Salerno arrive and didn't know how long he'd been watching him.

"I was only—" he began. But what was he doing? As far as Salerno knew, he had merely been sitting there. Was there something wrong with that?

Salerno looked at him as if he knew better.

"What were you doing?" Salerno asked.

"Deciding how to capture it on your map," he answered. He was surprised at how easily the lie fell from his lips.

Salerno looked at the Vortex, then back at the Mapmaker. The Vortex pulsed and hummed. "Shall we go?"

The Mapmaker followed Salerno back through the tunnel leading to Amon Tunde, hands shaking the entire way.

As the five-year anniversary of the first meeting with Salerno approached, the Mapmaker was desirous for another celebratory feast. He wanted to show the others the beautiful illustrations of the places he had been, places Madera and Eala had never seen.

But they had not been to Amon Tunde in so long he had to go looking for them.

He found them at the Rock of Light. It was a towering stone structure with an immense flame burning within its tip. He came to the door of the little enclave at its base, but they did not invite him in, talking outside instead.

Overlooking this perceived rudeness, he proposed a feast. They did not respond as expected.

"I'm afraid I won't be able to attend now," Eala said. "I have much work to do and time is not on my side."

She did indeed look more than merely old. She looked fragile and the Mapmaker wondered how much longer she'd be on the earth to do whatever it was the Phoenix was asking of her.

"I'm very sorry," Madera said. "I cannot go now either. Perhaps next spring?"

"But that is not the time of our anniversary," he pressed.

Madera and Eala exchanged glances.

"We have not celebrated the anniversary in so long," Eala said. "I hardly think Salerno will notice."

The Mapmaker furrowed his brows.

"In the spring," Madera said, putting her hand on his arm. "We'll make it grand."

"I see," he replied, pulling his arm away. "I did not realize Salerno no longer mattered to you." He felt his face growing hot.

"Of course he—"

"Now that you have your precious Phoenix," he said, gesturing to the Rock of Light, "you no longer need him." He saw Madera's surprise and he was surprised at himself, but his anger rushed through him like a storm. "Never mind that you couldn't do your little tricks without his training to start with."

"Now see here," Eala began.

"Please," Madera said contritely, silencing Eala with a glance. "It isn't that. Of course we're grateful to Salerno."

Her sincerity calmed him slightly.

Madera considered him. "I'm sure if you only knew for yourself how..." she paused, searching for the right word. "How *grand* the Phoenix is. How grand its Order."

"Not as grand as the Vortex," he said simply. "I've seen it."

Madera's blue eyes grew wide and her expression froze. "Not so," she said.

Here the Mapmaker caught onto a wild idea. "Would you like to see for yourself?"

Madera's eyes grew even wider and she grabbed his arm again. This time he let her. "Salerno is inviting us?"

"*I* am inviting you."

The Mapmaker did not know if Salerno would allow Madera and Eala into the Shoals. He knew he should probably ask, but didn't want to risk being told no. If these women were going to see the most extraordinary thing they were ever likely to see, he wanted to be the one to show them.

The greatest explorer in history. Truly.

He sensed Madera's hunger. "You want to see it, don't you?" he asked.

Madera nodded, her full head of hair bobbing eagerly with her.

"Could we really see the Vortex?" Eala asked, the raw desire in her voice betraying her.

"It is far," he said, explaining they would need to gain entrance to the Shoals through the Golden Canyon.

Looking dispirited, Madera said, "Such a long journey. That will take days."

Eala smiled. "Unless, of course, we fly."

Fifteen

Eala flew the great distance to the Golden Canyon with Madera and the Mapmaker lying close together on her back and clinging to her massive, feathered body. Madera had never been in the air with Eala before and spent most of the journey stunned by the expansive views. However, the most glorious sights awaited them at the Golden Canyon. A sparkling mountain lake lay cradled in a fertile, green valley, bordered on one side by soaring golden cliffs.

Before Madera could fully enjoy it, the Mapmaker yelled, "There! That ravine down there."

Madera's heart leapt into her throat and she tightened her grasp as Eala went into a dive. What power this old woman had in the form of a bird.

Following the Mapmaker's instructions, Eala slipped through a dark crevice into a tunnel filled with soft light. "Keep going," he said. "It's back nearly as far as we've come, underneath Amon Tunde."

Though they flew more slowly now, they still made impressive progress.

"How much easier my explorations would be with your speed," the Mapmaker said with a laugh.

There was a hitch of uncontrolled wildness in that laugh. It was the same dangerous thrill Madera felt in her own breast.

They came to first one fork, then another. Madera memorized their path as best she could, fearful they would get lost in the labyrinth of tunnels and never get out.

Part of her wanted to go back. Part of her wondered if they ought not to be down here. But her wish to see the Vortex silenced the rest of her. She had to see it, just once.

Finally, the tunnel opened into a cavern so massive Madera would have had to arch her neck to see the top of it, and she would have if she hadn't been so captivated by what lay in the center. As Eala landed on the rocky ground, Madera slid off the feathered body without removing her eyes from the marvel they had come to see. Eala transformed and together they stared at the Vortex.

It was almost more than Madera could stand. The Vortex hummed and swirled in a pulsating multitude of colors. She felt the pulsing in her own veins. Her heart ached as she took in its brilliance and sheer, raw power.

The Mapmaker smiled and gestured. "You see?"

Madera nodded. She saw. She saw it and felt it and understood clearly why the faeries rarely came here. It was too sacred. It was in a realm all its own. She felt it in the air, in the very earth.

"I don't think we should be here," she said.

"No," the Mapmaker said, "perhaps not. Perhaps I shouldn't have brought you." But he looked at each of them with a satisfied smile. "After all, Salerno only invited me."

Likewise captivated by the Vortex, Eala kept her eyes upon it. Madera marveled at the way its colorful light gave the old woman's face a more vibrant, youthful appearance. "But why did Salerno invite you?" Eala asked.

The Mapmaker's eyes hardened and he stepped in front of her, the Vortex pulsing behind him. "Why me? A man with so little magic?"

"I didn't mean—"

"Who else could make a map of the Shoals? Answer me that."

"I'm sorry. I—"

"A map?" This now from Madera, who longed to soothe the Mapmaker. She did not remember him having such a volatile temperament. She had not thought much of it back at the Rock of Light, but here it was again.

It felt a sinister thing to face, deep in the bowels of the earth as they were, and before this grand thing she could not help but feel they should not have come to witness.

"Are you truly mapping this place?" she asked, managing to keep her voice steady. "How do you keep it straight?"

He reached into his inner breast pocket and retrieved a small folio. "See for yourself."

Madera took the folio he offered her. It was bound in soft leather, the interior pages slightly uneven but thin. There were dozens upon dozens of rough layouts of the Shoals. She turned page after page of them, with symbols in the margin that, she assumed, linked one section of the map to the next.

"You did all this?" As she looked through it, the multicolored light from the Vortex flashed on its pages. Each page looked as complicated as the last. "How did you not get lost?"

"I've never been lost."

He looked gratified, but then he glanced at Eala and his face grew dark.

Eala was not looking at his little folio of maps, still in Madera's hands, but rather gazing at the Vortex.

Madera wanted to look at it too, but she was held captive by the expression on the Mapmaker's face. *We should go,* she thought. *I want to go.*

"I suppose," he said quietly, "you find maps unimpressive."

Eala slowly brought her gaze to him. "Thank you for bringing us. We should go now."

Eala turned away and headed back to the tunnel's entrance, breathing hard. "Come," she said without looking back, "let us go."

Yes, Madera thought and hurried to Eala's side.

But the Mapmaker didn't follow them. Madera turned back and saw he had approached the Vortex and was beginning to circle it. He looked up at it with an expression that sent a chill through her.

Her heart beat in her throat, and her breath caught in her chest. "Come," she called to him, but he ignored her.

Eala stopped and turned as well. Together they watched as he continued circling. He disappeared behind the Vortex and reappeared on the other side. All the while, his eyes were on the whirling bulk of pure, raw magic in front of them.

Madera slowly drew near to Eala and took her arm. Neither woman spoke. Neither took their eyes off the Mapmaker.

He came full circle, stopped, and raised his hands. The colored light glowed on his arms and face.

He uttered an incantation Madera recognized, and a strand of blue flung out from the Vortex and struck him square on the chest.

The women flinched together as he curled into himself, the blue light absorbing into his body.

The old woman removed herself from Madera's grasp and ran to him, but Madera was locked in place, her feet bound to the earth, her hands clasping the little book of maps to her chest.

Her entire body pounded with the rhythm of the Vortex and the shock of his action.

Leaning over him and putting her hand on his back, Eala called his name again and again, but the Mapmaker remained hunched over. Eala looked at Madera with a frightened *what-do-we-do-now* expression.

That was when the Mapmaker began slowly unfolding.

Leave, Madera thought upon seeing his face. *We must leave.*

Seeing him, Eala put her hand to her chest and exhaled in relief. "Are you alright?" she asked, but the last word diminished as he came to his full height and looked at her.

Now Eala's face reflected what Madera already felt.

We must leave. We must leave.

The Mapmaker reached out and put his hand on Eala's shoulder, hanging his head as if he were about to faint and needed the old woman's frail frame to keep him upright.

"Let us go," Eala said, but it came out more like a question. "Let's get you out—" Swallowing her words, she knit her brows in confusion. Her eyes grew wide. Her mouth gaped open in pain.

The Mapmaker seized her other shoulder then raised his head sharply. He glared at her as if he would devour her with his very eyes, and he was muttering something.

That got Madera moving. She raced toward them. "What are you doing?"

Eala's head arched back and she screamed.

"Stop! Stop! What are you doing?"

As she came to them she heard his incantation. It was the same one he'd used to take a piece of the Vortex into himself. What was he doing?

"STOP!"

But this was not from Madera, and this time the Mapmaker truly did stop. He released Eala and spun toward the sound of Salerno's voice.

Eala stumbled and Madera caught her, the woman's frail body leaning heavily into her.

"Salerno," Madera exhaled in relief. "He took it. He took part of the Vortex. Salerno, please."

The Mapmaker laughed. "Don't listen to her."

He stood there calmly. So calmly. Eala slowly straightened, better able to stand.

Salerno looked from Eala to Madera, and from the Vortex to the Mapmaker.

"A thief," Salerno said with realization. "A thief in the earth."

"A thief?" The Mapmaker glanced back at the Vortex. "It is not yours to hoard, Salerno."

Now Madera wondered if even Salerno could defend them. The Mapmaker felt different to her. He did.

"We should fly," Eala whispered in her ear.

"We can't leave Salerno," Madera whispered back.

"This place was never meant for humans. I've been foolish," Salerno said, watching the Mapmaker carefully. "This is a terrible thing. Terrible."

The Mapmaker grinned. "Terrible for someone, maybe, but not for me. Terrible," he said, spinning on Eala, "for those who thought they were better than me."

With the Vortex behind him, his face was a contortion of shadow. "You are wild," Madera said. "You are not yourself."

He scoffed, unconcerned by her accusations.

"Salerno," she pleaded, "what do we do?"

Facing the Mapmaker, Salerno had a look of dark determination Madera had never seen on anyone, faerie or human alike.

"You."

That was all Salerno said.

Just as when Salerno said a name and encapsulated all he understood about a person when he said it, Salerno said "You," and in that one word communicated his disgust, his disillusionment, his broken trust, his wrath.

"I should never have shown you," Salerno said lowly.

The Mapmaker narrowed his eyes, raised his hands, and said an incantation. His arms began to tremble, glowing faintly with the magic he'd stolen. Eyes locked on Salerno, the Mapmaker looked like a madman. A madman with a magic Madera could feel from here.

A similarly shocking transformation claimed Salerno's countenance. She had never feared Salerno, but he looked fierce now, like a wild animal protecting its young.

"*Sunsitsu!*" the Mapmaker shouted.

A rush of energy flew out of the Mapmaker in all directions. It sent Eala and Madera tumbling to the ground. Behind them, a low groan resonated from deep within the Vortex.

Salerno remained standing, lips pressed together. "No," he said. "No, this is not to be."

Madera heard the horrible, cracking sound before she located its source. Likewise, the Mapmaker looked all around before glancing at his feet and flinching.

Thick coils of what looked like tree roots seemed to appear out of the very air and were encircling his legs. He tugged at the wood, but it continued to thicken and snake up his body. He said an incantation, but the roots were impervious to his spell and rapidly climbing his stomach and chest.

Madera and Eala backed away toward the tunnel, stumbling backward until they were at its entrance, where they stood transfixed by the horror of it all.

A root hooked one of the Mapmaker's arms, pinning it to his side. He screamed. The terrifying sound echoed again and again in the immense cavern.

A root curled around his neck and climbed to his jaw. The Mapmaker gasped, apparently struggling to take in a breath.

His gaze locked on the brilliant Vortex spinning in front of him and there it stayed. The Vortex spun and hummed as its lights flashed blue, purple, and yellow in his eyes. In another moment, they went blank.

The Mapmaker was dead.

The roots covered his face, enclosing him completely, and fell still at last, their job finished. Madera felt cold all over.

Salerno turned toward the women. He wore the same frightening look he had before he destroyed the Mapmaker.

"Salerno—" Madera began.

"No human will ever step foot in the Shoals again," he said.

She did not argue with him. Eala transformed into a Tulaga, grabbed Madera with her talons, and they were gone in an instant.

Only when they'd navigated their way out and escaped through the narrow fissure near the Golden Canyon did Madera realize she was still clutching the Mapmaker's folio.

After studying the little folio of maps and piecing the pages together to reveal a more complete picture of the Shoals, Madera uncovered the last secret of the Mapmaker.

Marked on one of the pages was what looked like another entrance. This one was far from the Golden Canyon, clear on the opposite side of the Shoals. In the Mapmaker's clean hand, it was labeled simply, "Desert Entrance."

Though it was located in a foreign land, Madera went anyway. She worried the Mapmaker had told others about the Shoals and that someone else may try to take the magic found there. She remembered the madness in the Mapmaker's eyes and ran cold with it.

Like the one in the Golden Canyon, the Desert Entrance was hidden deep in a ravine, as if the canyon on top of the earth had accidentally gone too deep and touched the outer edge of the Shoals.

At first the Desert Entrance looked like any other cave, but eventually it turned into a tunnel with walls made of the strange, impenetrable rock found in the Shoals. She followed the forks and turns, using the map to navigate.

Before reaching the Vortex, however, Madera came to a shimmering mass that blocked her way. It glowed green and resonated with faerie magic.

Unable to pass through or remove it, she decided Salerno must have erected a barrier to keep humans away from the inner depths of the Shoals. She would later determine that he had placed it at the edge of the boundaries of Amon Tunde. Even deep within the Shoals, Salerno would not leave the realm of the faeries.

She did not know if Salerno knew about the Desert Entrance, or if he had simply created a barrier in every tunnel that reached the edge of Amon Tunde. She would never know, but it didn't matter. For the first time since everything had happened, Madera felt relief.

The inner sanctum of the Shoals was safe.

Like Salerno, Madera felt the Vortex must be guarded from human knowledge and human greed. And it was. She could rest now. She could rest at last.

She made the long journey out of the Shoals and home to the Rock of Light. Only then, while conducting a bit of routine magic using Phoenix ash, did a disturbing thought occur to her.

She had a few specks of ash in the palm of her hand and stood there considering it. Even just resting there on her skin, the ash exuded a kind of power. Unique in its own right, it allowed otherwise ordinary magical humans to do extraordinary things.

Each branch of the Order practiced a distinctive variation of magic using the ash, but the very structure of the Order prevented—indeed, forbade—the branches from sharing magical secrets with one another. Madera thought she knew why. Magical power had to be more than just carefully nurtured.

It had to be carefully protected.

Journeying to the Golden Canyon, she went through the entrance and navigated the maze of tunnels until she came, as she suspected she would, to another glowing faerie barrier at the edge of Amon Tunde. It was just like the one she'd found when she went through the Desert Entrance.

This time she inspected the faerie barrier more closely. It confirmed what she'd feared.

It could not be breeched with ordinary human magic. It required faerie magic to get through, and Madera already knew from her own experience that humans could not duplicate such magic. Salerno understood this as well, so as far as he knew, his barriers made the Shoals safe from the humans he no longer trusted.

But Salerno did not understand the power of Phoenix ash. With Phoenix ash, the faerie barrier could be broken. Madera knew exactly how to do it, if she so chose.

She considered returning to Amon Tunde to warn Salerno of this danger but was too frightened of him to try.

Meanwhile, Eala and the other Tulaga had chased away the dragons that liked to roost in the area near the Golden Canyon and began the work of making it their home.

When Madera had asked her about this, Eala simply said, "I cannot go off and leave the entrance unguarded. I have to know it's safe." Eala had likewise been concerned about keeping the Shoals a secret and wondered who else the Mapmaker may have told.

It was then Madera understood the true purpose of her branch. They had already begun other magical work, work they would continue. But Madera decided their most important obligation was to keep the Shoals safe.

The fertile valley near the lake at the base of the Golden Canyon would become the home of her branch as well. Together, she and Eala would stand guard.

They agreed secrecy would be the final layer of protection for the Vortex. They determined only future Heads of their branches would know of it, so they would always understand the importance of maintaining a presence there.

In the same spirit of secrecy, Madera never told Eala about the Desert Entrance or the faerie barriers she'd found.

Instead, using magical principles she'd learned from the Phoenix, along with a portion of her branch's ash, she wove a concealment spell and dropped it over the Golden Canyon Entrance like a veil. It looked—and felt—like the land itself and hid the entrance from view. She called her magical disguise the Veil of Madera and placed another over the entrance away in the desert.

Because the Veils of Madera required periodic strengthening with Phoenix ash, she established a second, secret residence for her branch near the Desert Entrance. These dual residences allowed her branch to maintain the Veils.

Nearly a decade passed before she found a body near the Veil in the desert, along with notes and a map indicating that some poor soul had spent years looking for an entrance he must have heard about from the lips of a boasting man.

It confirmed her fears that knowledge of the Shoals and the Vortex was lurking out there somewhere. It strengthened her belief that while the Madera branch was useful in many ways, its true purpose was to keep an ancient, powerful magic out of unsuitable hands.

Thousands of years later, as the Madera grew desperately low on ash, the Order was unable to help. Even if they knew the most critical function of the Madera branch, and they did not, the ash of each branch was bound to that branch only. It could not be shared.

And so, with only a small amount of ash left, the Head of the Madera branch gathered up his followers and their families and went off to an unknown location, where they became lost.

Extinct.

Gone forever.

Or so everyone believed.

Sixteen

"Let's go, wizard." The guard opened the iron door to Corren's cell and it clanged against the stone wall. He was accompanied by another guard, who stared at Corren with a grim expression. In the dim light, the marks on the men's foreheads were dark as shadow.

"Hurry up," the man said, gesturing. "Lord Tivoli wants to see you."

Corren followed him in silence, the second guard taking up the rear. Neither of these men concerned him; his thoughts were on the impending meeting with Lord Tivoli. It's what he had spent the last two days waiting for.

He hoped it would not all be for nothing. Based on what he had found in one of Aradia's folios, he suspected she had made the long journey to Hathmirr and talked to Lord Tivoli herself. He had reason to believe there was a connection between this group and the ash of the Madera branch stuck on the altar in the Rock of Light, but he didn't know what. If all went well, he would find out soon.

Leaving the musty chambers behind them, they climbed a narrow staircase and emerged into a stark hallway. At the end of this, a wooden door led to the more widely used areas of the Orsini Colony headquarters.

Elaborate tile work covered the floors, and ornate, hand-painted designs framed doorways and climbed pillars. Some walls were a crisp white, but others were cobalt, deep orange, or lavender.

In spite of the intricate beauty so typical of Hathmirrian design, the surroundings here lacked the vibrancy he'd felt elsewhere in the country. The few Orsini Colony members he saw lent an oppressive mood, as if casting the entire place into shadow.

As he and his guards progressed through the complex, Corren took note of their path, just as he had when he'd been led to the chambers a few days ago. He wanted to make sure he knew his own way out, just in case.

They came to a large room that rumbled with the low murmurings of the many men and women gathered together. It appeared nearly every member of the Orsini Colony was here. Each forehead was marked with a variation of the gold symbol that distinguished their society. Corren glanced around for the woman, Lini. He did not see her, but there were so many people present he easily could have missed her.

Corren wondered if this was to be a meeting or a lynching.

He kept his staff close as they led him deep into the crowd. Members stepped aside and kept some distance from him, but he stayed alert for any sign of attack. The more they progressed into the group, the more the gathering quieted.

Lord Tivoli waited in the middle. He wore multilayered robes of orange over plain trousers and rested his hands on top of his stout staff. It was the only staff among them, so far as Corren could tell.

The guards bowed before stepping aside and leaving him alone in the center of the assembly.

"You are here to answer my questions, wizard," Tivoli said. "What is your name?"

Though Tivoli spoke to him as he would to a prisoner, Corren answered with the confidence of a guest. "Corren of Caedmonia."

"You said you are from Stonebridge."

"That is correct."

"Then you know of the Rock of Light?"

He did not need to be from Stonebridge to know of the Rock of Light, for its reputation spread well outside of Caedmonia's boundaries. It was not unusual for someone to think of it first if they knew anything about Stonebridge at all. However, Corren did not fail to wonder if Tivoli's question reflected more than a casual interest. He nodded in response to Tivoli's question.

A few members exchanged glances with one another but otherwise said nothing.

Tivoli looked pointedly at Corren's staff. "Clearly you are from the Order, are you not?"

The man to Tivoli's left scowled at Corren with particular venom. Unlike Tivoli, whose scalp was neatly shaved, this man's dark hair fell past his shoulders.

Corren looked back to Tivoli. "What do you know of the Order?"

Cries of outrage swelled in the air. Corren gripped his staff tighter and glanced at the people surrounding him. They were not coming upon him, but he'd obviously done something to anger them.

Tivoli's face grew harsh. "Brash! Impudent! Typical Caedmonian. I asked you a *question*." He raised a hand to settle the group but did so without removing his glare from Corren's face. The assembly grew quiet, but there was still some agitated shuffling.

"Are you," Tivoli said in a dangerously calm voice, "from the Order, or not?"

Corren took a steadying breath. It was going to take more patience than he'd anticipated to deal with this man. "I am."

"Corren of Caedmonia, you are a trespassing fool. We can, and probably will, execute you for witnessing the High Ceremony of the Way of Orsini. Is there any reason why we shouldn't?"

Corren slowly slid his hand higher on his staff and rested it there, a gesture meant to remind them he wasn't defenseless. He didn't know if he could fend them all off at once and didn't want to open that door regardless, but if they thought they could haul him off to the noose without a fight, they were mistaken.

"My people and I have been betrayed by the witch Aradia," he said calmly. Murmurings rumbled throughout the group. The man to Tivoli's left glanced sharply at his leader. "I understand she came to see you," Corren continued. "I have come to ask you about this."

Tivoli's heavy eyebrows drew down over narrowed eyes, giving him a particularly sinister appearance. "Did she send you?"

"No. I came on my own. Aradia is dead."

This did not seem to surprise them, since there was no reaction. The man standing to Tivoli's left spoke up. "How do you know she's dead?"

"I know because I saw her." Corren firmly pushed away the mental image of Aradia lying dead in the Realm of the Phoenix.

The man leaned toward Tivoli and whispered in his ear.

Tivoli lightly pushed him away. "It matters not, Bricker," he said. Then to Corren, "If Aradia is dead, our business is with her replacement."

"What business would that be?"

"What business is it of yours? Tell me, wizard, who is the new Head of the Order?"

Corren weighed his response, but ultimately decided it was better to reveal himself than not. Still, he braced himself for their reaction. "I am."

Rather than the uproar Corren expected, a dark silence settled over the group.

Lord Tivoli shifted his staff into one hand and took two slow steps toward Corren. The tip of his staff knocked against the hard floor.

Corren watched him carefully, holding his ground.

"How convenient," Tivoli said quietly. "Then you can be the one to give us the ash."

Corren felt a prickling sensation down his legs. His lips parted slightly as he started to speak, but nothing came out. He glanced at the gold mark curling on Tivoli's forehead. Corren furrowed his brows. "What ash?"

"The ash of the Madera branch that's been promised to us."

Corren shook his head slightly. Is that what this was about? "Aradia promised you Phoenix ash?"

142

Tivoli smiled a slow smile that did not reach his eyes. "Aradia? No, no, no. She's not the one who promised us the ash. The Madera branch did."

Corren's breath caught in his chest. The Madera branch promised their ash? Corren realized this could be the explanation for everything, the reason the ash would not lift off the altar for Kennard or Corren or any of them. At the same time, he ran through all the reasons why what this man said was not possible. And those reasons were many.

Corren scanned the hard faces all around him. Far to his right, he spotted Lini. After a brief moment of recognition between them, he resumed his examination of the people who surrounded him. They endured his scrutiny with quiet assurance. Every face in the room, hers included, seemed to already know the information Tivoli was sharing. And they believed it.

Corren turned back to Tivoli. Whether his followers believed it or not, Tivoli had to be lying. The Madera branch was long gone. With this thought, Corren felt a measure of calmness return. "That's not possible," he said.

"Oh," Tivoli said, "but it is."

"They couldn't have promised you anything," Corren persisted.

"Why?" Tivoli responded harshly. "Because they've been dead for four hundred years?"

Corren couldn't hide his reaction.

"You think I don't know? You think I don't know how the Order turned their backs on their own people and left them to die out? I know all about that. The Order claims to be about doing what's *right*, but they're not so different from us after all." Corren narrowed his eyes at this insulting comparison, but Tivoli continued without so much as a breath. "*We* agreed to help. We did what you and your precious, pretentious Order wouldn't—" and here he jabbed a finger into Corren's chest.

Corren shoved the man's hand away and instantly the people around him responded, jostling forward in one mass. Corren

143

raised his staff to defend himself, but Tivoli's shouts cut through the commotion, "Hold your places! Stand down!"

He stepped away from Corren and turned toward his own people, sweeping one hand over them in a half circle and clutching his staff with the other.

The members around him did not continue to advance but did not back away either.

"That ash belongs to us!" Tivoli said, pointing his staff at Corren.

Corren forced his breathing to settle, to not let the escalating tensions cloud his thinking. None of this could be right. Why would the Madera branch have gone to a group like the Orsini Colony? The Orsini Colony couldn't preserve them any more than the Order could.

"You're lying," he said firmly.

This brought more aggressive shuffling within the group, but Tivoli raised his hand and they held their ground. "Oh, you think so?"

Tivoli seemed to be getting his own breathing under control. "Well, you're not the first Head of the Order I've had to convince." With that he turned and walked away, disappearing within the group.

Everyone seemed to understand they were waiting for something, but what that something was Corren could not say. Whatever it was, the promise of it seemed to settle them slightly and they backed off a bit. The man who'd been standing to Tivoli's left, Bricker he'd been called, gave Corren a dark smile.

Corren looked at the people around him. Though there was certainly no hint of friendliness in their eyes (and the feeling was certainly mutual), they all seemed to be waiting for inevitable validation. Whether Corren thought they were lying or not, they clearly believed they had some sort of claim here.

But why would they think this? It had to come back to Aradia. She must have somehow led them astray. And now here he was (admittedly by his own doing), left with the potentially dangerous task of telling these people they had no claim on the Phoenix ash. He doubted Aradia had any intention of giving it to them, but why would she have made such a promise? What did she have to gain?

The group parted as Lord Tivoli made his way back at last. As he filled the little space in front of where Corren stood, the object he carried became visible. An old book lay open in his hands. The worn, brown binding looked like it had once been a dark green, for this was the color hiding in the creases.

Corren immediately thought of Lini, who'd been thrown in the chambers for looking in a book. He wondered if it was the one in Tivoli's arms.

Tivoli did not show Corren the interior pages and, in fact, seemed to be guarding them from anyone's view. Instead, he held the book up with both hands to reveal the cover.

"Here is my proof," he said calmly, "that what I say is true."

There on the cover were the words, "Magickal Histories, Incantations, Protections, and Obligations of the Madera Branch of the Order of Ceinoth."

Corren stared at it.

There it was.

The book Aradia had wanted. The book *he* now wanted.

He was right. This book was why she came to Hathmirr, but for some reason she'd failed to procure it. Why? She'd managed to steal the secret books of five other branches, the gold leaf from the Tree of Origin, and the potion recipe for the Gateway from the water faeries. If she knew where this book was, why didn't she take it?

And the fact that they had it, did that necessarily mean that what they said was true?

"How do I know you didn't steal that?"

Tivoli gave him a dark look. "Four hundred years ago, Dennilen, the last Head of the Madera branch, delivered this book to the Lord of the Orsini Colony. Dennilen created an incantation that guaranteed the secrets of their branch would survive until the Phoenix brought more ash. He passed their birthright to *us*. Dennilen *bound* their secrets *and* the promise of the ash to our group, and that binding was made complete when Lord Steele took this book into his hands. It has been

145

guarded and handed down through the centuries while we waited for the Song that would announce the impending regeneration of the Phoenix. When we heard your Song of Announcement, we knew the time was close. We sent some of our finest people to Caedmonia to claim what is rightfully ours, but Aradia didn't take them to the Rock of Light like she said she would. She took them to Thrayce Island and slaughtered all but one." Here he gestured to Bricker, who watched Corren darkly. "Now," Tivoli said, his eyes and voice firm, "the Head of your Order promised to honor the agreement of the Madera branch. Are you going to live up to what she said, or not?"

Corren was scrambling to process everything he'd heard. "That ash was not hers to give away," he said, but he wasn't really thinking about what he was saying. How could Tivoli know all of this if what he claimed wasn't true? And the book. How else did he get the book?

"Aren't you listening, wizard? That ash is *ours*! Bound to us whether you like it or not."

Corren perked up. He'd heard Tivoli say that word before. "Bound? What do you mean bound?"

Lord Tivoli smirked.

Something about that smirk allowed everything he'd heard to finally sink in and settle into something solid. Corren's skin crawled. "Magically bound?" he asked quietly.

"Now you see," Lord Tivoli said, nodding. "We *are* the Madera branch. They bound their secrets to us. We absorbed the Madera branch into ourselves. We want our ash. Now where is it?"

Corren only looked at the Lord of the Orsini Colony. No one made a sound. If the Madera branch had indeed made that kind of agreement, would the Phoenix honor it? The Phoenix's own Order tried replacing the Madera branch with the Guard, and the Phoenix would have nothing of it. They'd tried everything they could think of, and Kennard could not remove the ash from the altar. And there was no question that Kennard was worthy of it.

That was when Corren realized the answer was easy. If the ash wouldn't come off the altar for Kennard, it certainly wouldn't come off for the despicable man in front of him.

This was not for Corren to decide.

"The ash is not mine to give any more than it was Aradia's to give. It may not have been the Madera branch's to give. Right now, six branches of the Order have retrieved their ash from the Rock of Light, but as for the ash that remains, only the *Phoenix* can allow its removal. Even if you attempt to remove the ash from the altar, if the Phoenix doesn't want you to have it, there will be nothing you can do about it."

Tivoli listened to this calmly. "And how do you know this? Has someone else tried to remove the ash?"

Corren paused. He didn't want to admit that they'd failed in their attempts. Tivoli seemed to surmise his answer through his expression.

"Perhaps," Tivoli said, patting the open book he still held against his chest and looking victorious, "Perhaps that ash won't come off for you because it is meant for *us.*"

The room erupted in affirming shouts.

Lord Tivoli walked up to Corren, smiling. "I say you take us back to your Rock of Light and we find out."

More cheers followed this.

Corren realized they knew the way to the Rock of Light already and would likely go with or without him. Over his dead body, probably, if they had to. He could resist but sensed that even if he escaped, it wouldn't be the end of things.

Perhaps the best solution would be to let them try, and fail, to remove the ash from the altar.

He didn't know for sure.

He didn't feel certain about anything—except one thing. If the Phoenix didn't want them to have the ash, they wouldn't have it. Period.

Corren waited for the cheering to die down.

"I agree," he said.

Lord Tivoli laughed. "I thought you might."

147

Seventeen

Nicolai had trained many times with Salerno, but this was different. This had a new sense of urgency, and things weren't progressing nearly as fast as he needed them to.

He stood with his hands on the bark of the Old Oak. His forehead too. He could smell the rich scent of wood and dirt. He had learned to both sense and identify the many elements in the Old Oak—it had stopped being a puzzle at last—but controlling them was another matter. He'd seen, and felt, Salerno do it over and over. Yet when Nicolai attempted it, things began to break down.

His entire body ached from the strain of his efforts. Too weary to continue, he opened his eyes and dropped his hands. He didn't know why trying to heal a tree should be more exhausting than plowing a field, but it was.

"You are doing well, Nicolai," Salerno said.

He'd heard this before, but Nicolai had his doubts. He rubbed his thumb into his left bicep, trying to get a knot out of his muscle. They'd been at this for four days.

Four long, exhausting days.

How long was it going to take him to learn what he needed to know? Could Lily wait that long? Meanwhile, Salerno had determined the blackness was spreading in Keck, though he was not yet visibly ill.

Nicolai ran his hands through his hair, pushing firmly along his scalp.

Salerno's bright green eyes watched him closely. Nicolai knew this sort of scrutiny. Another of Salerno's distinctive abilities.

Was he trying to discern whether or not Nicolai could really learn to heal the Tree? Perhaps Salerno had been wrong and now realized his error. Perhaps he sensed some weakness in Nicolai he did not sense before.

As he felt Salerno reach into him, Nicolai attempted to reach back. He did not know if he could do what they all needed from him—he truly wished Corren and his staff were here instead of Nicolai—but neither did he want to stand idly by and do nothing.

He wanted to keep fighting and he wanted Salerno to know it.

"Janus tells me," Salerno said quietly, "there is a woman in your life."

Nicolai pulled back abruptly and raised his eyebrows. This was the last thing he expected Salerno to say. "Yes."

"You are close?" Salerno asked. "In love, as they say?"

Nicolai nodded. He could not help but smile at the thought of her. He leaned against the broad trunk of the tree, massaging a knot out of his neck.

"It is my understanding," Salerno said, looking grave, "that human couples tend to divulge things to one another. Share secrets."

Nicolai slowly dropped his arm. "Uh... yes."

Salerno nodded slowly, his eyes holding Nicolai in place. "Since I already know I cannot warn you away from her—"

"Warn me?" Nicolai said, straightening.

"—I feel I must remind you of a promise you once made. Faerie knowledge is only for faeries, Nicolai. Not humans. You are not to discuss your training or what you know about us with anyone. Not even this woman you love."

Nicolai could only stare in response to this exhortation. The king of the earth faeries looked sterner than Nicolai had ever seen him. The air was still and quiet in the shade of the towering oak, as if it, too, awaited Nicolai's answer.

"I wouldn't," he choked out at last.

"No," Salerno said. "See that you don't."

It had been over a week since the wizard was caught spying on the Orsini Colony. In that time, Lini and the other members had been busy with preparations. Preparations they were carefully keeping from the wizard. He did not know what was taking them so long to depart for the Rock of Light, and they surely weren't going to tell him. But the time was drawing near. Lord Tivoli and his chosen companions would be leaving with the wizard day after next.

Lini walked through the tiled corridors toward Lord Tivoli's office. He'd sent one of the orphans with a message for her to see him immediately.

She rearranged her head shawl and gathered the ends into her hands. She ran the lace trim nervously through her fingertips. Ever since he'd caught her looking in the Book of Madera, Lord Tivoli had treated her with a peculiar kind of animosity. He was still angry with her, and for good reason, but he wasn't punishing her either. He hadn't done worse than throw her in the chambers for a night.

The wizard got off easy too. He also wasn't staying in the chambers anymore but rather in a little room on the second floor. Of course they still kept him under guard day and night. After all, he'd spied on them during the High Ceremony of the Way of Orsini. Actually witnessed it.

A familiar unease settled within her as she thought of the ceremony. Three times now she'd gotten away with her rebellion. And no one had any idea. It was getting more and more difficult to keep up the act.

If Lord Tivoli found out, there would be no mercy this time. She was sure of that.

She had been fetched from a shared dormitory on the ground floor of the south wing. She was older now, so she bunked in a smaller room that she shared with only three other people. When she was younger though, she lived in "the cave," what she and the other orphans called the great room where they all slept. It could hold up to twenty-two children.

When she was around twelve, it was filled to capacity. When she was thirteen, it went up to twenty-four, leaving two to sleep on the floor. The contests to see who would be relegated to the floor had been particularly nasty. One girl was beaten so badly she slept the next two nights in the infirmary, so only one person, scrawny Sienna, had to sleep on the floor anyway.

That was before Lini knew Sienna. Before Sienna saved Lini from a beating from Lord Tivoli. He'd accidentally beaten a boy to death the week before, so everyone's fear of him was fresh and raw. This was when Lini made what could have been a fatal error.

It was the evening of the High Ceremony for the youth. Her second. The first had made her so ill she'd vomited the potion almost immediately upon consumption and was forced to take it again. She had kept it down but felt it working in her. She felt what it was doing to her. Not knowing any better, she'd thought it was going to erase her entire consciousness. She thought she would disappear completely, eaten by the black.

She'd spent the following week living in terror of the next ceremony. She slept poorly, ate little, and spoke rarely. Her memories of that time seemed to center on her sitting on the window seat in Raven Hall, knees pulled up to her chest, arms wrapped around her legs, and eyes staring helplessly at the barren branches of the maple in the courtyard.

She did not know at the time how common that reaction to the first ceremony was. It usually took a full month of ceremonies for the potion to work properly and for the drinker to adjust. Or, at least, resign. Which was the point. Lini had seen it countless times with their young recruits.

What was not common was Lini's behavior at her second ceremony. She'd never seen anyone do what she did, and for years she would look back on it with shame. Recently, she pondered this event more deeply. Why *did* she do it? What was it, exactly, that made her lash out at Lord Tivoli, fling the

151

potion to the floor where it pooled like blood, and rush the altar like she, and she alone, would stop this thing?

Was it the same thing that enabled her current rebellion? A rebellion that was known to no one and a mystery even to her?

Sienna, scrawny little Sienna, had come to Lini's rescue. Seeing Lord Tivoli's wrath, Sienna had cradled Lini in her arms, stroking her hair and arms like she was soothing a wild animal (which, in a way, she was), and said, "Please, Lord Tivoli, she's been feverish. Please, it's not her fault. Please, I should have told you she's sick. She's mad with fever. Please, your greatness, I should have told you. It's not her fault."

On and on she went until Lord Tivoli's attention shifted from Lini to Sienna, until his rage went from hot to lukewarm, until he watched her with a mixture of curiosity and admiration and revulsion. It ended with a backhand at Sienna's face so fierce it knocked them both over. The girls lay sprawled on the floor, their astonished faces watching the back of his bald head as he walked away.

The other leaders made Lini and Sienna clean up the mess and continued the punishment Lord Tivoli left behind. Lini was so sore from the beatings she could only sleep on her right side for a week. But Sienna slept in the bed with her, the two curled up together as one. Sienna's soft breathing warmed the back of Lini's neck, and her thin arm wrapped around her. It was foolish that Lini felt safe in that moment, but she did—for the first time since she'd been brought to the Orsini Colony. Sienna made her remember what life was like before. Before her world vanished and fear built up a little fortress around her.

Of course, she wasn't truly safe. Neither of them were. And though the potion would eventually claim her, something deep inside Lini survived intact. It was the tiny little part that managed, in spite of everything, to love Sienna as much as the sister she'd once had.

Wise as a serpent but harmless as a dove, Sienna was eventually enslaved by the potion like everyone else, but the black did not consume her. Lini knew enough to know that.

This was right before the first Cleansing of Lini's memory, when their overflowing room of twenty-four people (once that poor girl came back from the infirmary) was suddenly reduced to thirteen. It would be three more years and two more Cleansings before Lini learned what became of the others.

Once she knew, she was not surprised. How easily she had participated. It even made sense at the time. Necessary and for their good, just like Lord Tivoli said. It was merely part of the workings and survival of the Orsini Colony. That memory, like so many others, was under constant transformation these days. Lini felt differently about the Cleansings now. There was the guilt, yes, but also cold, black fear.

Lini approached the open door to Lord Tivoli's office and gave the doorjamb two sharp raps.

His key leaders were there: Bricker, Peridot, Routt, Jatvia. They fell silent when she appeared at the door. No one seemed surprised by her appearance. Tivoli stood over his desk, surrounded by maps and books and papers.

"Lini," he said. "Pack your things. Keep it to one saddlebag. You're coming with us."

He gave her a gesture of dismissal, and the groups' attention went back to whatever they were discussing before.

Lini wanted to ask, "Why? Why me?" But she knew that was not allowed. She turned and headed back to her room, her unasked questions swirling in her head.

Eighteen

Though they had not taken Corren back to the chambers, his little room did not feel any less a prison. They brought him his meals and restricted his activities. He would have preferred to keep the door to his room shut but kept it open to show he wasn't afraid of them.

Across the hall was another room with a table and a few chairs. At first Corren thought members were simply gathering there, one or three at a time, until the first time he tried leaving his room. The man across the hall jumped up and took care of that notion. That's when Corren realized that room was never empty and the door was never closed.

When he asked if he could go outside to walk on the grounds, his current guard (they changed regularly) said he'd already proven himself untrustworthy. Corren couldn't argue with that, especially since he knew perfectly well he'd investigate further if given the chance.

During the day, the hall was often busy with passing members, including—Corren was surprised to note—the occasional child. Corren tried to ignore them all, but if he happened to meet the eye of a passerby, he was careful to look unconcerned. He kept his staff nearby but did not keep hold of it.

He busied himself, at first, with notes in his journal. Aradia had taught him well and he was a meticulous note taker. There was only so much he could say, however, and that activity soon wrapped itself up.

Several times he wandered into the room across the hall and tried talking to the guards, without success. Some were overtly hostile; others were more benign but still tight-lipped. No one gave him any information or any opportunity to go exploring.

Of course, even if he were to sneak away from his guards, every member in the compound knew of his existence. He wouldn't be able to investigate without someone noticing. What was he looking for anyway? If Tivoli was to be believed, he had his answer.

If Tivoli was to be believed, he'd found the Madera branch.

After waiting for over a week, Corren grew impatient and insisted he talk to the leader. The guards tried to stop him, but his staff kept them at bay. Finally, they escorted him to Lord Tivoli's office, who was none too happy to see him. Some half-dozen people were in the room with him, preparing, he said, for the journey.

"When do we leave?" Corren asked.

"Tomorrow or the next day," Tivoli said, looking over the papers on his desk. "There is much to do. You have food, don't you?"

"Yes."

"Well then," and he gestured for Corren to leave.

Corren obeyed; he got what he wanted anyway. They would depart soon enough.

That evening as he went to close his door so he could sleep, he noticed who was sitting at the table across the hall. The same woman he'd met in the market. The one who'd been in the chambers. Lini, she was called.

Their eyes met and he arrested his movements in the doorway, one hand on the knob. She was wrapped in a colorful robe, shawl, and skirts but was not wearing a head scarf. Black as night, her hair flowed in a straight sheet down to her waist. It reminded him of Aradia, whose long hair was just like it, only silver. This stirred up the pain he felt whenever he thought about Aradia, but he automatically pushed it back down. Lini did not look like Aradia in any other way, with her olive skin and large dark eyes.

She crossed her arms and looked away.

He checked the hallway. It was deserted. The compound was winding down for the evening. The window behind him was black and the small oil lamp burned feebly in a corner. Her room contained a chandelier, in which four lamps were lit. The warm orange light flickered on her face, reflecting off the gold mark on her forehead.

He stood in his doorway, contemplating. Here was one person, he thought, who might actually talk to him. Someone who might have more information.

He crossed the hallway slowly, as if approaching a wild animal he did not wish to startle. She glanced at him sideways, arms still crossed.

He approached a chair and put his hand on the back. "Alright if I sit down?"

She looked at him. Not quite a scowl. Not a smile either.

"I'm getting tired of the same room."

She shrugged and watched him as he sat down. Watched him like a cat.

He found it difficult to look away from her eyes.

As he searched for an opening line, he realized every situation in which he'd seen her was something she probably did not want him to bring up. *I remember seeing you in the market, while you were running from the guards.* Or, *Remember when we were locked up in the chambers together? What did you see in the forbidden book?* Or what he really wanted to ask, *Remember the ceremony? Did you really do what I think you did?*

He suddenly realized he'd left his staff in his room across the hall and glanced back. It was leaning against the wall, right where he'd left it. If the hall still had people in it, he wouldn't hesitate to go back for it. In fact, if that were the case, he probably wouldn't have left it at all. But with it being just him and this woman, it somehow seemed foolish to go back. Also foolish to leave it.

"Go ahead," she said.

He glanced at her. She said it without malice.

"I would if it were me."

He no longer felt he needed it but got up and retrieved his staff just the same. He came back and settled himself at the table.

"Lini?"

She scowled.

"Isn't it Lini?" She continued to scowl at him. "I heard the guard call you Lini…"

"Oh." Her look softened. Perhaps she thought he'd obtained her name through covert means. "Yes," she said.

"I'm Corren."

She looked at him. "Everyone knows who you are."

She did not seem happy about who he was. Withholder of the ash, no doubt. Potential repeater of Aradia's treachery. And indeed, he would keep the ash out of their hands if he had anything to say about it.

She took to staring at the opposite wall.

"I'm sorry," he said, and in that moment, he meant it. He did not want to be at war with this one. It wasn't her fault either. "Aradia betrayed me too."

She looked at him. "Why? What did she promise you?"

He shook his head. "It wasn't like that. She raised me."

Lini narrowed her eyes slightly, as if trying to discern whether he was lying or telling the truth.

"I didn't know who she was. Back then."

Lini's expression did not change.

"I guess sometimes people aren't who they seem," he said.

"People are almost never who they seem."

He frowned. "That seems a dim view."

"It's the truth. Better to know it than to pretend it's something else. They can't get you that way."

He thought back to the ceremony. "Who can't get you?"

She didn't answer but went back to staring at the wall. Already he'd pushed her too far.

She glanced at him, as if she couldn't help herself. They studied each other. Her eyes were so dark he wanted to lean in and look at them more closely, to find out if he could see her pupils or if her eyes truly were just a deep black.

Her eyes flicked to the top of his staff, still wrapped in cloth. She looked like she wanted to ask him a question, and he felt what he did back at the market: that she sensed there was more under the cloth than wood.

He had to resist the illogical impulse to whip off the covering, reveal the hardened ash at the tip, and boldly ask her what she did during the ceremony. But he didn't do any of those things. He approached the wild animal with caution.

"Does only your leader have a staff?" he asked.

She considered him, cautious herself. "Yes."

Those eyes.

"Is it the same for you?" she asked.

"Apprentices can make a staff once they're trained. If they wish."

"Why wouldn't they?"

"Not everyone is able. Making and using a staff is complicated."

She examined his staff again, her expression relaxing, like an animal slowly coming uncoiled. "Is it more than just wood?" she asked.

He nodded. "There are other things inside."

Their eyes met again. He had strangely opposing feelings. On the one hand, he felt he could ask her, just ask her what he wanted to know. But on the other hand, he knew she had no reason to answer.

"May I ask you a question?"

She raised her eyebrows in response.

"It's just..." he scooted up on his seat, leaning forward. She did not back away. In fact, her face softened a bit. Again he thought she may actually answer him. "I wonder if you could tell me... when you perform magic, do you have to say an incantation?"

Her expression froze, save her eyes, which narrowed slightly.

He wanted to scoot back but didn't move. "I mean," he said carefully, "aloud."

They stared at one another a moment, him leaning over the table, her gazing at him with narrowed eyes.

"Of course," she said.

He looked down at the table then flicked his eyes back up to hers. "You've never performed an incantation without saying it?"

She stood abruptly, her wooden chair scraping across the floor. Corren sat back. "You're mad," she said. "Mad. Get back to your room." She flung her arm toward the door, eyes darting, face hard.

"I'm sorry, I—"

"Get out!" She pulled her shawl tightly about her shoulders.

He retreated back across the hallway, cursing his stupidity. Before he reached his room, she called out, "Don't—"

He turned. She hovered in her own doorway. He could not read the expression on her face. Was it anger? Fear?

"Don't... talk about things like that with people," she said. "It'll get you into trouble."

With the look on her face, he half expected her to say, "*Please.*" Instead, she just stood there, staring at him.

He turned, glanced at her once he got inside his room, and shut the door.

Bricker waited at the cove on the shoreline for most of the afternoon until Faatin finally came to the surface. "The Head of the Order is here," Bricker told him. "We're going to Caedmonia to get the ash. I'll come to you again when we get back."

The water faerie shook his head. "No. I'll meet you there."

Nineteen

At long last, Corren and a party of Orsini Colony members started the long journey back to Stonebridge. It was only the first day—it would take over two weeks to get there—but Corren was glad to finally be on his way. Once outside the city, they spent most the day crossing the same flat prairies he'd traveled through to get here. They were accompanied by a team of horses and a couple of pack mules loaded with supplies.

The group was far larger than Corren would have liked. Nearly a dozen in all. It seemed less like an embassy to collect the ash and more like a potential war party. Indeed, he worried about what would happen when they got to the Rock of Light and the ash refused to be removed from the altar.

He feared more what would happen if the ash came off after all.

As evening drew near, they approached a large estate with an olive orchard in the rear and flowering bushes in the front. Like much of the vegetation in Hathmirr, these plants were unfamiliar to Corren, with thick, waxy leaves and bursts of purple blooms.

The group slowly came to a halt, bridles jangling and the horses' hooves sending up puffs of dust from the dry road.

A man came out the front door, which was a faded lavender. He wore simple trousers and a plain, maroon tunic. There was no gold mark on his forehead. When he saw the assembly gathered at his front path, a look of pure fear slipped over his expression.

"We didn't do anything," the man said, shutting the door behind him, as if to protect the home's occupants. "We didn't do anything."

Lord Tivoli merely frowned and said, "Who the hell are you? Where's Vickter?"

"Vickter sold us this property a month ago."

A few of the men chuckled.

"Ah," Tivoli said. "Welcome to the wayhouse of the Orsini Colony. I hope you enjoy your stay."

The men laughed again as Tivoli dismounted. He hefted his pack over his shoulder, unleashed a plain, wooden box from the back of his horse, and grabbed his staff. Setting the tip on the ground, he turned back to the man. "What's your name?"

"I am Gregor."

"And who is in your household?"

The man hesitated, looking from Tivoli to the men all down the line. He looked at Corren with the same apprehension he did everyone else, pausing only long enough to furrow his brows at the unusual sight of Corren's black cloak. His eyes landed on Lini and Sienna, the presence of whom he seemed to find slightly reassuring.

"My wife and my three little girls."

Tivoli groaned. "Keep them out of the way."

He pushed past the man, who seemed too afraid to argue, and swung open the door. Tivoli paused and looked back at the group, who were still mounted on their horses. "What are you staring at? You have your assignments."

The group began to dismount and got to work, some leading the horses around back, others joining their leader inside. Routt came to fetch Corren's horse, gathering the reins. Corren grabbed his bag and staff and went up the path in search of Tivoli.

Inside, a worn but elaborately woven rug covered the floor of the front room, which held a few squat chairs and a couch and little else. A simple lantern hung from the ceiling, but as the day still had enough light left, it was not lit. The home smelled of the sweet spices typical in many of the Hathmirrian dishes.

Beyond the front room was a kitchen where Lini opened one cupboard after another, inspecting the contents. Sienna was heading down the rear hallway, remarking to her fellow, "They have no cook staff and no gardener. It's no wonder this place is in such a state."

"She'd better not be late with dinner," Jatvia replied.

Bricker was making his way back up the hall and spoke to them in passing. "You and Routt are in this room here," he said to Jatvia, pointing. "Sienna, you and Lini are in the servants' quarters down the way."

He exited the hall and poked his head in the kitchen. "Lini. Servants' quarters."

He didn't wait for a reply before coming into the main living area and stopping short at the sight of Corren.

"Oh, right," he said. "I forgot. Well, rooms are full. You can sleep here on the couch." Bricker jabbed his thumb toward the lumpy couch behind them. With that, he disappeared through the front door, hollering out room assignments.

A woman came rushing down the hall, herding two small children in front of her and carrying a third. They gave him a wide berth, the little ones clinging to her colorful skirts and looking at him with wide, fearful eyes.

Passing into the kitchen, she said, "Oh! Oh!" at the sight of Lini going through her cupboards.

"We need dinner for a dozen," Lini said, "as soon as you can get it done. I suggest the shank. There's plenty and it'll cook up fast."

Corren left them and went down the hall, looking in first one room and then another until he came to the largest bedroom at the back. Lord Tivoli was sitting on the blue-and-yellow embroidered bedspread, his staff against one leg. His dirty pack and the wooden box sat next to him. The lid was slightly ajar, giving Corren a glimpse of the open Book of Madera within.

Tivoli glanced at Corren, shut the lid to the box, and went back to the folio he had in his hand. "Bricker will tell you where to sleep."

"What are we doing here?" Corren asked.

Tivoli looked at him like he was thick. "We're not riding all night."

162

"These people didn't even know we were coming."

Tivoli shrugged, writing something in his folio. "The previous owner should have explained how it works. They'll figure it out. Though they better hope they have enough food on hand."

"And if they don't?"

Tivoli set his folio on his leg and gripped the top of his staff with one hand. He looked at Corren, exasperated. "Is there something you need?"

Corren scowled at him. Why, *why* did the Madera branch seek refuge with these horrible people? What could this group do for them that the Order had been unable, or unwilling, to do? Could the Phoenix really be saving the ash for the likes of Lord Tivoli?

Corren huffed and retreated back down the hallway as Tivoli chuckled lowly behind him.

Corren woke to the sound of hushed voices and the faint light of predawn. He had a kink in his back from sleeping on the couch, which was too short. His bag was under his head and his staff lay next to him, his arm resting loosely over it. He must have woken up four times in the middle of the night, aching and restless.

The house was quiet, save for the voices coming from the kitchen.

"There aren't enough eggs," one voice said in a panic. Corren recognized it as the woman of the household.

"Serve them as a side." This voice belonged to Lini. Like the woman of the household, Lini spoke softly so as not to wake anyone. "Make oatcakes for the main dish. There's enough here."

"But what about the meat?" The frantic whisperings of the woman cut through the air. "We have no ham. He said he wanted meat."

"Madam," Lini said firmly. "Use the cutlets."

"That isn't a breakfast meat."

"He won't care."

From where Corren lay, he could see the block wooden table in the center of the kitchen. Corren heard some soft banging then saw the woman come to the table with a cleaver and begin slicing the raw meat.

The woman looked distraught. Lini brought a pan to the table along with some potatoes that looked freshly rinsed. She watched the woman, whose hands were shaking so badly Corren thought she might cut herself.

"I have to get back," Lini said.

The woman nodded, but Lini did not move.

"We'll be gone soon."

The woman stopped and looked at Lini then, "Please," she said. "My daughters—" Her voice broke and Lini held up her hand.

"We're not recruiting," Lini said quietly, "and taking your daughters would be more trouble than the lack of breakfast meat. Keep your head down. Stay calm."

The woman took a shaky breath and nodded, returning to her slicing.

Lini pulled something out of her pocket and handed it to the woman. "Keep it out of sight."

When the woman looked at her hand, Corren saw the gold coin.

Without looking at the woman again, Lini left the kitchen but halted in the doorway. Her eyes landed on Corren where he lay in the near darkness. As they looked at one another, both understood he just witnessed something he shouldn't have.

With a quick glance down the hall, she came over and knelt down. Her long dark hair cascaded over her shoulder. "For their sakes," she whispered, "say nothing of this."

Gone were any hints of her earlier animosity. She hovered near him, waiting only for him to agree.

Corren didn't know what to think of this woman, but he didn't want any harm coming to this family either.

He said nothing, only nodded, and she fled down the hall without another word.

As they rode through the next day, Corren had plenty of time to ponder what he'd seen and heard that morning in conjunction with everything else. He wanted answers; now he thought he knew how to get them.

Lini stayed clear of him all day, her dark eyes occasionally meeting his across the way before looking elsewhere or adjusting her head scarf to keep him out of view. They wouldn't have been able to talk anyway, for they were never alone.

They stopped again for the evening at a rambling estate that looked like it had seen better days. The owner was neither surprised nor happy to see them. He and his household (five family members and four staff) cleared rooms, barned animals, and provided dinner with little comment. Lord Tivoli and his crew ignored their hosts in kind.

The estate had so many unoccupied rooms that they were each able to take a room with plenty left to spare. Lini, he noted, was in a room two doors down from his.

When everyone went to bed for the evening, Corren lingered just inside his room. He leaned his ear toward the closed door and waited for the hallway to go quiet.

Lini had just finished washing her face and hands at the washbasin when she heard the door open behind her. Turning, she expected to see Sienna. Instead, the wizard Corren slipped inside and shut the door with a soft thud.

"What are you doing in here?" she hissed, not wanting anyone to hear. "Get out."

He held up his free hand—the other gripped his staff—and said, "I came to talk." He, too, kept his voice down.

"I'm not available to talk."

He glanced around the room. Aside from the silk-print wall hangings, there were only the washbasin, a narrow bed with carved wooden posts at each end, and a stuffed chair that was tucked in the corner. He caught sight of the chair and sat without comment.

She'd spent the entire day wondering if he was going to use his knowledge of that morning's events against her and now she knew. She folded her arms, came around, and sat on the bed. "What do you want from me?"

"I only want to ask you some questions."

"They'll kill you if they find you here talking to me."

"Then we'd better keep our voices down," he said, though he didn't look at all concerned. In fact, that was one of the things about him that irritated her. He was supposed to be their prisoner. He put up with all their second-rate treatment, and yet he didn't seem remotely afraid of any of them. Not even Lord Tivoli.

He scooted to the edge of his chair and leaned closer, his staff angling slightly. "Why did you get in trouble for opening the book?"

He didn't ask it like a man interrogating her. He asked almost as if... as if they were allies. Co-conspirators. That was the other thing that irritated her about him: he acted as if he knew her and had a right to talk to her. And she kept letting him. That irritated her too.

She narrowed her eyes. "Why should you care about that?"

He shrugged. "Aren't you allowed to look in it? The Madera branch bound the book to the Orsini Colony. Doesn't that include you too? Or was it only bound to your leader?"

"Only Lord Tivoli looks in the book." It was a safe answer.

"Then why did you look in it?"

She huffed. "I was curious."

For some reason, this brought a half smile to his face. "Only that?"

Oh, what did he want from her? "Curious and stupid and reckless, yes. Is that what you came to hear me say?"

166

He raised his hands, "Alright. It's alright. I understand."

"No, you don't."

He smiled fully and this caught her by surprise. She had not seen the wizard smile. It disarmed her and she sat there feeling exposed for some reason. "I understand curiosity well enough."

She furrowed her brows and scooted away to the edge of the bed, wrapping one arm around the hard post. She felt better then. Alone and safe.

His face grew serious again as he watched her. She watched him back. As she absently rubbed a thumbnail in a groove on the post, she thought she knew what his next question would be. But she would not answer it. She'd rather be hung for slipping a coin to the housewife.

"The High Ceremony," Corren began.

"Say no more, wizard."

"I saw you."

"I swear to you, do not say another word or I will tell Lord Tivoli about the housewife myself."

They held each other's gazes, each measuring the other. This time the wizard sat back. "Fair enough," he said.

He sat quietly for a moment, hand loosely on his staff. She looked at the tip again and the coarse wool covering. She felt that strange sensation once more. She wanted to unwrap it and see what lay beneath it. He thought he had her with blackmail. He didn't know she would tell him a great deal just to know what was really at the tip of his staff.

"One more question," Corren said quietly, "then I'll leave you in peace."

She dropped her arm and placed her hand next to her on the bed. He leaned forward again. Again, he looked at her as if they were confidants.

"When the woman mentioned her children," he whispered, "you said you aren't recruiting. What did you mean by that?"

That vulnerable feeling returned. Lini did not move away. "She—" His eyes held hers. He waited. The quiet of the house and the quiet of the room enveloped her. "What will you do if I tell you?"

He furrowed his brows. "You mean will I go to Lord Tivoli and tell him all I know?" He shook his head. "He won't know we talked unless you tell him yourself."

She looked at him.

"I hope you won't do that," he said.

"She... the housewife... she only wanted to know her children would be safe. Because of the orphans. We train up the orphans." She wanted to say it without saying it. He kept looking at her with that look of his, and she could not seem to extricate herself from it. She gripped the edge of the bed.

"The children I saw at your headquarters," he said. "Those are orphans?"

She nodded.

He raised his eyebrows. "You care for orphans?"

How noble it sounded when phrased that way.

"It's part of the work. We can't recruit adults and we cannot... have children of our own. So it must be the orphans."

"Ah. Not as a service to orphans. You seek them out. And also other children? That's why the woman was worried?"

She was gripping the edge of the bed with both hands now. "There can't be any family ties. It's not allowed. So they have to be orphans."

"Then why—"

His face went slack, but his eyes held hers.

Realizing he was starting to understand, she found herself wanting to explain. She leaned forward, moving a bit closer. "Maybe some man has been causing us trouble," she whispered, "or didn't pay what he owed us. Sometimes things are bad enough the only thing to do is get rid of him, but then you have trouble with revenge from other people in the family. They would cause problems. People know to stay out of our way, but with family ties, it's different. People don't think as much when family is involved. Their emotions get in the way. It's why we suppress emotions ourselves, so... if someone has to go... we can't leave family behind. Spouses, older children. It has to be clean."

She said it. Said all the words she'd been taught so many times, but they felt different when spoken to an outsider. Of course, everything had felt different for months, but it was so much worse saying it to this wizard she was supposed to hate. She had tried to say it all with conviction, as if she believed it still, but all the pretending she'd done for the last few months did her no good now.

In the face of this wizard, her words came out weak.

"If children are young enough, like the housewife's, they live and we bring them in. If they can acclimate, they get to stay."

Leaning forward on his seat, hand gripping his staff firmly, he looked horrified. She couldn't blame him. It was horrifying.

"And... if they don't acclimate?" he asked.

She thought about the Cleansings. She could not say it. She couldn't. But the look on his face told her he guessed the answer on his own.

His face grew hard. She wanted to shrink back but was frozen in place. "That ash," he said lowly, "will never come off the altar for the likes of you."

With that he stood and left as quietly as he came.

She found herself hoping he was right. But she doubted it.

Twenty

Marcellus and Janus had come to Amon Tunde to see how things were progressing. Now he sat in the clearing above ground, waiting while she visited Lily and the two other faeries who had fallen ill. Salerno and Nicolai stood under the giant Old Oak, hands on the bark, eyes closed. It had been too long since Nicolai's face had been seen at the castle. Marcellus worried about the damage that was causing to Nicolai's reputation, but there was nothing to be done. Nicolai was needed here.

Marcellus felt the warm lifting in his chest that was Janus' call to him. She was finally on her way back up.

"Gently," Salerno said to Nicolai. "Invite it to follow your will." They fell to silence again, both pressing their hands against the tree, eyes closed, doing something or other.

Even after everything he'd been through over the last several months, this sort of thing still felt strange to Marcellus. He knew well enough that magic was real, but he didn't really understand it. *How* was Corren able to make things happen with just a word? *What* exactly was Nicolai trying to do with that tree over there?

Janus came into view, walking slowly across the soft grass that flourished in the aboveground realm of Amon Tunde. She looked worn. He imagined she was concerned for her fellow faeries, as they all were. She caught his eye and smiled, picking up her pace as she crossed the clearing.

Salerno and Nicolai opened their eyes and stepped away from the tree. Nicolai frowned at it, wiping perspiration from his forehead and panting slightly.

"It won't listen to me."

Salerno gestured to the ground near Marcellus. "Sit, Nicolai."

As they came over, Janus settled next to Marcellus. Nicolai sat heavily on his other side. Marcellus gave him a hearty pat on the shoulder and Nicolai smiled at him weakly.

"Nicolai," Salerno began, "you already know how to do this. What you struggle with now is not knowledge; it is fear. It is that human part of you. You must let go and not be afraid of what will happen when you truly control your element."

Janus leaned forward and rested her chin in her palm, furrowing her brows.

"I thought being part human was supposed to help me," Nicolai said.

"It will. But you still must overcome the weakness of your race." Salerno pressed his hand onto the green grass in front of them. He made a gesture and Nicolai imitated him, putting his hand on the ground as well.

"The earth is trying to talk to you, but you are too afraid to listen," Salerno said. "You must let go."

As exhausted as he clearly was, Nicolai earnestly focused on Salerno. Likewise, Salerno was intently focused on Nicolai. Marcellus was grateful to be outside their attention, because Nicolai was not the only one trying to take it all in.

Marcellus glanced at the ground and lightly rubbed his open hand along the grass. The soft blades tickled his palm.

What Salerno said about the earth trying to talk to Nicolai felt familiar. Marcellus felt something like that every time he went in the water. How many years did he ignore the feeling that he could stay underwater without breathing? It wasn't until the water faeries gave him no choice that he was forced to recognize such a thing was truly possible.

He still had not tried to do it on his own. He wasn't sure he knew how.

Now he wondered. What if all he had to do was listen?

171

Janus walked with Marcellus toward the edge of Amon Tunde. Her hand was in his, but her mind was on Lily and the others. Especially Lily. In spite of Salerno's regular healing, she grew worse by the day. Janus had found it difficult to leave her.

She glanced at Marcellus. She knew he expected her to go back to Stonebridge with him. She had expected to go back too, but the further away she got from Lily, the more she wanted to turn around and go back.

She stopped and he looked down at her. "I... I think I'd like to stay a little longer."

"We can stay a bit longer if you want."

She appreciated his willingness but knew he'd been gone too long already. "No, I mean... I want to stay a lot longer. You should probably go back without me."

He nodded slowly. "Alright. Did you... want to... go back home?" Home meaning Amon Tunde. "To live?" Though he was trying to act as if he would not mind it if that's what she needed to do, she sensed how much he did not want that himself.

She did not want it either. Though part of her did not want to leave Amon Tunde with things in such a state, neither did she want to stay. Perhaps that made her selfish. Perhaps not. But her home lay elsewhere and had for a long time.

"No. Besides," she said lightly, "how will I make it to our nightly meetings at the spring if I'm here?" She squeezed his hand and he squeezed in return. "No, I just want to go back to Lily for a while."

"Of course," he said. "I understand." They started walking again, this time more slowly.

Through the trees, their horses came into view. Hers was tied to a young ash, just beyond the border, but Ryafan had stayed without being tied. The sunlight dappled his white coat as he nibbled contentedly on the grass.

Janus had a habit of looking at that horse sideways. It was like Marcellus was riding on a little bit of the ocean everywhere he went. For some reason, she hesitated to comment on the horse's unusual origins. Likewise, Marcellus never discussed it, as if Ryafan's existence were as natural a presence as the existence of his own arm. Marcellus would never think to say, "Why do you suppose my arm is here?" Yet that was what Janus wondered about the horse.

They stopped again. It was time for goodbyes, but they both lingered.

"It's strange," Janus said, her thoughts returning to her friend again. "Lily seems so confused. She asked me at least three times why I'm wearing human clothes."

"Human clothes?"

Janus nodded. "She doesn't like it. It was like she kept forgetting that Elana has died and I've left. I had to explain and watch her be hurt about it all over again." She glanced up at Marcellus and shrugged. "The last time I couldn't bring myself to tell her the truth."

"What did you tell her?"

Janus gave a slight, mischievous smile. "Oh, I told her Elana and I stole the bag of a human caught in a pixie circle and found the clothes inside. She scolded me for causing trouble. It seemed to make her happy."

She smiled fully now and Marcellus smiled too. "I would've liked to see that."

"I'll bet."

"I don't suppose you could act it out for me?"

"Just you never mind." She glanced behind them to make sure no one was around and stepped closer to give him a kiss. As she pulled away, he slid his arm around her waist and brought her back against him. He gave her the kind of kiss that left them both a little short of breath. The kind of kiss that said he wanted her to come home with him. But when they pulled away, he only said, "Stay as long as you need to."

She didn't know how long she needed to stay. She thought of Lily and the others. All fading.

"Don't worry," Marcellus said firmly. "I'm sure Nicolai will heal the Tree soon."

Janus nodded, but Nicolai, for all his diligence and trying, wasn't making progress. Even Salerno could not help them. What if that black magic could not be stopped?

Janus felt the little bloom of illness that had hooked deep within her chest two days ago. She felt the new blackness, hoped Marcellus could not sense it within her, and sent him off with a smile.

Salerno had gone down to check on Lily and the others, so Nicolai sat alone in the clearing. He was not next to the Old Oak though. He was out from under its canopy, his back to it. He concentrated on the earth in front of him, which was far more cooperative than the Oak was. A few days ago, Salerno had taught him techniques to manipulate the earth and Nicolai was practicing.

Or perhaps perfecting.

This was a task he found far easier to perform.

He heard Janus approaching—sensed her too—and nodded at her in greeting before returning to his work.

She sat next to him, watching as he pulled the earth into a smooth mound and caused soft grass to spring up and cover it.

"This is new," Janus said, surprised.

Nicolai shrugged one shoulder. "Salerno thinks it might help if I practice other skills." He waved a hand over one side of the mound and formed it into a ridge. It was almost ridiculously easy.

She stared at his handiwork, mouth slightly agape.

"*This* I can do," he said. "Frustrating, isn't it?"

She straightened. "Well, don't be too hard on yourself. Trees are the most difficult to manipulate. They think they own everything."

He gave a little laugh. "What?"

174

"It's true," she said. "Just look at them." She lifted her arm and he followed her sweeping gesture, taking in the expanse of trees stretching as far as he could see.

He smiled. They did seem like they were spreading out and claiming everything within reach. He turned and looked up at the massive canopy of the Old Oak. His smile faded. "Well," he said, turning back, "they're getting the best of *me*, that's certain."

"Yes," she said, "I've been thinking about that. The fault may be Salerno's, not yours."

He glanced at her. "How could it be Salerno's fault?"

"Well, maybe not *fault*. But... Salerno is training you like a faerie. And you are part faerie, but you cannot deny your human side."

Nicolai smoothed out the mound of earth and stood, ignoring his aching muscles. "But what does that mean? What am I supposed to do?".

"I don't know," Janus said, standing too, "but something I've noticed about humans is their strength. Their inner strength and resilience. Instead of letting go, the way faeries do, maybe you need to take hold of things. Be the master of them."

"Salerno said those are human weaknesses, to be so stubborn and controlling. He said I need to conquer that and stop trying to force things."

She nodded slowly. "Maybe. Maybe not. Salerno has his fair share of stubbornness, you know. That's not a trait unique to humans."

Nicolai gave a half smile. She'd conveniently neglected to mention she was another faerie known for a certain measure of stubbornness.

Still... he thought he might understand what she meant.

He looked at the Old Oak. It towered above everything in sight. If any tree had cause to think it owned everything, this one did.

He slowly started walking toward it. Was that what he was doing wrong when he first started training? Trying to own the tree? Thinking back, it did seem that way.

That hadn't worked, which was why Salerno told him to let go. Since then, Nicolai had been almost submissive to the elements. But that wasn't working either.

Nicolai moved under the shadow of the tree's canopy, beginning to sense the elements within the tree though he was not yet touching it. Slowly, the things Salerno had been trying to teach him merged with what Janus had just said and started to fit together in his mind.

Salerno told Nicolai to let go, to listen to the tree instead of forcing it to listen to him. Nicolai realized he had been thinking of it like a conversation. Either he talks and the tree listens or the other way around.

He took another step forward raising his hand, not near enough to touch the trunk yet.

Maybe it wasn't like a conversation. Maybe it was more like a dance, with Nicolai and the tree moving together. Maybe he needed both the sensitivity of the faeries and the will of humans.

He drew closer and already he felt the elements responding to him. He not only sensed the healing elements in the tree, he had hold of them. He gently but firmly eased those elements out of their places in the branches and gathered them down into the trunk.

His hand reached for the bark, willing the elements to come to him. Fingertips not quite touching, a flash of light sparked in the space between his hand and the tree.

He hopped back, heart pounding.

He did it.

"I did it," he said, stunned.

Janus rushed to his side and clutched his arm. "Nicolai!"

"Ha!" He pulled her into a bear hug and spun her around. "I did it! I did it!"

"Put me down, you lunatic!" she said, but when he set her on the ground she wore a grin as wide as his.

He laughed and put his hand on the Old Oak. He wanted to

do it again. And he knew he could. "Salerno." He had to tell him.

Grinning, Janus gave him a little shove. "Go."

Salerno had been healing Lily and the others nearly every day, pushing the blackness inside them as far back as he could. Today, for the first time, Nicolai did it.

Though he was relieved to be making meaningful progress at last, when he healed Lily, he was reminded that part of the blackness within her could not be healed. And that blackness had been growing over time. Even after her healing—which Salerno said was as good as he could have done it—her leafy hair remained withered and a few of the leaves were dark. Dead.

If Corren and his staff were here, surely this could all be done with. But Corren wasn't here.

Salerno led Nicolai down Oak Bone Tunnel, where a major root of the Old Oak was partially exposed in the roof above.

Salerno put his hand to the root and looked at Nicolai, who followed the implied instruction. He put his hand to the root as well. Immediately he noticed how different the tree's elements felt here.

"The Oak knows how to take nourishment into itself," Salerno said. "It knows what to do. You begin by bringing healing into it. You must give it something good it can feed on. You will pull healing from the earth all around it and direct it into the roots."

He'd known Salerno came here to heal the Old Oak after drawing healing powers out of it. The fact that its roots were exposed to allow for healing was one of the reasons they could use it so frequently. Its size was the other reason.

Nicolai considered all this more deeply now. "Can trees only be healed through their roots?"

"It is the only way they can absorb it. The trunk and limbs above ground will not allow it. You feel the differences, no?"

Nicolai nodded. "But can I get to the roots of the Tree of Origin?"

A shadow crossed Salerno's face. "Unfortunately... no. The roots are well protected."

Nicolai dropped his arm. "Then, how can I heal it?"

"That I do not know for sure. I trust you will find a way, Nicolai."

"But..." He thought Salerno had a plan. He thought he knew what to do and only had to teach Nicolai how to do it. But no. For the first time, Nicolai said aloud the quiet fear he'd had all along. "What if there *isn't* a way?"

Salerno looked at Nicolai soberly. "I do not know all things, Nicolai. However, I do believe you can help us."

Nicolai ran his hand through his hair in frustration. What if the damage Aradia had done could not be undone?

He looked at the root. It was almost as big around as he was.

"Do you trust me, Nicolai?" Salerno asked sincerely.

The king of the earth faeries stood there in his thick, mossy cloak, with that long hair that would have looked human had it not been so wild. His eyes, the same shade as the most brilliant green moss, watched Nicolai with his trademark calmness. Perhaps most humans would be startled by the appearance of this king of the faeries, but Nicolai had always sensed his magnificence.

So it was the first day he met him and so it was now. Salerno had never led him astray before. "Of course I trust you."

Salerno put one hand on the root.

Nicolai took a deep breath and placed his hand next to Salerno's.

And so they began.

Marcellus retreated to the isolated natural spring on the castle grounds. It was still light out but not by much. He was earlier than usual but came today with a different purpose.

He dove off a rocky ledge and swam under the surface for the length of the spring. He came up and took a breath, shaking the water out of his hair. There was a ledge just under the water, and he sat on it now, leaving only his head and shoulders above the surface.

He thought about what Salerno had told Nicolai about listening to the elements. He cupped his hands together, raised them above the water and watched it slowly leak out between his fingers.

He'd spent most of his life convinced magic was some sort of elaborate trick. His experiences with his stone, not to mention everything else he'd seen recently, had changed all that.

Still, he was no wizard. Not part of the Order. He had no desire to be. Magic, if he had to admit it, even scared him a bit.

But his element. The water. It drew him in against his will.

Marcellus dropped his hands and closed his eyes. His awareness of the water touching his skin intensified. It wasn't just water. It was more than that.

He tried to let go of any resistance. To listen. He allowed himself to feel the water, deeper than he ever had before.

He opened his eyes. He looked at his hands resting below the water's rippling surface. Again, he cupped his hands and brought them out. He wanted the water to stay in his hands. To not leak out.

And it didn't.

He looked at his hands and the water cupped within. It stayed in place. He felt himself keeping it there.

He flinched and flung the water away.

Heart pounding, he lingered on the ledge, hands pressed firmly on the rock. He could not bring himself to try again, but did not leave the water either.

Twenty-One

Lord Tivoli, Bricker, Sienna, Lini, and a few others walked along the edge of a ravine, with Tivoli taking up the lead. They had left the rest behind at the wayhouse they'd used for the night, sneaking out before anyone else awoke. No one dared ask what they were doing, but Lini could tell they were all wondering. She and Sienna kept exchanging curious glances with each other.

Everyone was wearied from the last two weeks of traveling, Lord Tivoli included. They'd cross the border into Caedmonia soon, then in another three days be in Stonebridge at last. So Lini had to wonder what was motivating Lord Tivoli to add this secret detour to their itinerary. It'd taken them close to two hours to get here—wherever here was—and they apparently still weren't done.

The ravine hadn't been too noticeable until they were practically upon it. The dry, rocky desert in this part of Hathmirr simply opened up to reveal a narrow ravine that wound like a snake for perhaps two furlongs.

The hot, desert wind whipped around them as they made their way along the edge. Tivoli gripped his staff in one hand, using it as a walking stick. In the other, he held the Book of Madera open in front of him. They had seen the book enough to know it was open to a map, but he wouldn't let them look at it more closely. He carried it against his chest, consulting it from time to time, while the rest of the party trailed behind.

Eventually he located a ridge that led down into the ravine. A gust picked up as Tivoli followed the ridge down. Lini held on to her layered wraps, which were flapping violently in the wind. The wind quieted as they descended below the rim and Lini

180

was glad of it. The canyon was deep and promised a fatal fall to anyone who went over the edge.

They had not gone far when the pathway, if it could be called that, narrowed severely. Lini wasn't sure they could safely continue. Apparently, Lord Tivoli wasn't sure either for he'd come to a halt, considering things.

He turned toward the group and looked at each until his eyes landed on Sienna.

"Sienna," he barked and gestured for her to come to him.

Everyone shuffled aside as Sienna made her way forward. She glanced at Lini as she passed. Lini saw her apprehension, but of course, neither of them said anything.

She approached Tivoli and stopped.

"You first," he said and stepped aside.

She went forward without hesitation, but Lini knew she had to be frightened underneath the forced obedience. Lini was frightened for her.

Tivoli watched as Sienna pressed herself against the cliff wall. She turned sideways, her colorful wrap flicking in the light breeze, and advanced along the path one careful step at a time.

Watching, Tivoli said nothing. Apparently, Sienna was one among them he was willing to sacrifice for whatever his purposes were. If the path was unstable, she would be the one to fall, not him.

Narrow though it was, the ledge was comprised mostly of solid rock and seemed sturdy enough. She made it through to the other side where the path opened up again. Tivoli moved forward, held the open book to his chest, and gestured for the rest to follow.

Lini watched as Tivoli and Bricker flattened themselves against the wall and moved along sideways.

Lini was next. She approached and looked down. The ground sloped sharply away from the narrow path, with abutments of rock jutting out all the way down. At the bottom was barren, rocky ground and one spindly tree, long since dead. If she fell, Lini did not doubt she'd end up right next to it.

"Move," Routt said behind her.

She forced herself to go forward. Too much hesitation could raise questions. She backed against the hard cliff wall. Her hands ran along the surface behind her, seeking something to hold on to, but it was too smooth. The only cracks and bumps she felt were too slight to do her any good.

She took one step to the side. The tip of her shoes nearly reached the end of the ledge. Beside her, she noticed, Bricker's larger feet extended slightly over.

Holding her breath, she took another step. Then another. Her shoes scraped against the rock. One careful step after another brought her at last to the widened path. Bricker advanced in front of her and she followed, relieved.

And so it went. The path widened and narrowed and widened again, taking them deeper and deeper into the ravine. They were in shadow now. The air cooled and smelled of damp earth.

Suddenly, Lord Tivoli came to a stop.

The group stopped, too, shuffling so they could look around one another to see what he was up to.

He pressed one finger on the map in the book, then examined a wide fissure in the wall of the ravine. He looked up like he was searching for something. Still looking up, Tivoli smiled.

Lini looked up too. The lip of the ravine stuck out over them, creating a bit of an awning. The rock above was streaked with ripples of red, brown, and yellow. It was a stunning sight. They had seen layers like this elsewhere in the ravine, but for some reason these meant something to Lord Tivoli.

"This is it," he said.

"What's it?" Lini wanted to ask, but she kept her mouth shut along with the others.

Tivoli went through the crack in the wall face. One by one, they followed. At first it seemed they were wedging themselves into a tear in the earth, the hard rock walls close on either side. However, the sides soon fell away and they found themselves in a cave.

The party's line relaxed and they walked two and three abreast, taking in their surroundings. They came to a breathtaking collection of rock formations that rose out of the ground like columns or hung from the ceiling like spears. Lini and the others ran their hands over the smooth surfaces as they wove their way around the pillars.

They followed the tunnel back and back. It was cool inside the cave, and she pulled up her head scarf for extra warmth. They went a short distance when Lini realized they should have been encompassed in total darkness but weren't. None of them carried a lantern. Yet the tunnel seemed to exude its own soft light.

They walked on.

Tivoli stopped but for no reason Lini could see. The party gathered round him, looking—as he was—at the tunnel that stretched away from them.

Lord Tivoli shuffled the book into his other hand so he could flip a few pages past the map. There, Lini saw a page with an illustration. As if realizing there were prying eyes all around, he glanced over his shoulder. "Stay back."

The group took several steps backward.

He examined both the tunnel and the book, at one point going back in the direction they'd come and examining the side of the cave wall.

He smiled and looked at them. It was a familiar, dark smile of satisfaction.

He raised his staff just slightly. "*Alehess*," he said firmly. "Say nothing of this. Back we go," and he pointed in the direction they'd come.

Once again, Sienna took up the lead, with Lini now behind her and Tivoli in the rear. Lini's head was buzzing with questions, and she was going nearly mad with the knowledge that she couldn't ask any of them. What on earth had this been about? She wanted to get her hands on that book now more than ever.

They exited through the narrow gap and came into the ravine once more. They climbed and climbed, navigating the path that narrowed and widened, narrowed and widened. Every time the path narrowed, Lini's breath shallowed as she pressed herself against the cliff wall. Every time it widened, she relaxed.

Each narrow stretch of path felt increasingly worse than the last, however, because they kept getting higher, the floor to the ravine dangerously far beneath them. Sienna and Lini took to clutching each other's hands during the perilous parts, an action they hid from the others.

When the way widened yet again, Sienna drifted out to the center of the path, leaving room now between her and the wall, and between her and the edge. Lini was close behind.

Suddenly, a huge section of the path just under Sienna's feet fell away, and down she went with a scream.

"Sienna!" Lini grabbed her wrap at the shoulders.

Sienna screamed and lurched backwards.

Hanging on, Lini went down hard, landing just on the path and her shoulder nearly tearing from the socket as her arm hung over the ledge. She had Sienna precariously by the fabric of her wrap, while Sienna had managed to grab Lini's upper arm by both hands.

Their eyes met. Loose rock skitted down the incline below Sienna, who was dangling above the harrowing drop, screaming and twisting.

Lini was vaguely aware of the shouts and commotion from the others behind her.

"Don't let go!" Lini said, but she was sliding forward herself. With Sienna gripping Lini's arm, Lini tried to find an anchor with her other, but the ground slipped slowly and steadily beneath her.

Sienna screamed again and Lini heard Lord Tivoli shout "No!" behind them.

Lini's shoulders went over the edge, and a sharp rush of fear consumed her as she imagined the two of them tumbling into the gaping ravine to their deaths.

Sienna's eyes were wide with horror. Her feet scrambled in vain to find a foothold, and her hands clutched Lini's arm fiercely.

"Grab her!" Tivoli shouted and someone had Lini by the ankles. Their momentum stopped. Lini had both hands on Sienna now, the one hand still clutching a wad of fabric from her wrap and the other grabbing her by the shoulder.

The grip on Lini's ankles was firm, but still the two women scooted forward an inch, then another. With every movement, they screamed and the men behind them hollered.

"Don't let her go," Lord Tivoli said. "Pull her up!"

"I'm trying!" It was Bricker. They slid another inch. More loose rocks cascaded over the edge in an arc. The rocks spun in midair before crashing on the ground far below, tumbling and cracking into pieces. "They're too heavy."

"Bricker, please!" Lini yelled.

"Lini," Lord Tivoli shouted, "let go of Sienna."

Lini and Sienna locked eyes, wide and fearful. Sienna screamed again. Lini held her fast. On the ground beside Lini, Lord Tivoli's shadow reared. She could see him raise his staff, holding it in the middle. Lini cried out. She knew what was coming.

"*Alehess*, Lini!" Tivoli hollered. "Let go of Sienna!"

No. No. No. Sienna's shocked eyes darted from Lini to Tivoli and back. Lini tightened her grip, trying to pull Sienna up, but she couldn't lift her. The two slipped another inch. "No!" Lini hollered.

Lord Tivoli positively roared. "*Alehess*, Sienna! LET GO!"

Sienna's hands released Lini's arm, and her wrap and shoulder yanked out of Lini's grasp. Lini scrambled for her, but Sienna plunged downward.

Lini screamed and closed her eyes, unable to watch.

Sienna screamed again and again, suddenly cut short by a bone-crunching thud that made Lini cry out and her heart clench. The horrible sound of the impact and Sienna tumbling to the bottom resounded in Lini's ears.

185

Her skin crawled with terror. *I'm next, I'm next.* She tried to reach back for the cliff's edge before Lord Tivoli could command Bricker to release Lini next, but her hands only clawed against the crumbling ground.

"Pull her up!" Tivoli said and this time Bricker was able to gain traction.

Next thing she knew she was on her back on the ledge, her heart pounding in her ears. Bricker was on his hands and knees next to Lini, panting. Lord Tivoli stood just beyond, glaring at Lini, still gripping his staff by its middle.

She looked up to the sky. Blue sky with a whiff of thin cloud and the ravine sides soaring up on either side of her. In spite of being on solid ground, she had the sensation of falling, with the sounds of Sienna's screams echoing in her ears.

Twenty-Two

Janus knew this forest like she knew herself. She knew every tree. Every sapling. Every shrub. She could close her eyes and navigate her way to the Old Oak just as well as with her eyes open. But the forest, with all its familiarity, felt strange to her now because she felt strange in it.

This illness had a peculiar hold on her. Though she managed to carry herself with the same erect posture and keep her stride as long and purposeful as she ever did (at least she hoped that's how it appeared), her body felt weak and soft. But she would not allow herself to slow her pace. She feared if she gave into it at all, it would take over.

Before the tree came into view, she sensed Nicolai there. She'd hoped he would be with the Tree of Origin, which is where he usually was. It'd only taken him two days to learn how to put healing back into the Old Oak, but after a week of trying to heal the Tree, he still hadn't been able to do it.

She wondered why he was above ground instead of below. Perhaps he was at the Old Oak because he was healing Lily or one of the others, but reaching out she sensed he was alone. She considered waiting until he left, but so long as Salerno was not nearby, it should be safe enough.

She came to the clearing and saw the Old Oak. Its branches waved and dipped in the gentle breeze. Nicolai sat next to the trunk, hands on the bark, eyes closed. His spirit continued to grow in strength, she could sense that from here, but would it be enough?

He opened his eyes and turned toward her, having sensed her before he saw her. She'd noticed he'd been using the faerie sense more and more. As he came out from underneath the canopy, she asked, "How are things going?"

187

He looked terribly worn, as he so often did these days. "Alright. I'm trying to see if I can draw healing into the Oak through its bark. If I can figure out how to do it here, maybe that will help me with the Tree of Origin."

She looked at the Old Oak doubtfully. There *was* no way to pull healing into a tree through its bark. She knew that. But Salerno was convinced Nicolai could do things no one else could. Maybe this was it?

She nodded and said, "That's good, Nicolai."

He was furrowing his brows at her. "Are you feeling alright?"

She felt a twinge of panic. Did she *look* ill? "Of course," she said, smiling.

He reached out and took her by the arm, looking into her eyes. Then she felt it. He was sensing her just the way Salerno would.

She wanted to pull away before he could discover her secret, but she was too struck by the fact that it was Nicolai doing it. This new ability startled and mortified her, but it also gave her hope. If he could do this...

"Nicolai..."

"Oh, Janus," he said, releasing her. He looked at her with a pitiful expression. As if her fate were decided already.

"Please don't tell Marcellus."

"He has to know."

"No." She took a step back. "It isn't bad yet."

"But—"

"There's nothing he can do!" she said sharply.

He stopped, watching her.

She closed her eyes and placed her fingertips on her temples. She took a deep breath, smelling the clean vibrancy of the forest. The place of her birth.

She opened her eyes. He was watching her. "Please, Nicolai," she said, softer now. "You know how he'll worry."

He sighed and looked off in the distance. She could see he was relenting but wasn't happy about it. "I'm wearied by carrying everyone's secrets."

She raised her brows. "How many do you have?"

188

"Amon Tunde counts for at least ten."

She laughed a little, but he did not.

"Come here," he said and turned toward the broad trunk of the Old Oak.

She *had* intended to pull a tiny bit of healing from the tree, so long as no one was around to see her. But doing it herself felt different than Nicolai doing it. Things weren't that bad yet. They weren't.

Janus stayed where she was. "I don't need your healing." He turned back with brows raised. "I am not sick."

It was a ridiculous lie and she knew it, but she said it for the same reason she walked with a quick stride through the forest. She said it for the same reason she didn't want anyone to know. She felt her will was the only thing keeping the blackness at bay.

Nicolai looked at her. "I just need someone to practice on," he said. "I thought you'd like to help."

She didn't think she'd ever heard Nicolai tell a lie before now.

"It's just that..." he said, "I hate to bother anyone else. With my practicing."

She stood there, wavering. She knew he could heal her more deeply than she could herself, but...

"Please," he said. His voice was soft, but his eyes held her firmly.

She hesitated, then took a step forward.

They kept their eyes locked on each other as she approached the tree. She placed her hands on the rough trunk, closed her eyes, and felt him come next to her. Not waiting for him, she began the healing on her own, drawing what elements she could into herself.

"Stubborn faerie," he said softly, then placed his hands gently on top of hers.

The healing she'd been pulling from the tree gained new intensity, humming with energy. Nicolai pulled it through her body and toward the blackness that infested her like a weed. It lessened and retreated in response.

She didn't realize how tightly she'd been resisting the sickness inside of her until she felt the restorative powers pulsing through her body. She relaxed, feeling almost dizzy with relief, leaning her forehead on the bark as the blackness retreated further and further.

The light pressed against the darkness until the darkness held its ground. It was still there, but smaller than it had been in some time. It was as much as Nicolai would be able to do.

He slowly removed his hands.

She straightened and looked at him, blinking back the tears that sprung rebelliously to her eyes.

"Thank you," Nicolai said softly, then walked away.

Corren saw the dust on the horizon first and was waiting on the porch by the time Tivoli and his crew pulled their horses alongside the gate. The other Orsini members who had been left behind slowly gathered on the porch as well. Tivoli and the others dismounted, looking more somber than usual, but not before Corren noticed Bricker had been pulling a horse with a saddle but no rider. That's when he noticed Sienna's absence.

Tivoli climbed the steps to the porch, his staff knocking on the wood. The box that Corren knew contained the Book of Madera was tucked under his arm. He looked at no one.

"Where'd you go?" Corren asked.

"That's none of your concern."

"Where's Sienna?"

The others in the group looked at him sharply, all except Lini who kept her head down.

"Wizard," Tivoli said firmly, "I don't answer to you. Mind your own business."

Corren narrowed his eyes as Tivoli and the others walked past him. He followed them into the house. "There's been an accident," he announced to his followers. "Sienna is dead.

190

That's all you need to know." With that, Tivoli disappeared down the hallway. Lini was nowhere in sight.

Later that evening, Lini showed up for dinner, but she was like a wraith. No one spoke to her, including Tivoli. Those who had gone with her and Tivoli during the day did not even look in her direction. Those who'd been waiting at the house cast curious, furtive glances at her and questioning looks to one another, but no one said anything. She took little for dinner and ate even less, excusing herself early and disappearing down the hall. Lord Tivoli's face was stone and he ate his dinner deliberately, one bite at a time.

At the end of the meal, Tivoli stood and said, "Get a good night's sleep. We leave in the morning."

For the second night in a row, Corren was relegated to the house's tiny loft, with only a thin mattress placed directly on the floor. It was the only time the entire trip that they'd stayed more than one night in the same place.

He lay there staring at the slanted wood ceiling, wondering where Tivoli and the others had gone and what really happened to Sienna.

More than anything, he kept thinking about the haunted expression on Lini's face.

Lini could not sleep.

She lay on the bed, curled on her side, eyes staring at the wall. It was the same position she and Sienna used to sleep in when they were children. Every muscle was clenched and her breathing shallow. Her heart beat rapidly against her chest, like a frightened rabbit.

She kept seeing it all over again. The terrified look in Sienna's eyes, the moment she opened her hands, Lini scrambling after her, and the sound of Sienna hitting the ground—it all kept going round in her head.

Her back and ribs ached where Lord Tivoli had kicked her. She tried to tell him she hadn't heard his command to let go, that she only heard Sienna screaming, but didn't know if he believed her until the beating was over and he looked down at her, huddled in the dirt, and told her to get moving.

She heard her door open, saw it out of the corner of her eye, but did not look at her visitor. She closed her eyes in case it was Lord Tivoli. If he changed his mind and decided to kill her after all, she didn't want to watch him do it.

She heard the door close. Heard footsteps approaching. Heard someone kneel down. She shook. She couldn't help it.

"Are you alright?"

She opened her eyes to find the wizard Corren, with that look on his face, so near to her.

"No questions," she said. She sounded so small and pitiful, even to her own ears. "Not tonight. I can't—" her voice broke.

"No, I... I didn't come to interrogate you," he said softly.

She looked at him.

"Are you alright?" he asked again.

Something welled inside of her. Something she hadn't felt in a very long time. But, oh, she remembered this feeling. This horrible feeling. Hot tears leaked out of her eyes.

"It was my fault," she whispered. "My fault." She pinched her eyes shut and clutched the edge of the mattress. She wanted to cry, to scream, but instead she held it in, in, in, and it threatened to break out of her anyway.

He put his hand on her shoulder. It was so steady and warm and comforting.

That was what did it. The last of her strength gave way, and she cried openly, pushing her face into the pillow, contracting further into a ball.

Oh, how she wished for the potion now. Wished there was another ceremony. She needed something to deaden this horrible pain. She wished she had never resisted the potion to start with. But then, she realized, she would have let go when Lord Tivoli issued the command. Sienna's death was bad enough, but if Lini had let go on purpose—

The wizard rubbed her shoulder. "I'm sorry," he said once, then let her cry in silence. She cried until she felt empty and drained.

Eventually, she quieted.

She felt vaguely embarrassed for displaying such emotion in front of him, but when she opened her eyes, that feeling vanished. He looked genuinely concerned for her. Such a strange person to understand, this wizard.

"We were on a ledge," she said, her voice raw. "There was this ravine and the ground fell out from underneath her."

His hand was still on her shoulder, where it had been since he first put it there. "So it was an accident," he said.

She shook her head firmly. "I tried—" her voice broke. She grabbed the fabric of the cloak on his chest and started again. She needed someone to hear it. Someone, anyone. "I tried to hold on, but we kept slipping and slipping. I couldn't stop it. We had hold of each other, but..."

He held her eyes and waited, listening, his hand still on her shoulder, her fist still grabbing the fabric of his cloak. "She let go," Lini said, her hand softly beating against his chest with each word. "She let go and I couldn't hold her."

The tears came again, flowing freely down her cheeks. She looked at him, imploring.

"It wasn't your fault," he said quietly.

She nodded. "It was—"

"It was an accident."

"If I'd grabbed her arm instead. Or... or something. She fell so far." Lini closed her eyes again, wishing she could erase it all from her mind. "I heard her hit the ground..."

"I'm so sorry."

A fresh wave of tears came and she cried as if she had never cried the first time. She clung to his cloak and cried until she was once again empty.

At last she released him and lay there quietly, her hand hanging loosely over the edge of the bed. She looked at the way the folds of his cloak fell over his chest. She listened to him breathing. Her muscles were heavy and her mind numb. Her heartbeat still raced with the trauma of it all, but she was numb even to that.

He gave her shoulder a firm squeeze then rearranged himself so he was sitting on the floor, one knee up, his arm resting on his knee. He looked at her. Calmly. Just waiting. She looked at him back.

"We were orphans together," Lini said. "But she was the good one."

More warm tears leaked out of her eyes. There was no end to them.

"No matter what they did to her, she was always the good one."

"I'm sure she was," he said softly, and he said it like he believed her.

This brought a small measure of comfort. She closed her eyes. She'd stopped crying and let the tears dry on her cheeks. Her hand still hung over the bed. She could sense him nearby. Her heartbeat was slowly settling down, and her breathing slowed with it. After a time she noticed that their breaths were in time with one another. Breathing in and breathing out.

She lay there with her eyes closed, her body still and heavy on the bed, and listened to their breathing until she fell asleep.

Twenty-Three

Nicolai hurried down the Vein of the Earth, the tunnel that led to the Tree of Origin, propelled by the force of a new idea and the hope that he'd found the answer at last. For weeks he'd been trying to bring healing in through the Tree's bark or even the leaves without success, all along knowing it had to be done through the roots. Salerno said the Tree's roots were well encased, but what if Salerno was wrong?

As he entered the cavern, his blood pounded through his body with each heartbeat. The shimmering light from the golden Tree glittered on the rocky walls, and the earth surrounding it was blanketed in soft, luminous grass. The only flaw in this magnificent scene was the increasing blackness at the top of the Tree. In addition to the five dead branches, others nearby were deeply marred with streaks of black. One branch, Lily's, was nearly all dark and many of her formerly golden leaves were dead and wilted.

Nicolai rushed under the gleaming canopy and fell to his knees by the base of the golden trunk. For the first time, he focused not on the Tree itself but on the ground underneath him.

He ran his hand over the emerald-colored grass, sensing the elements in the earth. He recognized many, but there were many he'd never encountered before. He assumed they must be unique to the earth here by the Tree.

Still, he thought he could manipulate it as he did the earth above.

He swept his hand over the surface, and a shallow depression formed, obeying his command. His heart leapt into his throat. *This could work.*

Almost as soon as the depression formed, however, it filled back up, the little blades of grass springing back into place.

He sat back on his heels, suddenly remembering something. The very first time he'd come to the Tree, needing a single leaf, he'd initially tried removing it with a common throwing spear. But it was the spear that had been cut, not the leaf. When the shard of the blade fell on the ground below, the earth swallowed it up in one smooth motion.

Nicolai swept his hand over the earth again. He again formed a hole—this one deeper than the first—but the earth almost instantly filled it back in.

"No," he said firmly. He only needed to expose one section of the Tree's root. That's all he needed. There had to be a way.

With both hands, he tried to work more rapidly, attempting to hold the earth at bay long enough to get to the root. The earth worked almost as quickly as he did, restoring itself to how it was before.

"I'm trying to help you. You're as stubborn as everyone else."

Again and again he tried, even digging his fingers into the cool soil, trying to hold it back with his hands. Nothing worked. The earth would not allow him any deeper than a hand's depth. The earth was reforming and restoring itself as if it couldn't help it. Just how black was the magic infesting the branches if the Tree could not likewise restore itself there?

Then he thought of the unique qualities of the spear he now wore strapped to his calf. It was the same one the earth had given him, borne from the walls of this very cavern and the only thing that had been strong enough to cut a leaf from the Tree. What if all he needed was more strength?

He grabbed it and dug a line in the dirt using the spear. Again the earth smoothed and rearranged until it looked exactly as it had before.

The hopelessness of the situation began to close in on him. He tore into the earth with his spear, with his hands, with his magic. *No, no, no.*

Shaking, he clenched the handle of the spear with both hands, roared, and plunged it into the ground in front of him.

Panting, eyes closed, leaning forward, he knelt under the canopy of the golden Tree and thought of all the faeries in Amon Tunde who were depending on him.

He took a deep breath, sat back on the grass, and rubbed his face with his hands. He looked at the spear, still sticking out of the earth.

Every day Lily looked at him with a desperate kind of hope. She was dying. And Nicolai didn't know if he'd be able to stop it.

The day after Sienna's death, Corren and the band of Orsini Colony members neared the Caedmonian border. Corren knew they should reach it by the end of the day and wondered how much further over the border they would get before being discovered by Caedmonian troops or the Guard of the Order or both. He'd already decided how he would handle each occurrence but was not looking forward to it, all the same.

The group traveled in relative silence. Lini had not said anything to him, not that there had been any opportunity to talk, but their eyes had met more than once and she'd held his gaze.

As he watched her fall asleep the night before, he thought of her not as a member of the Orsini Colony, not as the perpetrator of all their horrible acts, but as an orphan. Most likely a kidnapped orphan. He imagined her as a young girl in the foreign halls of the Orsini Colony, surrounded by people such as that. He wondered how many people had been in her family and what they'd done to offend the Orsinians.

Nevertheless, traveling in this pack of Orsini members and knowing they had all presumably been orphans once did not change who they were now. It did not—could not—erase the evil he sensed all around him.

Early that morning, Lord Tivoli had sent Bricker and Jatvia ahead of the group, and Corren was about to discover the reason why.

They came over a ridge to find a large campsite with several tents, many horses, and what looked like some forty people. Corren searched for the telltale gold marks and there they were. On every last forehead.

Those in the camp were gathered around a large cook fire, most sitting and eating, a few standing. They caught sight of Lord Tivoli and his party and started to get up.

The only one who seemed surprised by the sight of this encampment was Corren. He sped up to the front of the line where Tivoli led the way. "What is this?" Corren asked.

Tivoli glanced at him but did not answer.

"Tivoli, I said what is this?"

Lord Tivoli led them into the camp, brought his horse to a stop, and dismounted. The others followed his lead. "Carry on," Tivoli said to those who'd been waiting. "You can serve us up while you're at it."

A few people got back to the cook fire, dishing some sort of stew out of a large pot and putting it into clay bowls. Several people went back to lounging on the ground. Many cast Corren curious glances.

He ignored them all and dismounted.

"Tivoli," he said firmly. He felt the reverberation of his own voice in his staff.

The company stilled and Tivoli turned.

"I demand an explanation," Corren said.

Tivoli narrowed his eyes. He marched up to Corren, stopping directly in front of him. "I'll give you an explanation. The Head of your Order promised she would deliver what rightly belongs to *us* and she lied. She lied to me and she killed my men. We've been waiting four hundred years for our ash and we're going to get it. With or without her and with or without you. I've been sending my people to the border for weeks," he said, gesturing. "They've been scouting and rounding up supplies. I was due to join them anyway. You showed up *sneaking* around, so lucky you, you get to come with us. Now sit down and shut up. I don't want to hear another word from you until we reach the Rock of Light."

Without waiting for a reply, Tivoli turned and marched to the campfire. Corren noticed a few smirks on the faces of those around him, but he did not bother with them.

He'd had enough.

He spun around and marched past everyone until he was several paces away from camp, then turned to face them.

With a broad wave of his staff, Corren called up a streak of fire. In an instant, he fashioned a blaze twice as tall as he was. The Orsinians cried out and shuffled backwards. Tivoli raised his staff, but Corren drew his own staff in a circle. The fire raced along the ground, encircling the encampment of the Orsini Colony until they were contained in a raging ring of fire.

Through the roar of the flames, he heard their shouts and commotion. Several spells hit the inner wall of the fire, but they did no good. Corren stood on the outside, glaring at the flames until the group within quieted.

He took one step, two steps. Corren walked through the wall of fire and appeared on the inside, directly in front of Tivoli.

No one spoke a word. Every eye was on Corren and Corren's eyes were on Tivoli.

"Your gang goes no further," Corren said. "I will take *you* to the Rock of Light like I said I would. You will try—and fail—to remove the ash from the altar, and then you will take your band of criminals back where you came from. If anyone else steps foot on Caedmonian soil, I'll make sure it's the last thing they do."

Tivoli's eyes blazed as fierce as the fire that contained him. "I'm not going on alone."

"You're not coming with *them*. You're welcome to go back home now if you want."

Tivoli's grip on his staff tightened and Corren answered with nary a word. He caused a shimmering barrier of heat to materialize between them. It was enough to let Tivoli know that Corren was finished with his antics.

Tivoli's eyes darted over the heat barrier between them, then looked back to Corren. "Me and one other person. You cannot begrudge me that simple protection."

"Oh, can't I?"

Tivoli briefly closed his eyes. "I only ask," he said in a subservient voice Corren knew must have cost him dearly, "for one person to watch my back."

Bricker, his right-hand man, stepped forward. The hulking man inclined his head toward Corren, his long, dark hair slipping over his shoulders. "I would cause you no trouble," he said.

"Not you," Tivoli said. "Her." And with that, he pointed at Lini.

Lini's eyes widened, but Tivoli did not turn to look at her.

Corren narrowed his eyes. He glanced at Lini, who looked at him frankly.

"Why her?" Corren asked.

"I thought you'd feel less threatened by a woman."

He thought of Aradia, huffed, and said, "Bring her."

With that, he waved his staff, extinguished the ring of fire in a puff of smoke, and walked away.

PART II

The Book of Madera

One

The three-day journey from the Caedmonian border to Tower Hall South had a significantly different feel to it. Not long after Corren, Tivoli, and Lini crossed the border, they ran into the Guard of the Order. Corren told them where to find the Orsinian camp so they could keep an eye on the situation and make sure no one tried to come into Caedmonia, then brought two other members of the Guard with him to help keep watch over Tivoli and Lini at night.

They'd brought along a couple of packhorses for supplies and camped out in the open. On the first night, Tivoli complained about the barbaric conditions and said he, at least, knew how to provide a roof over someone's head. Corren looked at him dispassionately, then set the stack of logs for the fire ablaze with his staff.

Tivoli only sat there looking grim and clutching his box with the Book of Madera inside. He never let it out of reach. Only Corren's honor kept him from taking the book right then. He would first let Tivoli try to remove the ash, as promised.

Lini said little. She seemed as confused about her presence there as the rest of her group had been. She and Corren held their gaze with one another every now and then but did not speak. Only once, on the second day, did Corren risk speaking to her during a brief moment alone. "Why did he choose you to come?"

"I don't know," she said.

That was all they had the chance to say, and Corren didn't know if he believed her. Even if she knew why Tivoli wanted her along, would she tell Corren the reason? Just because he had comforted her, or tried to, in a moment of compassion he himself wondered about, it didn't change anything. Tivoli and

Lini were here for the ash, but Corren would never let them have it. Let the Phoenix roast him where he stood. If the ash came off the altar for Tivoli, Corren would pry the ash out of his hands or die trying.

They arrived at Tower Hall South late on the evening of the third day. Corren would have been relieved to be home at last, were it not for the two people he had in tow.

"This isn't the Rock of Light," Tivoli said, as Corren escorted them through the stone halls of the west wing where they would stay under guard.

"No. I'll call the Heads together and we'll go to the Rock of Light then. We can't perform the ceremony without everyone present."

Tivoli looked at Corren suspiciously, as if his true intentions were to keep them prisoners forever. In truth, Corren couldn't get them out of Tower Hall South fast enough.

In spite of the late hour, he sent messages to the other Heads. That would allow them to meet at the Rock of Light the day after next. In his message to Kennard, he asked him to bring extra members of the Guard with him.

In addition, a message went to Marcellus and Nicolai, though this one went by way of a royal messenger who had, apparently, been at Tower Hall South for weeks, waiting for Corren to show up so he could send word of his return.

Corren was too tired to ask the reason. He was too tired to pay a private visit to Lini to see if he could find out more about why Tivoli wanted her as his escort. He could take care of all those things tomorrow. For now he retreated to his room where he removed the covering from his staff at last, collapsed onto his bed fully dressed, and fell into a heavy sleep.

Marcellus and Janus had fallen asleep on the couch in his office again. It was the second night in a row and the second time he'd allowed himself the impropriety of it. After all the care he'd taken to make sure no false rumors swelled up around their courtship, when the evening came, he could not send her away. She did not seem to want to go either, and he feared it was for the same reason.

She was not looking well.

She seemed more pale than usual, but it was hard to tell. He hoped it was merely the invention of a worried mind. That really, everything was fine and he was just imagining things. He was afraid to ask.

Instead, they worked together on various matters of the kingdom throughout the day, talked and entwined themselves in each other's embrace through the evening, and fell asleep together at night. Underneath it all, Marcellus felt an undercurrent of panic. As if he were clinging to the last of something.

He was asleep on the couch, Janus lying with her head nestled onto his shoulder, when the knock came at the door. Having been in a restless sleep to start with, Marcellus jolted awake.

Janus startled and lifted her head. "What is it?" she mumbled.

A second rap at the door.

"Yes?" he called, still coming out of the fog of sleep.

In came a messenger, who apparently took Marcellus' reply as an invitation to enter. The messenger caught sight of them both and stopped abruptly, bowing.

"King Marcellus, please forgive me," he said. When he straightened, he kept his eyes on the floor. "I went to your chambers, but they thought you would be here. I've come with a message."

Marcellus and Janus rearranged until they were sitting up, but the damage had already been done. He sighed. "Yes?"

"Sage Corren has returned."

Someone was pounding on Corren's door. He groaned and scrunched up his face. He couldn't have been asleep more than a couple of hours. The pounding continued. "Corren! Corren, wake up!"

Was that Marcellus?

"Corren!"

"What on earth?" Corren mumbled. He peeled himself out of bed and stumbled to the door, Marcellus pounding on it all the while.

"What?" he said, opening it. Before him stood not just Marcellus, but Nicolai and Janus as well. He knew immediately that something was desperately wrong.

Corren stood in a clearing in Amon Tunde, with the Tree of Origin far beneath him. Nicolai, Marcellus, and Janus stood apart, watching him circle over the grass, his black cloak billowing behind. He'd caused a ball of light to hover over the area and scrutinized the softly illuminated ground with his staff held aloft. It was in this staff that Nicolai placed his faith. Lily lay elsewhere in Amon Tunde, nigh unto death. Janus pretended all was well out of sheer stubbornness, but even she could not hold her sickness at bay forever. For weeks, Nicolai had been longing for this moment. They needed this.

The forest was quiet and still. The blackness of the night pressed against the faint glow Corren had provided and the silent spectators watching him work.

When he began at last, Nicolai felt the magic in the air resonating in his very bones. Corren said not a word. He took his staff into both hands, raised it high, and struck it against the ground. A rush of energy flew out in every direction and the earth trembled and rumbled.

The party watching stood still. Corren himself did not move. The low rumbling of his magic retreated into the distance and faded away. All was silent once more.

Corren knelt, putting one hand to the ground.

Unstuck, Nicolai rushed next to him and did the same thing.

Nicolai could feel the luminous magic of the Tree of Origin far below. From this exact location, Aradia had cast her dark spell to remove a single leaf from the Tree of Origin, leaving blackness in her wake.

And that blackness was there still.

An hour later, Nicolai and the others left the clearing and headed for the border of Amon Tunde. Corren had attempted to heal the Tree until he was so exhausted he was leaning on his staff as if it were the only thing keeping him upright. At that point, Marcellus put a stop to things. "You can come back tomorrow, Corren, after you've had some rest."

Corren agreed, but insisted he see Lily first. He knew they expected her to pass at any time and wanted to see if he could offer any healing.

He did, in fact, cause the illness to retreat further in her than they'd been able to do in over a week. The rest of the blackness that had claimed her was immovable, but he'd bought her time, and for that, Nicolai was grateful.

Next, Corren had turned to Janus and likewise offered healing for the illness he'd sensed within her. Janus' face fell when she realized her secret was out, but Marcellus only watched Corren heal her and quietly thanked him when he was done.

Two

Corren led the way up the winding stone staircase of the Rock of Light. Behind him, the Heads of the Order and Lord Tivoli followed. They emerged into the upper room, encircled about by large openings roughly hewn out of stone. These presented views of the bay, the city of Stonebridge, and the Cliffs of the Realm. In the center, the altar presented the Phoenix's massive flame. It lent warmth to the room and made the steady sound of a sure wind. On the stone ledge of the altar, a single glass orb reflected the dancing light of the fire.

Within, the ash waited.

The white-robed Heads of the Order circled the altar and stopped in their places, like they had done so many times before. This time one among them stood out. The light flickered on Tivoli's shaven head and the many layers of his orange robe.

He leaned his stout staff against the altar. Corren and Bellamy did the same with theirs. Normally, they would have left their staffs elsewhere, but this situation was far from normal.

Kennard, at Corren's request, waited outside the circle, watching with a dark look on his face. Lord Tivoli wore a dark look also, except instead of scowling, he was smiling. Smiling directly at Corren, as if he knew something Corren didn't. As if he were triumphant already.

Corren glanced at the others, all watching him with wariness. No one had wanted to do this, Corren included. No one fought him harder than Kai'Enna. But he felt, and everyone eventually agreed, that if they didn't at least let Tivoli try to remove the ash, there would be war for sure. Corren glanced at the ash, waiting in the glass orb that glinted in the light of the

Eternal Flame. Surely the Phoenix would not let it come off. Surely not.

Tivoli's former words came back to Corren, "The ash is bound to us."

Magically bound.

If that were true, did the Phoenix have to honor that bond? Would the Phoenix allow the ash to go to this horrible man? But the Phoenix did not control everything; otherwise, Aradia never would have become Head of the Order to begin with. What if the reason the ash would not come off the altar before now had nothing to do with the Phoenix's will and everything to do with some sort of magical spell by the Madera branch itself?

Suddenly, Corren did not want to go through with it. What would he do if Tivoli were able to lift that orb?

Tivoli smiled again. "Shall we?"

Corren hesitated. His fingertips rested on the rough stone of the altar's ledge. This close, the heat from the flames was almost too much. He closed his eyes briefly, listening to the roar of the fire. He opened his eyes and began.

"*Illio tetha.*"

"*Illio tetha,*" the others chanted after him. Corren heard Tivoli's voice among them and felt a chill in his bones.

"*Ah mae alla,*" Corren said, and the others repeated it.

"*Immath ay, Immath ay, Immath ay,*" Corren said, and Tivoli placed his hands on the sacred orb.

This was the moment Corren had been dreading since he began the journey with Tivoli and the others weeks ago. This was the moment the Phoenix would make known its will.

All eyes turned to Tivoli. He was an enemy among them, Corren was certain of it, and he was here in this room with his hands around the orb.

And the orb was still on the altar.

Tivoli's smirk fell into a scowl. He tugged on the orb, yet the orb stayed.

Corren managed not to laugh with relief.

Tivoli glared at him. "You stay out of this." He thought Corren was magically holding the orb in place.

"It isn't me," Corren said. The circle began to relax as members exchanged relieved glances.

Tivoli was grunting, pulling at the orb again and again.

"The Phoenix doesn't want—" Corren began, but Tivoli grabbed his staff from where it had been leaning against the altar.

"*Expath!*" he shouted, pointing at the orb. It vibrated harshly and the rattling sound of the glass thrashing against the stone rippled around the room.

Corren and Bellamy both grabbed their staffs and Kennard started to come forward.

"What are you—" Corren said, but Tivoli seized the orb with both hands and again shouted, "*Expath!*"

The orb blazed red and Tivoli screamed, jumping back and holding out his hands. They were covered in swollen, red blisters and charred black on the fingertips.

The circle fell to chaos. Chandra, who'd been closest to him, moved forward to help but he stumbled backwards, shouting at her to stay away. He was heading toward one of the low openings to the outside, and the group shouted at him to stop and look out and watch behind him, but he only gaped at his hands, screaming and scrambling backwards.

"Wait!" Corren hollered, just as Tivoli's heel hit the bottom ledge of the window. He tipped back and flailed his arms. Kai'Enna gasped as he went over, but Corren sent a spell to catch him.

Everyone fell to stunned silence. Tivoli hovered in midair, half outside the opening.

Corren brought him back inside, where Tivoli fell to his knees, his burnt hands trembling in front of him. Corren slowly approached. The others silently stepped aside. Tivoli moaned and rocked forward and back on his knees.

Corren glanced at the orb on the altar. The glass had returned to its normal color. Corren turned back to Tivoli and waved his staff over him, thinking the healing spell that dissipated his burns and left his hands only slightly pink. He set the tip of his staff on the stone floor with a firm click and watched Tivoli dispassionately.

Tivoli, for his part, looked up at Corren and glared. "You injure me only to heal me?"

"It wasn't me," Corren said, his voice hard. "Your own spell did it."

He slowly got to his feet where he leered unsteadily. "You can't be trusted," he said and looked around at the others. "Any of you. You had no intention of giving me the ash."

Corren could not deny that but said nothing.

"I would ask why you bothered to bring me here," Tivoli said, "but I know what you want."

Corren thought of the book. The book that, as far as he was concerned, rightly belonged to the Order now that Tivoli wasn't able to retrieve the ash.

"It belongs to us," Corren said.

"You'll have to kill me to get it."

Kai'Enna came up beside Corren and said urgently, "We cannot let them leave with the book."

Corren thought of Lini downstairs. "I don't intend to," he told her, then to Tivoli, "It's over. We're taking the book and you're going home. You are not to return."

"I don't take orders from you," Tivoli spat.

Corren sent a magical spell to bind him.

"Stay here," he said to the others. "Kennard. Come with me."

Corren descended the stone stairs in the Rock of Light, wondering how on earth he was going to do what he needed to do. He needed that book and would use any means necessary to get it, but would Lini give it to him? The thought of forcibly taking it from her...

He and Kennard came to the base of the stairs, went through the Order's empty chambers, and into the anteroom where Lini sat with her guard. The box rested on her lap. She stood as they

211

came in. When Kennard shut the door, she looked to Corren. "Where's Lord Tivoli?"

"He's still up there. The ash wouldn't come off for him."

Wide-eyed, she looked from Corren to Kennard to the guards, as if not knowing whether or not to believe him. She turned her frightened eyes back to him. He kept his eyes on her but slowly rested his staff against the wall. He didn't want her to be frightened of him.

Corren slowly approached and she took a step back. "I'm sorry, Lini, but the book needs to stay with us."

Lini circled around the chair and backed against the wall, clutching the box close to her.

He stopped, not wanting to bully her. "I need you to give me the book."

She looked fearfully at the door then back at Corren. "Where's Lord Tivoli? I want to see him."

Corren exchanged glances with Kennard, who lingered by the door, staff loosely in both hands. "I'll bring him down after you give me the book."

He slowly stepped forward, their eyes on one another, until he was right in front of her. She gripped the box with both hands, looked at him with those soft, dark eyes, and faintly shook her head no.

"Lini, I'm sorry," he said quietly. "That book belongs to the Madera branch of the Order. The Order is charged with protecting the Phoenix and our magic. The magic in the Book of Madera is not meant for the Orsini Colony." He lingered, so close he could reach out and embrace her. "Please," he said. "Hand me the book."

Just as quietly as he had been speaking to her, as if she felt as badly as he did, she said, "You'll have to take it from me by force."

Holding her eyes, he gently placed his hands on the rough, wooden box. "If I must."

He lightly pulled, watching her, pleading with her not to make him use magic against her. As they held each other's gaze,

212

her expression softened and relented. Her grip loosened and he slowly pulled it free.

She briefly closed her eyes. He placed one hand on her shoulder, squeezed, and stepped back, the Book of the Madera branch of the Order in his hands at last.

⸙ ⸙ ⸙

Lini watched Corren go, wondering at herself. How could she be more loyal to this wizard than to her own people? How could she allow him to affect her as he did?

As he turned away from her, she glanced at his staff, which she had first seen uncovered when they'd journeyed to the Rock of Light that morning. The wood at the tip curled around a dark substance she'd never seen or felt anywhere. No one told her what it was and she didn't ask, but somehow felt she knew.

Corren's back was to her, but she heard the creaking of the lid as he opened the box.

He spun, eyes narrowed, holding out the open box to reveal nothing. Nothing. It was empty.

She stared at the empty box in shock. When had Tivoli done this? She quickly realized she had not seen him with the book itself since they'd left the Hathmirrian border. She only saw him with the box. Did he leave the book back at the border?

"You tricked me," Corren said lowly, a flash of anger in his eyes.

"No—"

"You tricked me!" he yelled and turned his back on her. His anger seemed to come off of him in great waves. Even his guard Kennard looked alarmed.

"I didn't know," Lini said. "I swear I didn't."

"As *if*," Corren said in a frightening voice, "I would ever believe someone like you."

"Sage Corren—" Kennard began, reaching out his hand.

But Corren slammed the lid shut and flung the box toward the wall where it burst into flame and puffed out with a whiff of smoke before it ever touched the stone.

They all stood there watching him, equally frightened of him, or so it seemed to Lini. No one seemed to want to move. They all just watched him standing there, head down, pinching his eyes closed, and taking slow, deliberate breaths.

At last he lifted his head and looked at Kennard.

"Take them to Tower Hall South," he said in a voice that sounded more like his own but seething, nonetheless. He retrieved his staff and walked outside without a backward glance.

Three

Corren marched down the stone hallways of Tower Hall South, heading for the west wing where Tivoli and Lini were under guard. He had already searched the rooms they had stayed in, but of course the Book of Madera was nowhere to be found. He could send the Guard to go looking for it, but it could be anywhere. He needed Tivoli or Lini to tell him where it was. The other option would be to surround and forcibly search the camp at the border.

He was considering it.

Kennard was willing to do it.

But would that bring an all-out war between their two groups? He wanted to prevent that if he could. The two groups had only avoided war in the centuries before now because they were far enough apart to stay in their own territories and leave the other alone. They'd never had a reason to bother each other. Until now.

As if one crisis weren't enough, there was also the matter of the Tree. He'd gone back to the Tree the day before and was no more able to heal it after a solid night's sleep than he'd been before. He'd spent the rest of the day looking through Aradia's folios for some clue about what she'd done to the Tree so he could know how to undo it. Lily and the others were hanging on, but Corren could see there was no time to waste. He may have been able to offer more healing than Nicolai and Salerno had, but his was no more permanent.

Meanwhile, he couldn't neglect the situation with Tivoli either. Over fifty Orsini Colony members waited at the border for the return of their fellows. He could only imagine what they would do if they waited too long.

Everything was a mess.

He was embarrassed by his outburst at the Rock of Light. He hadn't meant to lose control like that. He wasn't exactly sure why he had. But even now, his face burned with anger when he thought about it. It was more than not having the Book of Madera. As important as that was, as much as he needed to figure out a way to get that book back from the Orsini Colony, as much as he hoped the book would help him understand what they needed to do to restart the Madera branch, it was more than that.

He had trusted Lini. As if Aradia's treachery had taught him nothing. When he had every reason to know Lini was no different than the others, why had he thought she was? Because he saw her crying one night?

He shook his head in frustration. He'd been a fool. Again.

Corren came to the wooden door, behind which Tivoli sat in confinement. Two Guard members stood watch. Lini was in the room next door. Though he expected it to be fruitless, he had decided to talk to Tivoli first.

Corren opened the door and stepped inside. Tivoli lay on his bed, unconcerned.

"Where's the book?" Corren asked.

Tivoli laughed.

"I'm not walking away from this without it," Corren said.

Tivoli gave him an evil grin. "What are you going to do? Torture me until I talk? Search every mile between here and the last place you saw it?" He went back to staring up at the ceiling. "It's safe enough from you, I made sure of that."

Corren wondered what Tivoli had done to keep the book safe. A book he was so protective of he never let it out of reach, even when surrounded by his own people. He thought about Lini getting in trouble for looking in the book. Corren scowled. No, of course Tivoli couldn't trust his own people. None of them could be trusted. So what had he done with it?

Search every mile, Tivoli had said. *Did* he hide it somewhere on the way down? But when would he have done that? He remembered watching Tivoli read the book at their last stop before hitting the border, back when Tivoli seemed fairly certain he had Corren under his control.

He looked at Tivoli smirking on the bed now. Corren had no doubt Tivoli *still* thought he had Corren under his control. Corren wasn't sure he was wrong.

"This is what's going to happen," Corren said. "You're going to stay here until you decide to deliver the book to the Order. When it's back in our care, we'll escort you and Lini to the border and you can return to your home in peace. Don't test me. I have no hesitation about keeping you here as long as it takes."

Tivoli looked at him darkly. "You think my people at the border will just wait and wait for my return? They'll come looking for me."

"We can handle your people at the border just fine." Corren turned to leave. "Don't bother calling unless you're ready to talk."

With that he left and shut the door, certain Tivoli would be more than happy to call his bluff. They would, in fact, need to decide what to do about the Orsini Colony waiting at the border. And what would stop that group from heading home and coming back with more people? Who was to say they hadn't already sent for reinforcements?

If Corren couldn't get Lini to talk, he would have to turn things over to Kennard. He and the Guard would need to get to the border as quickly as possible to conduct a search.

He lingered in the hallway, knowing he had to talk to Lini. The Guard members looked at him expectantly.

He reached for her door handle, then pulled back.

Gripping his staff with both hands, he took a steadying breath. Then he straightened, pulled himself together, and grabbed the handle.

Lini was sitting on the window ledge, watching the lush grounds fall to shadow as the sun set, when she heard the latch lift on the door. In came Corren, staff in hand. He shut the door and leaned against it. Crossing his arms, he looked at her with what she thought was a carefully neutral expression.

She wanted him to know she didn't trick him, but it probably wouldn't matter what she said. He didn't trust her. She wasn't sure she trusted him either. Tivoli insisted Corren prevented the ash from coming off the altar. Maybe so. But why did Corren save his life? Why not let Tivoli fall to the ground?

"I know you want the book," she said, "but I don't know where it is."

"Why would I believe you?"

She fussed with the ends of her crimson shawl. "Don't believe me; I can't help that." She looked at him firmly. "But even if Lord Tivoli had told me the box was empty, he wouldn't have told me where he hid the book."

Corren looked at her skeptically. That look of his made her chest hurt. Why couldn't she stop caring what this wizard thought of her?

"Tivoli chose you to come along with him. Why?"

"I already told you, I don't know."

"Is it because he knew you could help him hide the book?"

She sighed. "I didn't help him hide the book. I don't even know when he did it, though it seems it must have been before you—"

She looked at him. *Before you scared us all half to death,* she thought. She didn't even know how to describe what he'd done with the fire. "Before we left the others," she finally said.

He scowled at her. She wished he would stop. She dropped the ends of her shawl and scowled back at him. "Look, I don't know what you want me to say. I don't know where the book is."

"Did he hide it that day you all snuck away? The day your friend—"

He stopped.

She turned back to the window but didn't really see what was on the other side. She was back in the ravine, surrounded by the sharp smell of dirt and terror. She felt again Sienna letting go and her wrap jerking out of Lini's grasp. She saw again the look on Sienna's face as she fell. Lini closed her eyes now, as she'd done then, and sitting here on the stone ledge in Tower Hall South, heard again the bone-crunching sound of Sienna hitting the ground.

"I'm sorry," Corren said.

She glanced at him. He still stood against the door with his arms folded, but the scowl was gone. Though he'd tried keeping his distance, when their eyes met, the space between them seemed to vanish.

"The Madera branch did not bind themselves to us," she said. And she couldn't believe she said it. She hadn't meant to.

He raised his brow and dropped his arms, one hand loosely on his staff. "They didn't?"

She sighed and shook her head.

He took a step forward. "But you have the book. Did you steal it?"

She nodded. "Four hundred years ago, our people found the last of the Madera branch near the Hathmirrian border. We weren't looking for them."

Corren slowly made his way toward her, listening intently.

"Lord Steele, the leader at the time, had been scouting the border. I forget why. Something to do with establishing a second compound in that area. Anyway, it never happened. The Madera branch, they were a pretty small group." She shrugged. "Compared to ours." The details weren't important.

Corren sat on the chair near her, his brows furrowed and his eyes on her. She could see his mind trying to work it all out.

"We captured them and stole the book, among other things. They didn't give it to us. They supposedly protected it with some sort of spell, but I don't know what."

"What happened to the branch members?"

"Lord Steele disposed of them, but he saved a few of their children for recruits."

"The Madera branch had their families with them too?" Not waiting for her to answer, he said, "It makes sense. When they ran out of ash, they abandoned their headquarters and moved somewhere else, though no one knew where. But then..."

He looked at her sharply. "The descendants. We have to find the descendants. Maybe that's who gets the ash."

Lini shook her head. "There are no descendants. Orphans are sterilized."

Corren sat there in his dark cloak, considering things, absently tapping his staff with one finger. "So there's no magical binding giving you claim to the ash?"

Lini shook her head.

"There's just some sort of spell on the book?"

She nodded. She went back to fussing with her head shawl, running her fingertips along the gold lace trim.

He furrowed his brows at her. "Why are you telling me this?"

She shrugged. She didn't know herself. "We're not getting the ash anyway." She thought again of the way Corren surrounded her entire group with fire. What were they supposed to do against something like that?

They looked at one another again. Considering each other. Such a strange combination of connection and uncertainty she felt for this wizard.

"And the ceremony?" he asked quietly.

Lini pressed her lips together and shook her head. She did not want to speak of the ceremony he'd witnessed. She'd said enough.

Not far from the Hathmirrian border, Tivoli, Lini, and their escort of ten Guard members made camp for the night. Kennard made it clear that's as far as they would go unless he was able to get the Orsinians on the other side of the border to agree to a trade.

Not long into their journey, Tivoli had told Lini he had no intention of remaining their prisoner. "These wizards are not as powerful as Corren. I have," he had whispered to her darkly, "a plan."

What that plan was Lini had no opportunity to discover. Kennard saw them whispering together, broke it up, and kept them separated for the rest of the trip.

While Kennard may not have been as powerful as Corren, Lini suspected he was a formidable wizard in his own right. She could not see any escape attempts being successful under his watch. He kept a particularly close eye on Tivoli and had, she could see, no kind feelings for her lord and master.

His interactions with her, by contrast, were neither kind nor cruel. They were perfunctory and no more, but she had several times caught him watching her curiously. As if she were a puzzle he was trying to figure out.

Lini could see Tivoli had not abandoned whatever his plan was. She knew that brooding, determined expression. She couldn't work out how he planned to do it. They were wildly outnumbered and under constant watch, even at night. The Guard had confiscated his staff and kept it strapped to one of the horses. Still, if anyone could find a way, it would be Lord Tivoli.

She wondered if he would escape with her or leave her behind. She didn't even know which she wanted to have happen.

Now they sat camped near the border, gathered around a sizable fire, while the Guard members discussed their plan for negotiating the book in exchange for their prisoners.

"They'll never agree," Tivoli said.

The Guard members scoffed, but Lini thought he was probably right. If he left the book in someone's care with the command to keep it safe sealed by the *Alehess* spell, they would die before disobeying.

Just like Sienna.

* * *

221

Kennard and his negotiation party departed not long after dawn. That left only four Guard members with Tivoli and Lini. Still outnumbered. Still under constant observation. Still seemingly secure, but Lini watched Tivoli closely. If he were going to try anything, wouldn't it be now?

She was not disappointed in her prediction.

Tivoli stood, held out both hands toward one of the Guard members, and shouted "*Puum umptu.*"

Sparking and popping, a purple light flew toward their captors, who answered with raised staffs and spells of their own. They deflected Tivoli's purple light, which went high into the sky—the only place it could go, Lini knew—then sent a binding spell to Tivoli. As he fell on the ground, they directed a binding spell toward Lini for good measure.

She fell on her back with a perfect view of Tivoli's beacon, sputtering and crackling in the air where it could be seen and heard for miles.

The Guard members with Lini and Tivoli apparently considered the possibility that Tivoli had sent some sort of signal. They moved to a new camp, kept Lini and Tivoli magically bound as a precaution, and sent out scouts to watch for any potential problems. That potential problem manifested itself as two dozen Orsini Colony members stormed the camp from three different directions.

Lini and Tivoli lay helpless, bound by the spells, until all of a sudden, they were free. She sat up, got a better view of the battle, and saw several bodies lying on the ground. Six were those of her fellows and two were Guard members, including the one who had cast the binding spell. The spell must have been released at his death.

The fighting continued, but Tivoli sprinted for his staff. When he had it in hand, he lunged for Lini, seized her by the wrist, and took off. She struggled to keep up at first but then found her stride, and Tivoli let go as they ran side by side, the sounds of the fighting fading behind them.

Four

Marcellus stood in front of the hidden spring, still dressed. The crisp, morning air chilled him slightly. The sun had not yet broken the horizon and the sky was a dusky blue. The surface of the water swirled gently, as it ever did.

He'd dreamt of this water.

Dreamt of commanding it—every single drop.

He'd woken from his dream with his heart pounding. He lay on his back, staring at the ceiling until his room began to lighten.

Now here he was.

He flexed his fingers then rubbed his palms against the thick linen of his tunic. He did not take his eyes off the water.

He thought of Janus, sleeping in her room; he could feel her from here. These days, a flame of fear licked his heart every time he thought of her, but he tried to ignore that. Corren or Nicolai would heal the Tree soon. They had to.

He'd been watching Nicolai becoming more and more the master of his element, which only served to remind him how much he, Marcellus, was holding back with his own element.

But something about the dream made him want to let go.

Marcellus raised his hands. He felt the elements on the surface of the water and tried to take hold of them. They began to roil. He reached for the elements deeper in the spring too.

Churning and rocking, the water threatened to spill beyond the boundaries of the pool. He raised his arms and the surface of the water lifted higher and higher. The watery mass, big as a barn, swirled and spun above the rim of the pool.

Ah! his heart cried. *Look at it!*

He wanted to form the swirling mass into a smooth ball. He exerted his will upon it, but it was too forceful. Too much. Too something.

He lost control and the mass of water exploded. The force of the wave that came his way knocked him backward, and he stumbled to regain his balance and keep from falling as the water rushed past him.

When the deluge ceased, he wiped the water off his face and looked around. Water puddled on the ground. It glistened on the rocks. It dripped from every limb in sight.

"That... didn't go as planned."

Foolishly, he reached out toward Janus and sighed in relief to feel that she was still in her room sleeping, as if she could have witnessed his error from there.

Still, though. He'd done *something*.

He walked along the edge of the spring, feet slapping on the water-soaked ground. He looked down. The water level was only half what it normally was.

He ran his hands over his wet hair, the excess water trailing down the back of his neck. He heard the water all around, drip, drip, dripping from the trees.

He felt every last bit of it.

Giving the water a stern look, like a commander preparing to call his troops to battle, Marcellus reached out his arms once more.

He gathered the water off the branches, bringing it down in flowing ribbons where it joined the water on the ground. The ribbons of water flowed toward the spring, meandering along the ground and over the edge of the pool.

Marcellus gathered and corralled the water until every branch was dry and the pool restored to its former level.

The surface of the water swirled gently as it ever did.

Marcellus watched it... and smiled.

224

Late on the evening of their escape, Lini and Tivoli arrived at a wayside house within Hathmirrian territory. Only Bricker and five other members waited for them there, as they had for the last eight days. After Corren's frightening display with the fire, Tivoli had ordered these six to sneak away and wait for him. And what did they bring with them but the Book of Madera.

Bricker now brought it to Tivoli, who took it into his arms and ran his hand along the gilded letters on the cover. He glanced at Lini, then the others. "Routt, you stand guard. If you see any of those wizards coming, we don't fight, we run. Rendezvous at the Wiedemann house if we get separated. Get some sleep. We leave early tomorrow."

"Leave for where?" Lini asked.

Tivoli gave her a hard look. He was in no mood to be questioned, obviously.

She remembered to bow her head deferentially. "I am sorry, Lord Tivoli."

"To bed," he barked. "Lini, come with me."

She followed him into the room where he'd be sleeping. He instructed her to sit on a nearby stool while he sat on the edge of the bed, the book tucked securely under his arm.

"You are to tell me," he said, "everything you discussed with the wizard."

She answered promptly, careful not to hesitate or seem like she was thinking. She said Corren tried to intimidate her, but she insisted she did not know where the book was. Which was true. To her surprise, Tivoli did not question her further. Instead he stood, handed her the book, and asked, "And would you give it to him now? Now that you have it? *Alehess*, Lini, answer honestly."

"No," she said.

"Who is your leader until death takes you?"

"You, Lord Tivoli."

"What gives you life and purpose?"

"The Orsini Colony, Lord Tivoli."

"Are you fading in the Ways of Orsini?" he asked.

225

"A little," she answered, because it's what would have been true anyway.

"We will handle that in the morning."

"I will be grateful for it, Lord Tivoli."

"Lini," he said, "open that book and tell me what you see."

Knowing she should not hesitate, she opened the cover to reveal the yellowed title page. "It is the Book of the Madera branch—"

"Not that," he said, squatting down and turning several pages until he came to what he was looking for. He stopped at the illustration of the map he had used to lead them down into the ravine and the cave. "Does this mean something to you?"

She furrowed her brows and looked at him. "My Lord?"

"Tell me what you see."

She looked at the pages spread before her. "I see a map, my Lord. It looks like the place we have already been."

"It is," he said, taking the book from her and sitting on the bed with it open on his lap. He turned a page and fell to reading. She watched him, confused. He waved a hand at her and said without looking up, "You may go. Be ready for the High Ceremony in the morning."

She stood and left the room, pondering.

Lini lay awake long after the house went quiet. Eventually she sat up, kicked her feet over the side of the bed, and stared at the floor. The idea that had been forming in her mind since their escape from the Guard had been growing and growing until it was all she could think about.

It would put her life at risk. Again. But then, what was one more thing? She was beginning to wonder if she weren't looking for a quick end to her own life.

But this felt different. This was about something bigger.

The room was dark, but enough moonlight crept through the windows to guide the way. She stood, careful not to let the bed make any noise. On bare feet she padded to her door, put her ear against it, and, when she heard nothing, carefully lifted the latch.

The hallway was dark, untouched by the moonlight coming in the front windows. She tiptoed down the hall, ears perked, eyes searching for any sign of her fellows. The front room was empty. Everyone was asleep, as far as she could tell, except for (one would hope) the guard out front.

She went to the window and pulled back the drape. She did not see him at first, but then he shifted in his seat and put his feet up on the railing of the fence that ran along the road. He was a good distance from the house.

She did not remember Tivoli ordering a guard for the rear of the house. The main thing was to watch the road, and even that was just in case. How would the Guard know to look for them here? They were in their own country, and they had plenty of rabbit holes like this one. They were as good as gone.

Lini went to the back of the house anyway. There was no window, so she had to open the back door in order to check the surroundings. No one. She closed the door and returned to the front window. The guard by the road must not have heard her open and close the back door; he had not moved at all.

Lini stood and let the drape fall back into place. She felt her heart beating against her chest as she made her decision.

Her breath was shallow. Tense.

Still in her bare feet, she crept to Tivoli's room. Hand on the doorjamb, ear against the door, she heard him softly snoring. She wondered if the door would creak. She wondered if he would buy her excuse if he woke up and found her in his room.

She swung the door open with just the slightest creak, but it sounded like a blast in her ears. She froze, watching him for the slightest reaction. He lay on his back, mouth open. A low snore escaped him. She let a soundless breath of her own escape her lips and glanced around the room.

She located the book on the table next to the bed. It was still open, as if he'd fallen asleep reading it. She would have to go right next to him in order to get it.

She hesitated, rethinking everything. She could turn around and go back to her room right now and no one would ever know. And in the morning... what then?

She made up her mind for the tenth time that night. She had to at least try.

The more she lingered, she knew, the more likely she was to be discovered. Proceeding as quietly as possible, she forced herself to take one step after another. She drew closer and closer, with one eye on the book and one on Lord Tivoli. He seemed to rear up and loom before her the nearer she came. She imagined him waking suddenly and seizing her.

Too afraid to even breathe, she came to the table, put her hands on the book, and lifted it soundlessly, eyes wide on her leader.

She held her breath as she crept back out of the room and slowly shut the door. Breathing again and walking faster now, she waited until she got back to her room before closing the book for fear the spine would creak—which it did. She grabbed her bag, which she'd already packed with her cloak and shoes, and continued barefooted to the back door.

Kai'Enna led Praea and the rest of their girls through a series of aerial maneuvers. They picked up on her signals and moved into position smoothly.

As one, they practiced gathering the element of air in front of them. It billowed together like a cloud. Thickening and strengthening it, they hovered behind it and held it in place. Like a shield.

Which, of course, it was.

They were not yet ready to fight dragons, but they knew how to defend themselves from them. That would have to be enough.

Now that she knew a man like Lord Tivoli held the Book of Madera, she could not wait any longer.

They had to scout out the Golden Canyon and find out what dragons still lived there. If they were to return and stand guard over the Golden Canyon Entrance, they needed to know just what they were up against.

Tivoli sat in the rear courtyard of the wayhouse. They'd spent the last several days looking for Lini with no luck. The first place he checked, of course, was the entrance to the Shoals. There was no evidence she had been there. Would she have gone back over the border? Somewhere else in Hathmirr? It made him boil to think of it. How dare she!

But more than that, he brooded, how *could* she? She was free from the Ways of Orsini; that much was clear. She had probably lied to him at the ravine as well. But *how*? How was she able to achieve it?

He thought back to the High Ceremony that the wizard Corren had witnessed. Tivoli was fairly certain they'd given Lini her dose before the whole thing came to a halt, so she would have received the potion then. Besides, they'd held another High Ceremony before leaving the compound.

He sat with his hands steepled under his chin. If Lini could do this, who else could? He'd already tested the members he had with them. They were still held by the magic, and many of them had self-inflicted wounds to prove it.

But what of Lini?

He thought of the entrance to the Shoals. Lini must want the magic that lay deep in the Shoals as much as he did. Why else would she steal the book? Did she think she could steal the magic in the Vortex? Beat him to it? Perhaps use her new powers to supplant him?

Well, he knew she wasn't yet in the Shoals, and he'd left two members near the entrance with orders to kill anyone who approached, unless it was him.

On Tivoli's lap was the small leather folio he kept in his bag. In it were the transcriptions he'd taken from the book. After all, he'd needed a copy he could access on his own. He'd transcribed the most important things first: the map to the entrance, the interior map of the Shoals, key magical properties of the Vortex. He'd gotten far enough along in his note taking that he'd started transcribing less important things in the book, with the intent of eventually having a complete copy.

It looked like that wouldn't happen now. Within three days, he'd lost both his hopes for getting the ash and the Book of Madera. Originally, getting the ash had been a goal unto itself. He knew the Phoenix ash would give the Orsini Colony even more power. Of course they'd wanted it. But his recent examination of the Book of Madera revealed a much more enticing reason for obtaining the ash. And even though he knew he could no longer hope to use the ash to breech the barrier inside the Shoals, he also knew there was another way.

Bricker came into the courtyard and bowed.

"Is our watery friend still waiting near Port Malado?" Tivoli asked.

"As far as we know, Lord Tivoli."

He stood and walked toward the door. "Good. Let's get going."

Five

Janus sat on the soft, moss-covered bench next to Lily's bed. Instead of wearing her knight's uniform, she'd taken to visiting Lily in her *undanna* cloak, which puddled softly at her feet. It seemed to bring Lily some measure of comfort. When Lily was awake, Janus told her old stories or entertained her with elaborate flower-blooming demonstrations. Sometimes these elicited a faint smile; other times she'd watch with a vacant expression.

Mostly, Lily slept. And this would be when Janus, exhausted from keeping up the act, would lay her head on her arm and fall asleep herself.

Praea, Kai'Enna, and their young Tulaga flew low over the Mountains of Vitra. As they neared the realm of the dragons, Praea gave the signal and the girls tightened their formation, flying nearly wingtip to wingtip. They flew over the ruins of mountain villages the Tulaga had once protected from the dragons. Praea had taught the girls the characteristics of the six different types of dragon and told them the purpose of this scouting mission was to find out which ones (and just how many) they'd have to displace from the Golden Canyon before they could, once again, call it home.

Of course, their ultimate goal went far beyond that, though only Praea and Kai'Enna understood this.

Just two nights ago, she and Kai'Enna sat in a broad elm with the moonlight shining down through the many branches. Here,

Kai'Enna revealed the last of their branch's secrets. Praea had already known how their founder combined what she had learned from the Phoenix with what she had learned from the faeries to design the first Tulaga transformation. And Praea knew *of* the Mapmaker, but she did not—until recently—know of his end. But within the branches of the elm, Kai'Enna told Praea about the Shoals and the Vortex and the Mapmaker's theft. Thus, Praea discovered the true reason the Tulaga settled the Golden Canyon: to guard the entrance into the Shoals.

"I wasn't going to tell you," Kai'Enna said. "I had hoped the knowledge of the Vortex had finally been lost. But the Orsini Colony has the Book of Madera." Kai'Enna's aged face was mottled with moonlight and shadow. "They know about the Vortex and how to get to it. Tivoli is not the kind of man to let that lie."

Praea and Kai'Enna weren't keen on bringing their girls into a potentially dangerous situation, but they both agreed they shouldn't delay. Rather than spend time training for each kind of dragon, they'd find out what was there then go back and prepare.

Their instructions to the girls were simple: stay together. If they encountered dragons, they were to fly away as one. If necessary, they would form a shield to protect themselves until they could escape.

As they went deeper into the mountains and through the corridor leading toward the Golden Canyon, the Tulaga slowed down, scanning for signs of dragons. They came around a bend where the broad canyon presented itself. On one side of the flat bottom of the canyon was a lake that was once surrounded by mountain villages, along with one of the outposts of the Madera branch before they disappeared. The lake had been terrorized by a Silver Spikeback dragon for years before the inhabitants finally gave up and abandoned their homes to the wild.

Beyond the lake was the river that carved a gorge deep into the far end of the canyon. The river was a wild tributary full of rapids and roaring waterfalls, and somewhere in the gorge above was the entrance to the Shoals. Far above the river and the gorge, carved out of the red rock in the side of the sheer canyon wall, was the Golden Canyon.

Praea was unprepared for its grandeur. It was more striking than the grandest palace she had ever seen. Even from this distance, she could see its ornate columns and delicate terraces, the plants and trees of which had grown wild without caretakers. There were no steps or paths leading up to it. This was a place one could get to only in the air. It truly could belong to only one of two creatures: the Tulaga or the dragons.

They slowed their approach, sticking close together and keeping a watchful eye out. Dragons tended to sleep this time of day, but who wanted to sneak up on a sleeping dragon?

They flew the perimeter of the lake first, looking for any signs of dragon habitation and finding none. It was both encouraging and unnerving. There were many places that would have made for ideal dragon-roosting grounds. But maybe they'd migrated elsewhere.

Having checked the lake, they rose to the Golden Canyon itself. As they flew across the gorge and to the stronghold carved out of rock, Praea knew this would be the most dangerous part of the mission. They would have to go into the complex and search the rooms to see if any dragons were there.

The front courtyard was flanked on either side by towering columns of rock, and the slate floor was littered with debris. Dead leaves skitted across the stone as the Tulaga flew in and landed. They transformed back into their natural form— Jesaray's dark ringlets an amusing comparison to the golden bird she had been just minutes before—and headed toward the grand double doors. The doors hung open and were broad and high enough that they could have flown through. One door was in pieces, the stone having cracked long ago. The remnants lay scattered on the floor at its base.

Even in its decrepit state, Praea was in awe at the sheer majesty of the place. It took the Tulaga over a hundred years to build it; now Praea understood why. How hard it must have been to let it go. Even in its current neglected state, Praea already wanted to stay and never leave. For the first time, she felt the weight of their history. This was their rightful place. It was home.

They passed through the doors into a tall entryway with an ornately carved ceiling. Natural light flooded through sheltered openings in the high walls, letting in light while still protecting the interior from wind and rain. In spite of the decay—more debris littered the floor, though to a lesser degree—the openness of this interior room kept the air from being musty. It was almost as fresh as the air outside.

From here they could go in one of three directions: to the grand rooms on either side or up the broad stairway deeper into the mountain. The rooms to either side were likewise lit by openings that let in the sunlight. The area at the top of the stairs and beyond, however, was dark as a cave. All Praea could see were the faint outlines of old, grand chandeliers hanging from the ceiling. Of course, in bird form, they could see well enough in the dark. Still, Praea wasn't looking forward to those explorations.

If a dragon wanted a place to call home, the dark cave of abandoned rooms up the staircase seemed a likely area. However, the rooms to the right and left were mere gateways to more rooms, some of which extended along the face of the mountain, and others of which went deeper into it.

Praea looked at Kai'Enna for direction, but she was already heading to the left. Praea and the others followed. They proceeded slowly, looking all around and listening for any movement.

The Golden Canyon was silent as a tomb.

They passed through room after room. They were largely empty, but there was the occasional armoire or chair, broken and rotting in a corner. Iron lamp fixtures protruded from the walls, which were otherwise empty.

Most of the rooms branched off into yet more rooms. They had all studied the maze-like map of the Golden Canyon, and Praea tried to keep it all straight in her head now that they were there. Everything was so much bigger than she'd anticipated.

She made notes in her mental map, hoping she remembered it correctly.

Kai'Enna led them through the front rooms lit by natural light until she reached the end. At that point they turned around, went back the way they came, and explored the front side of the opposite wing. No sign of dragons.

As much as Praea wanted to think the Golden Canyon was now dragon free, that they wouldn't have to chase any away after all, she was too acutely aware of the many dark rooms they'd passed that retreated further into the mountain.

They returned to the entryway and began ascending the stairs. Approaching the dark landing, they drew more tightly together.

Jesaray whispered to Praea, "I'm not afraid."

"I know you're not, honey." Whether foolish or not, she probably wasn't. She had more gumption than most of the other recruits, as if determined to make up for her small size. "Still, stay by me."

When they reached the landing, Kai'Enna gave the signal and they transformed into birds. Now able to see through the dark, the cavernous maze of rooms opened up before them. The ceilings were high and the hallways broad—truly designed for their flying inhabitants—but they wanted to proceed as soundlessly as possible and so stayed on the ground.

Following Kai'Enna's lead, they kept their heads down and eyes alert as they went deeper into the complex. Those in the rear looked behind more than they were looking forward. Necessary though it was, Praea couldn't help but feel this was too dangerous. Could these girls use their defensive magic in such a closed-in space? Gathering air into a shield was easier to do when leveraging larger air currents. Here, anything they managed to pull together wouldn't be as strong.

But what other option? How else would they be able to claim the Golden Canyon and watch over the entrance to the Shoals if they didn't first rid the area of dragons?

The quality of the air began to change. It grew cooler and there was a sharp scent suggesting something was rotting nearby. They continued cautiously, skirting a large chandelier that had long ago fallen from the ceiling and crashed to the floor.

Farther ahead, curious shapes came into view on the ground. Praea couldn't quite make them out, but they weren't moving. As they carefully drew closer, she saw what they were: the bones of a deer, the feathers of an eagle, the crushed skull of some unidentified animal. Kai'Enna stopped briefly, glanced at Praea, and kept going.

Soon after, they came to a large nest. Woven with thick branches and as large as their little group, it was empty.

Praea knew this had to belong to a Flying Jasmine, the one dragon she dreaded seeing more than any other. Fierce and fearless, this was the worst kind of tenant to try to evict. The only good news was they would only have one dragon to contend with. Flying Jasmines did not share their space. It explained the lack of dragons around the lake. Even other dragons avoided the Flying Jasmine.

The fact that the nest was empty did little to encourage her. The entrails on the ground were too fresh to assume this was an old site. Her only question was: why wasn't the dragon here?

Then she remembered. An oddity among dragons, Flying Jasmines were the only ones to build nests, warble like a songbird, and sleep during the day rather than at night. That meant...

Praea heard the ominous flapping of great wings—far too great to belong to a Tulaga—along with the warning cry of the girls in the rear. She turned and saw the massive beast sweeping down the hall toward them.

Kai'Enna gave the signal and they gathered the air into a shield, gray as smoke, as the dragon sped toward them. More than a shield, though, they needed a way out.

Praea remembered from her studies of the map that if they escaped to the chamber to the left, they'd end up in a dead end, but if they went to the right, that would lead them through a series of rooms to the front of the complex and their escape.

Kai'Enna obviously remembered as well. She gave another signal. The Tulaga and their shield shifted towards the right as the dragon came to them.

The room lit up as the dragon shot fire in their direction. Praea caught a glimpse of its brilliant crimson scales before the fire overtook everything in sight.

The swirling gray shield held, but only barely. It deflected the flames away but could not absorb the full measure of heat. Several of the girls tucked their heads under their wings in defense.

The dragon reared on its hind legs, as if recharging for another blast, which it probably was. Praea gave the signal for the girls to strengthen the shield, then noticed one girl was missing.

Frantic, she looked at each one, then turned her attention back to the shield as they withstood another scorching blast from the dragon. *Jesaray*, she thought. *Where's Jesaray?*

Kai'Enna looked around frantically as well. One of the girls gave a crying shriek, indicating an area behind the dragon. That's when Praea saw her.

Jesaray was huddled behind a pillar, her head sticking out. She must have gotten confused and gone the wrong way at Kai'Enna's command, but now the poor girl was so frightened she had even changed out of bird form.

Her little hand rested on the pillar and her wide eyes looked up in horror at the dragon towering high above her. A dragon that was, for the moment, oblivious to her presence.

Jesaray must have remembered the rooms on that side of the hall were a dead end, for she kept looking from the dragon to her fellow Tulaga, as if wondering how she was going to get across.

Praea and Kai'Enna glanced at one another. Kai'Enna gave a sharp cry that Praea understood to mean, *Get the girls out,* then sent a powerful blast humming through the air toward the dragon's head—an offensive spell the girls had not yet mastered.

More irritated than hurt, the dragon jerked its head back and it howled in rage. The room rumbled and vibrated in response.

While the dragon reared, Kai'Enna flew out from the protection of the shield and to the other side toward Jesaray.

Resisting the urge to follow, Praea knew her first duty was to get the rest of the girls to safety. Spreading her wings and urging them back, they took flight, speeding through the darkened rooms. The dragon came after them quickly, but the one advantage they all had over the dragon was speed.

Praea called to them in sharp trills, commanding them to fly hard. As they advanced ahead of her, Praea hung back slightly. She hoped to stay just close enough to lure the dragon out of the complex so Kai'Enna and Jesaray could escape behind it undetected.

The walls and ceiling of the hallway lit up orange as the dragon sent fire toward her. Unable to outfly the blast or create a strong enough shield on her own, she took a hard right into another room. This gave her some protection from the fire, but it also put her too near the approaching Flying Jasmine for comfort.

Its claws scratched at the stone walls as it came around the corner after her. She flew hard now. The dragon flew hard after her.

As she raced for the bright openings ahead, she heard its massive wings and sensed its bulk filling the space behind her. She could smell the charred scent of its breath.

Into a front room, through an opening, and into the bright sunlight at last, she saw her young recruits sailing over the clear surface of the lake. The dragon roared behind her as she cleared the exterior porches and steadily increased the distance between them. A plume of churning fire shot in her direction but she was out of reach now. The flames dissipated as she sped ahead.

She looked back and saw the dragon fly past the grand balcony, leaving the entrance open where, indeed, Kai'Enna and Jesaray—back in bird form—emerged. But as Praea looked back, so, too, did the dragon. Sensing a better opportunity, it turned course and flew back at Kai'Enna.

Kai'Enna and Jesaray split in two directions, already too few for a shield and now even more defenseless. Ignoring Jesaray, the dragon followed Kai'Enna, who was starting to gather the elements for an offensive attack. The dragon pulled its head down and opened its massive jaws wide. Praea turned back without thinking, for she knew the second before it happened who was going to be the victor of this battle.

Fire poured out of the dragon's mouth and engulfed Kai'Enna in flame. She dropped and tumbled wing over talon, a fiery ball, down and down into the gorge below the Golden Canyon.

Praea screeched, diving for her. The dragon swung its great head in Praea's direction. Furious and frightened, she gathered the wind into a blast and sent the swirling mass toward the dragon's snout. It huffed and paused momentarily, but she knew it'd be after her in moments.

Still tumbling out of control, Kai'Enna transformed back into her natural form and hit the river with a sickening splash. As Praea dove down, she spotted a blackened Kai'Enna rolling about in the waters below.

Praea swooped down and scooped her up but was stunned by how hot she was and nearly dropped her. Ignoring her burning talons and the sound of the dragon flapping and roaring behind her, she sped over the surface of the river. She raced along the winding canyon until the screeches of the dragon fell away, and she was free of it at last.

Praea looked down at her mentor and saw in a moment that she was lost. Her withered body was misshapen and nearly unrecognizable.

Praea looked away sharply, unable to bear it. Her cries echoed again and again off the canyon walls.

Six

Praea awoke in one of the rooms in Kai'Enna's cottage. In the bed with her was Nicolai. He held her from behind—her back and legs pressed snugly into him—breathing softly as he slept.

Her first destination, after escaping the mountains with Kai'Enna's body in tow, had not been the cottage. It had been Tower Hall South. She went there for so many reasons: to seek direction from Corren, to keep Kai'Enna's body away from the girls, and to see if he knew how to reach Nicolai. They wrapped Kai'Enna's body in a linen shroud, then Corren swept his staff over Praea's feet and healed her.

But there was nothing he could do to heal her heart. He said he would notify the rest of the Order and she left for Kai'Enna's cottage.

When she arrived, Praea found the girls, including Jesaray, shaken but unharmed. She got there just in time, for they were about to go back to the Golden Canyon to conduct a search in case Praea and Kai'Enna were injured but still alive.

After the girls retired for the night, she returned to Tower Hall South to see if Corren had been successful contacting Nicolai, and sure enough, there he was. Nicolai returned with her and held her until she fell asleep.

Waking now in the face of a new day, Praea felt the weight of what had happened. Not only had she lost a dear friend and mentor, she was now in charge of her branch. The new Head. And she wasn't ready. There were still so many things Kai'Enna had to teach her.

It would not be the first time in the last few hundred years an apprentice had to complete her training on her own. That had been the risk of having only two Tulaga at a time, the only way they could have made their small amount of ash last. As a result, her branch had too frequently been on the brink of extinction. Now here she was. While they at least had new recruits now, they were yet again left without a fully trained Tulaga to take over as Head. She'd thought once they had a normal supply of ash and brought in new recruits, they wouldn't have to face something like this again.

The cottage was still and quiet, Kai'Enna's absence a tangible thing in the air. It was up to Praea to finish training herself, continue the work of rebuilding their branch, and somehow protect the entrance to the Shoals.

Praea wrapped her arms over Nicolai's, closed her eyes, and took a deep breath. Thus cocooned in his embrace, she resolved to find a way.

Nicolai found Praea sitting at a small wooden table under a cluster of aspens at the edge of the meadow. A narrow mountain spring trickled nearby. He assumed this was the only place she could get a moment's peace as Kai'Enna's house was filled to the rafters with her fellow Tulaga. She was leaning studiously over a massive book, her forehead resting in her palm.

He quietly approached and placed a single orange poppy on the page.

She looked up as he pulled a chair next to her and sat down. "It's lovely," she said, bringing the poppy to her nose. He put his arm around her and she leaned into him.

"How are you?"

She shrugged weakly. "I don't know. Tired."

He rubbed her back as she twirled the flower between her fingers. The water gurgled gently behind them. Across the meadow, a sparrow hopped and pecked at something on the ground. In the freshness of the morning, Praea rested her head on his shoulder and his heart broke for her. So much death in her young life. In less than a year, she'd lost two brothers and now her mentor. Her father, while not dead, wasn't exactly here for her either. "What can I do for you?"

She shook her head. "Nothing right now." Her hand reached for his and he took it. "When do you need to go back?"

He'd explained last night that, much as he wanted to, he could not stay during the day. Of course, he couldn't say why, but she hadn't asked. She said she would fly him back to Tower Hall South in the morning when he was ready. "In a bit, but would you like me to come back tonight?"

She set the poppy on the table next to the book. "No. Yes. I don't know. I don't know what I need."

He squeezed her hand again. "I'll be at Tower Hall South again tonight anyway," he said. "If you need me, I'll be there. If not, that's alright too."

She smiled faintly and exhaled. "Thank you. I'll see how today goes."

"Have you eaten?"

She shook her head.

"I'll make you and the girls something. Then we can go."

She smiled gratefully and he gave her a kiss on the forehead before heading back toward the house. He was halfway across the meadow when she called his name.

"Nicolai?" She said it so quietly he almost didn't hear her.

He turned.

She was standing now, next to the table, and holding the flower in one hand. She was looking at it with furrowed brows. He walked back in her direction. She did not move. She only stared at the flower as if it held the key to some puzzle she needed to solve.

"Praea?"

"The poppy," she said faintly. "I'd forgotten."

"Forgotten what?"

She looked at him with the same expression she'd been giving the flower. "You made one bloom. Down in the gardens. A poppy just like this one." She seemed to be talking to herself

242

more than to him, like she was trying to put something together in her mind.

He thought he knew what it was. His skin began to prick.

Long ago, it seemed now, she had observed him in the king's gardens. Thinking he was alone, he'd gently stroked the bud of a poppy until it bloomed. It was only a small bit of faerie magic he assumed would go unseen. But Praea had been on an upper terrace and seen him. He'd been able to avoid her questions and since forgotten about the incident. Until now.

"I was walking on a path above and you were below—" looking back at the flower now, "—and you made it bloom. I saw you do it." She held up one finger as if to ward off any potential denials on his part but did not look at him. Instead, she paced several steps away, the cursed poppy still in her grip. "But that flower had nothing to do with the Phoenix and your stone, did it?"

"Praea—"

"All the strange things I'd seen from you when we first met," she said, "once I found out about the Phoenix and the prophecy and all the rest..." She spun and looked at him square on. He wanted to make her stop. "I thought it explained everything, but I'd forgotten about the poppy."

Nicolai's heart pounded in his chest and his skin crawled. "Praea—"

"And then the man in the forest. You knew each other." Her voice was strong now, as if she was done putting the pieces together and had come to a conclusion.

She stepped toward him. He actually took a step back. "Please—" he said.

"You once said you aren't a wizard, and you aren't, are you?" She drew closer still. "Old legends speak of a people who lived under the earth. A people who could make things grow, just as you did." She stopped right next to him, holding his eyes. "You're an earth faerie. Aren't you?"

He could not speak. He could not say yes or no. He could not lie, could not admit. Here she was, right in front of him, saying aloud the secret he had sworn to keep.

"It's true," she breathed. "I see it in your eyes."

"Praea, please."

"That's why. That explains it all. That's how you know Salerno."

He blinked. Those words out of her mouth were as shocking as the others. "How do *you* know Salerno?"

She looked slightly alarmed, as if she'd been caught inside of her own secret. "The legends..." she said. "The legends talk of the earth faeries and their king, Salerno." Her eyes grew wide. "The king. Why have you been pretending to be King Clement's son?"

"I *am* King Clement's son." But she turned away, not listening. He could see her trying to take it all in.

"And King Marcellus, does he know? Why does he think you're his brother? Oh, why didn't I see this sooner?"

"Praea, *listen*," he said firmly.

She stopped, reacting to his tone of voice more than anything. She watched him expectantly. The stream gurgled and the birds chirped and he thought of the different lies he could tell to cover things up, but he could not. Aside from the fact that he did not tell her of his origin with the faeries—she'd figured it out on her own—he refused to lie to her any longer.

He took a deep breath. Enough was enough. "Come," he said gently. "Sit down. I'll explain everything."

Late in the afternoon, Corren followed Delossa across the grounds of Tower Hall South. Still unsettled by Kai'Enna's unexpected death, he wasn't sure he wanted to see whatever it was Delossa had to show him. The serious expression on her face was enough to make him leery. And he didn't need one more thing.

He still couldn't believe Kai'Enna was gone, and it seemed so senseless to start with. What was she thinking, taking so few of them into a dragon stronghold like that?

At last, Delossa stopped. "Over there," she said, pointing to an alcove created by some piney hedges.

And indeed Corren saw. Lini. Lini who was supposed to be at the border with Kennard. And no Kennard in sight.

Corren halted. They were still some distance away. Lini saw him but did not move either.

"Where's Kennard?" he asked Delossa.

"She didn't say. She just said she wanted to see you."

Lini watched him with those eyes, and he couldn't tell if she were glad to see him or frightened of him or both. She did not look like she came to make trouble. But how could he know?

"You left her here unguarded?"

"I know," Delossa said quietly. "But... she looked too frightened to be much of a threat. I think she just wants to talk to you."

Maybe so, Corren thought, *but where's Kennard?*

"Wait here," he said and approached Lini, his staff in hand.

As he neared she withdrew farther into the shelter of the hedges. He paused, wondering if she were luring him into some sort of trap. Then, from underneath her scarlet wrap, she produced the Book of Madera and held it out to him.

He drew closer, staring at it. There it was, right on the cover:

Magickal Histories, Incantations,
Protections, and Obligations
of the Madera Branch
of the Order of Ceinoth

Corren turned slightly to Delossa and indicated she could leave. Back to Lini, "You *did* know where it was."

She shook her head, "No," and held out the book a little more. "Here."

He hesitated, wondering what this was about, then reached out and took it into his hands. He had it. The Book of Madera. The answer, he hoped, to everything.

The leather was so worn it no longer felt cool to the touch as new leather does. He ran his fingertips along the engraving on the cover.

He sensed magic on it, on the book itself, but felt nothing about it that warned him. "There's a spell on the book," he said, remembering what Lini had told him earlier.

She nodded.

He opened it carefully, the worn cover cracking open. "Do you know what kind of spell it is?" he asked.

She played with the ends of her head scarf and shook her head. "The spell may be too old to work anymore. It doesn't seem to be doing anything."

He closed the book and held it to his chest. "Thank you."

She blinked and offered a tentative smile. "You're welcome."

"But... where was it? Where's Kennard?"

She proceeded to tell him how they broke away from the Guard while Kennard was gone and how she stole the book from Tivoli that night while he slept.

She made the journey back on foot, barely sleeping or eating. She did, indeed, look weak and worn. "Come," he said. "Let's get you something to eat."

"No!" she said, taking a step back. "I won't go in there."

He would have argued, but she looked determined not to go any farther. Maybe it was best to keep her out of sight anyway. He couldn't make up his mind what he thought about her. She brought him the book, but it was more than that. Being with her made him want to trust her, even though there were so many reasons not to. Even now, even with the book in hand, he couldn't help but wonder if it were some kind of trick.

"Here, sit and rest. No one will see you. I'll bring you something to eat." As he turned to walk away, holding the Book of Madera to his chest, she placed her hand on his arm to stop him. His heart rate sped up. He gave her a questioning look and she nodded toward the book.

"I know you'll read it, but here..." She reached over and took the book. He marveled that he let her do it. She opened it and turned the aged pages until she found what she was looking for. Plucking a small sprig of pine needles from the hedge, she marked the spot before closing the book and returning it to him. "Begin there."

He wondered at this all the way back to his office where he locked the book in the cabinet, and wondered still more as he returned with food from the kitchen. Sitting on the grass, she took a great swig of the water first, followed by eager bites of leftover lamb and a small roll.

Pitying her hunger, he sat down next to her, grabbed an orange, and started peeling it. Its fresh scent mingled with the rich scent of pine. He watched her and she glanced at him too. He held out a segment of the orange. She took it and when her fingers brushed his, his heart sped up again. They looked at one another while she ate.

It was in this moment that Corren realized what he felt when he looked at her. He looked into those dark eyes and knew what it was. Help him, he felt... he was afraid to think it even. How could this happen? And now that he recognized it, it seemed to grow. He felt the warmth of it spread through his chest and face and through his entire body. He was aware of how excruciatingly close she was to him. He wanted to touch his fingertips to her cheek.

Their eyes locked on each other. He could not look away. It seemed like she could not look away either. They were in this shadowy alcove, and he felt like a completely different person here.

But was she a different person? Member of the Orsini Colony.

He glanced at the gold mark on her forehead and forced himself to look down at the remnants of orange in his hands. Scraps of the peel curled in his palm. Out of the corner of his eye, he saw her bring the bread to her mouth.

He sat there unable to move. He didn't know what was wrong with him. Why was he so drawn to her?

She finished eating and took a small drink of her water.

"Did you get enough to eat?" Corren asked without looking at her.

"Yes," she said quietly. "Thank you."

He stood and she stood too. She was right next to him. *So close*, he thought. *She's too close.*

"Where will you go now?" he asked.

She shrugged. "I don't know. I can't go back. I won't." She pulled her wrap more tightly around herself as she said it.

She looked so small and alone but also determined. How frightening it must be to so suddenly be without home or allies. He wanted to put his hand on her shoulder and comfort her as he'd done once before.

He wouldn't. He wouldn't do that.

But he could offer encouragement. There was no harm in that.

"Lini."

She looked at him.

"You've made it this far on your own. You don't need them. You're strong. You'll be okay."

Her dark eyes latched onto his.

"You're strong," he said again and he found himself placing his hand on her arm, almost without thought. He didn't mean to touch her. But now that he had, the energy between them changed.

As they stood so close together with his hand on her arm, the warmth in his chest grew hot. His heartbeat accelerated. His breathing shallowed. He sensed the same thing in her.

Whether he was moving toward her or she toward him, he couldn't tell. Perhaps both. An inch at a time. Closer. He looked down at her lips and back up to her eyes. Is this what it feels like to want a woman? How had he never felt this before? It was incredible.

But... but... a frightening chill began to break up the heat, to swirl with it. It made him slightly dizzy. Whether he felt drawn to her or not, she was a member of the Orsini Colony. A group that killed people who got in their way and took their children to boot. Did she participate in that?

But she had been one of those children once. And she had brought him the book.

But... but...

He thought of Aradia. As much as he had loved and admired Aradia, look what she had done. Look at how well she'd hidden her true intentions. All for her own purposes.

He halted, his lips inches from hers, and narrowed his eyes. What were her purposes?

He put his hand on her shoulder, shoved her away, and stepped back with one accord.

Her eyes widened and her face fell. She looked shocked and hurt, and he felt hurt, too, but he was also angry.

"You're staying here," he said firmly, "as it was before. Until I know there's no trickery."

"Trickery?" she said, eyes blazing now.

But he wanted no more of it. He couldn't take any more. "Let's go," he said. He turned his back to her and walked away.

Seven

Corren sat in the chair in the corner of his office with the Book of Madera on his lap when Delossa swept through the door.

"The message to Kennard is on its way, and someone in the kitchen will bring you something to eat," she said.

"Thank you."

"Apprentice Lampert still wants to talk to you about the Silent Circle."

Restorations to the Silent Circle had been completed shortly before Corren had left for Hathmirr. One of its functions was to help overcome magical blocks, and since the Apprentices were still struggling to learn nonverbal magic, Lampert suggested they use the Silent Circle to help. It wasn't a bad idea, but it was the least of Corren's concerns. "That can wait."

"That's what I told him. Are these ready for me?" she asked, opening a ledger that sat on his desk. He gave a sound that meant yes while she glanced through the notations he'd added earlier in the day.

Looking at her, it occurred to him: Delossa was a woman. For the first time he looked at her the way he supposed a man would look. He was surprised to realize she had a certain loveliness about her. A very lovely woman indeed. And smart and capable and kind and not remotely connected to a sinister group of people he wished he'd never laid eyes on.

Yet, while he liked Delossa and considered her a friend of sorts, he had no desire for anything beyond that.

He wondered if he could conjure it up. He tried to imagine being with her. Putting his arm around her. Kissing her. He furrowed his brows. Even in his imaginings, it was awkward and ridiculous.

She caught his eye and straightened. "Why are you looking at me like that?"

He turned back to the book. "Nothing. Thank you, Delossa."

She gathered up the ledgers and left without a word. The door clicked shut and he sat back in his chair, exhaling. Chastising himself for yet more foolish behavior, he returned to his task.

He'd been reading the Book of Madera, beginning with the page Lini had marked, and done little else since she gave it to him that afternoon. Normally, the Head of the Order wouldn't be privy to such information—Aradia wasn't, thank goodness—but since there was no Madera branch, he hoped it would help him solve the mystery of the ash still stuck on the altar. He soon realized the problems went far beyond that.

The more he read, the more he understood why Lini told him to start where she did. Which made him wonder—he couldn't help it—whose side was she on?

The room was beginning to grow dim. He glanced at the chandelier hanging from the ceiling, thought the incantation to set the wicks within ablaze, and went back to work.

Hours later, an empty plate sat on his desk, and Corren's mind was a tempest of worries that would not still. His thoughts darted from one thing to the next: the Vortex, Tivoli, the sickness in the Tree, Janus, Kai'Enna, and Lini. He and his brothers had planned to meet every few days to discuss the Tree, and tonight was one such night. He expected them any time and he needed them. He needed someone he could talk to about everything.

They arrived in short order. "I'm glad you're here," he said as they came through the door.

"Did you find something?" Marcellus asked hopefully, gesturing toward the open Book of Madera.

"No. Well, maybe." Corren grabbed a small volume on the corner of his desk that he'd been looking through this afternoon before Lini came. "Take a look at this." He handed the book to Nicolai and showed him the spell he'd marked. "I don't think you can duplicate it, but this does interesting things with the elements in tree bark. I thought it might give you some ideas. Maybe this could help you find a way to bring healing in through the bark."

Nicolai read through it and they discussed the magical concepts together, all the while Corren was fussing with the binding on the Book of Madera. Even while talking about the Tree, his other concerns were not far from the surface.

"I'll give it a try," Nicolai said at last. "Thank you."

Corren nodded mutely.

Marcellus had been scrutinizing him. "What else?"

"Hmm?"

Marcellus looked at him expectantly. He obviously knew Corren had something else to say. Why was Corren delaying? He already knew he needed to talk to them. "This," he said tapping the book, "is the Book of Madera."

Both Nicolai and Marcellus raised their eyebrows and Corren began filling them in.

He told them the key information contained in the pages Lini marked. It was information he normally wouldn't tell outsiders, but it concerned the faeries as much as it did the Order. And all three of them were half earth faeries. He told them about the Mapmaker and the Vortex, the Shoals and the faerie barriers. He told them about the Veils of Madera that helped conceal the entrances and how the Madera branch knew about a second entrance—the Desert Entrance—that even the Tulaga didn't know about.

"Can you imagine if Tivoli *did* get the ash?" Nicolai said.

Corren nodded. "But the Veils of Madera still need to be restored. The Madera branch believed the faerie barriers had a weakness. Based on my reading, I agree."

He proceeded to tell them how he came to have the book. When he explained how Lini delivered it to him that afternoon, Nicolai said, "She *did* have it!"

Corren shook his head. "She stole it from Tivoli and brought it to me. Or at least that's what she says. I don't know if I believe her. I can't think straight." He hadn't planned to go into his confusing feelings about her but seemed unable to stop. "She has me turned around."

Nicolai and Marcellus exchanged glances.

"I don't know if I can trust her."

Marcellus leaned forward, furrowing his brows. "So you don't trust her," he said. "So what?"

"Well..." he still didn't know if he wanted to say what else there was. Even to them.

Nicolai was leaning back in his chair, using that familiar, penetrating stare of his. "Well what?"

"Sometimes... sometimes it seems like I *can* trust her. But I wonder if... if that's just because I..." he absently turned a few pages of the book. Why was he saying any of this to them? So they could talk sense into him? He had bigger things to worry about, and yet he couldn't seem to stop himself from confessing, "I feel... funny... about her."

Marcellus' eyebrows shot up. "Funny?"

Nicolai's head slowly dropped. His shoulders began to shake. Corren stared at him in disbelief. "Are you laughing at me?"

Nicolai looked up, clearly trying to keep a straight face for Corren's benefit but not succeeding very well. "Of all the things you know, you can't even think of the right word for it."

Marcellus looked at Nicolai, confused. "What's so funny?"

"I guess wizards *can* fall in love."

Marcellus' eyebrows shot up even further, and he looked to Corren for confirmation. Corren felt a rare emotion toward Nicolai then: annoyance.

"She's a member of the Orsini Colony. I hardly think this is a laughing matter."

"I agree!" Marcellus said.

"I know, I know," Nicolai said, settling down and growing more serious. "I'm sorry." He tried to look sheepish, but a grin peeked out anyway.

"But why did she bring the book back?" Marcellus asked.

"That's what I wonder, too." Suddenly Corren found his tongue and ended up telling them everything, from meeting her the first time to witnessing her act of kindness toward the lady

253

of the house to comforting her after her friend's death... even how he almost kissed her and ended up shoving her away instead. They listened with serious expressions, not even trying to interrupt him. "I don't know what to do," he said at last.

Marcellus sat back with a thud against the back of the chair. "Well," he said. As if that were all there was to say.

Nicolai nodded. Apparently, he had nothing to contribute either.

They were no help at all. "What do I do?"

"Nothing," Marcellus said decisively. "You do what you need to do for the Order and the Tree. This problem will still be here waiting for you afterward, but maybe with time, things will become more clear."

Corren sighed. Somehow, it wasn't the sort of advice he was hoping for, but he knew Marcellus was right. And he did feel better for having talked about it.

"While we're revealing things," Nicolai said, "Praea knows who we are."

"Wait, what?" Marcellus said. "I thought we agreed no one would know about us yet. I have no idea how the kingdom's citizens are going to react to their leaders being half faerie. And didn't Salerno tell you to keep it a secret too?"

Nicolai raised a hand to stop Marcellus' protests. "She figured it out on her own. I just filled her in on the details. Don't worry. She knows how to keep a secret." Nicolai gestured to the book on Corren's desk. "After listening to this, I think I understand what she's been keeping from me as well. And it explains why Kai'Enna risked their lives over the Golden Canyon."

Corren sighed and rubbed his temples. Poor Kai'Enna.

There was so much to think about. What did they tackle first?

Praea did not come back to Tower Hall South that night, which was just as well. Nicolai spent the rest of his evening with the Tree of Origin, ultimately determining Corren's suggestion wasn't going to help. Nicolai wasn't surprised. He needed to get to the roots. He knew that.

As he left the golden light of the Tree and made his way down the Vein of the Earth, he pondered all he'd learned from Corren that night. The revelation that such a thing as the Vortex existed, and that a man such as Tivoli knew about it, was enough to keep his mind occupied for a week. What would they have been dealing with if he'd been able to remove the ash from the altar? At least Corren had the Book of Madera now. That was *something*. And right now, they needed any measure of success they could get.

Nicolai came out of the Vein of the Earth to find Salerno waiting in the golden Throne Room with the news Nicolai had been dreading for weeks.

The blackness on the Tree had claimed Lily at last.

Eight

For thousands of years, a little alcove in the underground realm of Amon Tunde was known to the faeries as the Key Chamber. Following Aradia's attack on the Tree of Origin, the faeries changed its name to the Mourning Chamber and buried their five fallen under soft mounds of earth covered in vines and flowers. Five stone pillars, fashioned out of the earth and with the names of the dead engraved in silver, marked the head of each grave. Nicolai watched numbly as Salerno created a sixth.

This done, groups of faeries rotated through the small room to add their share of the vines and flowers that would cover the mound. Salerno and Nicolai watched over this in silence. Nicolai judged the Mourning Chamber could hold four or five more graves. And after that? Would one room after another become a memorial to the dead until Amon Tunde itself was nothing but a tomb?

Janus had been with Lily when she died and came into the Mourning Chamber still wearing her *undanna* cloak. She slowly drew near, spread her hand over the freshly turned earth, and caused more vines and flowers to grow up onto Lily's grave. Nicolai examined her. She was pale and clearly weak but refused to lie down or even acknowledge this thing that was happening to her.

She glanced at him and caught his expression. "Don't look at me like that," she said, turning away. "I'm still here."

Keck and the others who were sick did not come. They were too ill to attend and would be next, Nicolai knew, if they couldn't heal the Tree.

As the last of the faeries came through and filtered out of the cave, Nicolai thought again about the Vortex somewhere in the earth below. What would it be like to see such an unimaginable source of raw power and magic? He felt similar wonder for the Shoals. It was somewhat unsettling to think of them, somewhere underneath his feet, and he found it difficult to imagine a network of tunnels so vast they stretched from Sakkara to Stonebridge. They lay under his old farm, under the castle, under Amon Tunde itself.

Nicolai furrowed his brows.

Under Amon Tunde.

He considered the blanket of vines and flowers covering Lily's grave.

"Under Amon Tunde," he said aloud.

He turned to Salerno. They were the only two left in the chamber. Salerno looked sadly at poor Lily's grave.

"The Shoals," Nicolai said.

Salerno turned to him with widened eyes. Nicolai didn't know if he'd ever seen the faerie king look so alarmed. "What did you say?"

Nicolai shook his head impatiently. "I know about the Shoals." He was too in the grips of his new idea to want to explain how he knew or ask why Salerno had kept it a secret even from him.

"If the Shoals run under the Tree of Origin, we can get to the roots."

"No, we can't," Salerno said, partly recovering his calm demeanor. "You cannot get to the roots of the Tree of Origin from the Shoals. They do not reach into the tunnels down there. There is nothing there like Oak Bone Tunnel. How do you know of this, Nicolai?"

Nicolai shook his head quickly. "I can explain later. Let's go. I want to see if there's a way."

"No," Salerno said firmly. "You must trust me, Nicolai. There is no way." He turned to leave.

"But what if there is?" he said to Salerno's retreating back. Salerno kept walking.

"I'd like to see for myself," Nicolai said, raising his voice.

Salerno turned, looking surprised at Nicolai's tone. Nicolai had surprised himself, but as he stood at the foot of Lily's grave knowing everything else had failed, he wasn't going to be told no. "Maybe you're right, but maybe you're wrong. You haven't been able to stop this either." He gestured at Lily's grave and Salerno grimaced. "You keep saying I'm supposed to figure things out, then let me figure them out."

Salerno furrowed his brows. "It's not like you to be so animated, Nicolai."

Nicolai narrowed his eyes. "What do you think I'm going to do?"

"It is not about you, Nicolai," Salerno said, though he didn't sound so certain.

"Have I not earned your trust by now?"

"I do not wish to repeat former mistakes. The Vortex is for no man."

"I am not only a man, I am a faerie. I don't care about the Vortex. I want to get under the Tree. I need to get to those roots. You know I do."

"The earth there is not subject to the magic of the faeries. If I thought it would help you heal the Tree, I would take you."

"Would you?"

Salerno did not answer.

Maybe Salerno was right. Maybe it would do no good. Maybe it was just one more dead end. But Nicolai wanted to at least try and wasn't going to overlook any option just because... because why? Salerno thought he'd be another Mapmaker? Because he thought Nicolai shouldn't know about the Vortex? He was tired of so many secrets and secret knowledge.

Nicolai would not be moved. "I want you to take me under the Tree of Origin," he said calmly but firmly. "Are you going to show me the way or shall I find it on my own?"

The tunnels that comprised the Shoals were cavernous in places, winding and narrow in others. There truly was something different about the earth here; Salerno was right

258

about that. It already seemed impenetrable. The rock walls reminded Nicolai of those surrounding the Tree itself. It looked like rock but wasn't mere rock. It was magic and the earth melded into one.

Salerno led the way, his mossy cloak hanging heavily from his shoulders. Tunnels branched off in different directions, leading this way and that. Many tunnels looked exactly like their fellows, but Salerno seemed to know the way.

At a fork, they turned left and the tunnel grew more and more narrow. The ceiling overhead dipped lower and lower until Nicolai and Salerno nearly had to hunch over to keep from hitting their heads.

Just as Nicolai was beginning to wonder if the tunnel would shut them out completely before they reached their destination, Salerno stopped. He looked up, his wild hair falling away from his shoulders, his angled face slightly shadowed in the faint light of the Shoals.

"It is there," he said.

Nicolai looked up. The rock above them had the same smooth, hardened surface that lined every other tunnel they'd seen so far. It felt as impermeable as ever. "I can't even feel the Tree," Nicolai said.

"Nor I. But I know where we are. The Tree of Origin is far above us."

Nicolai's hopes started to deflate, but then he thought of Lily's fresh grave. There had to be a way to get to the roots of the Tree. Some way to get closer. "Are there no other tunnels we can try? Something that maybe gets closer to the Tree from the side?"

Salerno shook his head. "The Tree is well encased. I've told you this already."

Nicolai leaned heavily against the wall.

"Nicolai. I am sorry. We must learn how to heal it from above."

"Salerno," Nicolai said quietly, sitting on the ground. "There *is* no way to heal it from above." He lay all the way back, pressed his palms on his forehead, and stared at the ceiling.

Salerno sat next to him, but he was not looking at the ceiling. He was looking at Nicolai. "There must be."

"Why must there be? Because we want it so badly?" Nicolai closed his eyes. "I don't know what else to do."

Salerno put his hand on Nicolai's forehead. Nicolai looked at him. "You are trying," Salerno said. "That is all anyone can ask."

Nicolai looked back at the impenetrable rock hanging above him. What good was trying if he wasn't getting anywhere? Maybe what they really needed to do was face facts.

Salerno patted Nicolai's forehead. "Let us go," he said quietly.

Nicolai stared at the ceiling, as if willing it to part and let him pass.

Salerno stood. The hem of his cloak brushed Nicolai's arm as he started back down the tunnel.

Nicolai let him go and pulled himself into a sit. He placed his hand on the rock wall, the smooth surface cool to the touch. He closed his eyes and felt the elements within. Such a strange combination they were.

He could no longer save Lily.

He may not be able to save anyone.

But if he failed, it would not be for lack of trying.

"Come, Nicolai." Salerno had stopped and was waiting for him.

Nicolai stood and Salerno turned to leave. "I'm not going yet," Nicolai said, putting his hand on the ceiling. He glanced at Salerno who looked about to argue. "You don't have to stay. I remember the way. I just... want to try."

Salerno clasped his hands together. Nicolai could not read the expression on his face. "I will wait with you."

Not knowing if Salerno was staying to be supportive or to make sure Nicolai didn't go looking for the Vortex, Nicolai took a resolute breath and turned back to the ceiling. Like the ground surrounding the Tree of Origin, it had elements that felt familiar mixed with magical elements he hadn't encountered anywhere else. He could see why it was not subject to the magic of the faeries. He could sense it.

Yet that didn't stop him from looking at it as he'd once looked at the Old Oak after weeks of failure. After Janus had helped him learn how to leverage both sides of him: the faerie *and* the human.

Since that time, regardless of the troubles with the Tree, Nicolai's ability to learn new things and control his element had blossomed.

Maybe this rock could not be moved. Maybe it could. But he would never know unless he tried.

He called up everything he understood about the earth, gathered all his will, and exerted it onto the elements under his hand. Nicolai took a deep breath... and pushed.

The crunching sound of rearranging stone sounded in his ears.

He jerked his hand away. There, just where his hand had been, was a small indentation. He watched it, waiting to see if the earth in the Shoals would restore itself just as the earth around the Tree had done.

But it stayed.

Nicolai's heart started pounding.

Salerno drew next to him, looking at the rock in astonishment. "Nicolai," he whispered.

Not only had Nicolai moved the rock, it *stayed.*

Nicolai clapped his hand on the ceiling once more. He pushed again and again it moved.

"How are you doing this?" Salerno asked.

Using both hands now, Nicolai rearranged the earth until he was able to pull himself up onto a shelf he created.

Heart still pounding, he worked hurriedly, digging and climbing. Before long he could feel it. Salerno was right. The Tree was right above him.

Nicolai pushed the stone aside like water, reshaping, reforming, climbing and climbing, until his hand brushed against something other than stone.

Nicolai froze. He took his hand away. Before him was not stone, but wood.

Standing upright now, he smoothed the stone away with both hands, revealing a section of root as big around as he was. Veins of gold ran through it, shimmering as if the blood of the Tree itself pulsed through the roots.

"Oh," he whispered, leaning his forehead against the root. "Here you are." He felt the same majesty and pure light he felt in the presence of the Tree. It hummed against his forehead.

He exhaled a shaky breath and put his hands on either side, pressing against the root. Thus he began. He felt the elements within, then felt his way all through the root system. It was massive. It seemed to go on and on forever, as if the roots of the Tree stretched as far as the boundaries of Amon Tunde itself.

Nicolai felt his way up the broad trunk of the Tree and into all the branches, hundreds of them. His heart ached with the beauty of it. The rawness.

As he felt each branch, he could see the face of the faerie to whom it gave life. He felt each one of them deeply. Faeries he barely knew became real and tender to him. The faeries he did know, his heart ached for. Janus. Keck. Salerno. His brothers.

He felt his way all the way to the top, and here, the blackness seeping within the upper branches of the Tree pressed so heavily on him his knees weakened and he tightened his grip on the tree, hanging on.

Just as he'd learned to do with the Old Oak, Nicolai reached beyond the roots into the earth surrounding them, gathered the healing elements he found there, and drew them into the roots. He guided that healing along the roots and up through the trunk, seeking the branches laced with poison. He wrapped the healing elements around the blackness. He pushed against the blackness and it pushed back.

No.

Pressing against the blackness, he simultaneously gathered more healing from the earth surrounding the roots and drew it in. Straining with effort, Nicolai's head slid off the root as he fell to his knees, but his hands remained on the wood. He looked up at the veins of gold pulsing through it.

Come on.

Still holding the healing against the blackness at the top, still feeling it resisting his efforts, Nicolai guided yet more healing elements up through the roots to the trunk and branches.

He sent the healing like a surge to that black magic, and the very edges of the blackness began to give way.

His heart started pounding.

Struggling to his feet, Nicolai exerted all his will against the black. Claiming it. Forcing it to retreat as the healing spread further and further and restored vitality to all it touched. He pushed the poison up and up, out and out. It retreated into the branches that were already dead and past saving.

As the last bit of poison was swallowed up in healing light, the Tree seemed to shudder. The vibration from the Tree traveled from its branches, to its trunk, and down to its roots where it resonated in Nicolai's arms.

Nicolai sensed, almost as if he were seeing it with his own eyes, the dead branches fall from the top of the Tree and crash onto the ground. The golden Tree shuddered once more, its leaves rustling like little bells.

Then everything went still. The root under Nicolai's hands and forehead hummed with absolute purity. It illuminated everything inside him. He lifted his head, let his weary arms fall to his side, and looked at it.

Covering his face with his hands, he swelled with such emotion he didn't know if he were going to laugh or cry. "Salerno," he said, too softly to be heard, yet too exhausted to say it any louder.

He gripped the root and planted a kiss on it. His energy surged. "Ah!" he cried. "Salerno!" He scurried back down the hole he'd created, restoring the stone and hollering for Salerno along the way. "Salerno! It's done!"

But when he got to the bottom, Salerno was gone.

❖   ❖   ❖

When Nicolai reentered Amon Tunde, he was greeted by a commotion unlike any he'd seen in this ordered world. The faeries gathered around him, all smiling and thanking him at once. Upon seeing each face, Nicolai felt a surge of tenderness, remembering what it was like to feel their branches.

Keck approached, looking healthy once more. His short, spiked, humanlike hair looked normal again, not the coarse gray it had become. His light blue eyes were vibrant and nearly twinkling, which brought a smile to Nicolai's face. Keck was not the twinkling sort. Keck did something he'd never done before. He took Nicolai's hand and gave it an awkward shake. Nicolai smiled broadly. "Thank you," Keck said. "Thank you, Nicolai."

Nicolai felt like hugging him but didn't want to alarm him. Where was Janus? That's a faerie he could hug if she were here. Though when he thought of Janus and imagined her looking as fresh faced as Keck, he couldn't contain himself. He pulled Keck into a hearty embrace. He was rewarded with laughs from the crowd and Keck's shocked expression.

Finally Janus arrived, still in her *undanna* cloak. He didn't even need to try to take a hug from her. She gave him one.

Through it all, he reached out for Salerno. He sensed him in the Throne Room. Alone.

When Nicolai finally made it there, Salerno would not look at him. "You have done well, Nicolai. I am sorry I did not tell you about the Shoals before."

"Well..." Though Nicolai truly was tired of everyone's secrets, he could see the anguish on Salerno's face. Maybe he should have told Nicolai, but Salerno had diligently taught him everything he could. Everything he thought would help. Nicolai did wish Salerno had told him, but neither could he blame him. After all, Nicolai had, in fact, done something no one else in Amon Tunde could have. "You didn't know."

"If I had told you, we would still have our Lily."

Nicolai opened his mouth to speak, but Salerno held up his hand. "I do not wish to talk, Nicolai. Please leave me."

Nicolai lingered a moment, then turned and left Salerno in peace.

Nine

Tivoli and his group of followers stood at the mouth of a cave that faced the gray sea, just within the borders of Hathmirr. At the back of the cave, four men held the water faerie fast, though it was more for show. Faatin was not struggling; he was smiling.

"It won't work with me." That's what Faatin had said. After some heated discussion, in which Tivoli wondered if the water faerie were just trying to save his own skin, he came to the conclusion that the water faerie was right. This creature was scarred, cursed. Ruined at his own hands. He was useless to Tivoli, unless he kept his word.

How ironic that Tivoli now needed him so badly.

"How do I know," Tivoli asked, "that you won't leave and not come back?" If Faatin wanted to get lost in the depths of the sea, there would be nothing Tivoli could do about it.

"Look at my face," Faatin said. His scarring was grotesque even in the dim light of the cave. "I have no pride. No home. No future. I want what Aradia promised me. I want to be healed. I will be back," he said darkly, "because I want the life I used to have. You're the only one who can give it to me. We have no choice," he said, "but to trust each other."

"Are you certain you can deliver what we need?"

Faatin shrugged. "I'm certain I can try."

Tivoli turned from the water faerie and paced away. He was stuck. He needed what Faatin said he could provide. They couldn't go forward without it, but the thought of letting that slimy fish back into the water made his blood run cold. Still, what else could he do?

An unpleasant thought occured to him. He slowly looked over his shoulder at the creature and narrowed his eyes. "How do I know you won't take the magic from the Vortex yourself?"

Faatin looked amused, as if Tivoli had just made an outlandish suggestion. "What makes you think I can get to it?"

Tivoli faced him fully now. "The Mapmaker. He said part of the Shoals disappeared into the water. Doesn't it go to wherever you water faeries live?"

Faatin's expression grew dark. He nodded slowly. "Yes. It does."

Tivoli straightened to his full height. So he'd been right. The creature *did* intend to steal the magic himself. But then... if he were going to do that, why hadn't he done it long ago?

"Their realm is in ruins," Bricker said uncertainly, looking at the water faerie as if he were trying to figure out the puzzle as well. "He told me so himself."

"Yes," Faatin said. "Naida is only a shadow of what it once was. But the Shoals have never been open to us. The tunnel leading to it is no bigger around than my arm."

Tivoli furrowed his brows, not sure if he believed him or not. "Why can you not get to it while the earth faeries can?"

Faatin's grotesque face stretched into a slow smile. "Perhaps the earth has always known our true nature. We are wild and untamable, like the sea itself. Perhaps the earth has never trusted us."

Tivoli felt a dark chill. He turned away from the faerie once more. He did not know what the earth may or may not intend—or even how such deliberate intentions were possible—but whether this water faerie's interpretation of things was correct or not, his statement had underscored a truth they both understood.

This particular water faerie could not be trusted.

Another truth had been understood as well. While the earth faeries selflessly guarded the Vortex, the water faeries—or this one, at least—would not hesitate to steal its magic.

Whether or not the earth could truly know of the lengths Faatin would go to preserve his own self-interest was irrelevent.

267

Tivoli knew it. Faatin admitted it. And that was where Tivoli had him. Faatin, bound to the sea as he was, needed Tivoli's help. To get it, Faatin would have to deliver.

Without turning around, he gave a signal to his men to release Faatin. He looked out at the sea, as gray as the storm clouds hovering above it. Faatin came to his side. Tivoli looked at him.

"I will fulfill my end of the bargain," Faatin said. "You fulfill yours."

Though Tivoli had already promised he'd lift the curse from the water faerie, it was an unsteady promise. Tivoli didn't know for sure what he'd be able to do once he stole the magic from the Vortex. But if the water faerie would help him do it, why not throw the creature a tidbit of the spoils?

"If you deliver the goods," Tivoli said, "I will do what I can to heal you."

Without another word, Faatin looked at the sea, dove silently from the rock, and disappeared under the water.

Corren went to the Rock of Light feeling hopeful after the celebration of the night before. While Nicolai's healing of the Tree came with a bitter taste—it was just hours too late for Lily, the timing of which Nicolai and Janus found heartbreaking—it also brought immense relief to everybody.

After Nicolai's success, Corren hoped the trend would continue. Kennard was back from the border. Corren would give him the Book of Madera and, thus, the knowledge he needed to properly restart the branch. Which couldn't happen too soon. While the Shoals were still guarded by the faerie barriers and Tivoli didn't have the ash he would've needed to get through, the sooner Kennard could restore the Veils of Madera, the better Corren would feel.

He would not allow himself to think of Lini, still under guard at Tower Hall South since the day before. Neither would he allow himself the indulgence of seeing her.

Shortly, Corren and the other members of the Order were gathered in the Cloister. The circular room sat at the base of the Rock of Light. One door led to the winding staircase and up to the Eternal Flame. Opposite, another door led to the anteroom and then to the outside. High-backed chairs sat in a circle, the symbol of each branch embroidered on the fabric. This was Praea's first meeting as new Head of her branch, and she sat in Kai'Enna's chair awkwardly. Corren knew the feeling.

They first discussed final preparations for Kai'Enna's funeral, then turned to the matter of the Madera branch and its ash waiting on the altar.

"I believe," Corren said as he walked over to Kennard and handed him the Book of Madera, "this is what the Phoenix wanted you to have before you could remove the ash." He headed back for his chair. "You will soon discover the reason why. You'll need to restore the Madera branch as quickly as—" Corren sat and stopped mid-sentence when he saw Kennard.

He was struggling with the book. Actually struggling with it.

"Why won't it open?" Kennard asked, turning it about in his hands as if looking for a latch.

Corren walked over, took the book, and opened it. He and Kennard exchanged awkward glances. Silently, Corren returned the book. Kennard held it open in his hands then slowly closed it. He tried to reopen it but couldn't.

The other Order members began to shuffle in their seats. Kennard closed his eyes briefly, then held out the book for Corren. "It's me," he said.

In those two words, Corren felt Kennard's utter rejection.

"It had nothing to do with needing the book," Kennard said matter-of-factly, trying to mask the emotion underneath. "The Phoenix just doesn't want me to have the ash. Here," he said. "Take it."

Corren took the book but furrowed his brows. "Sage Kennard. The Phoenix is a mystery. It always has been. But it's not you at fault here. I'm sure of that."

Kennard nodded, keeping a strong face, but Corren saw the self-doubt underneath.

"Sage Kennard," Corren said firmly, "no one here questions your loyalty." This good man had done nothing but show his devotion to the Phoenix, and Corren hated to think of him doubting himself. "Don't you think this is something against you. You fulfill your duties toward the Phoenix with honor and valor. You only want what is best for the Order and our purposes. You've made that clear. I would trust you with my life, Sage Kennard. If I could know of your goodness, there is no doubt the Phoenix does as well."

Kennard's eyes locked on Corren's, wide with surprise at Corren's passion. He drank in Corren's words as if he had never needed to hear anything the way he needed to hear this.

With a brief smile, Kennard looked down and nodded. "Alright," he said. "What now, Sage Corren?"

Corren took a breath to recover from his impassioned speech, then passed the book to each member in turn. None of them could open it.

"Maybe the ash is for you," Praea said to Corren. "Why else can you open the book?"

He returned to his seat with the book in hand. "I couldn't remove the ash either. Maybe I can open the book only because I'm Head of the Order."

"Then who?" Sage Bellamy asked.

Then Corren remembered. There was one other person he saw open the book: Lini.

Corren approached Lini's quarters with a pounding heart. Everyone had agreed: they would see if Lini could remove the ash. Everyone also agreed: the idea of any member of the Orsini Colony having the ash of the Phoenix was unsettling. But after he had shared some of what he'd learned about her (minus

270

details that were far too personal), and after they considered that she'd been the one to return the book, there was hope that maybe she was not like her fellows.

They'd come to an uneasy decision: they'd let her try and let the Phoenix be the judge.

Corren knocked on her door. She answered and his heart started pounding harder in response to the sound of her voice. The last time he saw her, things had not gone well. In fact, they'd gone horribly wrong. He lifted the latch with moist palms.

She was sitting at the desk under the window. She had asked for various supplies: quill and ink, paper, an additional blanket. Each request had gone through Corren's approval, but she hadn't asked for anything that caused concern and he'd denied her nothing. Other than her freedom, which she reminded him of now just by the way she looked at him.

He shut the door behind him. He gestured to a nearby chair. "May I?"

"You're asking me?"

He sat and she put down her quill, crossing her arms and watching him. Looking at her, even in her anger, he could not help but feel she *was* different from the other Orsini Colony members. But... he could not let go of his fear that he was terribly wrong. What if he was as wrong about her as he'd once been about Aradia?

Being with her now, he knew the word he couldn't say before with his brothers. He did feel differently about Lini than he ever had about anyone. He loved other people: he loved his brothers, he loved his fellow Order members, he'd loved Mother Taiven, King Clement, and, yes, he had once loved Aradia. Truth be told, he had loved Aradia more than he'd loved anyone.

He looked at Lini now and felt a troubling mixture of hope and fear. Why had he fallen in love with this woman?

Lini's hair was down. It was long and straight, as Aradia's had been, but black as night and as beautiful as she was. He had not much considered the beauty of women before, or at least, he had not before been so *impacted* by the beauty of a woman. He didn't know if he thought her beautiful when he first saw her or if it came to him later. Now she sat there with her arms crossed, her honey-colored skin offset by the bright colors of her robe, her dark eyes glinting at him, the gold mark shining on her forehead. Help him, even that looked beautiful.

He thought of the way she'd helped the woman so fearful of their presence in her home, the night he'd snuck into her room to comfort her, and how she'd risked her life to return the book.

Or did she?

"I have a question," he said at last.

She raised her eyebrows as if to say, *Go ahead then.*

"Did you ever see Tivoli open the book?"

She scoffed. "You saw it yourself. He was always reading that thing."

Corren nodded. "I saw him reading it, yes. But I never saw him open it. Did you?"

She opened her mouth then halted. Her antagonism switched to thoughtfulness. She looked at the ceiling and he could see her mind working. "Um..." she said. "I..."

She looked at him, the hurt feelings between them gone for the moment. "I... I only ever saw him reading when it was already open. Even when I took it off the night table, the book had been open." She paused again, furrowing her brows. "It was closed when I got in trouble for looking at it though."

"So, it was closed and you opened it?"

"Yes, but just for a minute. I closed it again as soon as he caught me."

"So if you closed it again, he must have been able to open it later."

She narrowed her eyes. "Why are you asking me this?"

"Because..." he swallowed. Did he trust her enough to tell her why? "Because... no one seems to be able to open it. Except me. And you. And, I suppose, Tivoli."

Which meant it wasn't Lini. If Tivoli could open the book yet could not remove the ash, then the fact that Lini could open the book meant nothing.

Corren exhaled in frustration. It was all so confusing.

Lini shook her head slowly. "No," she said. "I don't think he could. He made me open it again." Then she explained the way he'd dared her to open the book. She thought it was his way of underlining her defiance. His way of tormenting her before he condemned her to her punishment. "But it wasn't that. He walked away with the book still open."

"He made you open it?"

"And he did it again, after we escaped from the Guard and Bricker returned the book to Lord Tivoli. He pulled me aside and had me open the book. He asked me a couple questions about it, but the whole thing felt a little strange. Maybe... he just wanted me to open it... without me knowing that's what he wanted."

"So *that's* why when he left the book at the border..." Corren said, thinking he understood at last.

"...he chose *me* to come with him to the Rock of Light," she finished for him.

"He separated the lock from the key."

They smiled at each another with the joint satisfaction of solving the puzzle. But her smile didn't last long. "But what does it all mean?" she asked. "Why can't he open it? Why can I?"

Then Corren remembered something else. "What happened during the ceremony?" he asked.

She pressed her lips together but kept her eyes on him. He wasn't sure she was going to answer. "I'm not sure," she said. "I'm not sure how I did it. But..." she took a deep breath. "That ceremony is the High Ceremony of the Way of Orsini. The potion we drink binds us to one another, but most especially to Lord Tivoli. It's... supposed to make us one, but it's... it's dark. It makes us obedient. With the right command, Tivoli can—"

She looked away scowling. "I hate him," she said, tears pooling in her eyes. "He ordered Sienna to let go of me and she couldn't help it." She looked back at Corren. "She wanted to live. She wanted to live and Tivoli made her let go because he could and because he doesn't care about us or about anyone. I hate him and I hate the potion and I didn't want to take it anymore so I didn't."

He looked at her, waiting.

She took a few deep breaths, settling herself. "I don't know how. I just... *thought* it and kept it away and Tivoli never knew. No one ever knew. They would kill me if they did." She shrugged. "They'll kill me if they find me anyway, so there's no harm telling you now."

"You just... *thought* it?"

She nodded.

"Nonverbal magic," he said quietly.

"Maybe that's why I can open the book. I'm not controlled by the potion?" She furrowed her brows as if that explanation didn't make sense even to her.

Corren had a different thought.

"When did this happen?" he asked.

"What?"

"The first time you resisted the potion. When was that?"

"A few months ago. It's been getting more and more difficult to pretend."

"Was it before or after the last Song of the Phoenix?"

She furrowed her brows, thinking. "Um... after. Yes, it was after."

"You're certain?"

She thought some more, nodding. "Yes."

"How long after? Were there any ceremonies after the last Song of the Phoenix when you hadn't yet started to resist?"

"I... well... no, I don't think so. No. No, it was during that time when Tivoli was so upset about the fact that our people hadn't returned with the ash. He was especially difficult to please during that time. I was only a little afraid though... the potion sort of... numbs you to things. But I remember being in the ceremony and I remember the cup coming to me and I thought the same thing I always thought: 'I don't want that.' And this time, I didn't take it. I just... didn't."

Corren looked at her. When the Phoenix resurrected itself, when it gave Corren the gift of nonverbal magic, did it also give that same gift to Lini? Was she really meant for the ash, and the Phoenix gave that gift to prepare her?

The hopeful part of him was winning out, but the fearful part hadn't gone anywhere. His free hand shook on his lap; he stood so he could grip his staff with both hands.

"Lini," he said, "The Order requests your presence at the Rock of Light."

Ten

For the third time in as many months, the Order gathered around the stone altar of the Eternal Flame, glancing at one another with apprehension. The sound of the massive fire filled the otherwise silent room. Corren looked at Kennard, who stood away from the circle and watched the stranger among them carefully.

Distinct from the white robes of the others, just as Tivoli had been, Lini stood in her colorful wraps, eyeing the glass orb in front of her. In spite of Corren's assurances that this ceremony would not harm her as the High Ceremony of the Way of Orsini had done, she had been little calmed. "Tivoli was singed, wasn't he?"

"I think he was harmed by his own spell. He was trying to force the ash off the altar. Even if it won't come off, you won't be harmed."

She had looked doubtful, and he had to admit he was a bit doubtful himself. They were dealing with unprecedented circumstances and had been all along. They had been merely feeling their way in the dark. As he looked at the faces around him, he could see everyone was worn out by the situation.

He felt that strange ache in his chest as the firelight reflected in Lini's dark eyes.

For so many reasons, he needed her to lift that ash off the altar.

And so he began. "*Illio tetha.*"

Lini looked at him, alarmed. He tried to give her a comforting nod as they all repeated after him, "*Illio tetha.*" The sound of Lini's voice resounded in his ears.

"*Ah mae alla,*" he said.

As the others repeated it, Lini looked down at the orb with dread.

"*Immath ay, Immath ay, Immath ay.*"

All eyes swung toward Lini. She slowly raised her hands, paused, then gingerly placed them around the glass orb...

...and the moment stretched out. For one eternal second, he didn't know if she had not yet tried to lift it or if it was staying fast to the altar as it had for all the others... that second pounded in his heart, and he had to resist the urge to grip the stone in front of him.

Please.

...the moment shifted, and then he knew. He sensed it in the members around the altar. He saw it on Lini's face.

The ash would not be moved.

This time Corren did grip the altar. He held onto it with straight arms, dropped his head, and closed his eyes. In his mind, he still saw it: Lini here in the Rock of Light with her hands around the ash, when clearly the Phoenix didn't want her.

His doing. This was all his doing.

He heard someone rush past and the door fling open behind him. Without looking, he knew it was Lini, and he let her go. No one said anything. One by one, he heard person after person leave the room. He did not want to look at anyone. Did not want to talk to anyone. Did not want to think about what any of this meant.

Someone came next to him. "If it's any consolation," Kennard said, "I thought it would be her too."

Corren nodded and Kennard left without another word.

At last he opened his eyes. The room was empty, save Praea, who had drifted close to him, her brows knit with concern.

He stared at the stone in front of him, his hands grasping the edge, the light from the flame dispassionately illuminating all.

"I don't understand it," he said.

"Neither do I."

"What more?" he said, standing upright, his voice louder. "What more are we supposed to do? I have no idea, do you?

We've tried everything we can think of. *I've* tried everything I can think of. I've done almost nothing else for the past three months, and we're right back where we started." He pounded the stone altar with his hand and paced away to a window. In the distance, the formidable Cliffs of the Realm reared into the sky. "Three months. Three months as Head of the Order and every last one was a failure."

"Corren—"

"Maybe I'm not supposed to be Head of the Order. Maybe that's the problem."

"Corren, that's enough."

Her tone was so firm he couldn't help but look at her. Though she stood there in the white ceremonial robe of the Order, he did not see a fellow Head but rather a friend who'd fought alongside him in the Realm. "We all know you're supposed to be Head of the Order. How can you say that? You must know it's true."

He sighed. "I suppose. But why can't I figure this out? If there's someone meant for that ash," he said, gesturing, "I don't know who it is." There the glass orb sat still.

The fiery reflection on its smooth surface morphed into the likeness of the Phoenix. It was as if the Phoenix were telling him, *This is important.* As if he didn't already know. He'd been carrying a sense of dread about that ash for months. The shape of the Phoenix dissipated, leaving nothing but formless reflections.

He looked away, frowning. "I thought..." Fears or not, he did think it was Lini. Or hoped it was. Or something. Which was it? "I don't trust my own judgment. I can't even tell if people are good or bad."

"What nonsense."

Again, he looked at her, speechless.

"You certainly *do* know whether someone is good or bad. As much as it's possible for anyone to know such things." Though it was sometimes easy to forget this gentle woman's inner strength, he had no trouble remembering it now. Praea radiated

278

a firmness and conviction so tangible he could almost reach out and touch it. "Don't you remember what you said to Kennard? You told him he's a good man, did you not?"

"Yes, but—"

"Do you doubt Kennard's goodness?"

"No, but—"

"Do you doubt your judgment of him?"

"Well, no."

"How is this different?"

"I... I don't know. I don't know. Aradia tricked me. Lini could be tricking me too."

Praea looked at him sympathetically. "Aradia fooled a lot of people," she said softly. "That was a fault inside of Aradia, not you."

He looked away. "Maybe." He knew he wasn't responsible for what Aradia did, but he still felt he'd been a fool. That somehow he should've known better. "But what if Lini is the same way?"

Praea drew close to him. "Do you really think she is?"

He feared it. He did. But as much as he feared it, and as much as he knew people could always be something other than what they appeared, he did not think Lini bad. He did not think she was like Aradia. But... but then why the ash?

He exhaled with exhaustion. He didn't know what to do. Why wouldn't the Phoenix just tell him? The Phoenix made him Head of the Order. Gave him all this knowledge. Why wouldn't the Phoenix help him now?

He furrowed his brow and looked toward the top of the Cliffs of the Realm. The smooth surface of the rock reached high into the sky. Somewhere up there was the Phoenix.

Corren needed guidance. Maybe all he had to do... was ask for it.

"Praea?" he said, turning to her slowly. "Will you help me with something?"

◆　◆　◆

279

Corren and Praea landed on hard earth, which exuded heat like a rose releasing its scent. Corren had forgotten how hot it was in the Realm of the Phoenix. The golden Tulaga changed back into her natural form, then leaned over and placed her hands on her knees, panting. Scaling the Cliffs of the Realm was no small feat, even for her.

"Are you alright?" he asked, already feeling the moisture gathering on his brow.

Praea waved her hand in weary dismissal and straightened, still trying to catch her breath.

They stood in front of the pyre of the Phoenix, or what had once been its pyre. The *detanae* tree with its flat top held the charred remains of the Phoenix's recent regeneration, but there were no signs of the Phoenix itself.

Corren looked around. It was nothing but barren desert as far as he could see in every direction.

"Maybe the Phoenix only comes here to resurrect itself," Praea said.

"Maybe."

"So then where would it be now?"

Corren didn't know, but when his eyes landed on a spot of ground not far from them, his heart clenched. He came to the Realm for the Phoenix, but he'd forgotten what else lay there. It had only been three months since the Phoenix's regeneration. Three months since Aradia was killed and they left her to rot... just over there.

There were scrubby, heat-scorched bushes dotted all around, and a few blocked his view of the place where Aradia died.

He didn't want to see it and yet he did. His feet propelled him forward all while he cringed internally. Anywhere else and she would have been eaten by wild animals. But what happened to her, here in this Realm that had its own rules? Corren remembered Marcellus' horse. It also died in the Realm but was, seemingly, resurrected as the water horse Marcellus called Ryafan.

Corren came to a sudden halt. What if Aradia had been resurrected too? What if she were still out there in another form?

He thought of Lini with her long, Aradia-like hair. He thought of his draw to her, his fear of her. Heart pounding, Corren could not move another step. His skin crawled.

He felt Praea come to his side. "Corren?"

"Go see," he said. "Tell me if she's there."

"Of course she is."

"What if she isn't?"

Something in his voice must have communicated his need, for she put her hand on his arm and squeezed before going forward.

She couldn't have taken more than a dozen steps, and yet to Corren it seemed she would never get there. She just kept going and going while his heart beat in his ears.

She stopped short.

"Is she gone?" he called.

"No, she's here. She's just..." She turned and he saw the look of shock on her face.

"Decomposing?"

"Not exactly."

Corren found his feet at last and rushed across the rocky ground, at Praea's side in an instant. There Aradia lay, just as they left her. But it was as if she had become part of the earth. She was now made of something so hard and smooth it almost looked like rock. It was darker than the rest of the earth, as if declaring that something evil had been there.

But was it only rock, or was she really in there?

He looked up, got his bearings, and continued on, this time in search of Marcellus' horse. He remembered where it had been killed as well, but when they came to the spot, there was nothing. No corpse. No petrified formation of earth. Not even any sign of blood loss.

"The Phoenix is such a strange creature," he said as Praea came up next to him. The body of the horse, which did indeed seem to be resurrected in Ryafan, was no longer here, but

Aradia's body was. So she wasn't resurrected. She was still dead. Would always be dead. Corren took a deep breath, as if he were safe from Aradia once more. He felt a bit foolish, fearing a dead woman.

"Well," he said, taking another breath. "There's that."

They started wandering back to the pyre. "Where do you suppose the Phoenix would be?" he asked.

"I'm not sure. It could be anywhere."

"I really thought it would be here."

They approached the *detanae* tree with the blackened remnants of the pyre on top. He remembered exactly what it looked like when he plunged the tip of his staff between the rough sticks, thinking it would be the last thing he would ever do.

Yet, here he was.

They'd destroyed Aradia, saved the Phoenix, and managed not to lose their lives in the process. It was over. Or was supposed to be. So why did it all still seem so alive in his breast?

A shadow passed over and he looked up. There, high in the sky, was the Phoenix, descending straight toward him. Even from this distance, it was massive and stunning. Its brilliant feathers were so bright they almost seemed on fire.

His eyes landed on the face of the Phoenix and its eyes, glowing like embers. He felt captured by it. Closer and closer the Glorious Bird came until it consumed his entire vision. Warm wind wrapped around him and a bright light sprung up between them. He could neither see, hear, nor feel anything but light and wind and swirling warmth.

The next thing he knew, he was on the Phoenix's back with his arms wrapped around its neck. He looked at the ground, which was rapidly falling away, and saw a stunned Praea shielding her eyes with one hand as she looked up at them.

The wind rushed past them and they rose higher and higher as the Phoenix pumped its massive wings. A deep hum of air reverberated with every beat. Warm feathers brushed his cheek. He spread his fingers wide over the soft plumage and looked up to the clear blue sky.

Swirling wind appeared again, in blues and purples and yellows and reds. All he could see was the colorful wind streaking past and the Phoenix, whose feathers shone like firelight.

They came to a halt and the colorful wind dissipated to reveal new surroundings. They were on land again, but this land was green and lush, dotted with strange trees that reminded him of the *detanae* of the Realm. The long branches swooped down from the tops, each bursting with flowers the size of his head. He was standing on grass in bare feet—he vaguely realized his shoes had gone somewhere—but the sensation of it seeped through his skin and into his legs and chest. It was warm and tingling like liquid gold.

I... I...

Even his thoughts were arrested by the majesty of his surroundings. It all took hold of him, and that place in his chest that sometimes ached began aching again. He tried pushing it down, but it bloomed like a drop of blood hitting water.

Something inside him cracked open.

He clapped his hands over his face. A torrent of thoughts and emotions threatened to carry him off or consume him where he stood. All the once-happy memories of Aradia that were now tainted by the truth, all the hot pain, all the anger, all the fear, it burst out and he couldn't stop himself from feeling it.

He sensed the Phoenix behind him.

There appeared in front of him—or was he the one who'd moved?—a plant as high as his waist with dark, waxy leaves. At the top was a coral flower as large as his face. On his knees now, he cupped the soft bloom with unsteady hands.

He sensed the Phoenix behind him. Tears wet his cheeks and they fell onto the petals, where they sizzled like water on a hot iron. That place that hurt... it hurt and hurt and he thought now that the wall inside him had been shattered, there would never be an end to what came pouring out.

He sensed the Phoenix behind him.

Illl... UUUMMM... aayyyy.

Did he think it? Was it the Phoenix? It didn't matter. It was the second time in his life this spell came to his mind. It meant *deliverance* and he felt the power of it echoing in his bones.

The pain that seized him started to relax its hold.

Still cupping the flower, Corren closed his eyes and inhaled. It smelled like fire. The gentle heat of it entered into his lungs. He began to let go and as the pain began to drain away, golden light from the grass beneath him spread upward into his body.

The warmth from the grass and the sharp scent of the flower and the lingering hum of the spell and the magic of this place saturated the part of him that had hurt.

Eyes closed, he took another deep breath of the flower. Warm and rich, he felt lightheaded with it. His body grew still. Calm.

He sensed the Phoenix behind him. He knelt on the ground, eyes closed, the warmth of this place wrapping him up... and lingered in complete stillness. He felt he could stay like this forever. He felt maybe he *was* staying like this forever. On and on it went, until he felt he had never been anything but calm and whole.

In his mind, he saw Aradia. He remembered a time she'd hovered near, showing him some wondrous piece of magic and he, as a young boy, alight with her excitement. Another memory, the expression on her face as, wild and drunk with desire, she extracted the Phoenix's spirit from its body, determined to take its power and life into herself.

He remembered the way she stood in front of a class or addressed an assembly or even walked into a room. Her mere presence commanded awe in others. Her magic and power seemed to linger on her very skin, and he'd wanted to be just like her.

Corren remembered again lying on the hard ground, held immovable by her spell, while she gently placed her hand over his throbbing eye and healed him.

Not for the first time did such a collage of memories blossom in his mind, but now these things caused no agony. No pain. They just... *were*.

When he opened his eyes at last, the flower was gone and he stood on the earth. The land, with its blossoming trees and flowers and lush green grass, presented itself to him like a gift.

He turned and looked up at the Phoenix. Its eyes like burning embers looked down at him.

What a glorious creature you are.

A vision came to his mind. He saw the ash on the altar.

Oh, he thought, understanding at last.

A soft wind swirled up from his feet and slowly gained speed. It grew into a rushing wind of purples and blues and yellows and reds that swirled around them until all he could see was the light and the Phoenix. All he could feel was wholeness and peace.

When the light left him, he was standing in the Realm in front of the vacant pyre on hot, barren earth. He looked down, grateful to have his shoes again.

He turned to his left where Praea stood gaping at him. He smiled. "Shall we go?"

Eleven

When they returned to the Rock of Light, the Order was outside waiting for them. They had seen Praea and Corren flying to the Realm and waited to find out what happened. He was glad they were still there, but who he was really grateful to see was Lini. There she stood in her colorful shawls and with the gold mark on her forehead, lingering apart from the crowd. Behind her, the waves crashed along the rocky shoreline. Her face was unreadable.

Corren asked the Order to wait inside the Cloister, assuring them he'd explain soon. He needed to talk to Lini alone.

He went toward her. When she noticed the Order members disappearing into the Rock of Light, she marched up to him. "Ash or no ash," she said, "Tivoli is still out there, and if there's a way for him to get to the Vortex, he'll find it. I want to know what you're going to do to protect it."

He wanted to scoop her into his arms. He wanted to tell her everything would be okay. He wanted to say he was sorry.

Most of all that he was sorry.

"Well," he said, slowly. "We're going to restart the Madera branch. They'll help protect the Vortex as they always have."

"There isn't time for that," she said. "How long will it take you to find the right person to remove the ash? *You* need to do something about that entrance, Corren. Right now. Tivoli will not wait for you to worry about the ash."

He nodded. Gone were his feelings of doubt and fear, but he now understood the magnitude of pain and anger she felt from all the things that had been done to her. This was, he knew, too much for her to overcome alone. And he'd added a little bit to that hurt, even if only in a small way. He wished he hadn't.

"I'm so sorry," he said.

She furrowed her brows and crossed her arms. "Sorry for what?"

"For pushing you away."

She blinked in surprise, but then her scowl deepened. The waves roared behind them and the wind rushed past.

"I mean, not just for... pushing you. I'm so sorry about that. But also for... acting how I did. It... it wasn't about you. I'm sorry."

"I have more important things to think about than you, Corren."

"I know. And we're going to take care of it. I only wanted you to know I'm sorry. And..." This was harder than he thought it would be, but he knew he had to say it. "And I wanted to say that if... that..." He took a deep breath. "I wouldn't push you away again. I promise."

Lini narrowed her eyes. "I'm not here for you, Corren. I'm here to protect the Vortex."

He nodded and took a slight step back. "I understand," he said. "I want the same thing. I won't speak of the other again." And he meant it. He couldn't expect anything from her, especially not now and maybe not ever, no matter how much that caused a whole new kind of ache in his chest. He'd said what needed to be said. Now that that was done, he agreed with her on one thing. They needed to restore the protections to the entrance to make sure the Vortex was safe.

"There is something I think will help," he said. "With the Madera branch, I mean. With..." He took another breath. He still could not seem to get his words to come out correctly. "Lini, that ash belongs to you. I know it does."

She threw her hands up. "Corren, you're such a *stubborn... insufferable...*" She gestured towards the top of the Rock of Light, her crimson shawl blowing in the wind. "It won't come off for me. The Phoenix doesn't want me to have it."

"What I have to suggest will help whether it's you or not. If it's not you, I think this will help find the right person."

But the right person is you.

"Please. Will you try?"

287

She exhaled and he knew she would relent. "Try what? You haven't even told me what it is yet."

"This way." He turned and together they headed for the Cloister where Praea and the others were waiting.

Praea watched Corren return with Lini, looking for all the world like a member of the Orsini Colony. Yet, in spite of the traditional colorful robes and gold mark on her forehead, Lini did not seem like a Colony member.

But she did not seem like one of the Order either.

Corren said he was convinced the ash was meant for Lini, twice as much since his experience with the Phoenix. Praea's skin lit up at the memory of Corren rising into the sky with the Phoenix. She knew who he was and what he'd sacrificed for the Phoenix. For the Order. For all they held dear. She trusted him.

This woman standing before her, in spite of her rough edges, did not seem evil as Tivoli had.

She did not seem like an ally either.

But then again, how could she be? Being an outsider and from such a distant place, she couldn't know what the Phoenix meant to them. She couldn't know how precious its ash.

Maybe the ash waited for Lini. Maybe it didn't. But if Lini *were* to lift the ash off the altar, shouldn't she at least understand the gift she was being given?

It wasn't a very long flight from the Rock of Light to Tower Hall South, but when Praea finally landed on firm ground, Lini scrambled off and away. The terror of being so far off the ground still clung to her. She watched incredulously as Corren climbed down and the golden bird transformed back into a woman. Lini just looked at her, stunned. "That was horrible," she said.

Praea, who was nearly as golden and fair in human form as she was as a bird, said gently, "I wasn't going to let you fall."

"Horrible," Lini said again.

Corren only smiled. "Wait here. I'll go prepare the ash."

For a moment, she watched Corren retreating toward the massive stone complex of buildings that comprised Tower Hall South, then turned her attention to the sight before her. Rounded hedges about the height of her knees formed concentric circles, the center of which was just big enough for a person to stand in. A single path cut through the hedges, leading to the center. It looked harmless enough, but she sensed the magic in it.

"What is this place?" Lini asked.

"They call it the Silent Circle. The Layrin branch tends the hedges with their magic, and the Wysard branch does... whatever they do with it using their magic. I'm not sure what exactly."

Lini second-guessed the wisdom of coming. She didn't like the idea of something magical being done to her. "I don't understand what I'm doing here."

"Corren thought you should come."

Lini softened in spite of herself. Maybe Corren knew what he was doing and maybe he didn't, but she didn't think he would try to hurt her. She sighed. She was here. She could at least give this a chance. Whatever *this* was.

Praea was studying her. "What do you know of Corren?"

What did she know of him? He was powerful—frighteningly powerful at times—intelligent, determined, stubborn... and strangely comforting. She didn't say any of this to Praea though. Instead she shrugged and said, "I know he's the Head of the Order."

"But do you know why? Do you know how that came to pass? Do you know what the Order is really all about?"

Lini stared at her. No, she didn't know any of that. She didn't answer, but she didn't need to. Praea must have seen it on her face. "Perhaps knowing will be the best way for you to understand."

She began telling her about the Phoenix and the Order and how it had been a force for good and service for thousands of years. She told her about the prophecy and Aradia, about the stones and the Three brothers.

As Praea talked, Lini forgot to be suspicious of her, forgot to be careful of the woman she did not know. She had become enchanted with her tale.

When Praea told Lini about the sacrifice Corren made to bring the Phoenix back to life, Lini asked, "Did Corren really die?"

Praea nodded. "It seemed so. Yes."

"He knew that was going to happen and he did it anyway?"

"I don't know if I could have done it," Praea responded.

Lini turned away and saw Corren coming toward them across the lawn, holding his staff in one hand and a small, wooden bowl in the other. That man had thought he was going to die and did what he needed to do anyway. Praea may have doubts about whether or not she could have made such a sacrifice herself, but Lini didn't need to wonder. She knew she could never be that good.

Even if she wanted to be.

As Corren drew near, she looked inside the little wooden bowl in the palm of his hand. It held a dark gray paste.

"How this works," he said, "is I'll say the incantations while I place this ash mixture on your brow, eyelids, and temples."

She thought of the High Ceremony of the Way of Orsini, nervous once more. Would he try to hurt her?

"Then you'll walk to the center," he continued. "That's it. The Silent Circle will take over from there."

"But... what happens? What will it do?" She tried not to sound afraid but heard it there in her voice.

"It's different for everyone," he said gently. "Some gain knowledge or clarity about something. Some feel a deep sense of comfort. Some..." he stole a glance at Praea, "well, it can be a little emotional. A... cleansing kind of thing, I guess. Some have visions. Most of this I know from studying and the little we've used it since it was rebuilt. It takes a fair amount of ash, and we still tend to be cautious about that. This though. I think this was meant for you."

She looked again at the little rounded hedges. That circle, it was going to do something to her.

Corren leaned in and lowered his voice. "I cannot say it won't be difficult. But I promise you, it won't be *bad*."

She looked at Corren, feeling how she always did around him and remembering all Praea had said of him. She looked at the gray paste in the little bowl. She looked at the hardened ash at the tip of his staff. She looked at Praea, who waited patiently.

She realized that, in spite of herself, she trusted them.

She took a deep breath. "Alright."

Corren raised his hand, holding it flat so the little bowl sat on top. He held her eyes and said quietly, "Thank you."

He turned his attention to the ash then. Tucking his staff into the crook of his other arm, he scooped a bit of ash out with two of his fingers. She did not take her eyes off his.

She could not explain why. She wanted to cry.

"*Revia ayalla*," he said. His hand came to her forehead and gently rubbed the cool paste across her brow, right over her gold mark. As if it weren't even there.

Back to the bowl for more paste.

Now he met her eyes, fingers aloft.

She remembered what she was supposed to do. She hesitated, then closed her eyes. They could do anything to her now. Though she felt a little vulnerable, she kept her eyes closed.

"*Revia ayalla*," he said and the cool paste went first on her right lid, then her left.

She heard the folds of his cloak moving as he dipped into the bowl for more ash.

"*Revia ayalla*."

She felt the paste on her left temple. Then her right.

That was it, but she did not feel any magic pressing on her as she thought she would. She tried to be open to whatever might happen but could not help the resistance deep within her. That internal guarding against the potential for harm.

She opened her eyes. Corren was still right in front of her. He nodded in the direction of the circle behind her.

She slowly turned. The little rounded hedges looked no different. They felt no different. She took one step in, then another, slowly walking down the pathway toward the center. She still felt nothing.

Maybe it wasn't going to work for her. Just like the ash would not lift off that altar. Maybe Corren was wrong. Maybe too much was wrong with *her*.

She approached the center and stepped inside.

Here she felt the magic that brought her to her knees.

While still feeling as if she were in her body, she also saw herself as if from above. She saw herself kneeling in the center of the Silent Circle, head down, hands over her eyes. She saw Corren and Praea nearby, watching anxiously.

At the same time, she saw things as if she were standing in the center of the Circle looking up. And looking up she saw it.

More than a bird. More than anything she ever imagined. The Phoenix appeared before her with wings outstretched, as magnificent and terrifying a thing as Lini had ever seen. The wind from its beating wings swirled around her. She felt it but heard nothing. She was in a place deep inside herself.

And there on the ground looking up at the Phoenix.

And floating above herself as she received this vision.

In every place she was, it was perfectly silent.

The part of her standing in the Circle looked at the Phoenix, and it looked right back at her. It looked as if it could see and know everything about her.

Every. Horrible. Thing.

Raw and gaping, Lini felt the Phoenix *knowing* her.

All the despicable things she'd ever done. All the despicable things that had been done to her. Everything she'd ever felt and thought, cherished and despised. Everything she hoped for, wished for. How she wanted more than anything else to be safe and whole and loved. How she longed to be in her parents' arms, an innocent girl once more.

To start over and have a different life.

In the midst of this vision of the Phoenix, she finally understood how she had resisted the magic of the Way of Orsini. The Phoenix helped her do it. Somehow, it knew she wanted nothing of it, and for some reason it helped her.

As if independent of her own mind, thoughts came to her. But different even from that. Not thoughts with words, more like thoughts that *understood.* And they came from the Phoenix.

Lini thought back to her first time taking the potion of the Way of Orsini. Just a girl. A girl missing father and mother and the wide-open valleys that surrounded her home, terrified in a strange, new place. Had she sensed the evil in what they were giving her? Had she tasted that evil, sharp and bitter like metal on the tongue?

She had fought it, whatever it was, but at her second ceremony, as Sienna saved her from a deadly beating, Lini knew she would have to take the potion again or die.

Moments ago, Praea had talked about Corren giving up his life in a fight against evil. Lini, as a child, had in fact done something no one else in the Orsini Colony had ever done. She had tried to stop the ceremony and failed. On the heels of that failure, she chose to save her own life, even though that meant also choosing submission and evil.

She had never forgiven herself for it.

Here, now, she saw herself as the Phoenix saw her. She had pity on that child. She had admiration. She had forgiveness. She had only been a child, after all. Lini realized that even though she'd since grown into a woman, as long as the potion of the Way of Orsini had been in her, she had remained that child, frightened and huddling on the ground, waiting for the fatal kick.

Across earth and sea, the Phoenix had somehow swooped down and given her the ability to resist.

But it was more than that. What the Phoenix gave her was more than just what she could do during the ceremonies. It was something that came down to this very moment and every moment hereafter. She felt, at last, the full impact of what the Phoenix gave her: the freedom to choose. The ability to truly have that freedom.

She still had it.

She didn't have to go back to the Orsini Colony, but neither did she have to stay with the Order. She could go somewhere completely different, East perhaps, and build a whole new life where no one knew her or knew who she had once been. She could begin again.

Looking into the eyes of this mysterious, majestic creature, Lini did not know *why* the Phoenix had given her this gift, only that it had done so. And that her choices were her own forever after.

She saw the pathways of her choices in front of her as clearly as if she stood at the head of them even now. One path would take her away into a green country with soft, rolling hills and deep, deep quiet. This tranquility of the Silent Circle... that would be hers to keep. The other path would take her up a soaring mountain with backbreaking climbs but stunning, heartbreaking views.

She knew what each path meant. She knew each could bring her happiness. She knew the Phoenix would give her either one she chose.

She thought about that difficult but beautiful, mountain path. Only a few moments ago, she did not think she could climb such a path. She thought her past kept her from it. She thought she could not be good enough and could never be that kind of person, but now she knew that she could. The choice had always been hers; she just didn't believe it before.

She thought about Corren and his brothers and the stones that had come to them. They had been compelled to their paths. They didn't choose; the Phoenix chose them. The Phoenix *needed* them.

But this was different. The Phoenix held out its offerings to her like a gift she could accept or decline. And she felt the Phoenix would be happy for her either way. That's what astonished her the most. She could walk away from the Phoenix and the Order and live a life of rest in the green hills of the East. She could be at peace and happy at last, and the Phoenix would be happy for her.

Maybe the Phoenix already knew who else would climb that mountain if she chose not to.

There was no pressure, no expectations, no fear of the Phoenix coming to an end if she turned away. The Phoenix gave her a gift freely, presented her with her options, and left it to her.

For the first time in her life, Lini had both power and freedom to choose her own path.

The part of her looking up smiled at the Phoenix; the part of her watching her kneeling figure from above saw the tears slip beneath her hands and fall to her crimson skirt. The part of her kneeling sighed.

All three parts of her whispered, "Thank you," and Lini came together.

Whole again.

There in the Silent Circle, with Corren and Praea looking on.

Twelve

Lini followed Corren and the other members of the Order up the winding staircase with Kennard just behind her. The Order members had waited after Corren's assurances that Lini would be back to claim the ash. And here she was. But she still held the vision of the two paths in front of her.

As they came into the upper room with the Eternal Flame burning in the center, Lini looked at the orb of ash and knew that if she tried to lift it, it would be hers. Even as they gathered around the altar and took their places once more, she knew that the only thing left was to make her choice.

Which path did she want?

Corren, confident as he usually was, had brought her back and now began the ceremony without preamble. She heard the words lilting around in her head. She gazed at the Eternal Flame.

Before they came back to the Rock of Light, Lini had asked Praea about the lands in the East. They turned out to be Praea's own country, Sakkara. A quiet, green, peaceful land. No doubt full of pale people just like Praea.

Lini stood in front of the altar, wrapped in the colorful fabrics of her people with the gold mark of the Orsini Colony still on her forehead. Where it would always stay. Because her past would always be a part of her. And she could acknowledge it now without it darkening her future or her own vision of herself.

As she looked at the Eternal Flame, heard Corren chanting *Ah mae alla*, and chanted it back herself, Lini knew she wanted the path that would remember the past while allowing for a new future.

She thought about the ravine, the Book of Madera in Tivoli's hands, her friend Sienna, and how near they were to the entrance to the Shoals.

Corren said the final chant and the time was upon her to make her choice.

Lini placed her hands around the glass orb.

Then lifted it off the stone.

She lifted it higher and higher until it was above her head and she was looking up at it.

I choose this, she thought, not knowing if the Phoenix could hear but wanting to think it just the same. *I choose this.*

Come what may, if anyone was going to guard those Shoals from the evil of Tivoli, it was going to be her.

At the hidden spring on the castle grounds, the surface of the water undulated softly in the moonlight. Janus removed her shoes and sat cross-legged on her favorite ledge, waiting for Marcellus. Without him here to distract her by his constant attempts to get her in the water with him, which she never would, she was able to more fully enjoy the serenity found here. Especially now that she was back to herself, free from the blackness that had been consuming her.

Lily had not been so lucky. The whole thing made Janus remember what it was she loved about the human world: their bravery and joy in the face of inescapable death.

The wind swooped through the trees and brushed past her face and bare feet. She unfolded her legs and touched one toe to the water. She wondered if all earth faeries had an irrational fear of the ocean's water or if it was just her. But if she had done one thing over and over since leaving the faerie world for the human one, it was force herself to go forward in the face of fear.

She lowered her leg until her entire foot was encapsulated in the water. It felt so different from the water of the earth. Wilder.

She forced her leg to relax. The water swirled around her calf.

She considered putting in her other leg. Instead, she wrapped her arms around her shin and rested her chin on her knee. Bravery could go just so far.

She sat there for a time, until she almost forgot about the water swirling about her calf and the strange sensations it caused. Then she felt something. She straightened and looked behind her. "Marcellus?"

She felt him call to her. He was on his way. But there was something else. Something else she couldn't identify.

It felt like Marcellus, but not. Then she realized this strange feeling wasn't coming from behind her, but in front of her. She spun around but before she could jerk her foot out of the water, someone grabbed hold and pulled.

Yanked off the ledge, Janus disappeared beneath the surface, which riled and upheaved until everything went still and silent.

PART III

The Shoals

One

Marcellus sat at his desk, the balcony doors behind him hanging open to let in the cool, night air. He would have been down at the hidden spring with Janus this very moment, had he not been cornered by the Advisor of Finances. Tinogen was "highly concerned" about the rising costs of dam reconstruction at Kilona Lake. They weren't in any danger of draining the coffers, and Tinogen was the sort to be "highly concerned" even when there weren't unforeseen drains on the treasury, but that's what made him so well-suited to his position. With such diligence, the king of Caedmonia wasn't likely to be accused of waste.

Still, Marcellus found it tiresome to be here soothing Tinogen's nerves when he could be relaxing in the spring with Janus instead. When at last they finished reviewing various figures and Marcellus authorized a few necessary adjustments, he stood to indicate the meeting had reached its end.

Tinogen, who likely would've continued rehashing the evening's topics for quite some time, took the point. He stood and bowed. "Thank you, your Grace."

"I trust you feel the matter settled?"

"Yes, your Grace." He gathered his books, bowed once more, and left the room.

Marcellus retrieved a small ledger from the bottom drawer and made a few notes. He'd been taught that wise kings took measures to protect the treasury against thievery from within. This done, he left his office and told the page waiting outside his door that he could close things up for the evening.

The hall was quiet. Iron sconces along the walls softly illuminated the smooth stone. He would normally head to his

301

room to dress down for the evening before sneaking away to the hidden spring, but he'd had enough of delays. In his embroidered king's coat, with his jeweled sword still hanging from one hip and the water sword on the other, he sent the call to Janus to let her know he was coming.

When he reached out, he sensed something strange about her. Confusion and—a sudden sharp swoop of fear, then... nothing. He couldn't feel her.

Heart pounding, he stopped short. "Janus?" he said aloud. His voice echoed in the vacant hallway.

He reached farther, trying to find her, but she was gone.

He bolted into motion. His steps echoed sharply as he ran down the hallways and stairs. He tore through a side door of the castle and into the dark of night. His feet pounded the ground and the blood pounded in his ears. All the while he reached for her and found nothing.

Where did she go? Janus!

He flung open the iron gate leading to the hidden spring. It clanged behind him as he ran past darkened pines. The spring came into view and he saw Janus' boots on the ground next to the bench, but no Janus.

He sprinted to the edge and swept his eyes over the eddying surface of the dark water. If she were on the grounds, he'd be able to feel her, but what if she were in the pool? What if she fell in and couldn't swim?

Marcellus dove from the rock and plunged into the cool water. The weight of his clothes and weaponry pulled him down, but he manipulated the elements in the water to regain control. He scanned the rocky bottom and drew closer to a dark pocket, fearing he'd see Janus' lifeless form. But it was nothing but stone. He frantically continued his search along the length of the pool with no sign of her.

When he came to the deepest part of the spring, the water churned violently around him. Here the undercurrents were dangerous enough to drag down even a strong swimmer.

Janus.

Marcellus pushed through the currents toward the bottom and disappeared into the tunnel that would take him to sea.

It seemed she had been in the water for as long as she had been alive. Janus was surrounded by the dark and the deep and the wildness of an element that was not hers. She felt it sapping her of strength. She pulled and grasped at the arms around her waist, but they did not budge. She could not see her abductor. Whoever it was had her from behind, and they sped through the water, on and on and on.

Though she understood she was not drowning, she still felt as if she couldn't breathe, as if any moment her lungs would compress and squeeze the life right out of her. The longer she was in the water, the more her ability to fight against her captor waned. The dark beneath them deepened as she was taken farther and farther from home.

Finally, they began to ascend and rose through the water until her captor's head broke the surface. He stopped just short of allowing her to do the same. An orange light winked at her through the rippling water, and she heard the muffled sound of him talking to someone. Now there were two. She resumed her struggles, with no more success than before.

Suddenly she was out of the water, simultaneously lifted by her captor and grabbed by someone else. She took a great gulp of air, free from the sea at last. The man who'd lifted her out of the bay had dark hair that fell to his shoulders and a gold mark on his forehead. He tried setting her on her feet in front of him, but she had difficulty supporting her own weight and stumbled into the man's chest. He caught her by the shoulders and flung her away from him. She landed hard on the rocky ground.

They were near a cave of sorts, which glowed from a large campfire. Some six men gathered round looking down at her.

All had gold marks on their foreheads. She knew this identified them as members of a Hathmirrian group of wizards who had been causing a fair amount of trouble.

From out of the sea came her abductor. Seeing him now, Janus confirmed what she had already surmised. The grotesque scarring down his cheek and bluish-gray coloring of his skin matched Marcellus' descriptions of the water faeries he'd seen once before.

As the faerie looked down at her, she felt the element of water slipping away. Her strength was slowly returning, but she did not move. They were not restraining her.

The faerie looked at the man who'd pulled her from the bay. "Delivered, as promised."

"This is not who you promised. This is a woman."

The water faerie nodded. "This is even better, Bricker. She is an earth faerie. A *full* earth faerie."

The man called Bricker scowled down at Janus, as if deciding whether or not to believe it. "Is she now?"

While he was busy scrutinizing her, she took note of the details that most concerned her. None of the men had swords. She saw no weapon she could try to steal in order to defend herself. So far as she could tell in the light from the fire, the beach was free of driftwood or any other item she could use against them.

Underneath the rocky overhang, in addition to the fire, was evidence the men had been making camp here. Waiting, perhaps, for the water faerie and whoever he was supposed to capture instead of her.

A man, apparently. Then she understood. Marcellus. He'd come to the pool looking for Marcellus.

Janus narrowed her eyes.

Bricker knelt down as if studying some strange creature. Janus brought up a knee and kicked him hard in the temple. She reached to her right and pulled the feet out from under the man nearest her and he went down hard on his back. Hands and arms came at her from every other direction and she was soon pinned down.

"Get her up!" someone shouted.

She continued to struggle, but two men held her arms, which they twisted behind her. They lifted her wrists so high she had to bend over to keep her arms from snapping. The muscles in her shoulders strained and burned.

"Don't break her," their leader said flatly.

They yanked her upright.

The men were looking at her with a new kind of respect now. Respect and wariness. Clearly, no one wanted to get too close. Too bad because she was itching to kick someone else.

Bricker gazed at her darkly. He glanced at one of the men and jerked his thumb toward their campsite. The man headed over, understanding some unspoken command. The water faerie lingered on the edge of the shoreline. One step backwards and he'd be in the water and gone. As if he didn't trust the men any more than she did.

The man returned with a rope. Janus resumed her struggles but they came upon her with one accord, taking her to the ground and tying her up. Only then did Bricker come within striking range. He pulled back his arm and punched her solidly on the temple, then everything went black.

The trail in the water was so faint, Marcellus wasn't even sure if it was truly a trail or merely wishful thinking. He didn't know what it all meant, but after a quick search of the bay and finding no sign of Janus, the only other thing he could think to do was follow the one lead he had. The farther and farther he went, however, the more he wondered if this wasn't a mistake. Maybe this was just an old trail of some water faerie going wherever water faeries like to go and wasn't leading him to Janus at all.

He wondered if he'd missed her somehow. He questioned whether she was on the shore by the sea, or maybe she'd been in the woods near the spring. But why couldn't he feel her? He could only think of two reasons: either she was dead or she was in the water.

Marcellus sped through the bay, unable to contemplate the first option.

Janus awoke in the back of a wagon, with the moon lending just enough light to reveal the hulking shapes and hard faces of the three men riding with her. She was gagged and lay on her side, helpless. Her temple throbbed and ached and she briefly considered healing herself but decided against it. One of the men noticed her. He tapped one of his fellows with his boot and nodded in her direction. They all looked at her and she looked back, but no one moved. They turned away unconcerned. They had her where they wanted her.

She would soon discover just where that was.

The wagon came to a stop and two of the men hauled her out. They were in back of a squat stone house, its tiny windows lit by the fireplace burning within. Bricker came around and hooked a hand under her arm, yanking her forward. Still bound and gagged, she followed, resisting the urge to stick out her leg and take Bricker down. It'd be a fleeting victory and she knew it.

They entered the house where an old couple huddled in the kitchen corner, watching mutely as the troop passed by and into a living area. A bald man stood as they entered. He, too, had a gold mark on his forehead and held a staff with both hands in front of him. She had thought Bricker was their leader, but upon seeing this man, she knew she'd been wrong. She thought of Corren's staff and wondered what this man could do with his.

"An earth faerie, Lord Tivoli," Bricker said.

Janus knew this name. Leader of the Orsini Colony. What could they possibly want with her? Or Marcellus?

The man came close, running his eyes over her as if he were inspecting a horse at market. "She doesn't look like a faerie."

She took stock of the room: a sagging couch, two wooden chairs, a squat table, a few stubby candles in their holders, a broom leaning against the corner. What she wouldn't give for a sword.

Tivoli examined her temple, where Bricker had hit her. It felt swollen and no doubt had started to color.

He stepped back. "Looks like a mere wench to me. How do we know that slimy fish isn't trying to trick us?"

Perhaps the man was not really asking, for no one offered an answer and he returned to his assessment, looking her in the eyes. She watched him with distaste.

Tivoli smirked. "Release her."

"But my Lord—"

"Release her!"

The man behind her loosened the gag, which fell around her neck. As another started untying her bonds, Bricker stepped forward and caught her eye, giving her a warning glare. Clearly he didn't want any more of her aggression. She held his gaze, wishing she could put an arrow through the gold mark on his forehead.

Though her bonds were released, the man behind her still held her arms. She let him. Tivoli gave a gesture and Bricker came up and grabbed her left wrist, raising her arm out to her side.

"That's right," Tivoli said. The dark look on his face was enough for her. She yanked her arm out of Bricker's grasp but was restrained so fast by so many that she soon found herself back in the same position, struggling against her captors, arm held aloft.

Bricker offered a satisfied smirk, but her attention was soon drawn to Tivoli, who was stepping toward her and raising his staff. He placed the tip on top of her exposed bicep. The wood felt cool, but with a word from Tivoli, the cool sensation turned sharp and hot. Struggling anew, she was held fast and watched as the tip of his staff cut her arm like a knife, leaving a bloody gash.

Her arm burned as the blood ran freely onto the wooden floor below. He withdrew his staff and took a step back. She kicked the man behind her. Caught off guard, his grip around her waist loosened slightly, and she was about to take advantage of this when Tivoli's staff came bearing down on her neck.

Everyone stilled.

His hard face was inches from hers. The wood pressed on her skin. His dark eyes glowered at her as the tip of his staff rested over her artery, which pulsed against the offending object.

She watched him, still as stone. Her left arm screamed in pain.

"Play nice," he said lowly, "or I'll cut you until you're begging for death."

His eyes glittered with arousal at the idea. He stepped away and brought his staff in front of him, resting both hands on the tip. "Now," he said, calmly, "heal yourself."

Her left arm was still held out to her side, throbbing as blood poured from the wound.

"Unless you'd rather die," he said. "Heal it."

She did indeed need to heal it if she didn't want to bleed to death. Her fingertips were beginning to feel cold, and she was starting to get lightheaded. There was nothing she could do about her blood loss—she would need herbs or a tree to recover from that—but she could close the wound.

She tried moving her other arm, but the man restraining her wouldn't let her budge. "I need my hand," she growled, though that wasn't quite true.

Tivoli nodded and the man released her arm.

The Lord of the Orsini Colony watched intently as Janus placed her right hand on the underside of her throbbing bicep.

The slick blood ran onto her palm. She slowly raised her hand until it covered the gash.

Golden healing light seeped through her fingers and the pain retreated. The collective holds on her body relaxed as the men watched the evidence of her magic. Tivoli and his staff drew near. She continued running her hand up her arm in one smooth motion, revealing the healed flesh underneath.

He leaned closer, eyes on her arm. She knew it would cost her, but she struck her blood-soaked hand across Tivoli's face.

The group responded with outrage but she managed to elbow the man to her right before they had her restrained again. Bricker himself held her from behind now, his arm locked tightly around her neck. Her elbow smarted and she could barely breathe, but that didn't stop her from reveling in the astonished look on Tivoli's face.

He brought two fingertips to the dark blood smeared across his cheek, then lowered them enough to stare at the evidence of her assault. "That," he said to Janus, "may be the last thing you ever do of your own free will."

He glanced to the others. "Take her downstairs."

Two

The trail in the water eventually led Marcellus to the opposite side of the bay. An old campfire was still smoldering in the center of the dark cave in front of him, but it was not this evidence of recent activity that alerted him the most.

It was what he felt, very faintly. Janus. He could barely sense her off in the distance.

In spite of the dimly lit night, he headed in her direction, finding a path that led from the shore up onto scrubby grassland. He suspected he was somewhere on the eastern coast of Hathmirr. If he were, he should be grateful to be under cover of nightfall, given that his clothes clearly marked him as a Caedmonian of rank. However, he mostly cursed the lack of light for hindering his progress toward Janus.

He ran as silently as he could, his footfalls light and quick on the hard ground. Soon, dark silhouettes of buildings came into view. A few had lights burning within, so he turned to the right in an effort to skirt them. He quickly determined he was on the edge of a settlement, and further down saw a tall, sturdy structure he identified as a military outpost. A series of torches burned along the top and a few men stood guard.

He backtracked, hoping he could more easily go around the settlement in the other direction. A row of squat, adobe homes stretched before him, and he lost touch with Janus before he came to the end. He went back immediately, keeping her in range. The fact that he could barely sense her alarmed him, but not as much as the fact that she wasn't responding. What was going on?

Though he knew it'd be safer to go around the city, he couldn't risk losing touch with her. He carefully approached the row of darkened homes and slipped through a narrow passageway between two of them. All was quiet and still, except for a few chirping crickets.

Coming to the front, he checked his surroundings. Across a deserted lane were more dwellings, nearly all dark. He darted forward, but as he got to the other side, he heard a group of men turning onto the road, heading in his direction. Their rhythmic march told him they were Hathmirrian soldiers. There must have been at least a dozen, but they carried only two torches. Unseen, he hurried into the shadows between two houses, careful not to make any noise.

He kept close to the side of one house. Halfway along its length, someone holding a lantern opened a back door and a beam of light cut across a rear field.

Marcellus crouched low, pressing against the outer wall.

A dog ran out into the yard. It was a mutt of some sort with a mangy-looking dark coat, but it was a sizable animal. The kind men used for hunting or protection. Whoever opened the door seemed to be lingering there while the dog sniffed around, looking for a place to relieve itself.

Marcellus held his breath, waiting. Behind him, he heard the soldiers coming closer. If it was daylight, they'd be able to see him once he got into their line of sight. As it was, he was in the shadows and could only hope that would be enough.

The dog took to its business and, having finished, jogged toward the house. Nearly there, its ears perked up and it looked in Marcellus' direction. It stopped, sniffing the air.

The man at the back door whistled. "Come on, boy!"

The soldiers' march along the street continued. They were directly behind him now.

The dog drew near. Body tense, tail erect, its eyes glinted in the dark. As it spotted Marcellus, the hair on the back of its neck rose into the air.

March, march, march.

The animal issued a long, deep, rumbling growl.

The sound must have carried to the road, for the footsteps behind him fell out of rhythm and shuffled to a stop.

Marcellus wasn't about to wait to get caught and would rather deal with one dog than a unit of armed men. Staying low, he unsheathed his sword and bolted to the other side of the passageway, hoping for space to break past the dog. Several things happened at once. A soldier behind him yelled "Halt!" and some men started running. The dog let out two booming barks as it charged toward Marcellus. The owner of the dog came around the corner, holding his lantern aloft and further blocking Marcellus' escape route.

The dog leapt toward him and Marcellus struck it on the shoulder with the handle of his sword. It yelped and fell on its back, trying to scramble to its feet.

Marcellus broke into a full run, with the pounding feet and shouts of the Hathmirrians behind him.

"Move! Move!" he shouted to the man with the lantern.

Eyes wide, the man glanced at Marcellus' sword and stumbled backward.

Marcellus pushed past him and sprinted across the field with the soldiers running and shouting behind him. The dry ground was cloaked in darkness and crunched underneath his feet as he ran. He was pulling ahead but running somewhat blind. He hoped he wouldn't hit a hole or stumble over some object on the ground. The rear of another line of houses, and their accompanying passageways in between, came into view.

He pushed hard toward an alleyway, the distance between him and his pursuers steadily increasing. When he entered the darkened passage, however, he heard the commotion of more men running and shouting just ahead. They came into view, pouring into the narrow space in front of him.

More Hathmirrian soldiers. Four. Seven. Marcellus came to an abrupt halt, and in the next instant there were some ten men in front of him and another dozen closing in behind. The sides of the buildings lit up with the soldiers' flickering torches. And in that moment, it was over. Not only was he going to fall into these men's hands, but they stood between him and Janus and whatever was happening to her. He thought of the sharp swoop of fear he'd felt from her before she'd disappeared from the castle grounds, and the way that she wouldn't or couldn't respond to him even now, and had half a mind to cut through every last man in that alleyway to get to her.

But that could not be. Cursing under his breath, he sheathed his sword and raised his arms into the air, knowing a fight would only end in his death.

The ringing of swords echoed in the alleyway, and in a matter of moments he was surrounded by blades pointed in his direction.

"Weapons on the ground!" a man in front hollered in his thick Hathmirrian accent.

Marcellus hesitated. The sharp scent of the flames from the torches thickened in the air. He again recalculated the probability of success if he went on the offensive and again deduced inevitable failure. He pulled his jeweled sword out of its sheath and set it on the ground, followed by the water sword.

A few whistles escaped the group. Several of the men shuffled to get a better view. They all wore red vests and had long, dark hair in a tight braid down their backs, as was typical of the Hathmirrian forces.

"What's this?" One of the men picked up the sword forged by the water faeries and examined the wavy blade. Its surface seemed to ripple like water, and as he rotated it forward and back, it glinted in the torchlight.

Their leader, however, was scrutinizing Marcellus, not his sword.

With narrowed eyes, he stepped forward and looked him over. Marcellus regretted not taking the time to remove his coat at the hidden spring. He regretted not running left in the darkened field instead of right. He regretted not being at the spring with Janus earlier as planned. He regretted a lot of things.

"What have we here?" the man said.

"Who knew nighttime maneuvers were going to get so interesting?" the one with the water sword said.

There were a few appreciative chuckles, but the soldier in front of Marcellus continued to regard him with a calculating expression. Marcellus grimly wondered if the man knew just who he had.

"Yes," he said. "I think the commander will be very interested to see you."

In the earthen basement of the stone house, Janus was tied to a wooden table. The members of the Orsini Colony were gathered around, looming over her. There was one lit candle above her head and no more.

They had been chanting incantations while Tivoli held a shallow bowl aloft. After a time, the group went silent. The only sound was Janus struggling against the ropes and the trickling sound of Tivoli pouring whatever was in the bowl into a wooden cup.

Janus pressed her lips together even before he approached her, cup in hand. She turned away but someone forced her head back while another pulled on her jaw to open it. She tried to bite him but he gripped her lower teeth in one hand, her upper teeth in another, and wrenched her mouth open so fiercely she thought her jaw would break. Her vision was largely blocked by the man's arm and everything she saw was in confusion as they fought to subdue her.

Someone poured the bitter liquid into her gaping mouth and she gagged and gasped, swallowed reflexively and coughed, and it wouldn't stop, wouldn't stop, and she couldn't breathe and thought she really would drown this time. The deluge ended and they released her to swallow and gasp for breath.

"Devils!" she spat, but this only drew low laughter from the group.

They began chanting again, but Janus' attention drew inward. She could sense where the liquid was going inside her and could not tell if it was poison or a potion or perhaps both. She sensed the magic of it, dark and terrible. Because she was not a human, but a faerie, and had control of her body both inside and out, she forced herself to regurgitate the liquid all over the table.

This stopped the chanting abruptly, but she was still focusing inward. Part of the potion had already eked into her system and she couldn't get it out.

She tried quenching it with the healing light within, but it spread inside of her like smoke.

"Will it still work?" she heard someone ask. "Do we give her more?"

She felt a hand on her forehead but was unable to move away from it. She realized she had closed her eyes.

"It's working," Tivoli said. "Begin again."

The sound of their chanting washed over her. The magic within her seemed to move with the rhythm of their chanting. As if it were obeying them. Undulating. Capturing her from within.

It was as if the very essence of her life was being gathered out of her.

The chanting grew faint, like it was coming from far away. Now there was talking. Mumbling. They have enough, they said. They're leaving, they said. They said they'll leave her to die, and the old man of the household could bury the body himself.

Janus was left in the silence and darkness. Alone. Fading, fading, fading.

Three

Lini and Corren descended the central staircase in Tower Hall South near the main entryway. It was still predawn and as the general population of the Tower had not yet risen, the foyer was dark. It lit up when Corren cast the spell that set the massive chandelier hanging from the ceiling alight. They were on their way to the front courtyard, where preparations for their journey were nearly complete.

After Lini removed the ash from the altar late yesterday afternoon, she indicated she wanted to return to the Desert Entrance as soon as possible. She was relieved when Corren not only readily agreed but planned to come with her. Kennard—whose status as Head of a now-defunct branch of the Order had not yet been discussed—would escort them and offer protection, along with a handful of Guard members. Kennard and the Guard knew the purpose of the trip was to neutralize a potential threat from Tivoli, but they didn't know the details. Only Corren and Lini knew they were going so she could restore the Veil of Madera.

Corren opened the front door and held it for her. Kennard and the others were in the courtyard, securing the last few saddlebags on their horses. She hung back and Corren waited with her. "I've been thinking," she said. "Maybe we should tell the Tulaga about the Desert Entrance."

He let the door close, leaving them alone in the foyer. He thoughtfully tapped one finger against his staff. "I don't know about that, Lini."

"They could help us protect it."

Their voices echoed off the stone walls in the large foyer.

"The different branches are careful about sharing knowledge with each other for a reason," he said. "Too much knowledge by one person or group can lead to trouble. We've seen that before. And I can't tell you how glad I am that Aradia didn't know about any of this."

"But Praea already knows about the Vortex," she pressed. "Her sage died trying to protect the Golden Canyon Entrance. Isn't that worth something? Doesn't that prove they should know about the Desert Entrance too?"

Corren thought about it for a moment, then said, "I'm not sure, to be honest. It may be worth considering, but I don't think you should be too hasty to reveal something the Madera branch kept secret all that time."

She frowned, thinking. He made a valid point. She didn't know much about the ways of the Order. Maybe there were good reasons to leave things alone. She looked at him, still unsure.

"Let's think about it, alright?" he said. "We'll get to the Desert Entrance and restore the Veil of Madera, then you can decide how to go forward from there."

Well, he was right about that. She could make those kinds of decisions later. Restoring the Veil took precedence, and it was the Desert Entrance they needed to worry about first. Even though Tivoli knew about both entrances, he was much closer to that one and would have to cross half of Caedmonia to get to the other. Not to mention potentially facing the dragon that killed Kai'Enna.

Corren opened the door for her once more and they stepped out into the cool, morning air of the courtyard. Lini took in the scene before her. The men were quietly tying the last bags into place and checking the saddles to make sure they were secure. The horses bobbed their heads and knocked their hooves against the dirt. The air was crisp and still and a few birds chirped to one another in the treetops, blissfully unaware of the burdens this group carried.

When she chose to lift the ash off the altar, she imagined she'd be walking this path and trying to protect the entrances into the Shoals alone. She'd been willing to do so. But these people were right here with her. She understood they weren't coming only for her. Maybe not for her at all. These were good people, she was starting to realize, who would be doing all this whether she were here or not. But it bolstered her, it did, to know that they were with her and she with them.

With everything loaded up, Lini, Corren, and half a dozen Guard members set out before the sun crested the horizon. While she was worried about whatever Tivoli's plans may be—and sorely wishing the Veil of Madera were already in place instead of the Desert Entrance still being vulnerable—she also felt wonder that she should be part of something so good.

Nicolai rose at dawn as he usually did, little suspecting what the day would bring. The disappearance of King Marcellus and Janus wasn't discovered until shortly before breakfast. Of course, no one quite thought of it as a disappearance at first. More of a 'where has he gotten off to this time?' But after Nicolai reached for them in the faerie way and felt nothing—not even as far as Amon Tunde—he ordered a search. When they looked in all the regular places, with no luck save for Janus' shoes at the hidden spring, things grew dire.

Swimmers searched the pool as best they could, but the currents prevented them from going too deep. Nicolai, knowing where the pool ultimately led, feared the worst and sent knights down to the shoreline. An afternoon of looking turned up nothing.

Nicolai ordered search parties be sent on land in every direction, but he sensed they only followed his commands because they, too, wanted to find Janus and the missing king. Murray, captain of the guard, stayed close to Nicolai, shadowing him along with several other knights. Commander Donnelly kept close as well, and for that Nicolai was grateful. He seemed to be the only thing preventing the others from throwing Nicolai into the dungeon. If anyone had motivation to murder King Marcellus and hide the body, it would be the one who was next in line for the throne. The heir who had only been on the scene for three months to start with. Judging by the looks he got from nearly everyone he passed, few trusted him.

Nicolai knew he was in a dangerous situation, but that did not overshadow his concern for his brother and Janus and the fear that someone, somewhere, would find King Marcellus and Janus dead.

In a tiny, stone room with naught else but a narrow bed and small wooden table, Marcellus stood by a window no bigger than his head. It was nearly level with the ground and afforded him ample views of horses' hooves, soldiers' boots, and the haze of dust hovering over the earth. The clamoring of activity outside was a marked contrast to the quiet and stillness in the little room. Marcellus had not moved from this spot in over an hour.

He was under guard in a Hathmirrian outpost of, he was told, the King's Fifth Regiment. While the soldiers who had captured him realized they'd discovered someone of rank in the Caedmonian army, it was their commander here who took one look at Marcellus and identified him as king. They locked him in this room and he hadn't seen anyone since.

It gave him plenty of time to consider the things he might have done differently and worry that his capture, apart from endangering both himself and his country, may have also cost Janus her life.

The Hathmirrian couple who'd had the displeasure of hosting the Lord of the Orsini Colony and his consorts the night before now faced the daunting task of trying to save a dying woman. She lay limp and unconscious on the mattress they'd brought down into the basement, setting it against one wall while the table—from which they'd untied her—had been pushed to the other side. They suspected she wasn't Hathmirrian, and likewise deduced that whatever was wrong with her was the result of some dark magic the Orsinians were so famous for inflicting on their enemies. Afraid to seek help lest that should bring more misfortune upon their household, they tried to tend to her alone. She was alive, but only just, and unresponsive to their ministrations.

They began discussing how they could manage to discreetly bury her, when the inevitable moment came.

Lini and Corren and their escort galloped across a broad valley, pushing the horses as hard as they dared on their long journey.

She'd stolen the Book of Madera and left Tivoli seven days ago. Seven days. And she had no idea what he'd been doing during that time. What if they got to the Desert Entrance and restored the Veil of Madera after he'd already been there and gone?

Almost as bad as the possibility of missing him was the possibility of running into him. What would he do to her if he had half the chance?

She looked at Corren, who was riding next to her with focused determination. Kennard and the other Guard members might have been along for protection, but it was Corren in

320

whom she found comfort. If he decided to protect her—and she did not doubt that he would—there wasn't anyone who could bring harm to her.

Unless, of course, Tivoli found a way to steal magic from the Vortex before they could stop him.

There was always that.

As before, Lord Tivoli and his obedient followers descended the narrow pathway into the ravine, past where they'd lost Sienna a few weeks ago, through the crevice in the rock wall, and into the cave where the air itself seemed infused with its own soft light. Each person had a lantern tied to their belts, but they did not need them.

They came to the tunnel he had inspected once before. Last time he was here, he'd confirmed that the Veil of Madera had dissipated, leaving only the far-distant faerie barrier to contend with. Now that he thought he had a way through it, he was willing to make the long journey to find out.

This time, he and his followers kept going.

They came to a junction where the tunnel broke off into two directions. He pulled out his leather folio and flipped through it, the pages rustling quietly. He found his hand-drawn notes, taken from the Book of Madera, that would lead the way. He pointed with the tip of his staff and took the tunnel to the right. Behind him, his colony members were carrying packs and supplies, enough to last several days.

It would be a long walk in this underground maze called the Shoals, but once they made it through the faerie barrier, there would be nothing left to stop them.

Four

Marcellus awoke to another day still in the holding cell of the Hathmirrian's Fifth Regiment. Yesterday, the only information he'd gotten out of the little group of soldiers who'd come to deliver his one meal of the day was they were waiting for instructions from a high-ranking commander stationed elsewhere.

It was starting to look like today would be more of the same. The door to his cell didn't open until midday. He rose and stood by the window, unwilling to sit before any of his captors, and watched as four soldiers came into the room, with at least five more lingering in the hall. One man carried a tin plate with a small loaf of bread, a burnt potato, and an overcooked cut of meat of unidentifiable origin. He dropped it on the table with a flat clang.

Though Marcellus was hungry enough to eat everything on the plate, as well as the man who'd brought it, he did not move. His captors watched him with a mixture of glee, arrogance, and caution.

While each man was heavily armed, one in particular held Marcellus' jeweled sword and wore the water sword in a sheath around his waist.

The man wore a cocky grin and made a show of admiring the stones in the hilt. "The sword of Marcellus the Fierce," he said. "You don't look so fierce now."

He noticed they'd brought no fewer than nine men to deliver their sorry excuse for a meal to Marcellus the Fierce, but said nothing.

"I think this will make a fine addition to my collection," the soldier said with a condescending nod of his head. "I thank you."

"That'll do, Leif," came a stern voice from the hall. The owner of the voice swept through the door, his men stepping aside. He addressed the soldier holding Marcellus' sword. "I'm sure you meant that will make a fine addition to the collection of your king, to whom that plunder rightly belongs."

Leif bowed his head deferentially. "Yes, Commander Ryden."

Commander Ryden turned his attention to Marcellus. The two regarded one another for no more than a heartbeat, but it was enough. The man before him presented an air of authority and, when called for, ruthlessness. He was the kind of man Marcellus would target on the field if they were in battle.

And they were. But this was not the kind of battle Marcellus could win with his sword, even if he had it.

"Your swords are not the only booty bound for our king," the commander said. "We're transporting you to Port Malado where you'll board a ship that will take you to our capital. There, I will present you as a gift to our king."

Marcellus did not allow himself to reveal his reaction to this bit of information.

The commander turned to leave the room. "Give him ten minutes to eat his meal," he said, "then load him up."

The king of Caedmonia and his future queen had been missing for a day and a half, and though Nicolai suspected they'd gone through the tunnel that led from the hidden spring to the bay, he had no idea why and had no means to follow them. Meanwhile, those in the castle were beginning to openly speculate that the worst had happened.

Nicolai gathered key military leaders and several of the king's advisors around the mahogany table in Jade Hall to determine if the citizenry at large should be notified of the situation. On the one hand, Nicolai didn't want to create a panic or make his already precarious situation worse. As the person with the most to gain from the death of the king, he knew alerting the kingdom in general might do no more good than landing him in the dungeon. However, he felt the more people they had looking, the more likely they were to find Marcellus and Janus. He thus argued it was in the best interest of their king that they make circumstances public.

After some debate, with a few advisors wondering aloud what Nicolai stood to gain from a public pronouncement—in spite of Nicolai being present to hear such ruminations—they agreed the safety of the king and queen-to-be was paramount. The announcements went out at midday.

Following this, Nicolai suggested yet again that he search the shoreline himself. While he trusted the king's knights to do their jobs, he was tired of directing troops and search parties—something Commander Donnelly was capable of handling himself—and wanted to put his tracking skills to use instead. He didn't want to be here in the castle; he wanted to be out finding his brother and Janus.

Captain Murray took Nicolai's request as an opportunity to voice concerns he'd so clearly had all along. He leaned across the table and addressed Commander Donnelly. "Yet again he's trying to leave the castle. Why? Does he see we will not permit his coup to succeed? Is he trying to escape?"

"I just want to help look—" Nicolai started, but the captain spoke over him.

"Why are we permitting him to roam around at will?"

"What do you suggest, Captain Murray?"

"Get him in the dungeon where he belongs. We don't need his help to find our king."

"Unless he can tell us where to find the bodies," another knight said hotly.

Nicolai stood and everyone in the room stood with him.

"Now hold on," Commander Donnelly said. "We have no evidence of guilt."

"Who else would it be?" Murray asked.

"Who else has shown more urgency in trying to find the king and Commander Janus?" This endorsement, to Nicolai's surprise, came from his trainer, Commander Whittaker. "I admit we would be foolish to leave him alone, given the state of affairs, but I don't think he would murder the king." This was answered with grumblings from many of the men and Whittaker raised his voice. "I'm sorry, but I don't," he said firmly and the group quieted slightly. "Keep an escort with him, but let's not hang him just yet. He wants to help scan the shoreline? I say we let him."

"And what of that?" Lang spoke up. "Why is he so insistent we search the bay more than anywhere else? How would he know where to look unless he was involved?"

"Maybe the place to look is on land," said an advisor, "and he's trying to throw us off."

"We're looking on land," Nicolai said firmly. "We're looking everywhere we can. We're alerting the citizens to ensure every eye is searching, and I'm glad of it, even though that means every eye in that city," he said, pointing out the window, "will be looking at me with the same anger and suspicion as most of you in this room. I did not ask to be a prince of Caedmonia, but King Marcellus expects me to live up to the responsibilities of a prince, and I will do as he asks."

"Is that what you were doing for weeks on end when you were nowhere to be seen and the king himself would not say where you were? Maybe he *could* not say where you were because he did not know himself."

"King Marcellus has made it clear he trusts Prince Nicolai," Donnelly said.

"He's no prince of mine!" Captain Murray spat. "He's been back for three days and now our king is gone. No trace! How do you know this so-called prince wasn't away planning a coup all along?"

"I don't," Donnelly said, "and neither do you. Can you really look at this man and see someone who would murder the king in cold blood?"

"We're wasting valuable time," Whittaker said. "I say we let him help with the search on shore. There's no harm in that. Unless," he said, looking directly at Captain Murray, "you don't think your men can keep an eye on one solitary person long enough to prevent some sort of escape."

Captain Murray scowled at Whittaker and folded his arms. He gave Nicolai a dark look. "Oh, we can keep an eye on him."

"I don't think so," Donnelly said flatly. "The prince comes with me."

Some twenty Hathmirrian soldiers escorted the king of Caedmonia along the busy docks at Port Malado. His wrists were bound in front of him in iron shackles, and a soldier on either side held his arms. Curious citizens watched as the entourage passed by. Their destination was a large ship moored at the end of a long dock. Seamen were hauling crates up the gangplank and into the ship.

Noticing what Marcellus was looking at, the soldier next to him leaned in and said lowly, "I told them we should've sent *you* in a crate." This was Leif, the same one who'd taunted Marcellus with his own sword. The man still had it, strapped to his hip. Commander Ryden, ahead of them, had the honor of bearing Marcellus' water sword. "Of course," Leif continued, "we would've had to chop you into bits to make you fit. But I was alright with that."

Marcellus ignored him. He was taking note of the ship's location within the port, the other ships moored nearby, and the formation of the soldiers escorting him—oh, so kindly—to the bay. He had no intention of getting on that ship, in pieces or otherwise.

They marched down the dock, feet pounding on the wooden planks, and turned onto the gangplank, three deep. Nine in front, the rest behind. Commander Ryden leading the way.

The plank rose steadily to the high deck, where the captain of the ship and another half-dozen soldiers waited.

Marcellus glanced down at the dark water, far below.

The moment was now. He charged sideways into Leif, who stumbled and clung to Marcellus' arm more tightly as he attempted to regain his balance. Giving the man another firm nudge, Marcellus pushed him over the edge. Still hanging onto Marcellus' arm, he nearly took Marcellus with him, but the soldier on his other side, as well as another from behind, grabbed hold of Marcellus and Leif lost his grip. He plummeted down into the water with a splash.

Marcellus spun toward the soldier on his other side, and with both of his shackled hands, gripped the front of the man's coat and pulled hard, simultaneously hooking a leg around the man's knees. Marcellus leaned sharply backwards and they both careened over the edge, free falling through the air until they hit water at last.

Under the water now, bubbles gurgling all around them, Marcellus released the soldier and came to the surface. He noticed Leif nearby, trying to stay afloat in full uniform.

And with one sword too many.

Leif reached for a rope hanging down from the dock, intending to climb out. Marcellus caused the water to swell into a wave. Gathering both himself and Leif into the crest, he caused the wave to rise toward the gangplank where the soldiers there either scattered or ducked. As the wave carrying Leif and Marcellus arched over the plank, Marcellus grabbed Commander Ryden by the collar of his coat and yanked him off his feet. Down they all went, along with a few inconsequential soldiers.

Marcellus released the others so they could swim to the surface, but caused the struggling Leif and Commander Ryden to stay with him as he sped away from the ship and deep down into the bay. Ryden fought against the strength of the water that was holding him right where Marcellus wanted him.

Marcellus removed the water sword from the scabbard around Ryden's waist. Causing the sword to float upright, he ran the iron binding his hands along the shimmering blade and heard the creaking sound of the metal giving way. Hands thus freed, he replaced the sword in his own sheath and caused the water to jettison the commander back to shore.

He turned on Leif next. Leif gave him a panicked look and thrashed about in an attempt to get away. In a matter of moments, Marcellus regained his jeweled sword and confiscated Leif's uniform coat for good measure. Marcellus gave him a shove before releasing him and letting him struggle to the surface above them. That one, Marcellus thought, can swim back on his own.

Marcellus sped farther away, deep underwater. He'd made a point to keep his bearings since his capture the night before. He knew Port Malado from maps of Hathmirr and determined he'd been captured along the coast a short distance southwest of here. If he went in the opposite direction, northeast, he'd eventually reach Caedmonia's westernmost port on the bay. And safety.

Nevertheless, Marcellus went southwest, rushing through the water toward the place where he'd last felt Janus' presence.

Five

As Marcellus returned to the campsite by the shore and made his way into the little settlement where he'd been captured two nights before, he reached out for Janus as far as he could.

He felt nothing.

Broad daylight made it both easier to find safe passageways through the settlement and easier to be spotted. Leif's coat, though a tight fit, served as an improvised disguise, but Marcellus kept himself hidden as much as he could anyway. As he cleared the other side of the settlement and entered the desert, he stayed off the road but followed its path, thinking it the most likely route Janus would have taken.

His blood rushed through his veins, and his heart pounded with a fear that had nothing to do with the fact that he was alone in enemy territory and at risk, once more, of getting his country's king captured. No. It was the fact that he was past the point where he'd last felt Janus but felt nothing of her now. He didn't know if that meant she was too far or...

... he didn't want to think what.

He had to believe she was out there somewhere. But where?

Another few miles of barren desert and no hint of her had caused Marcellus' pace to slow, though his heart still raced frantically in his chest.

He was being selfish. He knew he was. If Janus were here, she would chastise him for endangering the safety of his country over one person. Any person. And she would be right to do so.

He knew how to do what was right for his kingdom even when that meant making sacrifices himself. He'd done almost nothing else for the duration of his young life, but the thought of going back to Caedmonia without her. Or without even knowing what happened to her.

He didn't know if he could do it.

He came to a stop and bent over, bracing his hands on his knees.

She'd survived the sickness in the Tree. And now this. Just when he'd thought she was safe. How could this be happening? *What* was happening? How did she even get here?

He stared at the tops of his dust-covered boots. A few scrubby weeds poked out of the dirt. He closed his eyes, panting. Caedmonia called to him. Caedmonia needed him to turn around and go back. But somewhere ahead of him could be Janus.

Janus.

Was she even there? He reached and reached for her.

Nothing.

"Fifty steps," he said aloud, straightening. Fifty steps, then he'd go back.

He took one step, two steps. Still reaching out for her, he pressed forward, counting and feeling the weight of each number. Seventeen. Eighteen. It was giving up and he knew it. He'd get to fifty and have to go home without her.

Come on, Janus, he thought, counting each stride. *Be there. Please.*

He went on, step after step after step. *Please.*

Then he felt her. On step one-hundred thirty-three, he felt her and she was not well. She felt, in fact, as if she were dying.

That's when the king of Caedmonia, disguised as a Hathmirrian soldier, broke into a run.

At the edge of a field next to a brown stone house, Marcellus slowed his steps just enough to give due caution. He didn't see anyone across the field and saw no signs of anybody inside, but he felt her enough to know she was in there. He drew his sword. He was going in and would not be coming out without her.

As he neared the house, a woman old enough to be his mother came around the corner with a bucket, saw him and his drawn sword, and jolted in surprise, water sloshing over the rim.

"Stop!" Marcellus said firmly, though it was hardly necessary. She stood frozen to the ground, gripping her bucket with both hands.

He continued toward her, feeling Janus draw closer and closer with each step.

"Please, sir—"

"Who else is in the house?" he asked, taking her by the arm and leading her around the corner.

"Just—"

An older man stepped out the back door, looking terrified at the sight of Marcellus, who raised his sword in the man's direction.

The man threw up his arms in surrender and the woman whimpered. "We didn't do anything," the man protested. "We didn't do anything. I swear."

"You have a woman here," Marcellus said.

Wide-eyed the man nodded. "Please, sir, it wasn't us. We don't even know who she is."

"Who else is in the house?"

"Just us—" and here the man glanced at the woman. "Please, sir, don't harm my wife."

"Step aside," Marcellus said, indicating with his sword the man should clear the entryway. He backed up and Marcellus guided the woman ahead of him. Stepping into the cool interior, Marcellus released the woman, who hurried to her husband's side. They were in the kitchen, which led into a living area. The rooms were quiet and empty. He glanced around for a door that might lead to a basement, for he sensed Janus somewhere below.

"Where is she?"

The man exchanged nervous glances with his wife.

"Where!" Marcellus said impatiently.

"Downstairs."

"Show me."

The man led him down a hallway and to a narrow stone staircase that took them into a dank basement. There she was at last, lying on a thin mattress next to a wall.

He rushed to her, his sword clanging on the stone floor as he fell to his knees. She was pale and drenched in sweat. If it weren't for the grimace on her face, he would have thought she was dead. "Janus! What is this? What's wrong with her?"

"I... I don't know, sir," the man said.

Marcellus knelt over her, putting his hand first on her cheek, then on her forehead. "So hot," he whispered. "Janus," Marcellus said firmly, patting her cheek. "Janus, open up. Look at me. Janus."

"She won't," the woman said.

Marcellus turned to them. They'd drawn cautiously nearer, seeming to realize he was here for her, not them. "I'm sorry," the woman said.

"What happened?"

"The Orsini Colony," the man said, as if that were all the explanation that was needed.

Marcellus scowled at him. "The Orsini Colony? What did they do to her?"

"I don't know. I heard their chants and their spells," and here the man closed his eyes briefly as if shutting away a bad memory. "I didn't understand the words. When they were done, they left."

Marcellus looked at her. This was from a spell? He thrust his sword back into its sheath and gathered her into his arms. He had to get her to Corren as quickly as he could. "A horse," he said.

"Sir?"

With Janus' limp, feverish body in his arms, he started climbing the stairs. The man and his wife followed behind. "You're giving me a horse. Get it ready now."

"But—"

"Now!"

They reached the top and the man hustled past him. Marcellus followed him out the back door and around to the barn. He looked down at Janus. Her head rested in the crook of his arm. Her brow was furrowed into a grimace.

"Janus?" She still wouldn't open her eyes. Days. He was days away. "Hold on, Janus. I've got you. Just hold on."

But Marcellus didn't need to wait for the man to saddle a horse. There, trotting up to him with his white coat gleaming in the sun, was Ryafan.

"Oh," Marcellus breathed. And though he hadn't known Ryafan was coming or that he could know how to find him, that didn't stop Marcellus from looking at this horse that was more than a horse and saying, "What took you so long?"

Janus dreamt she was floating on top of the sea, wrapped up in something warm and earthy. It smelled like Marcellus. She dreamt she opened her eyes. In her dream, the earth was Marcellus and she was in his arms. She smiled within herself. He was blurry and his voice came to her as if through water, "I've got you," he said. "Stay with me," he said.

I'm right here, she thought.

She closed her eyes, and while cocooned in the earthy warmth of his arms, she felt she was being carried off to somewhere. Though whether in this world or the next, she could not tell.

Even on Ryafan they were going too slowly. They'd gone in a northeasterly direction until they came to the sea and were now following the coastline as best as they could, hoping the westernmost port of Caedmonia wasn't too far. From there, the fastest way back to Stonebridge would be by ship. Even faster, of course, would be to take Janus back through the water. He trusted Ryafan could find his own way home, but Marcellus sensed he should not take her into the sea. He didn't know what it would do to her.

The old man and his wife gave Marcellus a small bundle of provisions before he left, but he was nearly out of water. Janus had opened her eyes once, and a few times he was able to get her to swallow a bit from the water bag, but he couldn't get her to eat or respond to him at all. The sun was dipping lower and lower toward the horizon behind them. Hoping the Caedmonian port was nearby, he urged Ryafan onward, holding Janus close.

After a time, he spotted a distinctive rock formation to the north and was able to orient himself more firmly. They'd managed to cross the border, but only just, and weren't as close to the port as he'd hoped.

He'd have to stop for water. He found a stand of cottonwoods close to shore. He carefully dismounted and laid Janus next to the trunk of one of the trees. Even though they were now in Caedmonian territory, he wanted to keep her out of sight, just in case.

He set the mouth of the water bag against her parched lips and tilted it upward, emptying the last few drops into her mouth. She swallowed then turned her head to indicate it was enough. It was the most movement he'd seen from her since they'd left the old couple's house.

"Janus?" He gently shook her shoulder. "Janus?" She didn't move. Hating to leave her for even a moment, he stood and hurried to the shoreline.

Ryafan was already in up to his knees, drinking the seawater. "At least I don't have to worry about you," Marcellus said. Seawater might be alright for a water horse, but it wouldn't do any good to Janus.

Marcellus went into the water and scooped some out with his hand. He guided it into the water bag, pulling the salt out as he went. The wind carried the granules off his palm, and they fell to the earth like sand.

After filling the water bag, he turned back toward Janus and froze. She was still lying on the ground, but one arm was stretched up, her hand resting on the base of the tree. A light emanated from between her hand and the bark.

He didn't know if he was seeing it or only sensing it, but a faint light washed over her while blackness seeped up the trunk of the tree. Marcellus stood watching, unable to move. Again it happened, in great waves, the light over Janus and the darkness over the trunk.

She opened her eyes, looking up to the top of the tree, which was slowly withering. Her skin regained its color and she sat up, with both hands on the trunk now, as the healing light surrounded her and the tree grew darker and darker.

At last, Janus pulled herself into a stand and removed her hands. Above her, the cottonwood's leaves were brown and withered, barely hanging on to the deadened branches.

Skin tingling, Marcellus slowly approached. He felt her strength now and, just as clearly, felt the sadness he saw reflected on her face.

Janus, healthy and strong, stood in front of the tree, looking at it with a regretful expression. "I'm sorry for it," she said.

"I'm not," Marcellus said, coming close.

"A tree in Amon Tunde would have survived."

He pulled her into his arms and closed his eyes in relief as he felt her embrace him firmly. He couldn't hold her tight enough.

He pulled back and took her face into his hands. "You know," he whispered, his face close to hers, "for an immortal being, you keep coming awfully close to death."

"Just keeping you on your toes," she whispered back.

He kissed her deeply then, and they clung to one other while the remnants of all the fear they'd had from almost losing each other washed over them. When they pulled apart, she rested her cheek on his chest, squeezing him about the waist. "How did you find me? I didn't even know where I was."

"Let's talk about it on the way," he said, leading her toward the shore where Ryafan stood waiting. "We need to get back to Stonebridge as quickly as we can."

When she saw the horse, she stopped. "Not that thing again! I'm not getting on that."

"Janus," he said. "You've already been on him."

"I have?"

The horse swung its head around to look at her.

She frowned at it, as if trying to conjure up an alternate form of transportation.

Marcellus squeezed her shoulders and nudged her forward. "Don't worry. He likes you."

Still frowning she said, "Who's worried?"

Six

Corren, Lini, Kennard, and the rest of the Guard members had stopped after another long day of traveling. They'd made good time in the last two days, and Corren estimated they would reach the Desert Entrance sometime tomorrow afternoon.

After a short and weary dinner, nearly everyone had retired to their bedrolls for the night. Only Corren was still up, sitting on the ground and leaning against a log, writing in his folio. A little ball of soft light hovered over his shoulder, giving him enough light to write by.

He heard Lini roll over and glanced at her. She was still awake. She lay there watching the campfire burning down to embers. She'd had trouble sleeping the night before, and he wondered if it'd be the same for her tonight. Not that he was doing any better. There was too much to consider and worry about. He didn't think either one of them would sleep well until the Veils of Madera were restored.

She glanced at him. He gave her a smile and went back to his folio. He had yet to write about his experience with the Phoenix a couple days ago, and meant to work on that tonight until his mind was tired enough to sleep, but was finding it a difficult thing to describe and hadn't gotten very far.

Lini sat up, apparently resigned to being awake for a while. He closed his book and watched as she quietly came over and sat next to him.

"Is my light bothering you?" he asked softly, not wanting to wake the others.

She shook her head. "I've been thinking about the entrances into the Shoals. What if there's a better way to protect them?"

337

"What do you mean?"

"I mean, they've been vulnerable all this time because the Veils of Madera require constant maintenance. The Madera branch did the best they knew how, and the Veils are truly extraordinary, but..." She looked at him tentatively and he furrowed his brows.

"But what?"

"Kennard says you're the most powerful wizard he's ever known," she said, gesturing to Kennard's sleeping form. His dark, bald head barely poked out of his bedroll. "He says you're even more powerful than Aradia."

Corren shook his head. "No. I assure you. That's not true."

"But..."

He leaned toward her and held her eyes. "Trust me on this. And Kennard should know better."

For a moment, he felt that connection to her that he was trying really, really hard not to feel. He promised he would not press her about... things... or bring them up again and, true to his word, he hadn't. He couldn't seem to keep those feelings from stirring around inside him though. He straightened and looked down at his book.

"Still," she said quietly. "I've seen what you can do. You have magic and power the Madera branch didn't have. You can't argue with that."

He shook his head. No. He couldn't argue with that.

"So, what if there's a better way to protect those entrances? Something that's permanent so we don't have to worry about this again. Wouldn't that be better?"

He furrowed his brow, immediately starting to consider her suggestion. *Was* there a way to block the entrances permanently?

"Will you try?" she asked.

He looked at her. She was so earnest. How desperately she wanted to protect the entrances into the Shoals. How did the Phoenix know she would be so good for this?

"Yes," he said. "I'll try."

She looked a little comforted and exhaled. She tucked her feet up, wrapping her arms around her legs and resting her chin on her knees. "I suppose we should get to bed," she said, watching the fire.

He nodded and extinguished the ball of light that had been hovering over his shoulder. They fell into darkness, except for the soft light from the glowing coals. "Do you think you can sleep?" he asked.

"No." She put her cheek on her knee, looking at him. "What if he's already in there?"

He sighed. "Well... then we deal with it."

"That's not very comforting."

"I'm not trying to be comforting," he said gently. "I'm trying to be honest. I know from experience things don't always go as planned. All we can do is the best we can. If something else comes up, we'll have to adjust."

She nodded in reluctant agreement. No one had done more adjusting in recent days than she had. "How early can we leave in the morning?"

"First light."

"Will the horses be alright?"

"These belong to the Guard. They're pretty hardy."

They fell to watching the coals, lingering.

"What were you writing?" she asked quietly.

"Well... I'm trying to record my experience with the Phoenix. I know I need to. Aradia always said thorough records serve you well, and I've found that to be true, but... I don't really know how to describe it. It seems to just... want to stay inside me."

"I've been trying not to ask you about it."

He gave her a questioning look.

"In case you didn't want to talk about it," she said.

He watched the coals for a minute. "It was..."

She put her cheek on her knees again, watching him.

It wasn't just the place and the magic he found difficult to define; it was what happened within him. "It was... beyond my understanding," he said at last. Then he started describing what happened, as best as he could. In order for her to understand—and he wanted her to—he told her about Aradia and how much he'd loved and admired her. He told her how devastating her betrayal was and how he hadn't been able to shake it.

"It was like it was always there with me, somewhere. Even when I was doing other things. Even when I forgot about it for a time. It'd come back and remind me, and I'd be angry about it all over again. I didn't want to be, but..."

She sat back, straightening her legs. "You couldn't help it."

He looked at her.

Her head was slightly cocked, as if she were really considering him. Not considering him. Seeing him.

"Yes. I found it so hard to..." He stopped, trying to find the right way to describe it. "I didn't want it to, but it was affecting so many other things. I doubted... people." *You*, he did not say. "I doubted myself."

She listened quietly, watching with those dark eyes of hers.

"I let Aradia haunt me," he said, finding the words at last.

"And the Phoenix made that go away?"

He nodded. And it was true. All the pain he'd felt anytime he thought of Aradia wasn't there anymore. "It was the most amazing piece of magic I've ever experienced."

She smiled softly. "I'm glad."

He smiled too but looked away. It was getting too hard to linger here, so close to her, feeling that connection between them as he had so many times before. Part of him wished he hadn't fallen in love with her. But he had.

"That's how you knew I needed the Silent Circle," she said.

He nodded. "Something like that."

He had to bring this moment to an end. He got to his feet and held out his hand for her. She took it and stood.

He hadn't planned to, but he held on to her hand. She stood right there in front of him, and he looked into those dark eyes and held on. She seemed to be holding on too.

Then he remembered his promise to her. He looked away and released her. "Sorry," he said quietly. "Good night, Lini."

He turned, but she called him softly, "Corren?"

When he looked at her again, she held his eyes with hers and all the feelings he had been trying so hard not to have for her threatened to burst out of his chest. It felt just as it did when they'd been in the little alcove of pines, but this time there was nothing holding him back. No doubt. No fear.

She stepped closer, and as before, he couldn't tell if he was leaning toward her or if she was coming closer to him. Wrapped up in the night, her hand slipped softly inside his, and he squeezed her fingers and leaned down and kissed her.

And it was a kind of magic he'd never known existed.

Janus and Marcellus were on a fast cog from the king's fleet, heading for Stonebridge. They'd reached the westernmost port of Caedmonia late last night and boarded the ship early that morning. As if riding on a horse that seemed to be made of the ocean itself weren't bad enough, she was now in the middle of the vast sea with nothing between her and the water but a few wooden boards.

But none of this occupied her mind as much as Tivoli and the strange ceremony she'd endured three nights ago. It nagged at her. Tivoli had taken something from her, she was sure of that, but why? What was he planning to do?

Tivoli and his group of followers were starting to lose their sense of time. How long had they been under the earth, surrounded by light both night and day? They'd slept here. They'd stopped for meals. They'd followed the map at every junction, every twist and turn. He started to have the surreal sense that they weren't really making any progress, that they'd somehow gotten stuck in a labyrinth of time and place and would never get out.

Still, he was not yet at the point of panic. The map marked the place they sought and he pressed them forward, following it. Finally, as if they'd reached it all of a sudden, they were there.

A green mass blocked their way. It looked like the end of the tunnel, and the rock was covered in nothing but spongy moss. It hung down in tendrils here and there. But ever so slightly, just under the surface, it shimmered.

The men behind him shuffled to a stop and they stared at it as one. Tivoli brought his hand near to it and felt the magic within. He felt the warning too. He didn't know what would happen if he touched it but knew enough not to try.

So this was it. The great protection of the earth faeries. The protection the Madera branch knew could be breeched with Phoenix ash, something the earth faeries did not take into account because they did not understand it.

Tivoli could not say he understood it either, but the Order was famous for the things they could do with that ash. It was powerful. Powerful enough that otherwise ordinary wizards could do extraordinary things. It's why Tivoli had wanted it.

Not until Lini opened the Book of Madera and he read their secrets did Tivoli realize an even greater power awaited him—far more than what ash alone could give. He couldn't believe the Madera branch had sat on it all that time. Protecting it when, instead, they could've had it for themselves.

He estimated they were half a day from the Vortex. Assuming he could breech the barrier before him.

He drew closer to it. He could see why breaking it would take something as powerful as Phoenix ash. Which, in spite of all his efforts, he did not have.

But, if he correctly understood the description of the faerie barrier in the Book of Madera, he suspected the faerie barrier could be breeched another way.

Tivoli held up the clear vial, filled with the serene, golden liquid he'd collected from the earth faerie he'd left to die. He lifted it in front of him, pulled the stopper, and said, "*Wyl ada.*"

The contents inside the bottle began to swirl. Slowly at first, then more and more rapidly. "*Expath,*" he said and the bottle hung in the air of its own accord. It began to vibrate violently.

The trembling bottle edged nearer the green barrier. Two of his comrades took a step backward. Tivoli tossed them a furious glare and said, "Stay where you are." They halted and he returned to the trembling bottle, directing it with his staff.

It edged nearer the glowing, green barrier. When it made contact, he shouted, "*Katath,*" the bottle shattered, and the glowing faerie essence splattered onto the surface, spreading and branching out over it like bloody veins.

The barrier gave way with a hiss and blast of cold air. It disintegrated until there was nothing left to see but the long tunnel before them.

Seven

As Lini approached the ravine, the wind tore through and bits of dust stung her face. She brought her hand up to shield her eyes and began walking down the path, with Corren, Kennard, and the rest of the Guard members following.

She and Corren had argued about whether or not it was necessary for everyone to traverse the dangerous path with her. She had not wanted to risk anyone's life but her own and thought she should go down and restore the Veil of Madera by herself.

Corren, however, insisted they were there to help and protect her. "What if Tivoli's down there?" he'd asked.

She had thought of this. In truth, she'd feel safer if Corren came with her and she wasn't inclined to argue the point. "Just you, then," she said.

But he hadn't agreed to this either. After a short-lived disagreement about whether he alone made for an adequate defense, he finally leaned toward her and said in that comforting but firm way of his, "Everyone here knows the risks. We're going with you."

But it was more than the danger that was bothering her now. As the path narrowed and the ridge line rose above them, her breathing constricted and her heart began to race.

Holding onto her wraps in the fierce wind, she came to the first thin ledge. The one Tivoli had made Sienna test first. Stepping onto the ledge, she went back to that day. She pressed her back against the smooth rock wall, shuffled sideways along the ledge, and saw Sienna in this very place, clinging to her wraps as the wind whipped against her, just as it was doing to Lini now.

On the long journey from Tower Hall South to the ravine, Lini had thought and worried about many things. But somehow she did not realize until this very moment—on a sliver of rock barely wider than her feet—that she was returning to the place where Sienna had died.

She felt slightly lightheaded. She shuffled sideways more quickly, hurrying to the place where the path widened onto solid ground.

Of course, the ground had seemed solid before it disappeared from beneath Sienna's feet.

Though it was no longer necessary, Lini kept close to the wall, putting hand over hand on the rock as if it could save her should the ground suddenly give way.

She glanced toward the edge of the path, and the canyon beyond gaped at her. She realized the place where Sienna died was just around the next turn. Its unavoidable presence loomed toward her.

She closed her eyes and came to a stop, her heart beating in her ears and the scent of the rocks thick in the air. Sienna's body was still down there somewhere. She was down there and Lini would have to walk right by her.

"Lini?" It was Corren, next to her.

She saw again the horror on Sienna's face as she fell down and down. She heard her screaming again and again. "It was here," she whispered.

"I know."

"I can't do it." She pressed her palms over her eyes. She heard again the crunching sound of Sienna hitting the canyon floor.

"Lini..."

"I can't do it." She saw again the rocks skitting over the edge and Tivoli's shadow rearing on the ground.

"Lini, look at me."

She opened her eyes. Corren was in front of her, leaning close. Real and tangible. She could smell him. She could reach out and touch him. The ghost images in her mind began to retreat as she looked at his face.

He put a hand on her shoulder, steady and comforting. "Take a breath."

She inhaled deeply as he held her eyes. A breeze slipped through and rustled the fabric of his cloak and her wraps. Out of the corner of her eye, she saw Kennard and the others standing back a pace, waiting silently. As the present world became more real to her, the echoes of the past faded.

"You can do this," Corren said steadily. He held her firmly by the shoulder.

She nodded. She could. She could do this.

As he saw her resolve return, he gently squeezed her shoulder and released her. "Alright?"

She nodded and took another breath. She could do this. She just had to focus on something else. Continuing on, still close to the wall, she decided to think about the instructions for creating the Veil of Madera. She thought of the words to the spell and tried to imagine what it would look like.

Rounding the turn, she recognized the place as soon as she saw it. She did not slow and did not look over the edge. She looked at the path in front of her—the dust and the little rocks—and listened to the scratching of a dozen feet behind her. She was still aware of the place; she knew when it was immediately to her left and when it fell behind as she passed. When it was to the rear of their little party, she exhaled sharply. She hadn't realized she'd been holding her breath.

Now that she managed to get past the place where Sienna had died, she returned to thinking about the Veils of Madera more easily. Her thoughts focused yet again, as they had so many times on the journey here, on what she came all this way to do.

And if Tivoli had already been here and gone? If they were already too late?

She did not know what they would do.

Tivoli, Bricker, and the others stood at the mouth of a massive cavern, gaping at the swirling mass of color known as the Vortex. The brilliant lights reflected on the walls as the ethereal form of the elements spun smoothly around and around. From here, the elements of earth, water, and fire flowed from the Vortex in steady waves. Though invisible once they left the core, the elements could still be felt. Tivoli sensed them vibrating in the air.

The low *puum* of the Vortex pulsed slowly. Rhythmically. It resonated throughout the cavern and echoed in his own chest. Cautiously, Tivoli approached.

The towering Vortex hovered above a wide pit. Shimmering light illuminated the sides for some depth, but the pit eventually fell to darkness, hiding the bottom from view. Tivoli questioned whether there were, in fact, a bottom.

The Vortex throbbed with power before him, and he felt the tang of longing on his tongue. He could reach out. Right now. He could reach out and take it for himself just as the Mapmaker had once done.

Bricker and the other group members drew closer to the Vortex as if they were being lured in. The colorful light danced across their faces and flashed off the gold marks on their foreheads. They looked up at it with hunger. "*Alehess!*" he barked. "Step back!"

They hustled backwards and he scowled at them. They could snatch the power within the Vortex as easily as he could.

"You are here only to serve the Lord of the Orsini Colony."

"Yes, Lord Tivoli," they said in unison.

"*Alehess,*" he said for good measure. "You will do nothing to betray me."

He turned again to the mesmerizing whirlpool before him. His hand itched with yearning. His heart swelled darkly in his breast.

The Book of Madera claimed the Mapmaker's rash theft from the Vortex caused him to go mad, but Tivoli thought he had a better way. One that was not so reckless as the Mapmaker's had been. Not for nothing had the Orsini Colony spent hundreds of years perfecting its powerful circle ceremonies. Tivoli would indeed seize power from the Vortex, but he intended to be the master of it.

He thought about Corren and the Order and the traitor Lini. *I'll slaughter them all*, he thought. *It's the first thing I'll do.*

He turned to his devoted servants, who were awaiting his command.

"We begin," he said.

They came forward and slowly surrounded the Vortex. It hummed and swirled in the center as they all looked up at it.

Tivoli nodded to Bricker. Bricker raised both hands and the others followed his lead, the bright fabric of their wraps slipping down their arms.

Tivoli's heart pounded. He held his staff by the middle, raised it horizontally before him, and cried out with a loud voice, "*Uum kata alli.*"

"*Uum kata alli,*" they repeated, their voices echoing in the cavern.

The Vortex pulsed outward and in, outward and in.

"*Uum kata alli.*"

The Vortex shuddered, the colors within rippling. Deep vibrations trembled throughout the cavern. The Vortex flashed brighter and expanded, rushing toward them, and they all jerked backward to avoid coming into contact with it.

Losing their magical grip on the Vortex, it ceased its pulsing. It hovered over the black pit, swirling and humming.

"Hold your ground!" Tivoli shouted, though he'd been unable to keep from backing away himself.

The Vortex was powerful and resisted their efforts to contain it. But they were used to resistance. They only had to keep going. It would bend to their will in the end.

It was inevitable.

"*Alehess*," he growled. "Keep chanting. Don't stop. All together now."

"*Uum kata alli*," they said in unison and the Vortex again pulsed inward and outward, inward and outward.

Tivoli bellowed, "*Uum kata alli!*"

Together, the men surrounding the Vortex raised their voices as the chant boomed through the air, "*Uum kata alli.*"

And that's what did it. It stopped its pulsing, bound by their spell. They now had the swirling Vortex in their grasp.

It was time to take his portion of its power.

"*Emotay!*" he shouted.

"*Emotay!*" the circle echoed.

The massive Vortex spun faster and a harsh wind began to howl around the cavern. The binding they'd placed on it held firm, but Tivoli was wrestling with the elements within. They wouldn't come to him as commanded. Within the Vortex, they collided as if warring with each other... and with him.

"*Emotay! Emotay! Emotay!*" all together.

The Vortex whipped faster and faster. Letting out a groan so loud his entire body vibrated with it, the Vortex slowly tilted to one side.

Tivoli's stomach fell to his toes.

Still whirring around, it swayed like a top run out of steam. The edge of the swirling mass scarcely brushed Bricker's chest as it went careening past. He crumpled upon impact but still chanted "*Emotay*," bound by Tivoli's command.

"*Emotay! Emotay!*" the circle of Orsinians shouted. The Vortex vibrated so violently the earth beneath Tivoli's feet began to quake.

He was no longer chanting. The Vortex reared in his direction and he scrambled backward. It swung around in a blinding circle and collided with a fellow member. He did not cry out. He did not keep chanting. He fell to the ground in a scorched, lifeless heap. The rank smell of burnt flesh bloomed in the air.

"*Emotay! Emotay!*" the others continued as the Vortex barreled toward them.

"No—" Tivoli said, but the Vortex swept through two more members and sent them crumpling to the ground. The swirling mass came screaming toward him.

Tivoli spun and sprinted back the way they'd come. Darting into the tunnel, feet pounding on the ground, he felt energy swelling behind him. Lights pulsed rapidly on the walls of the tunnel. He thought—too late—that he should have released anyone left in the circle before he ran. Before more damage was done.

Racing toward a junction, he scrambled around a sharp turn and bolted down the passageway. A blinding light flashed from behind and crashed against him. He collapsed and skidded on the ground, unconscious.

In the shadows of the ravine, the earth smelled cool and damp. The sides of the canyon soared up on either side as Lini and the others continued to descend the steep trail. A sudden rumbling somewhere in front of them brought her to a halt.

The others shuffled to a stop behind her as the rumbling sound increased.

"What is that?" Kennard asked.

Corren stepped next to her, staff raised, searching for the source of the noise. The rumbling swelled. A loud crack drew their attention to the canyon wall just ahead. A huge section broke loose, crashing and shattering on its way down to the pathway in front of them.

They scrambled back of one accord, everyone shouting "Run!" and "Get back!"

The sound of crashing rock bellowed in their ears and Corren shouted, "The walls are collapsing!"

They bolted up the narrow path and the earth jolted brutally, knocking everyone off their feet. Lini went down hard, knees and hands stinging against the rough ground. Another crack resounded through the air, this time from above. Before she had a chance to react, a massive boulder soared overhead and into the ravine below.

"Go! Go!" Corren yelled behind her, scrambling to his feet along with the rest. The ground quaked beneath them as they ran. The rumbling thundered in the air and seemed a tangible force about to swallow them whole. Coming to the narrow ledge, one person after the next pressed their backs against the wall and shuffled frantically along the edge, grabbing each other's arms for support.

Lini threw herself against the rock face as well, scraping her feet along sideways and gripping Kennard's arm in front of her. They cleared the ledge and ran. She glanced behind Corren and saw a plume of dust and the walls of the cavern sliding into the ravine behind them.

The dust cloud rushed nearer until it blew over them, stinging and scraping her skin. The dust caught in her lungs and she coughed and squinted and stumbled blindly over the hard earth, equally terrified of falling over the edge and being crushed from behind.

Unable to see the way, she reached out to her side, searching the rock face for guidance when the earth heaved and she lost her balance, slamming into the wall. Her wrist gave way and her shoulder screamed in pain.

A rush of hot wind blew in from behind and the dust lifted. Just as she regained her footing, Corren grabbed her arm and they ran forward. His staff was high in the air, and she realized he was creating a bubble of space to hold back the dust. The sound of crumbling rock seemed just at the heels of their feet and he shouted, "Hurry!"

Lini pumped her legs as fast as she could, her lungs burning. They seemed to be breaking away from the landslide at last. They outran the dust cloud and Corren lowered his staff, still running. The earth felt more steady as their feet flew over it. Nearly to the top, she and Corren slowed enough to sidestep their way across the final ledge, then emerged onto the rim of the ravine with Kennard and the others.

Turning back, they gasped for breath as they watched the walls deeper in the ravine collapse and slide into the space below. Rocks tumbled downward, cracking and breaking. On and on it seemed to go until, at last, the earth quieted and the dust began to clear.

The group was left to stand on the edge and wonder what triggered this degree of devastation.

But fearing they knew exactly what caused it.

And who.

Eight

Tivoli awoke in the dark. Everything was still. He ached all over but otherwise seemed unharmed. The light that had been in the tunnels on his way to the Vortex was gone now. He fumbled for the lantern at his waist, but a sharp edge of iron sliced his hand. He felt liquid on the ground and smelled the rank odor of the oil. The lantern was broken.

A slight tremor in the earth and a deep rumbling sound caused Tivoli to tense and arrest his movements. He braced himself, but it was over as quickly as it began. All was still and silent again.

Heart pounding, Tivoli slowly made his way in the dark on hands and knees. His shallow panting echoed in his ears. He feared for a time that the tunnels were dark because the Vortex had gone altogether—and wondered what horrible consequences would come of that—but eventually he came to a turn he vaguely remembered taking when he'd been running away. The junction led to more darkness in one direction, but in the other, to a pulsating light in the distance.

He continued on, the light at the end of the tunnel growing larger and the sound of the Vortex now whirring lowly.

"Bricker?" he called, surprised at how timid his voice sounded. He slowly pulled himself to his feet. Unsteady, he braced himself with one hand against the hard tunnel wall. "Bricker," he called again, trying to sound more certain. His voice echoed down the tunnel. The Vortex groaned. No one answered.

He cautiously came to the mouth of the tunnel. There it was again: the massive cavern, the black bottomless pit, and the

Vortex swirling above it. But it was rotating haphazardly, as if it had been knocked off its center.

Around the Vortex, the blackened bodies of his companions lay on the ground. All dead. Tivoli stared at the scene—the swirling Vortex spinning out of balance, the bodies of his followers—and did not know which horrified him most.

There, in the center of the Shoals, Lord Tivoli felt a dark chill.

Corren and the others pushed the horses at a gallop, racing south back the way they'd come. The earth rumbled sporadically as if it were contemplating opening up beneath them. The horses were skittish and difficult to control. Their riders weren't faring much better.

Corren knew the landslide in the ravine could've been just that. Nothing more or less. Certainly nothing sinister. But it had felt sinister and he left it all behind feeling full of dread. He didn't know how Tivoli could've caused such a thing, but neither could he believe it was merely a coincidence. As they tore across the plains of Northern Caedmonia, he struggled to piece it all together. He was missing something.

Lini thought they were on their way to check the Golden Canyon Entrance, but Corren had something else in mind. He needed to get to Amon Tunde and find out if the faerie barriers were still intact. If they were, he'd know the Vortex was safe.

And if they weren't? He had no idea what they would do next.

They came to a broad stream and made a hurried stop for water. Kennard and the Guard members spread their horses out slightly along the bank, too ill at ease for conversation. With their horses drinking eagerly next to them, Corren and Lini knelt down together to dip their leather waterskins into the stream. The water gurgled and sloshed over the rocky streambed.

"Something's wrong," Lini said quietly. "It's Tivoli. It has to be."

Corren was little comforted to hear her verbalize his own fears. As the cool water slipped into the mouth of his waterskin, he felt something peculiar, down in the earth.

He stood. The water dripped from his fingertips.

The stream gurgled along, but beneath it—or no, across the way—something under the earth felt wild.

Lini stood too. "What is it?"

On the opposite bank, an old tree drew Corren's attention. Its hollowed trunk had split open long ago, but now, colorful light shimmered from inside the opening.

Corren and Lini glanced at one another then looked back to the tree. The inside of the trunk shone with variegating colors: blue, purple, yellow, pink. All in constant motion.

It was beautiful, or would be if it weren't so disturbing.

And still, the wildness deep within the earth churned.

"Kennard?" Corren called loudly, not taking his eyes off the disquieting sight across the way. Out of the corner of his eye, he saw Kennard stand. One by one the rest of the group caught sight of the tree and rose to watch it.

He quietly handed his waterskin to Lini and slid his staff out of the loops on the saddle.

"What's happening?" Lini asked lowly.

"I'm not sure."

Next to him, his horse shuffled its hooves, its skin twitching nervously. Corren reached for the leather reins with one hand and held tight to his staff with the other.

The lights in the trunk flickered out.

Whatever wildness Corren sensed in the earth did not disappear, however. It grew.

Vines emerged from within the tree, curling and sprouting little blossoms of pink, purple, and blue. Expecting something more threatening, he almost laughed, but the peculiarity of the sight cut him short.

The vines poured out of the tree and raced down the trunk, flowers springing up along the way. They grew in fast motion, down the tree and to the ground, where they fanned out in all directions.

To the right, they crawled over the crumbling remnants of a fallen log until it was completely hidden. To the left, they encircled an aspen sapling, slinking up its trunk. The tree bent toward the ground as the vines overtook it, causing the leaves on the branches to shudder.

A great crack resounded through the valley as the tree snapped in half and its crown came crashing down.

Lini flinched. Corren's horse reared. He strained against the taut reins, trying to keep the animal from bolting, while yet not taking his eyes off the sight before them.

"Take it!" he yelled to Lini, who was backing away with her horse. She grabbed the reins and he raised his staff. The vines raced toward them. All along the bank, the others were backing away and hastily mounting up. Lini pulled the horses away.

He sent a spell to the vines but they only grew more rapidly, dipping down the bank and into the stream. The water bubbled and churned in response.

Corren sent another spell, but the elements of earth were in a strange, wild form he'd never felt before. And they weren't listening to him. The vines thickened and coiled around one another, advancing across the stream to the nearest bank and growing into such a large mass they were blocking the flow of water. Upstream, the water was slowly rising.

"Stop it," Lini said behind him. "Corren, stop it."

"I'm trying!" Staff held aloft, Corren's mind was working rapidly. The flow on one side of the vines was trickling to a stop while the water on the other threatened to overflow the banks.

Hastily backing up, Corren sent another spell, this one just as ineffective as the last. Raw and wild, the vines reared up as if driven by an unseen force.

"Corren!"

Out of the corner of his eye, he saw Lini approaching on her horse, but he hollered, "Stay back!"

"Let's go!" Kennard yelled.

The water overtook the bank and spread onto the ground where he and the others had been standing.

Corren cut his staff upward through the air and a ball of fire burst into life in front of him. The others backed away from the sudden heat, but Corren held his ground. When he caused the fire to advance on the front-most portion of the vines, the entire mass sharply contracted as if the whole of them had been struck.

Waving his staff, he sent flames racing over the surface of the quivering vines. He pressed the element of fire against them, and the wild force of the earth he'd been feeling began to relent. The flames whipped and roared. That strange wildness within the vines began to shrink and shrink until it disappeared completely. At last, the mass went still.

Astonished, and not understanding exactly what had just happened, Corren straightened and set the tip of his staff on the ground. He released the fire. The flames vanished, leaving a sea of scorched vines, with the stream puddling and bleeding around it.

Down the coast from Stonebridge, halfway between the Rock of Light and the Cliffs of the Realm, a steady stream of lava oozed into the bay. Great plumes of smoke rose high into the sky, a beacon to all on land and sea alike.

Word came to the King's office, as it usually does, via royal messenger. The message came, not as it usually does, to Prince Nicolai. He'd had a rare moment away from the various people trying to keep an eye on him, though a pair of knights subtly stood guard outside the door. They followed the messenger in, drawn by curiosity.

The young man stood in the King's office in his tidy red uniform, delivered his report, and watched the new prince skeptically.

Before Nicolai had finished digesting this first message, a second arrived. This one brought word of a "bizarre" occurrence on the shoreline not far from the castle. Here, apparently, fish were beaching themselves on the sand, creating a sea of flapping tails all up and down the shore.

While Nicolai wondered what on earth was going on and deciding what the citizens might expect the king (or his consort) to do about such things, a third messenger appeared. This young man ran through the door and bowed, panting and struggling to catch his breath. The commotion of his frantic journey through the castle apparently attracted Captain Murray, Commander Donnelly, and a handful of knights, for they poured into the room after him.

"Your Highness the Prince," the messenger said breathlessly—Nicolai still wasn't used to being addressed as such—"there's been a landslide in the Southern Quarter," he said. "A dozen buildings, at least, fallen away."

At this Nicolai rose, his chair scraping the floor. "Were there people inside?"

"Yes, sir. We're trying to rescue them now, but we fear there are casualties."

Nicolai looked sharply at Commander Donnelly, who understood the implied command. "My troops are on the way, your Highness," he said, bowing and rushing out of the room.

Nicolai came around from behind the King's desk and said to the page in the corner, "Prepare my horse immediately."

"Yes, your Highness," the page said, bowing, and darted out the door.

"You two come with me," he said as he strode across the room, indicating two of the messengers. They snapped to and hustled after him, but they weren't the only ones following.

"Wait a minute."

This was from Captain Murray, clearly miffed that Nicolai was daring to step left or right without his permission. Nicolai ignored him and addressed one of the messengers as they entered the hallway. "Alert Advisor Tinogen and tell him I want him to arrange for provisions to be brought to the Southern Quarter. Food and medicines. Understood?"

"Yes, your Highness."

"Go."

The messenger darted ahead.

"Stop," Captain Murray said, marching to keep up.

"You," Nicolai said to the remaining messenger, "alert the Royal Advisors and tell them where they can find me if they need me. Tell Lang I want him to investigate the lava flow you told me about."

The young man scurried off on his mission.

"Where do you think you're going?" Captain Murray said with a raised voice.

Having had his fill of Captain Murray and being in no mood for delays given the state of things, Nicolai spun and faced his opponent. "I believe you meant to say, 'Where do you think you're going, *your Highness.*'"

Murray, momentarily stunned, narrowed his eyes.

"Let me be clear, Captain," Nicolai said. "If you cause one more moment's delay in the rescue efforts of those citizens, you'll find yourself locked in the dungeon and I won't mind escorting you there myself."

The remaining knights in the hall grew still, and Nicolai realized he'd put his hand on the hilt of his sword without meaning to.

Nicolai sensed hesitation in the man in front of him. He wanted to leave no room for doubt about who was going to be the victor here. Knowing there were people in danger, he needed that fact established now.

"Back up," Nicolai said coldly.

Murray blinked and glanced at a few of the knights. Nicolai continued to glare, watching the sinking expression on Murray's face when he realized no one planned to assist him in his insubordination.

Murray looked down and quietly took a step backwards. "Forgive me, your Highness."

It was a move of self-preservation and not a gesture of true respect, Nicolai could see that, but it would have to do for now. Nicolai removed his hand from his sword and marched away, the Captain and his knights following at a respectful distance.

Down in the Southern Quarter, it was chaos. Buildings had slid halfway down the hill, collapsing and shredding walls and roofs along the way. Donnelly's knights and citizens alike dug through the rubble, searching for survivors. Some had shovels, but most were trying to heft boards or clear debris with their bare hands. The wounded and their frantic loved ones crowded the streets, along with a few bloody and mangled bodies.

Nicolai ordered Captain Murray to move the wounded to a neighboring boardinghouse for care and to establish a temporary morgue for the dead in a warehouse not far away. He sent a unit of knights to gather as many shovels and tools as they could find.

Riding around the perimeter of the disaster, he noticed several structures appeared to be at risk of collapsing. He ordered knights to evacuate citizens who were trying to haul out their belongings and sent for the city engineers to stabilize the structures and inspect a nearby water cistern for damage.

These things done, he called for a shovel, dismounted his horse, and climbed into the heart of the wreckage, looking for pockets that might hold survivors.

A few hours later, they'd rescued several citizens, sent mercifully few bodies to the morgue, and narrowed the missing down to only three.

Prince Nicolai, sore and hungry and filthy and determined to find those last three citizens, was unaware that many who were witness to his actions that day began to question whether they'd correctly judged the man. They began to wonder, if Nicolai was not the cause of their king's disappearance, then who was?

As Corren and Lini and the others rushed through the northern plains of Caedmonia, their journey was marked with more strange occurrences. Windstorms came and went, seemingly springing up out of nowhere and wreaking havoc over the land before vanishing and leaving an eerie calm behind. Like the vines, the wind did not respond to Corren's spells. At one point, their party was nearly run down by a stampeding herd of wild horses before Corren and Kennard managed to redirect them. Corren thought this *could* have a perfectly normal explanation—until they saw the dragon. A Flying Jasmine.

Its massive shape blocked the sun as it flew high overhead. Leathery wings outstretched, it continued on its way, but its appearance had no small effect on Corren and the others. They pushed their horses harder, eager to put more distance between themselves and the dragon.

"Since when do dragons leave the mountains?" Kennard asked.

Before they had time to think about it further, a swarm of Silver Spikebacks crested the treetops to their left and sent the party bolting into the thicket in the opposite direction. The dragons flew low overhead, the edges of their broad wings tearing through the foliage and sending branches swaying and debris falling.

The swarm continued on. One of the dragons roared as it retreated into the distance.

"What—" Kennard began, but Lini kicked her horse into a gallop and bolted back into the open, yelling, "Look! Look!"

A formation of Tulaga came into view. Lini hollered at them, waving her arms and trying to flag them down. They flew past but then circled around and landed, transforming smoothly from the massive golden birds into women. Or rather, Corren thought at the sight of them, one woman and several girls. Praea's oldest recruit looked nigh unto sixteen, and her youngest (a whip of a thing with curly brown hair) looked barely eleven.

"What are you doing here?" Praea asked.

"I was going to ask you the same thing," Corren said.

"We're tracking those dragons. They've never left the mountains before. I can't believe they've come so far." Looking at Lini's concerned face, Praea asked, "Is everybody alright?"

They told Praea about the many disturbances they'd seen, and before she could ask what might be causing it, Lini explained everything. Whether or not it was a good idea to tell Praea—not to mention the others—was a moot point now, but that didn't stop Corren from being mortified.

"I'm sorry, Corren," Lini said, "but Tivoli knows what's going on and that puts him at an advantage over us. Something's wrong and we don't have time to tiptoe around. They need to know what's at stake here so they can help."

She turned back to Praea who'd been listening with varying degrees of alarm and concentration. "We need to get to the Golden Canyon Entrance as soon as possible. I..." she hesitated, then turned to Corren earnestly. "I know we said we'd restore the Veil of Madera, but I think we need to go into the Shoals. I think we need to see if the faerie barriers are unharmed. That will tell us for sure if Tivoli's been there."

"I've been thinking about that too," he said, exchanging a meaningful look with Praea. While everyone present now knew the faeries had their own way into the Shoals—through the Way Beneath—only Praea knew Corren, as half earth faerie, could get to it.

"We can take you," Praea said, her eyes locked on Corren. "Though we may want to stop by the Wilds on the way."

Nine

Nicolai was helping to clear away the rubble of a knifesmith's shop—which had been reduced to two exterior walls and nothing else—in hopes of finding the last missing citizen, when he felt them. He stood abruptly and looked out toward the sun-drenched bay. There they were: Marcellus and Janus.

Dropping his shovel, he reached out and felt them respond in kind. They were on the bay, coming into port on a ship.

"There're back!"

A few people straightened and followed his gaze down to the sea.

"Who?" Commander Donnelly asked.

"The king and Commander Janus."

"What? Where?" This from Captain Murray.

Nicolai rushed to his horse and mounted up. "There," he said pointing. "The king's vessel coming into port."

Nicolai and the others were too far inland to see who might be aboard any of the many ships dotting the bay, but he was too sick with relief—and unexpectedly, anger—to explain. He only wanted to get to the docks. Away he went, his horse's hooves beating along the cobblestone streets, with Captain Murray, Commander Donnelly, and a dozen others trailing behind.

They raced through the city and down to the harbor. The ship had pulled into port, and the crew threw down the moorings, which thumped heavily on the wooden planks. Nicolai and the others thundered along the dock, bringing their mounts to an abrupt halt.

He looked up and there on the ship's deck was Marcellus. He leaned over the bulwark, one hand on the rail, and looked down at Nicolai with a troubled expression. Janus stood next to him.

Seeing them at last, clearly safe, he didn't know if he wanted to embrace them or pummel them. "Where the hell have you been?" he demanded. Then remembering who he was talking to and where they were, he hastily added, "Your Majesty."

"I'll have to explain later," Marcellus said, striding alongside the rail as the crew quickly lowered the gangplank. "I regret I wasn't able to inform anyone I was leaving, but Commander Janus' safety demanded it. What's happened?" He gestured to the landslide in the Southern Quarter, the general devastation of which was visible from here.

As Marcellus and Janus—and, of all things, Ryafan the water horse—marched down the plank, Nicolai explained what happened. Not stopping for a moment, King Marcellus continued down the dock with Nicolai and the others falling in with him. "Commander Janus and I require your assistance, Prince Nicolai," Marcellus said loud enough for all to hear.

Then, taking Nicolai by the arm and leaning into his ear, "We need to get to Amon Tunde."

On the Hathmirrian side of the bay, not far from the place Faatin was supposed to wait for Lord Tivoli's return, the sea churned as it does in a wicked storm, with fierce waves that no man can tame and that no water faerie wants to tame. For the sea is meant to be wild.

But this wildness was not now as it should be. Though far below the water's surface, where he would normally be safe, Faatin was tossed about in the deep. The sea abused him as if he were no more significant than man's little ships.

He alone could not calm it—for he had no control over the element of air that had invaded the sea and brought violence into its belly—and did not know that his fellow water faeries were elsewhere in the bay, joining their magic together to keep the sea from tearing asunder.

Even if he did know, he would not have gone to help. Instead, Faatin did what he did best.

He fled.

He fought his way out of the currents until he was far from the unnatural disturbance. He did not even turn back to look at the massive whirlpool churning in the deep.

As he sped through the water away from the chaos, he suspected that Tivoli had failed, though he did not know how exactly. Worse, he suspected this failure was even more horrific than Aradia's treachery had been and could affect far more people than Faatin alone.

But Faatin was not accustomed to empathizing for anyone but himself, and this moment of cowardice would be no different. He merely fled.

He fled until he was as he feared he would always be: cursed and alone.

Tivoli ran down a darkened passageway, his weakened legs working against him as much as his inability to see. His exposed skin felt raw from the waves of magic that had washed over him, as if he'd been scoured with grains of sand. His rapid, shallow breathing echoed in his ears. His eyes bugged wide, though he could see little. He had to get out. He had to get out. He stumbled, as he had so many times already, and caught himself before going down. Running once more, he thought it again and again. He had to get out.

He heard the earth rumbling, felt it shaking beneath his feet, and knew he was the one who set this lion loose.

With Stonebridge set on the hill in the distance and the vast expanse of the Wilds to his right, Marcellus raced along the bank of the Big Winding River, which churned wildly down the middle of the valley. Ryafan's hooves pounded over the ground, and the wind howled in Marcellus' ears. Not far off, a group of Tulaga swirled in the air, apparently trying to subdue the tempest that was pummeling the valley further north. Marcellus, Nicolai, and Janus had seen the billowing clouds on their way to Amon Tunde. They'd formed in a matter of minutes out of nothing but clear, blue sky.

But that wasn't as disturbing as what was happening in the Big Winding River. The water did not feel like the water of the earth. It felt like the water of the sea. He could sense the true river underneath it all, still there where it belonged, but the foreign elements in the surface rose and fell like the waves of the ocean. They swelled larger and larger, the waves roaring and crashing. Not far from the edge of the Wilds, the waves had already leapt the bank of the river and rushed over the land. Heading for Amon Tunde.

Marcellus didn't know what would happen if the waters from the ocean met the realm of the earth faeries, but he didn't want to find out. He raced along the bank and toward the water spreading over the land.

As it neared the edge of the forest, the water gathered into a great wave, while just beyond, the black clouds of the storm swirled darkly, the Tulaga small against its expansive mass. The violent wind tore at the rearing wave and water sprayed off the top.

Wet and wind whipped, Marcellus and Ryafan raced under the huge wave of water. He raised his hands, pushing back against the elements before it hit the trees.

The wave roared in front of him, as if held in place by an invisible wall.

Marcellus trembled from the effort. It wasn't just that there was so much of it; it was that the element of water was so raw and wild. It was nearly too much for him. He didn't know if this ocean water had come into the river all the way from the sea or if it'd sprung up out of nothing, like the storm. He didn't know what to do with it except push it away from Amon Tunde.

Marcellus' arms shook, threatening to fail him. The hovering wave of ocean water still churned and roared as it towered over them, but it rippled and quivered, as if it too were ready to give way.

With Marcellus clinging to his back, Ryafan reared on his hind legs. In one joint effort, they pushed hard on the elements in the water.

And the wave fell backwards, crashing onto the ground.

Retreating, the water dashed back into the river. Marcellus dropped his arms, panting. His heart pummeled his chest, almost as an afterthought. The ocean water churned upstream, leaving only the river water behind. The wind still whipping around them, Marcellus patted Ryafan's neck but stared at the river in disbelief. What on earth was going on?

Nicolai and Janus came tearing up on their horses. They looked between Marcellus and the river, mouths agape.

"What *was* that?" Marcellus said lowly.

"I can't believe you did that," Janus said. He'd told her about manipulating the water to help him escape the Hathmirrians, but she hadn't yet seen his new abilities. He couldn't fault her for looking stunned. He was stunned himself.

Add to this event the strange occurrences in Stonebridge, along with the foreboding communications Nicolai and Janus both sensed coming from Amon Tunde, and Marcellus was more than a little ill at ease.

The wind suddenly ceased. To their right, the billowing black clouds were beginning to collapse in on themselves, yielding to the magic of the Tulaga circling around.

Then, running along the plains in their direction, were Corren, Lini, and half a dozen others.

Lini held her wraps tightly about her shoulders. As she listened to Corren and his brothers hurriedly explain things to one other—the king and prince, too, had seen strange things happening with the earth—she felt more and more a sense of overwhelming dread.

Praea and the other Tulaga finished subduing the storm that had interfered with their journey to the Golden Canyon and came to join the rest of them. It was now rather a large group, Lini thought, as they began rushing along the edge of the forest and discussing a wildness within the earth that, it seemed to Lini, was too much for any of them. Even Corren's presence offered her little comfort. Something horrible was happening with the earth. What were they supposed to do about it?

It all had something to do with Tivoli and the Vortex. She knew it. But what exactly?

She wasn't sure, but she was eager to continue their journey so they could, hopefully, get into the Shoals and find some answers.

"We shouldn't delay," Lini said. "We need to get going."

This was when Corren revealed that they were really going to Amon Tunde instead. At least, he and his brothers and Janus. The rest would have to stay behind.

"Wait," Lini said, as Marcellus, Nicolai, and Janus dismounted their horses and hurried toward the forest with Corren. "I want to go too."

"I don't think you can," Corren said, without looking back. He and the others were breaking into a run, Lini trailing after them.

"If you can go in, why can't I? I want to help."

"I know," Corren said, not slowing, "but you need to stay here."

"But—"

"Lini, I'm sorry. There's no time to explain."

She stopped, scowling, and watched them disappear into the trees. The white horse drew up next to her, bobbing its head with agitation as if it wanted to follow its owner but knew it had been told to stay behind as well.

Lini marched back toward Kennard and the Guard, who were waiting with Praea and the other Tulaga. "Why do they get to go?" Lini said, not really expecting an answer. Surprisingly, Praea offered one anyway.

"They're friends of Salerno," she said, "but I don't know that he would consider us the same."

"Well, *we* didn't do anything wrong. I'm not going to just sit here."

Praea shook her head. "Don't worry. I'm not going to either." She glanced at Kennard and the other Tulaga. "Remember, there's still another way in."

In moments they were taking off from the ground, the king's white horse watching them from below.

When Janus and the Three reached the Grand Cavern, they were met with an eerie calm. The cavern stood vacant, not a faerie in sight. One section of the flowered wall was singed black. Water dripped from the skeletal remains of the plants and puddled on the floor.

The group came to a momentary halt. Janus' skin crawled. In thousands of years, she'd never seen such a sight in Amon Tunde. What was going so wrong with the earth that it was reaching them here?

"What happened?" Marcellus asked. "Where is everybody?"

She felt her fellow faeries, desperate and fearful, and hurried toward them. "This way."

The four of them sprinted across the cavern, their footsteps slapping on the wet floors, and headed down Emerald Tunnel. Here, too, scorch marks bloomed on the ceilings and the air was thick with the lingering hint of the element of fire. Here. In Amon Tunde. It sparked in the air like tiny, floating embers.

As they neared the end of the tunnel, the faeries came into view. It seemed as if all of Amon Tunde was here, gathered near the Way Beneath and overflowing into Emerald Tunnel.

At the rear of the group, Tyri watched Janus approach. She had long humanlike hair that flowed to her waist, as Janus did, but her eyes were the color of violet irises. She gave Janus a somber look. "You have come to die with us?"

Janus furrowed her brows. "What's happened?"

"The earth is destroying itself. It can't help it."

Janus turned back to the Three. They looked at one another with dark expressions.

"Where's Salerno?" Corren asked.

Janus led the way, the faeries' soft cloaks brushing her arms as she passed. One face after another looked at her as if she had come only to join them in their doom.

Salerno stood next to the Way Beneath. Rather than open to the spiraling tunnel that led down to the Shoals, the Way Beneath was now hidden by a woven tapestry of vines. As they drew up next to it, she watched Nicolai put his hand on a vine as big around as his arm and look the whole thing over with a grim expression.

Janus focused her attention on Salerno.

She had never seen such an expression of defeat on the man. Not even when the blackness on the Tree took Lily's life. "I have been to the Vortex," he said gravely.

The earth began to vibrate violently. Janus sensed the faeries around them reaching out with their magic to settle it, and she immediately joined in to help. Taking hold of the restless earth, they calmed it as one, but the mass of vines covering the Way

Beneath continued to tremble. The vines stretched and creaked, threatening to snap. Janus helped the others strengthen the vines against what was on the other side. Something that did not belong.

"What's happening?" Marcellus said.

"Is that fire on the other side?" Corren asked, leaning close to the vines.

It shouldn't be here, Janus thought.

Corren raised his staff, shouted an incantation, and the fire Janus had been sensing on the other side vanished. The vines grew still.

Salerno looked sharply at Corren. A dawning expression crossed his face. "You," he breathed. Janus sensed Salerno had a new idea forming.

"Will somebody please explain what's going on?" Marcellus said.

"The Vortex has been damaged," Salerno answered. "The elements in their raw forms are spreading where they should not."

Janus' skin tingled with this news. Tyri was right. The earth was going to destroy itself.

Marcellus furrowed his brows, still not understanding.

"The earth isn't absorbing the raw elements properly," Janus explained. "That's what's causing all the destruction. As earth faeries, we have no control over the raw elements of fire and water here, but we've never needed it."

"These other elements do not normally come to us from the Shoals," Salerno said. "Only the earth flows to us here. But you," he said to Corren now, "you subdued the fire."

Corren had been listening intently. Janus could see his mind working. "So this is all because of damage to the Vortex?"

"It is out of balance," Salerno said, nodding.

Janus suddenly realized what Salerno had in mind. "If we can help the Vortex regain its balance..." she said.

"Right," Corren said, understanding too.

If the earth faeries could control the element of earth, Janus thought, and Corren could control the element of fire, that left...

She, Corren, Nicolai, and Salerno all slowly looked at Marcellus.

He glanced from face to face. "What?"

"I sense you have finally opened yourself to your element," Salerno said.

Marcellus blinked.

"We need you, Blue Brother."

Marcellus' eyes widened with alarm, but Salerno turned back to the vines. Janus squeezed Marcellus' arm in reassurance and he turned to her. "Need me to do what? What are we doing?"

"We're going to the Vortex," Corren said, gripping his staff and watching Salerno.

Nicolai had been listening to the conversation with a grim, studious expression. "Once we get there," he said quietly, "will we be able to fix what's wrong?"

"That," Salerno said, "I do not know."

He swept a hand over the vines. They slowly untangled and spread open to reveal the charred tunnel of the Way Beneath.

Ten

The earth faeries closed the shield of vines behind them, and the Way Beneath fell to darkness. Corren felt a sinking sense of dread. He caused a soft ball of blue light to float in front of them, and they continued to descend the spiraling tunnel. Salerno led the way, Marcellus was at Corren's side, and Nicolai and Janus took up the rear. The passage curved down and down, the charred moss crunching beneath their feet. At the bottom, it leveled out and the walls turned into a unique kind of rock that resonated its own magic.

So these were the Shoals.

The ground momentarily trembled. The party stopped, alert. Their sharp breaths punctuated the otherwise silent tunnel. The earth remained still.

Corren and Marcellus exchanged glances.

Salerno pressed on.

He led them through a series of turns. The deeper into the earth they went, the more Corren felt they were descending into their own tomb.

Salerno's cloak rustled quietly in front of them. "It is near," he said.

Indeed, they rounded a corner and a distant opening flickered with light. Several more steps and Corren extinguished the blue ball; they were now illuminated by the shimmering colors dancing at the end of the tunnel.

As they drew yet closer, a blinding flash at the end of the passageway brought the party to a halt once again. They stood still, listening as a distant rumbling seemed to barrel through the earth, away from them. It rolled on and on before finally fading away.

"We should hurry," Nicolai said.

Salerno continued and they neared the opening. An immense cavern came partially into view. A droning, grinding sound cut through the air, and they caught glimpses of a massive object swirling into and out of their line of sight.

Another flash of light exploded in the cavern. This time a stream of some ethereal substance—glowing orange and green and blue—came barreling toward them. As it raced in their direction, Corren barely had time to sense it wasn't only one element but several. Pure, blinding, raw elements that he knew would be beyond his control except, perhaps, the element of fire, which was in such pure form it hadn't even taken shape as flame yet.

Salerno raised his arms and Corren raised his staff and it was nearly to them.

"Marcellus!" Corren shouted. "The water!"

"I know!" he said, raising his arms, and then it was upon them. A blast of scorching wind rushed overhead and Corren just barely managed to hold back the element of fire—unprepared for the force of it—and sensed Salerno, Janus, and Nicolai doing the same to the element of earth. The orange and green ethereal lights vibrated and groaned so loudly in response that the ground beneath them shook.

The element of water, however, broke over them. The blue ethereal form of it roared like the rushing of waves and clapped on their skin like a shock of ice water. The collective hold on the element of earth seemed to weaken.

"Send it back!" Janus shouted. "Push it back!"

"I'm trying!" Marcellus yelled.

Already struggling to control the element of fire in such a pure state, Corren tried to cause it to surround the blue, semitangible substance of the water element as sections of it rushed past them toward Amon Tunde. As he pushed the fire element against the water element, it curled back in response. He felt Marcellus pushing on his element more successfully now, and together, all five of them sent the collection of raw elements racing back the way they'd come.

The lights retreated into the cavern and dissipated, and they stood for a moment in the empty tunnel, panting.

"This is a death wish," Marcellus said.

"We will otherwise die anyway," Salerno said, then went forward and entered the cavern where the Vortex waited.

Praea and the other Tulaga sped toward the Golden Canyon with Lini and Kennard and the others on their backs. Unlike before, they were not bound for the lair of a dragon but rather the entrance to the Shoals, hidden deep in the ravine below the Golden Canyon. Praea went as fast as she thought her passenger could tolerate and Lini clung to her fiercely.

Along the way, they saw more evidence of destruction: sheets of ice crawling over the lowlands, lava bubbling near the southern edge of the Wilds, and fires raging on the mountain peaks in the distance. It was as if the earth itself were coming undone.

At last they came to the lake, their broad-winged reflections soaring over its glassy surface. Praea looked toward the ruins of the Golden Canyon and saw no sign of the dragon roosting there. They flew low over the surface of the water, across the flatland, and to the gorge beneath the Golden Canyon.

Finding the distinctive rock formation that marked the correct place, Praea dove toward the far side of the gorge, slowing in time to land on a broad rocky ledge overhanging the river far below.

Lini scrambled off and Praea transformed. The others landed and did the same. Lini took a few steadying breaths as Praea slowly approached a narrow fissure in the rock. Quietly, Lini and the others gathered around it as well.

Kennard eyed the opening skeptically. "Are you sure this is it?"

Lini pointed to a section of rock on the wall above them. "See the way those rocks look like dragon scales?" she asked. "And the column of pockmarked stone there? This is the place."

Praea turned sideways and slipped through the opening of the narrow crevice. The sheet of solid rock both in front and behind seemed to squeeze in on her. She forced herself to continue, expecting the path to grow too tight with every step, but it never did. Though it didn't seem it, there was room enough.

After a time, the fissure let out into a small cave. The floor descended rapidly and they had to be careful not to lose their footing on the way down. The crevice that led to the outside lent only a dim shaft of light. The rest of the cave was cloaked in darkness.

Kennard raised his staff and a soft ball of light bloomed in front of them.

Lini fussed with the end of her colorful head scarf and scrutinized their surroundings. "I thought the Shoals gave their own light."

"Maybe we're not in the Shoals yet," Praea said.

Brows still furrowed, Lini led the group further back into the cave until they came to the opening of a broad tunnel.

She exhaled definitively, as if the sight of it confirmed for her they were, in fact, in the right place. She stopped and pulled her bag around and withdrew the Book of Madera. When Lini opened the book, Praea was reminded that Lini had been almost the only one able to do so and the only one able to remove the ash from the altar. As she watched Lini turn to the maps in the Book of Madera, Praea understood that while she had no idea what they were getting themselves into, she found herself glad Lini was here.

"There should be a fork ahead," Lini said. "We'll need to go right."

"We're not walking are we?" Jesaray asked, at Praea's side as she so often was.

"No," Praea said. It would take days to get back to the Vortex if they walked, but as Tulaga they could get there quickly. "Provided we have room enough to fly. Let's see the map. It'll be quicker if we don't keep stopping so you can check it."

Lini came to Praea's side, holding the book open. The two women leaned over the map together, Kennard and a few of the others leaning in to see as well. Lini ran her caramel-colored finger along the route. "Right, right, left..." she recited as she came to each junction. Praea repeated it in her head, trying to commit it to memory. It wasn't that complicated and they could only get as far as the faerie barrier anyway. There, Lini would attempt to break it with the bit of Phoenix ash she'd brought in order to restore the Veil of Madera. The ash would serve a different purpose now.

Lini tucked the book away and Praea repeated the directions through the Shoals over and over in her head. *Right, right, left, right...*

She transformed and Lini climbed on. She hoped the tunnels didn't get too much smaller or they'd be walking after all.

As they rushed through the tunnels, Praea hoped she remembered the way correctly. If not, they could be hopelessly lost. The tunnels of the Shoals were sometimes broad, sometimes narrow, but so far were just big enough to permit flight.

After the last turn, Praea slowed slightly, watching for the faerie barrier that would be up ahead. Farther and farther they went and Praea slowed even more.

They should be upon it. Any moment now.

Another junction came into view and Praea suddenly realized why she hadn't yet seen it. They'd flown past where the faerie barrier was supposed to be.

But it wasn't there.

Before she could wonder about the reasons for this, a plume of fire came rushing down the tunnel toward them.

Eleven

Corren gaped at the Vortex with a mixture of horror and awe. He was unprepared for its massive size or for its raw, wild power. It swirled in a whirlwind of luminous light and color: the splendor of the elements in their purest forms. But its rotation was haphazard and violent. It groaned deeply as if it were about to burst open, and the sound echoed through the room, reverberating in his chest and ears. He feared it would consume them all where they stood if they got any closer.

Corren hastily scanned the scorched bodies circling the black pit. Now they knew. Whatever Tivoli and his followers were trying to do here, things went terribly wrong.

And if Corren and the others tried to tamper with the Vortex, would they be joining them? Yet they had no other option.

Two other tunnels led out of the cavern. A strand of elements in their ethereal forms shot out from the Vortex like an arm. It broke away and went careening down the tunnel opposite them. Rather than the invisible forms of the elements flowing smoothly out of the Vortex, the ethereal forms were escaping the core. They had to be contained.

As the Vortex roared before them, Corren exchanged dismayed looks with Janus and Salerno.

"What?" Marcellus shouted over the noise. "What do we do?"

The Vortex dipped and swayed toward them, and they all hustled back of one accord, pressing against the walls.

"Quickly," Salerno said loudly. "We must keep the elements in the core and try to bring it back into balance."

Corren agreed, but looking up at the immense whirlwind of light and raw power, he didn't know if such a thing could be done. He had struggled to control the raw form of fire when it came toward them in the tunnel, but now... there was so much more of it.

"We have to do what?" Marcellus shouted.

Before them the Vortex groaned and teetered.

There was no time to waste.

Corren raised his staff and tried to grab hold of the element of fire. While he was able to take hold of some of it, most of it continued to rush around in the Vortex, an unstoppable gale.

Meanwhile, Salerno, Nicolai, and Janus all raised their hands. He felt their will on the earth. They slowly spread out, working as a group to contain the element of the earth in its raw form. The three of them, together, had strength enough. The raw element of fire, however, slipped and skitted under Corren's grasp.

Another arm of elements shot out from the Vortex, careening down an adjacent tunnel, but it contained only the elements of fire and water. The element of earth stayed in the Vortex, held in place by the earth faeries containing it.

Marcellus was trembling as he strained against the element of water. Corren had no room in his mind to think about how on earth Marcellus could be expected to control such a mass of elements alone. Corren had his own element to think about.

Cursing under his breath, he wished the ethereal form he was so unsuccessfully trying to rein in was in the form of actual fire, which he knew he could control. He impulsively gave the raw element a spark.

The others gasped and hollered as the ethereal fire shuddered and bloomed into flame. Or almost flame. It carried the echo of flame-like shapes and threatened to return to its pure essence any moment, but with this slightly more tangible form, Corren was better able to contain it.

He extended his hold on the fire all throughout the Vortex, his arms and body aching from the strain. Salerno and the others were still containing the element of earth in the center.

The element of water, however, pushed and pulled against the others wildly.

As the Vortex continued to roar and groan, Corren glanced at Marcellus. He had never seen such an expression of horror on Marcellus' face. "Marcellus!" he hollered, trying not to lose control of his element. "Turn it into water!"

The pure, ethereal form of the element of water had all the power and violence of a hurricane. The agitated light from the Vortex flickered on Marcellus' face. His arms were raised and his legs slightly bent and trembling, as if he were trying to heft a boulder into the air and was in danger of being crushed by it.

"Try to make it become water," Corren hollered.

"I don't know if I can!"

He didn't know if Marcellus would be able to control the element once it took form—or if he could even change its form—but he did know he couldn't hold onto the element of fire much longer. Wisps of flame licked at the edges of the ethereal element of fire. "Try! Just try!"

Evidently Marcellus did try, for a tsunami appeared out of nowhere. Crashing and tumbling, it soared over the flames and the ethereal element of earth Nicolai and the others were controlling.

"Hold it! Hold it!"

Marcellus roared and his arms trembled from the effort. The water slowed its progress, churning slowly and strangely in the air, but it continued on its course. It loomed closer and closer, threatening to overtake them all.

"Marcellus!" Janus yelled.

Suddenly something brushed against Corren from behind. Ryafan came galloping to Marcellus' side, his white coat gleaming with the multitude of colors from the Vortex. The horse reared on his hind legs.

The churning water came to a halt.

The horse reared again, kicking at the air with his front hooves. His mane took on the appearance of foaming waves. His coat shimmered like sunlight on water. Marcellus pulled his arms back and pushed forward with a growl. The wave of water retreated and changed back into its ethereal form as it rejoined the other elements in the center.

Panting heavily, they held the elements in the Vortex as it spun and groaned.

The elements were contained, but they didn't feel in control either. It was taking all of Corren's strength to keep the almost-fire in its place.

"Now what?" Nicolai hollered.

Corren wasn't sure. There was still something in there that was wild and out of control. He was sure if they let go, the Vortex would go back to spinning out of control and the elements would violently release in every direction.

A stream of Tulaga shot out of the tunnel on his left, pouring into the cavern and rising into the air. There was Lini, on Praea's back, and Kennard and the other Guard members. Corren's heart clenched in horror. The Tulaga circled down and transformed instantly as the others climbed off.

"What is this?" Salerno asked.

"What's happening?" Lini asked.

"Get out!" Corren hollered. The swirling mass of elements threatened to explode any moment. He didn't want them in harm's way when the dam burst. "Hurry! Go!"

Praea's youngest recruit, Jesaray, was scrutinizing the Vortex with furrowed brows. "What's going on with the air in there?"

Praea likewise studied the whirlwind of elements.

Corren looked back to the Vortex and understood. It was the element of air they still needed to control. "Wait!" he said, though they'd made no move to leave. "Can you contain the air?"

Praea glanced at Corren and the others containing the elements, furrowed her brows at the sight of Marcellus' horse, then looked to her young charges. "Follow my lead," she said. She raised her arms, said an incantation, and brought them down in the form of massive golden wings. The glittering Tulaga took flight.

Her girls followed suit and soon a mass of Tulaga were high up in the cavern, circling the Vortex from above.

Things inside the Vortex began to shift. To settle. To smooth out.

The din of noise slowly lessened.

Now that the element of fire was more in harmony with the other elements, Corren was able to let it go back to its raw form while maintaining control.

But something was still wrong.

The Vortex pulsed violently, as if it would still erupt if they released their hold on it.

"Why isn't this working?" Janus said.

Lini began to circle the cavern, leaving Kennard and the Guard behind.

But she was not looking at the Vortex. She was looking at the bodies of her former friends.

She walked slowly, deliberately, her brow furrowed. The Vortex shimmered and trembled above her. The light glimmered on the gold mark on her forehead.

Corren's strength was starting to give way. He couldn't contain the elements much longer. "Lini?" he called.

She did not answer but kept walking. He could not read her expression. Was she mourning her friends or—he feared—was the temptation of the power from the Vortex too much for her, as it had been for Tivoli and, once upon a time, for the Mapmaker?

Corren took hold of himself. *The Phoenix trusts her,* he thought. *I trust her.*

"Lini," he said firmly.

She looked at him.

"What is it?" he asked.

"I think I know what they were doing." She looked up at the quivering Vortex with the same intense expression.

"Lini."

But this was from Salerno. He said her name in that way he had of saying a person's name as if he truly understood them.

382

The two looked at one another, human and faerie.

"Everybody here is here to help," Lini said.

"Yes," Salerno said. "I see that."

Corren's arms trembled as he struggled to keep hold of the element of fire. The ethereal element escaped in one small section, and Corren turned it into flame before causing it to snuff out. The others jumped and gasped in response.

Salerno turned back to Lini. "Do you know how to fix it?"

"I think so," she said. Then facing Corren, she said, "It's still bound from one of our rituals. I think I can release it."

"Do it," Corren said. "Please hurry!"

"Kennard!" she called. He rushed to her side, cloak billowing out behind him. She directed him and each of the other Guard members, telling them where to stand until they were circled around the Vortex. They had to step over and around the blackened bodies of the Orsini Colony members as they did so.

And what if Lini did not truly understand what she was dealing with any more than her fellows had? What if she and Kennard and the Guard were next?

"Repeat after me," she said, then raised her arms. Corren briefly pinched his eyes closed. His entire body felt ready to give way. He heard Lini holler, "*Alli uum aught!*"

"*Alli uum aught!*" Kennard and the Guard repeated.

Corren opened his eyes. There they stood around the Vortex. There Lini was with her arms raised and the light flashing off her face. Corren felt no difference in the elements in the core. His heart pounded and his body trembled with the strain. If this didn't work, what then?

"*Alli uum aught,*" Lini said.

"*Alli uum aught,*" they chanted.

The Vortex glowed more brightly, swaying in a slow, graceful arc around the room.

Corren squinted against it, his arms screaming as he tried to keep hold of his element.

"*Emoteth,*" Lini said.

"*Emoteth.*"

"*Emoteth, emoteth, emoteth.*"

They repeated the chant and the Vortex spun into a tight spiral, standing up straight and spinning rapidly, faster and faster. Corren frantically tried to keep hold of the fire.

"*Emoteth, emoteth, emoteth.*"

The elements pulled into the center of the Vortex so powerfully they were yanked out of the magical grasps of everyone present.

The light that erupted was so blinding they all had no choice but to duck their heads away and shield their eyes.

The sharp light faded. They slowly turned back of one accord.

There in the center of the cavern, the Vortex spun upright. Humming. Calm.

Balanced.

The Tulaga landed gently and transformed back into women.

The humans and faeries around the Vortex could only stand there watching it, breathless.

Twelve

Salerno, tentatively amending his former inclination toward secrecy and mistrust, led the entire party up the spiraling tunnel of the Way Beneath. They entered the inner realm of Amon Tunde and went down the Emerald Tunnel, Corren snuffing out bits of embers floating in the air along the way.

The faeries, having sensed the danger from the Vortex had passed, had set to work repairing the section of singed vines on the wall of the Grand Cavern. They had anticipated the return of their king and the Three but were not prepared for the emergence of over a dozen humans trailing after.

Both the leaf-covered and humanlike faeries of that underworld watched in silence and wonder, as the humans similarly beheld the glittering realm of Amon Tunde and its inhabitants with humbled awe. Even Ryafan, the horse born of the ocean, ambled through the earthen faerie realm.

For the second time that day.

As the party entered the Grand Cavern, Marcellus explained that the horse had sensed his distress and found his way to the Vortex, giving Marcellus the strength he needed to get the water elements under control.

Hearing this, Janus could not resist wrapping her arms around the neck of the watery beast and giving him a hug.

Though when he started nuzzling her in response, she gave him a perfunctory pat and said, "Yes, yes. That's enough."

Praea came to a halt next to the gurgling stream flowing through the center of the Grand Cavern. Hands clasped in front of her, she gazed at the ceiling far above. The flowing rock sparkled as if it had been dusted with starlight. She longed to take flight and brush its surface with her wing tips. Her eyes trailed downward along the wall covered with vines and an astonishing assortment of blooms. Many-petaled roses, vibrant purple orchids, and delicate white dahlias bloomed side by side with flowers she'd never seen before. One—an orange flower with long, teardrop petals—looked as soft and velvety as a horse's nose. The Grand Cavern was stunning in its beauty, even with one section charred and blackened, and the magic of the place hummed in her very bones.

It felt vaguely familiar.

Perhaps it felt familiar because she had previously witnessed faerie magic performed by her beloved Nicolai. Or perhaps it was because this glittering faerie realm was entwined with the origins of the Tulaga. The magical concepts of the earth faeries, combined with Phoenix ash, made it possible for her—a human—to transform into a magnificent golden bird.

And it all began long ago, when Eala set foot in the aboveground realm of Amon Tunde and made friends with the king of the earth faeries.

There he stood, across the cavern, watching her. His eyes were an emerald green, the same shade as the brilliant moss growing in the nooks of the cavern walls. His hair—nearly like a human's but infused with a wildness that brought to mind branches and leaves and running barefoot through the forest—fell past his shoulders. His slender frame was draped in a cloak that looked like it could be made of the mossy forest floor itself.

She did not fear him. She wanted to, in fact, embrace him. And thank him.

Whether he saw this on her face or not, she did not know. He gave a regal gesture indicating the party should follow him and turned to lead the way. He escorted them up to the forest, through their wooded lands, and to the boundaries of Amon Tunde.

Before bidding them farewell, he invited them all to return in a week's time.

They watched in silence as Salerno's cloaked figure retreated into the still forest.

Lini looked to her left, where Corren stood with his brothers. The king stood nearest to Lini, though he was not only a king any more than Corren was only a wizard. Together, they were the Three, and as she looked at them, she felt the weight and wonder of that fact in her breast. Look at what they had done since the stones first came to them, and there they now stood. They looked weary, yes, but also steady and strong and good.

Then again, look at what she had just done.

Would someone else look upon her and consider her brave or strong or good? Did the Three feel as disconnected from such grand notions about themselves as she would if someone thought such things about her? She didn't know and it didn't matter. She was content to merely be on their side and to have helped accomplish something good.

Just as the Phoenix said she could.

Corren looked at her. No longer one of the Three, he was to her in that moment as he so often had been since the day she met him. A kindred soul.

They gave each other soft smiles.

"Shall we?" he said.

This nudged the party into motion. Together, they turned toward the boundaries of the Wilds and entered the Rheita Valley and its water-drenched plain. As they walked, Corren drifted closer to Lini until his billowing cloak nearly touched the folds of her skirts. Without a word, he tentatively took her hand in his. They did not look at one another, but she smiled and gently squeezed his fingers.

His brothers did not fail to notice this subtle gesture. In unison, the two raised their eyebrows, came to a halt, and looked at one another in bemusement. Nicolai's face eased into a satisfied smile. Marcellus smiled as well, though his was more of a mischievous grin, for what good was it to have a brother if he couldn't tease him about a girl?

During the coming week, the Three and Janus and the Tulaga searched land and sea for signs of flood, fire, or earthquake, and did what they could to repair any damage and assist citizens affected by the catastrophes. They found the last missing person in the rubble of the landslide in the Southern Quarter and buried him with his fellows at week's end. The earth took care of righting some things itself. The lava flows stopped and the sea calmed and many reported the swarm of Silver Spikebacks crossing the plains with their long wings outstretched, heading for the southern mountains where they belonged.

Lini, for her part, continued to worry about the last remaining human entrance into the Shoals. One night while she sat in her temporary quarters at Tower Hall South, searching the Book of Madera for answers, she had a sudden realization. The book did not hold the key to permanently protecting the Golden Canyon Entrance any more than it ever did. The answer lay elsewhere. As she remembered what she'd witnessed at the Vortex, she jumped up and hurried through the stone halls to tell Corren of her idea.

Thus it was that she and Corren, and Praea and Nicolai, came to the Golden Canyon Entrance and set about the work of sealing the opening. Nicolai manipulated the earth within the Shoals, closing it off to the outside world. Since he was the only one in thousands of years to have had such an ability, they felt fairly reassured that this would keep the Shoals free from human intrusion, forever.

They took additional precautions anyway. Corren and Nicolai collapsed the cave in a deafening rumble of cracking rock and a plume of dust, thus rendering the most critical function of the Madera and Eala branches a thing of the past. This sealing of the Shoals lightened Lini's soul with relief. She had not realized the full weight of the burden she'd been carrying until it was gone.

The relief was so keen that it was still with her as, on the day appointed by Salerno, she and the others entered the Wilds and headed for the realm of Amon Tunde. They had agreed that since Lini had figured out how to permanently protect the Shoals from intruders, she should be the one to share the good news with Salerno.

And she was eager to do so. A human had betrayed Salerno long ago, and now, all these years later, humans had helped to make it right. She wanted Salerno to know they were on his side.

But perhaps he knew this already.

Deep in the forests of Amon Tunde, they came to a grove and discovered a magnificent feast laid out in their honor. Keck and half a dozen other faeries sat around... well, no one but Janus knew quite what it was. It might have been comparable to a circular table if this were a feast prepared by humans, but this was no human feast. A ring of entwined, golden vines offered up fragrant white flowers—which they would soon discover was a sweet delicacy—along with every kind of fruit imaginable. How the faeries managed such a thing, no human could say, but growing from the vines were clusters of strawberries, blackberries, grapes, and strange varieties of fruit many present had never seen before. Large leaves shaped into bowls held walnuts, almonds, and tiny edible seeds. Goblets—made out of wood so thin the sunlight cut through them—contained a light, golden nectar that bubbled like champagne.

Encircling this unique spectacle were soft stools of moss, some holding the few faeries willing to brave the world above ground, others vacant and ready for their invited guests.

And there at the head of it all, ready to greet his friends, Salerno stood, waiting.

Connect with the Author

Sign up for updates at: donnacookauthor.com
Twitter @DonnaCookAuthor
Facebook.com/DonnaCookAuthor